Relic
— of —
Darkness

Relic of Darkness

A James MacBridan Mystery

James S. Parker

TATE PUBLISHING
AND ENTERPRISES, LLC

Relic of Darkness
Copyright © 2013 by James S. Parker. All rights reserved.

No part of this publication may be reproduced, stored in a retrieval system or transmitted in any way by any means, electronic, mechanical, photocopy, recording or otherwise without the prior permission of the author except as provided by USA copyright law.

This novel is a work of fiction. Names, descriptions, entities, and incidents included in the story are products of the author's imagination. Any resemblance to actual persons, events, and entities is entirely coincidental.

The opinions expressed by the author are not necessarily those of Tate Publishing, LLC.

Published by Tate Publishing & Enterprises, LLC
127 E. Trade Center Terrace | Mustang, Oklahoma 73064 USA
1.888.361.9473 | www.tatepublishing.com

Tate Publishing is committed to excellence in the publishing industry. The company reflects the philosophy established by the founders, based on Psalm 68:11,
"The Lord gave the word and great was the company of those who published it."

Book design copyright © 2013 by Tate Publishing, LLC. All rights reserved.
Cover design by Allen Jomoc
Interior design by Jake Muelle

Published in the United States of America

ISBN: 978-1-62510-212-6
1. Fiction / Mystery & Detective / General
2. Fiction / Suspense
13.03.25

Dedication

For my wife and daughter,
Margaret and Mara,
for their love, their encouragement,
and their belief in the dream,
they are my blessings from God!

Last night I saw upon the stair
A little man who wasn't there
He wasn't there again today
Oh, how I wish he'd go away
"Antigonish"
Hughes Mearns (1875-1965)
American educator & poet

CHAPTER 1

1947

Although she didn't understand why or, for that matter, who they were, there was no doubt that they were after her. She'd never gotten a good look at them, fleeting glimpses at best. Yet more often than not, she could feel their presence nearby. She felt this way now.

Keeping a watchful eye, Jean stared out the window at the same dark, brooding skies that had draped across the Scottish Highlands for days. Officially, it was spring, but it had been far too long since they had seen the sun. The year had distinguished itself for snow; London had had flooding last week. Of course, for this time of year, the damp, cold weather wasn't really all that unusual. But Jean knew there was something wrong, something that didn't feel quite right.

"Is it still raining out there, Em?" Her grandmother called her Em because she said that she reminded her of her sister Emilia when she'd been a child. Safe and secure in her grandmother's room, Jean kept her vigil at the window, gazing across the manicured grounds of her family's estate.

"Drizzling actually, just more of the same dreary stuff, damp and gray. I do so wish it would clear up."

"Not to worry, my dear, it'll soon pass. You'll see."

For the past few days, a batch of light showers had kept them inside. More of an annoyance than anything, the light rain only served to thicken the mist that clung to the trees and bushes, swirling across the lane, surrounding the grand house.

"Grandmother, please, it's still my turn." Colina, Jean's younger sister, pouted. "I want to ask if I'll get to meet any movie stars."

Her questions were always about the movies; last month the spirits had been worried silly about the Black Dahlia's murder.

Their grandmother turned back and smiled into the child's soft blue eyes. She had the same dark curly hair as her sister Jean but was much more impatient. "Oh yes, of course, we must find out while the spirits are still talkative."

Jean and her sister, much to their mother's dismay, often played with an antique fortune-telling board when they were with their grandmother. Their mother hated the thing, calling it a witch board, but as it had been in the MacKinnon family for generations, there was simply no getting rid of it. So their mother had done the next best thing; she had forbidden them to play with it. Their grandmother, however, did not share their mother's feelings. So the only time they could use it was when they visited their grandmother, in her room, with the door shut, of course.

Jean once asked her grandmother about this, about why her mother felt so strongly against it. "Is it really a witch board? It couldn't hurt anyone, could it?"

Grandmother thoughtfully considered her questions and said, "Your mother is a lovely, caring woman. However, she is a Douglas by birth and does not have the sturdy, adventurous spirit of a MacKinnon. So as not to worry her, our time with the board will be our little secret." And so it had been, and on a day like today, it helped to pass the time. Sadly, no movie stars lurked in Colina's future.

However, it was more than just bleak weather and boredom that was troubling Jean. In fairness, there were many things on her mind, any of which would have easily explained the nervous tension that haunted her, following her wherever she went.

First, there was her grandmother's health. Jean dearly loved her grandmother, but the elderly woman had been seriously ill twice in recent months and was only now recovering from her latest bout with fever. She passed into sleep easily, her mouth falling open, her breathing shallow.

As worrisome as her grandmother's health was to her was her family's plan to leave Scotland. They were getting ready to move to America to live on a horse farm the family owned in Virginia. Although exciting and full of promise, the move came with its own list of worries. But as significant as these two things were to her, Jean knew they were not the core of the tension she felt.

With most of the problems that had come up in her young life, Jean usually turned to her grandmother. Though only eleven years old, Jean was quite mature for her age, mature and sensitive but not sensitive in the normal way of a young lady. No, this was entirely something else, something different.

Grandmother had spotted signs of this trait in her a few years back, realizing that Jean had the gift of the MacKinnon women flowing in her blood. This sensitivity had been passed down to many of the women in the MacKinnon clan for hundreds of years. Its beginning was rooted back to a dark and tragic time, many believing it to be a curse. Nevertheless, it only touched the women of the clan, some more so than others. In Jean, she knew it was strong and, in time, would need to be channeled. There were ways to keep the other world at bay. But Grandmother's sharp focus on these matters had dimmed during the war when the boundaries between the worlds were worn down by so many passing over, especially so many before their time. The fever took a further toll.

The past week had been difficult for Jean. No matter what she did to occupy her time or where she went in the house, this sense of uneasiness followed her, growing ever so slightly with no relief. Today was no exception. Even being with her grandmother, she found herself on edge, glued to the window, futilely trying to catch a glimpse of that which she was certain was hiding just beyond the scope of her vision, concealed by the mist, waiting, hiding.

She jumped as her grandmother's hand lightly touched her shoulder. "I'm sorry, my dear," her grandmother said. "I didn't mean to startle you. Colina is going to read now, and I think it is time for us to talk. Tell me, child, what's bothering you?"

Suddenly, Jean found herself close to tears, and she turned into her grandmother's arms. "I don't know what it is. Something is scaring me, but I don't know what it is."

Her grandmother held her close. "Don't hold back, child. You can tell me anything. Is there something outside that's scaring you? Is that what you've been looking for?"

Jean pulled away and turned back to the window. For several minutes, she remained still and quiet. Her grandmother stayed close to her, patiently waiting.

"Grandmother," said Jean, "can shadows move by themselves?"

The color drained from her grandmother's face. Her hands trembled ever so slightly as a forgotten fear began to fill her stomach. "Why do you ask such a question?" Her voice nearly failing her, just above a whisper.

"Because a couple of times I think I've seen them move, dart from one place to another, but I'm not sure. I've never been able to get a clear look at them, but sometimes, they seem to scoot around. It's always something I catch out of the corner of my eye. Each time, I stop and watch, but nothing happens. I don't know why, but it scares me."

Grandmother had not expected this from her, not before young womanhood, and it took almost more strength than she had to mask her emotions from Jean. "I wouldn't worry about it, not now. But if you see them again, you come and get me, and we'll both look for them."

Jean was growing up too quickly. In three months, she'd be twelve. Her grandmother didn't want to frighten her, but there were things she needed to know. It had been this strong three generations ago, and the family had loss a bonnie lassie to the other side, where shadow is more real than substance.

"Come along, Jean, don't dawdle. We must be on our way," scolded her mother.

Jean stepped up into the carriage and sat down next to her. "But where's Grandmother? Isn't she coming?"

"Not this morning, I'm afraid," answered her father as he climbed into the carriage. He sat down across from them between Colina and her older brother Elliot. "Unfortunately, your grandmother did not have a good night. We thought it would be best for her to stay in bed and rest. Frankly, this damp weather's not good for any of us."

The coachman, Mr. Ramsay, shut the carriage doo, then climbed up on to the front seat. The carriage lurched forward as Jean and her family started the short ride to their family's ancestral chapel, located on the estate grounds, not far from the main house. As they came around the side of the large manor house, Jean looked out the carriage window and up at the windows of her grandmother's room. She saw that the drapes had been pulled. The nervous tension that had dogged her every step was even more intense this morning, so much so that Jean snuggled in closer to her mother for protection. Near the house, a small older woman, dressed in black, was looking up at her grandmother's window.

"Are you cold?" asked her mother.

"A little," lied Jean. "I'll be all right."

On a clear day, the chapel could easily be seen from her grandmother's room or, for that matter, from any room on the second floor on the back side of the house. The gardens behind the manor house ran up to the tree line where a footpath began, winding its way through the grove of trees that separated the manor from the chapel.

In good weather, her father always enjoyed the short walk through the woods. It was a lovely, peaceful walk, and they used the path as often as they could. However, today, the light rain, along with the unseasonably cool weather, had negated any thought of going by foot.

The chapel, a magnificent structure, was actually older than some parts of the house. For many years, it had been the only church in the area. The MacKinnon coat of arms was proudly engraved over the broad solid oak doors. Many of the graves encircling the chapel held generations of the MacKinnon clan, as well as those of other people from important families that had lived in and around the estate. The large ornate headstones marking the graves competed for a prominence now lost to time, no longer of any importance, especially to their occupants.

Mr. Ramsay brought the carriage to a halt in front of the heavy, tall, wrought iron gates that stood open for this morning's services. Several other carriages, as well as a few automobiles, were already parked along both sides of the lane. Jean recognized two of them that belonged to her cousins.

As Mr. Ramsay helped them down from the carriage, he looked at her father and said, "If you don't mind my saying so, sir, it'll be a sad day to see you and the family leave Scotland."

"I appreciate that, Ramsay, it will be hard to say good-bye. But our business in America needs more attention than it's been getting," answered her father. "Therefore, we've decided that it'd be best to move there so that I can personally take over the reins of the operation."

Her father laughed heartily at his own joke, and Mr. Ramsay smiled along with him. It was a joke that he'd become quite proud of and had, of late, used repeatedly. Her mother's sigh of exasperation went largely unnoticed by her father.

Jean's great-great-grandfather had purchased the land in America about ten years before the American Civil War and had quietly supported the North. After the war ended, the family business in Virginia developed into a thriving venture, raising thoroughbred horses bred from Irish stock, as well as annually harvesting a large and profitable tobacco crop. In the early days, the money from their holdings in Scotland had kept the farm going, but after the war, it flourished, now producing a significant part of the family's income. During the recent war, the US government had purchased two sections of land from the MacKinnons for a substantial figure. The MacKinnons had initially resisted the sale of the land, but the United States needed to build a large complex in Langley.

Jean firmly held her mother's hand as they stepped out of the carriage and onto the gravel path, closely followed by Elliot and Colina, her father leading the way. As they passed through the gates, Jean looked closely at the sharp spear-shaped tips that arched across the top and at the tall stone walls that completely encircled the chapel and the rather large churchyard. Thick green vines seemed to smother the walls, alternating with patches of dark-green moss. Stones could be seen breaking through the vines at the top of the walls, resembling a jagged row of sharp discolored teeth. The round chapel's shape had been of interest to many historians; there were few of these left in Scotland, relics of the fourteenth century.

Her parents loved the old chapel, each visit bringing to mind several pleasant memories. They had been married in the chapel and had celebrated the christening of each of their children there. For generations, the old chapel had been used to commemorate many special events in the MacKinnon family. Jean, however, had never liked it. The chapel simply scared her. Her fear of the chapel remained the one secret she had not shared with anyone, not even her grandmother.

A couple of years ago, she had asked her father about the need for the massive walls and the heavy iron gates. She was worried because Elliot had told her, one night in her room, the tale of the gatherer, her family's version of the banshee. All across the Scottish Highlands, it was believed that when an evil person was buried in the churchyard, their spirit would become the new gatherer, wanting others to join it. However, should the gates to the churchyard be left open, the gatherer would roam the countryside, hunting others to come and join it in its hellish existence. Worst of all, it especially liked little girls! After hearing that, many of her nights had been filled with nightmares of a dark, nameless horror waiting to pull her down into the ground right in front of the chapel, the darkened chapel windows staring indifferently at her.

Patiently her father explained that the chapel had been built centuries ago. The walls had been put there to protect the MacKinnon family from raiders, Vikings, and sometimes even other clans who had once scourged the Scottish countryside in times past, times far more violent. His explanation had helped; it made sense to her, but it didn't erase the fear of the chapel that lived within her. On the other hand, much to Jean's delight, her father had punished Elliot for scaring her with such a silly superstition.

As she grew older, her fear of the chapel, the graveyard, and the gatherer lessened a bit, but it never fully went away. She felt nervous every time her family attended services. She had never once gone there by herself; she simply couldn't, and only in the past couple of years had she developed enough courage just to walk past the chapel on the lane where their carriage now waited for them.

The gravel path snaked its way around the graves, leading them to the solid oak doors of the ancient chapel. Over the doors, a Latin inscription read, "*Pauperes Comilitones Christi Templique Solomicici.*" She knew "paupers" meant poor, but poverty had never been part of her family's history since their rise at the end of the Crusades. Her family hurried to get inside, escaping the mist that continued to roll across the ground keeping everything wet and cold. Jean knew that Mr. Ramsay would join the other servants in the back of the chapel as soon as he parked the carriage.

She loved Mr. Ramsay, and it made her feel good to know that he would not be waiting for them outside in the cold. Likewise, Jean held a special place in his heart, and he treated her as if she were his own daughter. He always had time for her, and she loved his remarkable stories about the magical folk who lived and played in the forest.

Entering the candlelit chamber, Jean was surprised to find almost every seat taken. Several servants stood in the back, lining the walls. A hush fell over the gathering as the lord of the manor and his family proudly walked down the aisle, taking their place in the front pew. Her father took his regular place on the aisle, her mother next to him, then Elliot, Colina, and Jean. It was always this way. Usually her grandmother sat next to her, and today Jean missed her more than ever.

Today's service was to be a special one, which accounted for the large turnout. It would be the MacKinnon family's last opportunity to participate in services here for some time to come as they would be setting sail for America in the coming week. Today would be the last chance for many of their friends and family to wish them well and say their good-byes.

Jean had learned that morning that the only member of her immediate family not making the trip to America would be her sick grandmother. She worried over who would care for her. Jean's mother assured her that her grandmother would have the best of care and, in time, would join them in America. Still, Jean didn't feel right leaving her behind.

The tension that had been building up in Jean over the past few days intensified as they sat down. Surrounded by her family and their friends, she still felt exposed, threatened by something she couldn't see and didn't understand. They had no sooner sat down when she began to keep a close watch on the stained glass windows on both sides of the chapel, afraid that she would see the vague face of her fear glaring back at her.

One of the deacons, Mr. Odhram, approached her father. A short man, he was extremely overweight, and the overlapping folds of skin that gathered around his neck made it hard for Jean to look at him. The long flowing robe he wore gave one the impression of being a great white shell with a head sticking out of the top bobbing back and forth as he walked toward them like a grotesque turtle. "Good morning, Lord MacKinnon," he said a little too loudly.

"Good morning."

"It is so good to see you and your charming family," he said, ingratiatingly smiling at each of them in return. His face was flushed and his clean-shaven cheeks sagged down off his face hanging just below the jawline. Jean, Colina, Elliot, and her mother all acknowledged his greeting, appropriately smiling back.

"Thank you," said her father. "You are most kind."

"It is unfortunate that I have to inform you that we will be ever so slightly delayed this morning. Reverend MacRae is ill, but I'm told that Reverend Stewart from Urray is on his way and should be here shortly."

"That is unfortunate. Nothing serious I hope."

"That too is our prayer. Hopefully, it will pass, and he will be back up and with us in a few days. It shouldn't be much longer." With that, he bowed to Lord MacKinnon, turned, and disappeared through a door behind the altar.

As far as Jean was concerned, the deacon could not have delivered worse news. Now she had no idea how long they'd be stuck here, adding yet another layer of tension. Her nerves were in such a state that she really didn't know how to deal with them, resulting in her inability to sit still. Her mother's stern glance quickly caught her eye, telling her, without uttering a word, to stop it and stop it now. "Young ladies do not fidget." She'd heard it before.

Her father understood that of his three children, Jean usually had the hardest time sitting still, especially during church. It was clear that today would be no exception. Jean saw her father watching her, but rather than giving her another reprimand, he indulgently smiled at her. He then leaned over and whispered something to her mother. At first she did not agree with her husband, shaking her head no, dismissing whatever had just been suggested.

Then her mother motioned Jean over to her and said softly, "Your father has left his prayer book in the carriage. Would you like to go get it for him?"

"Yes, ma'am, I'd like to do that very much." Jean started to leave, but her mother stopped her, gently placing her hand on her arm. "Do not be gone too long. I do not want you coming in and interrupting once things have begun," directed her mother.

"Yes, ma'am, I'll be right back." And with that, she took off before her mother could change her mind. It took every ounce of her will power to keep from running down the aisle. Looking over her shoulder at her father, she smiled her thanks to him. He winked at her and then turned back around.

Mr. Ramsay saw her coming and moved to open the door for her. "And where would you be off to?" he asked.

"Father left his prayer book in the carriage," she explained. "I'm going to go get it for him."

Mr. Ramsay frowned and put on as stern a face as he could muster, hooking his thumbs into his vest pockets. "I see. Well, the carriage is pretty far down the lane, and I'm afraid the weather is not improving. Why don't I go and get that for you?"

"That's all right. He wants me to get it." Mr. Ramsay knew how strong willed Jean could be and that he was not going to be able to dissuade her, so he smiled and told her where he'd parked the carriage. Jean quickly scooted out the door.

The weather had deteriorated. The mist had thickened, crawling across the ground and clinging to the base of the headstones. A light, steady drizzle accompanied the dark, billowing clouds. Jean, however, didn't even notice, and she bounced down the few steps in front of the chapel. Walking as quickly as she could down the gravel path, she was anxious to get to the gate and, at least for the time being, leave the chapel behind. As she approached the gate, she could hear the heavy exhale from one of the horses stomping the ground with its hooves. "It must be terrible at times to be a horse," she reasoned, "always having to wait, always outside no matter what the weather was doing."

"Jean."

Jean stopped and turned back toward the chapel. Had someone called her? She thought she'd heard her name, but it had been so soft, like a whisper carried by the wind. Jean looked around but didn't see anyone. Turning back around, she continued to make her way toward the gate.

"Jean."

This time it had been louder, clearer, but still she'd almost missed it entirely due to one of the horses. She'd startled the poor creature as she came to the gate, and the horse had shied away, rattling its harness just as her name was spoken.

Again, she stopped and turned around, looking back at the chapel. The silent mist-covered churchyard stared back at her. A faint rumble finally drew her attention to the sky, and she noticed that the clouds were beginning to darken even more. The giant maples that stood near the chapel had blocked most of her view of the sky, and it wasn't until she'd made it to the lane that she could see that the weather was indeed worsening.

Shrugging her shoulders in dismissal, she stepped out into the center of the lane, quickly spotting their carriage. It stood off to the side, beside the churchyard wall that ran parallel to the lane. Mr. Ramsay had been right; it was a good ways away. Remembering her mother's warning not to take too long, she set off toward the carriage at a brisk pace. Despite this, she made a point to pet each of the horses harnessed to the other carriages as she went by.

Mr. Ramsay kept the wood of the carriage refulgent with polish. It was bigger, older, and grander than any other vehicle in the churchyard. It wasn't until she was inside that she realized how truly miserable conditions had become. Though not actually warmer inside the coach, it was dry, and once she closed the door, the wind and the dampness were blocked out, making it feel warmer.

Jean quickly spotted her father's prayer book. Somehow, it had fallen to the floor and had lodged as far back under the seat as it could go. Careful not to get too dirty, she knelt down on the floor. The whole time she kept trying to think of a way, some reason her parents would accept, for her to stay here and not return to the chapel at all. Perhaps she could claim the weather? Sadly, she realized that this would not be possible, especially today, and she sighed in resignation, knowing she had to go back.

Doing her best to keep her dress clean, Jean stretched her arm as far as she could without actually lying on the floor, her fingers only just reaching the prayer book. Without warning, the carriage shifted, just like it did every time someone stepped into the coach. At the same moment, she felt a cold breeze enter the carriage washing over her back lightly caressing her neck.

Jean froze. Had the door somehow opened? She was sure she'd shut it tightly; she'd heard the latch click into place.

Someone was behind her; she could feel it. The blood drained from her face and hands as panic teased at the edges of her young mind. She didn't know what to do; everyone was in the chapel and so far away. Had Mr. Ramsay joined her? Why didn't he say anything?

"Mr. Ramsay, is that you?" she asked, the fear in her voice quite evident. Her question went unanswered.

Jean's fear took over. She had to get away and get away now before whoever it was grabbed her. Summoning all her courage, Jean slid out from under the seat and spun around, ready to jump out the other door. The coach, surprisingly, was empty; the door closed. There was no one behind her, no one looking in the window. She was quite alone. Carefully she looked out both sides of the carriage; there was just the dismal weather and the cold mud-covered lane.

The experience had left her shaken to the point of tears. No matter how terrible the idea had sounded moments ago, now she wanted to get back to the chapel, back to her mother and father and to Mr. Ramsay.

Picking up the prayer book and clutching it to her chest as if it were a shield, she opened the door and climbed down onto the lane. Closing the door with more force than she'd intended, she started for the gate.

"Jean...come to me."

It was behind her. She could practically feel its presence touching her. She jerked her head around to look so quickly that she almost tripped herself. The lane was empty, nothing moved, except their horse, which stood there slowly swishing his tail back and forth. *Elliot. It had to be Elliot.*

"Elliot! Where are you? Stop it! Father will be angry at you."

Jean didn't wait for an answer but turned and ran as fast as her legs could carry her. The wind had picked up, stronger now, whirling the mist around her, its low moan filling the treetops. When she got to the gate, she stopped and looked back up and down the lane. There was still no one in sight.

Leaning on the gate, she slowly let out her breath, trying to calm down. Her shoes were splattered with mud, but she didn't care. She'd made it; she was safe now. Still shaken by the whole affair, she began to make her way up the gravel path at a rapid pace. Running in the churchyard, she remembered, was not allowed.

Behind her, the tall gates began to move on their own, solidly clanging shut. She whirled around and stared at the two heavy iron edifices. *How could they have moved like that? It must have been the wind, but could the wind really move something that big, that heavy?* Then, in stunned disbelief, she watched as the iron bar on the gate move on its own, sliding into the catch on the opposite gate, locking her in.

A deep, paralyzing terror welled up inside of her. Silent tears streamed down her cheeks. She took a couple of steps backward then turned to run the rest of the way to the chapel doors.

Jean had taken no more than a couple of steps when she saw them. They stood completely still, one on either side of the chapel doors. They looked tall, at least to her, even taller than her father. They were oddly dressed and looked like knights of old, their armor rusted and dented in places. Each had their hands resting on the hilt of their sword, the point of the sword touching the ground. On their chest, they wore a tunic, torn and tattered and stained with dirt, and yet the faint symbol of a cross could still be seen. Their heads were bowed as if in prayer. Each wore a cloak draped across their shoulders, the hood pulled up over their heads concealing their faces in the dark folds of cloth. They didn't move, but their very presence made it impossible for her to move.

Jean glanced around, but there was no place to run. Her whole body trembled. The two sentinels remained absolutely still, waiting. The wind continued to pick up in its intensity, but Jean didn't notice.

Then, impossibly, a third creature erupted out of the ground, slowly extracting itself, an inch at a time, from the clinging mud to stand between the other two. The creature stood on the path directly in front of her. This one was even more terrible in its appearance, its armor black, the sword larger, and the cross on its tunic a bright scarlet red. Like the others, the hood that covered its head hid its features, its cloak almost dragging the ground. It smelled awful. The odor of wet earth, decay, and death filled the churchyard just as densely as the mist.

Clear and distinct, the nightmare that stood before her hissed her name, "Jean." Jean couldn't move, holding her father's prayer book tightly, terrified beyond belief.

The temperature around her plummeted, turning deathly cold. The black knight slowly began to raise its arm. The folds of its cloak rose with it, but the hand was missing. In its place was a dark formless mass. An unseen force pulled the hood back, partially revealing the face, or at least where the face should have been. Jean stared at the dark countenance, unable to see it clearly. Its features were distorted, with dark patches where the eyes and nose should have been. It looked much the same as a face on a badly blurred photograph.

"Jean...come to me."

Unwittingly, Jean stepped toward the creature, somehow compelled to go to it. Her mind instantly rebelled, stopping her as a numbing panic set in bringing her to her knees. The rain that had been falling all day quickly soaked through her dress. In a last desperate effort to save herself, she began to scream, shrieking, "Father! Father! Help me, Father!"

The chapel door burst open. Jean watched Mr. Ramsay rush out, quickly catching sight of her and springing down the steps, coming to her aid. The two specters standing watch on either side of the door remained absolutely still. The third creature straightened up and turned, filled with rage at the interruption, and a sickly green light suddenly burned where its eyes had once been. Something inside Jean told her that Mr. Ramsay could not see the demon standing before him. She wanted to warn him, but her voice wouldn't respond. Raising its sword, the specter quickly glided across the ground and intercepted Mr. Ramsay on the gravel path. Jean watched in horror as the specter smoothly entered Mr. Ramsay's body disappearing from sight. He took only one more step before grabbing his chest, his face contorting in pain. Mr. Ramsay staggered then dropped to one knee. He looked at Jean, his expression one of shock and confusion. His entire body convulsed; then, he fell over, landing on his back.

The creature emerged from Mr. Ramsay and, once again, stood between her and the chapel. "Jean MacKinnon...arise... come to me. It is your time to serve."

Jean forced her eyes away from Mr. Ramsay's still form and back to the creature before her. Slowly, it began to glide toward her, reaching for her. Jean closed her eyes and began to scream again, collapsing into a curled up ball on the ground.

Suddenly, strong hands gripped both her shoulders, lifting her from the ground. Jean fought back, trying as hard as she could to escape, but she could not break free of the hands that held her.

"Jean! Jean! What's wrong? It's Daddy, sweetheart, everything's all right."

Her father's voice finally broke through the panic. Opening her eyes, she looked up into her father's strong face. She then saw that several other people had gathered around Mr. Ramsay, some of them kneeling. The chapel had nearly emptied.

Frantically Jean looked around, terrified that the creature would now attack her father, but it was gone, as were the specters that had stood guard beside the doors. She looked back at Mr. Ramsay. The man kneeling next to him looked up at her uncle and sadly shook his head. She heard someone say that Mr. Ramsay was dead. It was all she could take. Jean collapsed into her father's arms, sobbing uncontrollably.

CHAPTER 2

2008

MacBridan's plane glided in for a smooth landing, rolling into the gate right on time. The flight over to Richmond had been reasonably short and uneventful, his favorite kind. As usual, he'd carried his luggage on with him, avoiding the thrill of waiting forever for his bag to arrive. MacBridan shuffled through the crowded terminal and went directly to pick up his rental car. The airport was soon behind him as he started the fifty-mile drive to the MacKinnon farm. The gentle hills of the Virginia countryside were thick with trees, and he passed several small farms, steadily making his way into a rugged yet beautiful part of the state.

Having just returned from a short vacation, MacBridan had only been given the assignment a couple of days ago. Not one to argue with easy money, he had questioned Dolinski as to whether or not he was really needed. The team working the assignment was both capable and experienced, and frankly, he just couldn't see what he could contribute.

In short, the assignment was simply not MacBridan's forte, and the whole idea bored him to tears. It was a relocation project, not an investigative detail, and the security already in place was most impressive. Nevertheless, Dolinski explained that the MacKinnon family had been a significant client dating back to nearly the inception of the firm and that the Hawthorne Group had decided that it wasn't going to take any chances. Dolinski believed that their greatest area of vulnerability would be transporting the goods from the farm to the docks in Baltimore. If anything was going to happen, that would be the most likely time.

The Hawthorne Group was proud to have the MacKinnon family as one of its clients and had worked with them exclusively on all legal and contractual issues, in addition to their tax preparation. The family was now preparing to relocate temporarily to their ancestral home in Scotland while their home in Virginia underwent a radical renovation. The house was quite old, having been built prior to the Civil War, and was listed as a national historical landmark. Due to this distinction, each aspect of the renovations had to be cleared with the National Registry, the project potentially lasting two years.

MacBridan, lead investigator for the Hawthorne Group, had reported to Peter Dolinski for close to four years and enjoyed working for him. Both men were the product of military backgrounds, as well as having worked for different law enforcement agencies. It was because of this that MacBridan understood Dolinski's black and white, no-nonsense approach to things, as well as his often blunt and direct manner in dealing with people.

Dolinski's style, from the outside looking in, could often be perceived as being harsh or uncaring, but in reality, it was the unemotional fact-based perspective that the job required. All in all, MacBridan liked and respected the man. Most important was that Dolinski let him run his own show without constant interference or direction. MacBridan could not stand being micromanaged or the people who tried to do so.

If there was any difference of opinion between them at all, it was due to a vein of ruthlessness in Dolinski that had shown up before on various occasions. Not a consistent trait, it was always on the peripheral, never far away, and could spring up without warning. To MacBridan, Dolinski's personality during those times closely resembled the dramatic swings usually attributed to Dr. Jekyll and Mr. Hyde. In times of crisis, Dolinski would offer no middle ground and seemed to operate without a heart or conscience. However, at the same time and to his credit, it was important to note that Dolinski was very loyal to his people. He gave unwavering loyalty and expected no less in return.

The strong professionalism and intense focus that Dolinski's team often demonstrated was characteristic of many of the people who worked for the Hawthorne Group, one of the oldest and most prestigious law firms in the United States. The Hawthorne Group started over sixty years ago as a family-owned practice; their considerable wealth enabled them to cater to a select clientele of their own choosing. Over time, the firm grew in strength and power, earning a sterling reputation for protecting the special interests of its clients. Appropriately, as the demands of its clients grew in complexity, other divisions were added to support their needs.

A strong financial division, capable of working through the most delicate tax problems on up to the largest of corporate mergers, evolved over the years and worked closely with the legal teams. Dolinski had been brought on board to tackle various security challenges, as well as to lead the private investigative services division. Lastly, and often used to divert the media's attention, a public relations division had been created. Dolinski did not care a great deal for this particular area of the business. He often told MacBridan that its sole purpose was to cover up the shady side of their client's true character.

Based on its reputation in all the right circles, the Hawthorne Group had been able to attract top talent and has well positioned it to handle the most sensitive of issues. MacBridan had been one of the first investigators that Dolinski personally recruited into the firm. Based in New York, the Hawthorne Group fielded offices in five countries, along with six locations spread out across the United States. Sometimes, the jobs were intense. Today's job would be easy.

The directions to the farm given to MacBridan were very detailed, and he had no trouble finding it. In all, there were five entrances to the four-thousand-acre farm, all of which were gated with armed security. Normally, the security was much more passive, but Cori Hopkins, the Hawthorne Group team lead, reinforced it the day she arrived.

The MacKinnon's upcoming move to Scotland was not a secret by any means. The number of people going in and out of the farm on a daily basis, just in support of the farm's business, was significant. However, that number swelled dramatically as new teams arrived to catalog, count, and crate the household furnishings.

The primary concern for Cori's team focused on the extensive art collection owned by the MacKinnon family. Over the years, many pieces had been loaned out to museums across the United States. Therefore, in order to best protect the collection, Cori had brought in Dr. Bram Van Dych, an art historian and appraiser used by the Hawthorne Group. His job was to catalog the collection, authenticate each piece in coordination with an expert from Lloyd's of London, the company insuring the collection, and then supervise the packing of each individual item. A collection of this size and value, as well known and admired as it was in the art community, was a magnet for both fraud and theft. Although they did not anticipate any trouble, Cori had been directed to leave nothing to chance. Each crate would be sealed with its own unique number, which would be checked against an inventory once it arrived in Scotland.

MacBridan pulled into the main gate and was approached by two men, one a uniformed security man who worked for the MacKinnon family and the other a specialist from the Hawthorne Group.

"Good afternoon, sir, how can we help you?" MacBridan handed him his identification and watched as both men went through the process of verifying his ID. He quickly answered a couple of routine questions and was soon on his way, the security guard having given him directions to the main house. The park like appearance of the grounds verified all that he'd read about the farm in the MacKinnon file on the flight down.

MacBridan had talked to Cori prior to taking off and was looking forward to seeing her. They'd worked together before on some pretty tough assignments, and he respected her abilities as well as her attention to detail. Plus she was fun to look at.

Cori simply didn't fit the mold so often associated with women in law enforcement; in fact, she was quite the contrary. At five foot seven, her athletic figure was on the slender side and never failed to draw the attention of the men around her. Her hair was a dark auburn brown, which she often wore loose, letting it frame her face while highlighting her pale green eyes. Cori, more often than not, dressed like a Wall Street account executive in the conservative world of finance, but the clothes couldn't hide her curvaceous figure. Cori was capable, tough, and a deadly shot yet could easily grace the cover of any magazine.

MacBridan rounded a rather sharp curve, passed through another gate, and left the trees behind. A broad rolling lawn stretched out before him, surrounding the house that rested on the crest of a small hill. The MacKinnon home, though large, had a quiet, stately charm. A rambling redbrick colonial-style mansion, it boasted large white pillars, giving a distinctly Southern style touch to the porch that stretched across the front of the house. The lane forked, with the right-hand lane leading to the front door and the left guiding MacBridan to the rear of the house. There he found several cars parked next to one another on a gravel parking area, with two catering vans backed up to what he guessed was the kitchen.

MacBridan parked next to a small white pickup truck, taking the last available space. He got out and stretched, thankful that he would not be stuffed into any cramped airplanes or rental cars for at least the next week or so. Between the workout he'd done yesterday and today's trip to the farm, he found he had more than a few sore muscles. MacBridan worked at staying in good shape, for he knew that all too often the demands of his job could become quite physical.

MacBridan walked past the catering van and held open a door for two of the catering personnel who were bringing in large trays of sandwiches. MacBridan followed them into a very large kitchen that was being used as a staging area. He quickly crossed through the kitchen, heading toward two swinging doors on the other side of the room. Just as he started through them, he nearly collided with a woman coming through from the other side.

She was balancing two trays of dishes and, after several frantic gyrations, barely kept from dropping them. Glaring at MacBridan, she gently set the trays down before turning on him.

"How stupid are you? You never use the left-hand door, always the right. What is this, your first job? And why aren't you in uniform?" The faint trace of a French accent was unmistakable.

MacBridan just stood there. It wasn't that he was stunned by her attack on him; it was obvious that he'd committed a huge breach of catering etiquette. It was more the fact that he found himself face-to-face with an extraordinarily beautiful woman, an angry woman, but very beautiful. About six inches shorter than him, she had raven black hair pulled back into a ponytail that reached down between her shoulders. Her eyes were captivating, one green and the other brown with gold specs giving her face an exotic air. She had the tight, slender build of a dancer, well toned, filling out her catering uniform quite nicely, certain to inspire one's appetite.

Despite the strong reprimand, MacBridan couldn't keep the smile off his face, which didn't help the situation at all. "I'm afraid I'm not part of the catering staff, which probably means I'm not supposed to be back here. My name's James MacBridan. I apologize for nearly running into you."

The fire in her eyes burned even stronger, completely ignoring his apology. "I have already talked to the packing supervisor twice about you people coming into this kitchen. He knows, and so should you, that no one but my team is allowed in here!" She glared at MacBridan and finally took a deep breath. "All right, no harm done. Just get back to whatever it is that you're supposed to be doing, and I'll let it go."

Scolded and summarily dismissed, MacBridan was surprisingly at a loss for words, something he rarely experienced. Clearly not going the way he wanted it to, MacBridan said, "What say we start over because I'm not with the moving company either? I work for the Hawthorne Group, and I literally just drove in."

MacBridan held his hand out and turned his smile up several degrees, oozing charm. "Truce? I did apologize. I'd hate to think that you would hold a grudge or, worse, possibly put something in my food at some time over the next few days."

She studied MacBridan closely. Just over six feet tall, he was obviously in good shape, broad in the shoulders and, depending on the cut, sported a size 46 jacket. Despite his smile, there was a hard look about him. His thick dark-brown hair accentuated his penetrating blue eyes, which did manage to help take some of the edge off.

"The Hawthorne Group, so you work for Cori."

"She thinks so, but then we disagree on all kinds of things. In fact I was looking for her when I nearly ran into you."

She took his hand and said, "Well, Mr. MacBridan, apology accepted. We've had so many problems with the packing crew that I guess you really touched on a nerve." MacBridan was impressed with how firmly she shook his hand. She was surprisingly strong, which MacBridan attributed to the catering work.

"I'd certainly like to make up for that. Perhaps, when you get a break, we could have some coffee outside. What I've seen of this place so far is beautiful, inside and out."

She smiled up at MacBridan, and it took all he had to keep his professional demeanor in tack. "I don't drink coffee," she said. "But tea is always nice. We'll have to make time for that. Tell me, what do you do for the Hawthorne Group?"

"I'm in their investigative division."

"That sounds exciting. There aren't any problems here, are there?"

"Not that we know of, but then one can't be too careful."

She smiled again and said, "Excellent advice. I'll certainly make a point of passing that along to my crew."

MacBridan hadn't yet released her hand when a voice behind him cut in. "If you don't let go of her, there isn't going to be a lunch. And if that happens, there's an entire moving team out there that isn't going to be very happy."

Mac let go of her hand, turned, and smiled at Cori. "We were just talking about you," he said.

"Of course you were," said Cori. "I see you've already met Collette. She's in charge of the caterers that Lord MacKinnon engaged to keep everyone fed. Ms. Fortier, this is James MacBridan."

Collette was all smiles. "I'd better get to it or Cori's right, we may have a small riot on our hands. I'm sure I'll be seeing you." MacBridan watched her as she walked away exiting through the swinging doors. There was just something about a French woman in uniform.

Cori shook her head. "You do work fast. How did I know I'd find you in here?"

"Because you know how dedicated I am and that I never skirt any detail." Mac smiled as Cori rolled her eyes. "Truth is I came in through the wrong door. How are things going?"

"So far, so good. The packing is taking longer than I anticipated, but that's primarily due to Dr. Van Dych." Cori stopped and frowned. "No, that came out wrong. Come on, let's get out of here."

Cori led Mac back through the kitchen and out the door he'd entered by. He followed as she stepped out onto the lawn and began to walk toward the front of the house. "Don't misunderstand me. Van Dych's doing a good job. But it's—to borrow one of your expressions—he's turning out to be the one-lane bridge on the eight-lane highway."

"What's he doing to slow things down?"

"All of the jewelry, the artwork, and specific pieces of antique furniture have to be examined by him and the insurance agent before they can be packed. Many items have never been appraised. We are dealing with really old money here, and there are many of those kinds of items. Once authenticated, the object is then packed and crated, all in the same room. He observes each crate being closed and seals each one with a label bearing his mark. He's using some kind of labeling gun that not only numbers them but can't be removed without wire cutters. You can imagine how all that can bring things to a crawl."

"I'm sure you've thought of this," said Mac. "But couldn't you just bring in more people to move things along, no pun intended."

"Oddly, this is how the insurance company wants it done. Once they have the cataloged, they can determine their rates."

"It is their money we're gambling with. Now that I'm here, is there anything I can help you with?"

Cori stepped up onto the front porch. Several high back chairs and rockers were clustered in sets of four across the length of the porch, all overlooking a sloping valley with several pastures and barns off in the distance. Not too far off, MacBridan could see a rather broad stream flowing through one of the lower pastures with stands of large willow trees guarding its shore.

"Yes, there is. I would appreciate it if you'd take a look around at the security we've implemented. Never hurts to have a second pair of eyes look things over."

There were few things she could have said that would have surprised MacBridan more. He looked at Cori with puzzled concern. This was completely out of character for her. She was an experienced professional and one of the most methodical people he'd ever known. "Is there something specifically bothering you? I mean, let's be honest, you could do this assignment in your sleep. I told Dolinski that you'd resent my being here because you'd probably think I was being sent to check up on you."

Cori smiled, but Mac could see that she was holding something back. "Mac, I called Dolinski and asked if I could have you here for a couple of days. Don't laugh, but I'm pretty sure there is something I'm missing, and I can't figure out what it is. It's just a feeling, but there's something out of place, something wrong, and it's driving me nuts."

"Have any of your security teams reported any problems, anything that didn't seem right to them?"

"No, that's just it. Everything is running smoothly, yet I can't shake this feeling that something's just not right. Truth is, the biggest problem we've had has been with your little kitchen cutie and her catering team, and that's only because they've got to be the clumsiest caterers alive. At this point, the casualty list includes two full trays of sandwiches, one large pot of soup, and two tubs of dishes. That alone has to have eaten up most of the profit they were planning to make on this job."

MacBridan chuckled at this. "No wonder she got so upset with me. Inadvertently I almost put her into bankruptcy."

"Anyway, it is all probably much to do about nothing, but I'm glad you're here."

"Me too," said MacBridan, watching a few of the horses that had come up next to the fence. "It's tough getting back into the swing of things after being off for a while, but I got to tell you, it's not too often that I get this kind of a laid-back assignment. I'll take a look around outside and then join you."

"That'll be good. I want you to meet Van Dych. He's a bit of a character, but despite the pace he's setting, I do like him." Cori turned and started through the front door. She stopped and said, "You know, I appreciate your keen, all-seeing investigative eye, but do be careful where you walk. You step in something, we'd prefer you didn't track it into the house."

"Yes, Mother, I'll be careful."

MacBridan began his inspection with the front doors and the windows that ran along the porch. Once that was done, he stepped off the porch, continuing to work his way around the house. It was then he noticed that one of the catering guys had walked out and was standing next to his rental car. The waiter hadn't spotted MacBridan. He seemed nervous, glancing around as if checking to see if anyone was watching him. MacBridan stopped and waited, curious as to what he was up to. The waiter glanced around again then squatted down between Mac's car and the white pickup truck he'd parked next to, dropping out of sight. Mac started across the lawn for a closer look but stopped and smiled as he caught sight of the guy again. As the waiter stood back up, Mac could see that he'd lit up a cigarette. The guy had simply ducked out to take a smoke and apparently didn't want to get caught in the act. Having already experienced Collette's temper, MacBridan could only imagine what she must be like to work for. The waiter finally caught sight of MacBridan watching him, smiled rather sheepishly, and then turned his back to continue his smoke.

Mac continued on his inspection around the property. As expected, Cori had done an excellent job. Whatever was making her doubt herself, it certainly wasn't her work out here. All of the doors and windows had sensors secured to them. She'd mounted cameras, which kept everything under close surveillance and, in addition to help out at night, had set up motion sensors with changing wave patterns creating a virtually impassable twenty-five-foot-wide security moat. Assuming anyone could get by this without being seen or setting off an alarm, they'd have an equally difficult time getting back out.

It didn't take MacBridan long to finish his inspection of the garage, which was detached from the house. A large covered portico led back to the kitchen area. Mac decided to get some coffee and then go find Cori.

As he approached the kitchen, two of the waiters came out carrying a packing crate. It didn't appear to be all that heavy, but its size made it awkward to handle. The crate was rectangular in shape, roughly three and a half feet by five feet, but no more than six inches in depth. The way they were holding it blocked their view of MacBridan.

Mac stepped behind one of the pillars supporting the covered walk to watch and see what they were doing. The two catering vans were parked one in front of the other. Opening the doors of the van closest to them, they rested a corner of the crate on the van's floor. One of the waiters quickly jumped up into the van while his partner continued to hold up the other end. Together they began to wrestle the crate into the van.

Mac quietly moved in on the two men. As he got closer, he could hear something that sounded like metal moving on rollers but couldn't tell what it was. The men continued to work with the crate, maneuvering it inside the van. The second waiter didn't get in, blocking most of MacBridan's view, but as he drew closer, he could see what they were trying to do. The sound he'd heard had been a door on the inside wall of the van sliding open. Behind it was a compartment so cleverly concealed that a search by most security teams wouldn't see it or have any reason to guess it was there. The men worked as quickly as possible to maneuver the crate into the compartment but were having trouble getting it to fit.

That's one of the problems with thieves, thought MacBridan, *just no practical sense of spatial relations.* MacBridan stood directly behind the man leaning into the van. He was a little shorter than Mac with bristly blonde hair. "Need some help, guys?"

Without looking, the waiter slightly turned on his left foot and shot out a back kick. Had he not been off balance, leaning into the van, it would have connected with MacBridan just below the knee. Instead, the kick merely brushed against his pants leg. The move surprised MacBridan, and his adversary quickly spun around, coming at him with two quick punches—both were hard and well aimed. MacBridan quickly realized that he'd underestimated the men he was up against; these were not amateurs. MacBridan blocked both punches and countered with two solid hits to the man's midsection. This gave MacBridan a brief opening, and he connected with a left uppercut to the man's jaw.

The force of the blow spun the man around and into his partner who'd jumped out of the van to help. Both men fell down onto the gravel lot. Mac pulled his gun as the second man got up preparing to lunge at him.

"Hold it," MacBridan said, "game's over." The man MacBridan hit slowly got to his feet and stood next to his partner. Both men glared at MacBridan, but neither one of them looked the least bit concerned that they were being held at gunpoint. Bristly Hair, who'd first attacked MacBridan, looked to the other man for direction. "Don't overthink it boys, you have only two choices. Cooperate or I start shooting kneecaps, makes little difference to me. Now get that crate out of the van."

MacBridan's eyes showed no sign of mercy, so the men nodded and began to climb back inside the van. MacBridan moved in closer, standing to the right of the open doors.

"Move slowly, do the best you can to keep your hands where I can see them, and you'll get through this in one piece. Do anything I don't like and I'll start shooting. We clear?"

"Yeah," said Bristly Hair. A red welt had already begun to rise up on his face at the jawline. "We got it." The men maneuvered the crate out of the van. The waiter who seemed to be the leader of the two stepped out, and they lowered it down to the gravel parking area.

"Now, set it behind that wall," directed MacBridan. A low wall, a little over two feet tall, bordered the parking area, obviously there to keep cars off the lawn. The men did as they were told, lifting the crate and setting it behind the wall.

"Now turn around, face the van, and put your hands behind your head," said MacBridan. As the two turned around, MacBridan pulled out his cell phone and called Cori. She picked up on the second ring.

"What's keeping you?" she asked. "Dr. Van Dych is anxious to meet you. He has a couple of questions that he believes only you can answer."

"I'm in the parking area out behind the kitchen. Two of the catering staff were trying to steal what appears to be some artwork. I convinced them that it wasn't in their best interest."

"I'm on my way."

"We'll be waiting for you, but be careful. They may have friends we don't yet know about."

Just as MacBridan was putting his phone back in his pocket, a woman's voice said, "They do have friends, MacBridan, and they're right behind you."

Mac turned to find Collette and another waiter, both with guns leveled on him, not ten feet away. "Now slowly put your gun down at your feet."

The two men MacBridan had been holding lowered their hands, turned, and smiled at him. Their smiles were not friendly. Rather than putting his gun down as directed, MacBridan tossed it over the low wall and into the grass.

"Now that's not what I told you to do," said Collette. "Move very carefully, MacBridan. I am not being paid to shoot anyone, but I assure you, you wouldn't be my first."

"And here I thought we had something special."

She looked at the men by the van. "You two get that crate loaded back into the van and be quick about it."

"Sure," said Bristly Hair, "right after I teach Smart-Mouth a lesson."

The man came at MacBridan just as Cori and another one of the Hawthorne security men ran out the front door rounding the corner of the porch. "Nobody move!" she shouted.

Two more waiters had joined Collette, but if they had guns, they hadn't drawn them. MacBridan stepped into the man charging him and landed a hard roundhouse blow to his stomach, knocking the wind out of him. MacBridan caught Bristly Hair as he started to collapse and, using the man's own momentum, launched him into Collette and the other gunman.

Without waiting to see where they landed, MacBridan dove over the small wall and rolled back up against it for cover. Someone fired a shot, but Mac wasn't sure where it'd come from.

MacBridan heard Collette yell to her men to get out of there. Two more shots were fired, both at Cori and the security man, who'd taken up position at the corner of the porch. MacBridan wasn't wearing a backup piece. He spotted his gun but realized that it was too far away for him to be able to reach it without getting himself shot. As quickly as possible, he crawled along the wall, doing his best to move out of the crossfire.

Once MacBridan reached the end of the wall, he looked back at Cori. She was on her phone, alerting the other security teams. MacBridan heard doors slam, and one of the catering vans roared past him and out of the parking area, flinging gravel behind it. He got up and noticed that the van they'd been trying to hide the crate in had been left behind. They'd also left Bristly Hair behind. He was sprawled facedown in the gravel, so much for honor among thieves.

MacBridan ran to his car. Although reasonably confident that the van would be stopped, no matter which gate they tried to get through, he'd already underestimated them once and wasn't going to make that mistake again. MacBridan, keys in hand, slid in behind the wheel. Even though his rental didn't have the greatest pick up, he knew he'd be able to catch up with them. Slamming down on the accelerator, the car jerked hard to the side, and he had to fight with the steering wheel to keep it going straight. MacBridan struggled with the car. It felt like he was trying to drive through thick mud.

MacBridan hit the brakes, pretty sure as to what was wrong. Getting out, he walked around the car, confirming his suspicions. All four tires were flat.

Cori caught up to him and looked at the tires. "How did that happen?"

"We'll need to check all the cars before moving them," answered MacBridan. "I saw one of the waiters out here earlier pretending to take a cigarette break. He was actually putting spikes in front of each tire. I'll say this for them, they were well prepared."

"Terrific. We also have another problem." Mac looked at Cori; the expression on her face was not encouraging. "I can't get post number 4 to answer. I just hung up from sheriff's department. They're on their way."

MacBridan glared at the flat tires, mentally cursing himself for having been so easily duped. "Cori, I don't know who they were, but one thing's for sure, they were pros. Fortunately, they left one of their people behind, so it shouldn't be all that hard to find out who the rest of them are." MacBridan watched as the security man who'd come out with Cori put handcuffs on the waiter.

"We may also have a little more good news," continued MacBridan. "We'll need to check the inventory, but at least as far as we know, they didn't make it out of here with the art they were trying to steal." Mac pointed to the crate leaning up against the wall. Walking back to the house, MacBridan looked at Cori, smiled, and said, "And from my perspective, do you know the really best part about all this?"

"What's that?"

"As you're in charge, you're the one who gets to phone the report into Dolinski."

Chapter 3

The light from the early morning sun poured through the windows of the conference room so much that MacBridan had to adjust the window shades to keep from being blinded. The room was connected to Dolinski's office, and MacBridan and Cori were waiting to meet with him. It had been two days since the attempted theft at the MacKinnon farm, which had been followed by a flurry of activity. Before returning to New York, they had coordinated closely with the sheriff's department. The influence of the MacKinnon family, along with a well-placed call by the Hawthorne Group into the Virginia governor's office, secured getting deputies posted at each of the farm's gates. The actual move was scheduled to take place three days from now, and absolutely nothing was being left to chance.

"Good morning," said Dolinski as he entered the room. "We just got an update from the Virginia State Police on the two catering vans." As always, Dolinski was impeccably dressed. Never having personally been a slave to fashion, MacBridan had to guess that the charcoal gray double-breasted suit that Dolinski had on was the latest that Brooks Brothers had to offer. Although not a tall man, Dolinski was barrel-chested and could be very intimidating when the situation called for it.

"Just how hot were they?" asked MacBridan.

"They'd been stolen six weeks earlier off a used car lot in southern Maryland. Apparently, both had had extensive body and engine work done on them, one feature being the creation of the hidden compartment in which they tried to hide the crate containing the art."

"Someone put in a great deal of planning and money on this," said Cori.

"True," said Dolinski, "but we'll come back to the money. You don't know half of it. The second van was located yesterday in an old barn about five miles from the MacKinnon farm. Sheriff's department thinks that they'd been storing two cars there to make the switch from the vans and effectively vanish."

"What happened to the real catering team?" asked MacBridan, refilling his coffee.

"Absolutely nothing," answered Dolinski. "We believe that someone, an employee working at the farm, was paid to find out which catering service they were going to use. The day after the catering company was hired, Ms. Colette Fortier showed up and introduced herself as one of the MacKinnon family staff. She explained that due to the high security needed at the farm, she'd be coordinating the on-site staff. That said, Ms. Fortier was quick to assure the caterer that this would not in any way reduce the fee that had already been agreed to. The caterer was delighted with this arrangement. With not having to fool with the wait staff, they were suddenly looking at a much-broader profit on the job."

"They were always there," said Cori, "starting around six thirty each morning until about eight thirty or so at night. The way they operated, we never had a need to call their office. Each morning, a couple of them would take one of the vans and drive to Richmond, get restocked, and be back that afternoon."

"I didn't know they were staying at the farm," said Dolinski.

"They weren't," said Cori. "Colette told me they had rooms about ten miles away at a small motel. Still, Julia Harris did not impress me as being too careless. How is it that she accepted Ms. Fortier as the new caterer?" asked Cori.

"Ms. Fortier called Ms. Harris from the caterer's, introduced herself as the on-site leader, and went over all the details with her to make certain nothing went wrong. Ms. Harris told us that she could see from her phone that the call was coming from the catering service she'd hired and didn't think anything about it," said Dolinski.

"Who is Julia Harris?" asked MacBridan.

"She works for the MacKinnon family, pretty much manages the farm. She'll be staying on-site during the renovation," explained Cori.

"Pretty clever," said MacBridan. "No one knows a switch has been made, and our merry band of thieves has the real caterer preparing the food." He looked at Cori and smiled. "It would explain their clumsy behavior around the kitchen. I'd venture to say that most of them probably had more experience at serving time than serving tea."

"It was a bit of a rogues' gallery," said Dolinski. He opened one of the files he'd brought in and handed Mac and Cori their own copy. "The waiter you dispatched turns out to be a local hood, very familiar to the Richmond Police."

"He seemed to be a pretty tough, experienced sort of guy," said MacBridan. "Are they getting much out of him?"

"Depending on how this goes down, he could be looking at his third felony conviction. In an effort to avoid that, he's singing his head off."

"Very nice," said Cori. "So who is Colette Fortier, and why have they not caught up with her yet?"

"That is probably the most significant question that we need answered," said Dolinski. "In short, no one knows. All that our local hood knows is that Fortier called the shots and apparently demonstrated early on that she was not to be crossed. Exactly what she did to get that point across, he won't elaborate on. All but two of the crew were local, and she did most of the recruiting."

"He didn't know who he was working for?" asked Cori.

"Didn't matter to him. The money was too good," explained Dolinski. "He was paid half up front and was to get the other half upon the successful completion of the job."

"Even bad guys don't usually throw money around like that. Did his employer share with him how many pieces they were going after?" asked MacBridan. "It was just pure luck that we caught them when we did."

"If what he's telling us is true, it was a very targeted operation. He claims that they were after one piece and one piece only. The goal was to sneak it out, hide it in the side panel compartment of one of the vans, and slip away without anyone even knowing there'd been a theft."

"Interesting," said MacBridan. "So that would lead one to believe that the individual paying the bills is a very determined collector, who also has little in the way of conscience as to how he expands his collection. I'm not all that tuned into the world of art, but we know which piece they were trying to steal. With that tidbit of information, I'll bet there's someone out there who could make a pretty good guess as to who we should be going after."

"I have the inventory here," said Cori. "Which painting were they targeting?"

"Mac, I agreed with your line of reasoning, and it's exactly what I thought at first. Unfortunately, in this case, it won't hold up," said Dolinski. "The piece they tried to steal is a family heirloom that has been in the MacKinnon family for several generations. According to Van Dych, it was painted by the brother of the lord of the manor in the early 1820s, not long before he died. The brother had somewhat of a shady reputation and was looked upon as the black sheep of the family. He'd been at sea for years, and there were rumors when he returned that he'd sailed with pirates. Needless to say, his return to the estate in 1819 created a bit of a local stir. Not too long after that, he took ill and became so sick that eventually he was confined to his room. It was then that he began to paint and completed five paintings that we know of."

"What became of the other four?" asked MacBridan. "Are they at the farm also?"

"The other four are at the MacKinnon estate in Scotland where they've been since the day they were painted," said Dolinski. "Van Dych was able to get this information from Lord MacKinnon just after the failed attempt at the farm. This particular painting was brought to the United States by the family when many of the MacKinnon clan moved to Virginia, a piece of home so to speak."

Cori quickly thumbed through some files in a large box that she'd brought in. "Here it is," she said, pulling a file out and laying it on the conference table. "We have each piece numbered and photographed. This is the painting they tried to steal."

MacBridan and Dolinski studied the picture. For the most part, it appeared to be a rather normal, run of the mill landscape painting presented from the perspective of one looking out of an upstairs window. Part of the inside of the room could be seen, end tables on either side of the window, an oil lamp on one, and what appeared to be the corner of a box with numbers on it on the other one, as well as part of the windowpane. Most of the picture, however, was focused on the view from the window, a large and beautiful garden with a tall tree line in the distance.

"The information we were given dates the painting as having been completed in 1820. The scene has been identified as being of one of the gardens on the MacKinnon estate, one that he could see from his bedroom," said Dolinski.

"How sad," said Cori. "He must have really loved the gardens to have spent his final days painting them."

"Not to be unduly harsh," said MacBridan, "and I'm certainly no authority on art, but this doesn't appear to be that good of a painting. Not that I could do much better, but this seems to be the kind of painting that only a family, and a very loving family at that, could appreciate."

"When I was talking to Van Dych about it," said Dolinski, "he admitted his surprise that anyone would go to all this trouble to steal it."

"How much is this particular painting insured for?" asked MacBridan.

Cori looked through another file that she had and said, "Virtually nothing. Unlike many of the more valuable pieces of art, this is only insured for actual damage during the move, a cracked frame, a tear in the canvas, that sort of thing." She continued to read down the page she was looking at. "There is only five hundred dollars coverage on it in the event of theft. The family could put in a claim for loss, but the payout would be nominal."

"That shoots that motive in the head. So why all this effort to steal a valueless painting?" asked MacBridan. He'd read a detective novel as a kid about a really famous painting that had been painted over. Maybe the black sheep had hidden a Rembrandt or something.

"Why indeed. Now here's where it gets really interesting, bringing us back to a point Cori referenced earlier regarding the money to do a job like this. While there aren't any pictures on file with any law enforcement agencies, we believe, based on your description, Mac, that the thief's true name is Nicolette Cuvier, also known as Talon," said Dolinski.

"I've heard of her," said Cori. "Little over a year ago, I read about a huge art robbery in Vienna. If I recall, none of the pieces taken have ever been recovered."

"That's correct," said Dolinski. "Nicolette Cuvier has a remarkable reputation as one of best in the business when it comes to stealing priceless works of art."

"Did any of the cameras Cori have set up at the farm get a shot of her?" asked MacBridan.

"We already checked," said Cori, "and unfortunately, no. For the most part, she stayed in the kitchen area and away from the cameras. The only one where we got a partial shot was the one outside the kitchen door. Each time she passed by, she managed to shield her face."

"Nice work, Mac," said Dolinski. "Had your description not been so detailed we still wouldn't have any idea of who we're dealing with."

Before Mac could respond, Cori said, "Oh, he got a good look, up close and personal. Any closer and we could have lifted his prints off of her."

MacBridan's expression was one of innocence. "I assure you that my contact with Ms. Cuvier was purely investigative in nature, not to mention my being a thorough, hands-on professional."

"And as it turns out, so was she," said Cori.

"Nevertheless," said Dolinski, "you are both to be congratulated. You were able to prevent them from achieving their goal, and our client is quite pleased."

MacBridan started to ask another question as Ester King, Dolinski's administrative assistant, came into the conference room. "Excuse me for interrupting," she said, "but you asked me to let you know when Lord MacKinnon arrived. I have him waiting in the Dunbridge conference room as you requested." Ester King was a bit of a throwback to the fifties. Extremely loyal to Dolinski, she was very thin and dressed conservatively to the point of being a borderline nun. She always reminded MacBridan of the maiden aunt you didn't want to cross. Her personality was pleasant but distant and strictly professional in every sense of the word. In the years he'd worked there, MacBridan had never been able to get even as much as a trace of a smile out of her. One of his goals was to unmask the unstated, natural attraction that he was sure she secretly harbored for him.

MacBridan caught her eye and flashed his most charming smile, a smile so effective with women that at times he'd considered having it licensed. Her gaze remained fixed on him for a mere moment, but her somewhat dour expression never changed, and she turned her attention back to Dolinski. *Nearly got her*, MacBridan thought to himself. *You have to admire her self-control.*

"Thank you, Ester, that's excellent. We shouldn't be much longer here."

"Very good," she said. "I'll let him know that you'll be joining him shortly." With that, she turned and left. Cori had caught the brief exchange between Mac and Ester. Mac winked at Cori and gave a small shrug.

"Sir, before we meet with Lord MacKinnon, I'd like to talk about this a little more," said MacBridan.

"You have something else?" asked Dolinski.

"Well, unless Lord MacKinnon can shed some light on this, we have an extremely expensive conspiracy to commit a theft that, based on the value of the target, makes absolutely no sense at all. Not to sound too cliché-ish, but there's got to be more. For this to make any sense at all, we have to be missing a big piece of the puzzle."

"Are you driving at who would be the money behind all this?" asked Cori.

"That's certainly a part of it," answered MacBridan, "but the whole thing defies explanation or, for that matter, good business sense." He reached for the art inventory that Cori had pulled out. "It is well known that the MacKinnon family has several famous works of art at that farm. Look at this list.

Here are two Monets, three Picassos, a Rembrandt, and that's just the tip of a sizeable priceless iceberg. When you step back and review the facts that we have, why would anyone target that particular painting? If the goal had been to steal as many pictures as they could lay their hands on and then get out of there, that'd be one thing. Then I could understand that as luck would have it, they just happened to start with a poor random choice. But we've been told the exact opposite. This was a well-planned targeted operation led by perhaps one of the top professionals in the field to steal what is, for all intents and purposes, the equivalent of a nearly two-hundred-year-old paint by number."

"There is, of course, the chance that our thief is lying to us," said Dolinski, "but I seriously doubt that. I'm also certain that someone of Ms. Cuvier's reputation would not make such a careless mistake as to not know what was in the crate she was stealing."

"I agree. This is far from being a simple smash and grab," said MacBridan. "Someone went to a great deal of time, planning, and expense to pull this off."

"How much expense are we talking?" asked Cori.

"Easily well into the six-figure range," said MacBridan. "For as we all know, good Talon doesn't come cheap."

Cori grimaced, all too familiar with Mac's brand of humor. Dolinski stood up and said, "You raise several good points. Let's see if Lord MacKinnon can shed any light on this, shall we?"

"I also think it'd be in our interest to examine that painting far more closely, determine exactly what we're dealing with," said MacBridan. "I'll ask Van Dych to take the lead on that."

"Sounds good," said Dolinski. "Now let's go meet with our guest." Gathering their things, they followed Dolinski down the hall to the Dunbridge room, one of the smaller conference rooms on that floor.

Lord MacKinnon rose to greet them as they came in, with a cup of tea resting in front of him on the table. "Good morning, Peter," said Lord MacKinnon, shaking Dolinski's hand. "And so good to see you again, Ms. Hopkins."

Lord MacKinnon's accent was distinctly Scottish but not nearly as thick of a brogue as many of his countrymen. Clearly in his early fifties, Lord MacKinnon was a couple inches shy of being six feet tall and bald on top with thick white hair along the sides and back of his head. Clean-shaven, he had a prominent nose and a strong jaw, features MacBridan would come to recognize as being common with the MacKinnon clan. While in seemingly good health, he was easily carrying thirty pounds of extra padding at his waist.

"I'd like you to meet one of my top operatives," said Dolinski. "This is James MacBridan."

"Ah, yes," said Lord MacKinnon as he shook hands with him. "I understand that I owe you and Ms. Hopkins a debt of gratitude for stopping the thieves. You've got a good name, Mac Gille Bridhge, son of the servant of St. Bridget."

"It's a pleasure meeting you, sir," said MacBridan. "We were very fortunate that things went our way."

"I often trust to good fortune," said Lord MacKinnon as he set back down, "but as my family crest reads, 'Fortune Favors the Bold.' You acted quickly and intelligently. It's called being on top of your game, a trait I look for in all the people who work for me."

"Thank you," said MacBridan. "We certainly appreciate the compliment."

"At this point, I'm afraid that we still have more questions than we have answers," said Dolinski. "We were hoping you might be able to clear up a couple of items for us."

"Of course, I'll do anything I can to help."

"Before we get to that, I'd like to have Cori bring you up-to-date on all that we know," said Dolinski. "It may help you with the questions we have."

Cori proceeded to give Lord MacKinnon a thorough update, from the theft of the vans and duping of the catering company to the attempted theft. "The description given by the man we have in custody, along with the descriptions provided by Mac and me, has us believing that the leader of this gang is a woman named Nicolette Cuvier. Does that name sound familiar to you?" asked Cori.

Lord MacKinnon lowered his head in thought for a moment. "No, I can't say it does." He shook his head and added, "No, I've never heard of the young woman. Although I must say that I find all this simply astonishing. For this woman to have gone to all this trouble, it must have been an expensive venture for her."

"We quite agree," said MacBridan. "If we're right and it is Ms. Cuvier, then it will have been a most expensive venture, at least for someone. She has a reputation as being one of the top art thieves in the field today. She's better known by the law enforcement community as Talon."

"Rather fierce moniker for such a petite thief," said Lord MacKinnon.

"She's not known for her failures," said Dolinski. "To our knowledge, she's never killed anyone, but she has used violence when necessary, having taken out more than one security guard. She's expensive, somewhat lethal, and she delivers."

"Lord MacKinnon," said MacBridan, placing a picture in front of him on the table, "this is the painting that we believe they were targeting. We've been told that it was the only one they intended to steal. The hidden compartment they'd built into the side of the van semiconfirms this in that there was only enough room for one crate, a crate of the dimensions necessary to contain this painting and its frame. We understand that this was painted by one of your ancestors. Of all the art that you own, do you have any idea why they would have gone after this particular piece?"

Lord MacKinnon studied it for a moment and gave a small smile, almost embarrassed by the picture. "Heavens no! There are actually four more of these garish things, the others are on display at our manor house in Scotland. My grandfather brought one of them with him when they moved to America. It's just one of those things a family collects over the years, and my family is quite old. Then, for some silly and completely unexplainable reason, someone comes to cherish it, and it becomes a valued family heirloom. That painting is as worthless as the man who painted it. My aunt Jean and I have discussed it on more than one occasion. Well, discussed may actually be too calm of a word to use, but every time I talk about wanting to take it down and put it in storage where it belongs, she gets all over me for disrespecting my heritage. My aunt Jean is remarkably strong of character with very definitive opinions."

"Have there been any attempts on the other four, or for that matter, any of the art at your Scotland home?" asked Cori.

"The security at the estate is run by Marston Pierce, a most capable man. Naturally, I alerted him as soon as I learned of the attempted theft here. He's been with me for nearly six years now, and we've never had a single issue."

"I know Marston," said Dolinski. "He's not someone I'd want to go up against."

"Marston mentioned that you knew each other," said Lord MacKinnon. "I believe you met him when he was still with the SAS, isn't that right?"

"Yes," said Dolinski. "We worked on a case together. He's a good man."

"Our concern at this point is that she'll try again," said MacBridan. "As we stated earlier, she delivers. A failure such as this could tarnish her reputation, and that wouldn't be good for business."

"I appreciate your concern, Mr. MacBridan, but I have great confidence in the people around this table. Now that you know who it is that's trying to steal from me, I'm sure you'll be able to take the appropriate measures."

"You're right, of course, we have gained some advantage in knowing who we're dealing with," said Dolinski. "However, having lost the element of surprise, her next move will be escalated far beyond the more subtle approach she took here."

"I'm not sure I follow what you're saying," said Lord MacKinnon.

"Not to put too fine a point on it, I think her next attempt will most probably be head-on and as violent as it takes to achieve her goal," said MacBridan. "You only get one chance to surprise someone, and in that she's failed."

"Lord MacKinnon," Dolinski began, "our current assignment is to pack and move your household possessions to the docks in Baltimore and see to it that they are put on a cargo ship to Glasgow. Unfortunately, the circumstances have changed dramatically, and so should our plans. We propose that once everything is loaded on board, that Mac and Cori sail with the ship and accompany the trucks all the way to your manor house."

"You truly believe that's necessary," said Lord MacKinnon, more as a statement of fact than a question.

"Talon will take another run at this. You can count on it," continued Dolinski. "It's just a question of when and where."

"Very well," said Lord MacKinnon. He looked at Cori and MacBridan, smiled, and said, "I look forward to having you as my guests while you're in Scotland. I'm sure you'll enjoy my home as well as the quaint little village of Abbotsbury."

Chapter 4

With the setting of the sun, the thin, arid mountain air cooled quickly, so much so that he could now see his breath. It had taken Kaseem five days of hard travel to get here through steep and dangerous terrain. Few knew of the paths he'd followed. Deep in the Hindu Kush Mountains of northwestern Pakistan, the final leg of his journey now rose up before him.

The tribe had guarded the hidden path that worked its way up the mountain and had done so for centuries. Their fierce loyalty was grounded in religious fervor as well as a deep-seated fear. They had lived and worshiped here for hundreds of years and knew all too well the wrath of their demon goddess. Kaseem, a twice-born, stayed with them one full day before completing his journey along the narrow path to their god's one true temple. He spent that time talking and eating with the tribal elders, honoring them for their fealty and for allowing him to lead them personally through the dark rites. Despite his status, only the sacred scarring on his arms and back allowed him safe passage among them.

The temple sat high up on the mountain and had been built out from the edge of a steep, jagged slope. The ornate structure covered the entrance to a cave whose vast system of passages led deep into the bowels of the mountain, a mountain that had been home to a malevolent evil long before man ever ventured into the valley. The Old Religion had been practiced in the cave beyond memory, dating back to nearly prehistoric times, with only the drawings of the Horned God on the cavern walls to mark their followers' early existence. The temple building had been completed around 3,300 BC, and no one but the priests and their acolytes were allowed to pass beyond the altar and into the labyrinth of passages.

The primary chamber of the temple was windowless, but its walls were covered with intricate carvings of ancient symbols used in their rituals. The lower altar stood in the center of the chamber, and it is here that all sacrifices to their god were placed. At the far end, raised upon a dais, rose a large gilded altar. This is where the priests stood to bless the sacrifices and to lead their followers in rituals of praise. The entire chamber was filled with the heavy scent of marijuana, sandalwood, and the sweet tang of burnt flesh. But there was another odor here, the smell of something alien to human life and purpose, the pheromones of demons, the smell of snakeskin from Eden, as the banned books said, "By their smell you shall know them."

Close to three years had passed since Kaseem had been here, but he stayed in close communication. A tall man and powerfully built, Kaseem walked slowly to the altar at the far end of the chamber, knelt, and gave the ritual prayer. He had been born in the region and had grown up not far from the temple. Orphaned at the age of twelve, he was recognized by the ritual specialist in his village, who had seen his potential and had brought him here as a candidate for their priesthood. He was of the wrong caste to be initiated by the Hindus, too poor for the Muslims, but just right for the man who could do things. The long ordeal had been terrifying, extremely painful, and almost more than he could endure. Three of the scars on his back and arms were a grim reminder of the tests he had faced. Those who failed the tests of priesthood died in the process.

A score of other acolytes lined the walls, endlessly chanting the seed mantras that allowed the dark gods a foothold to this dimension. Their faces bore signs of idiocy from the prolonged contact with forces inimical to the clean life of this planet. Saying the words was like handling uranium; it took its toll on the flesh.

With the prayer finished, he stepped behind the altar and entered a long, narrow hallway that sloped downward. The hallway ended in a small chamber with heavy dark-red drapes covering the back wall. Parting the drapes, he felt the moist air of the cave wash over him and began his descent into the mouth of this enormous system of passages. The steps had been carved out of the stone floor and had worn down in places with the passage of time. The long stairwell was lit by oil lamps that hung from the walls.

It took him several minutes to finally reach the bottom that opened up into a large cavern, the top arching at least twenty-five feet above his head. Like the stairs he'd just descended, multiple lamps lined the walls of the cavern, but they were unable to illuminate the entire room, leaving much of it in impenetrable shadows. For centuries, the room had been used as a crypt for the high priests, and their cremated remains were placed against the right-hand wall in ornately carved urns.

Three smaller passages veered off from the cavern, each leading deeper into the mountain. Kaseem made his way along the left-hand side of the vast room to the first of the three. Two men, also priests, wearing the black and ochre-colored robes of their order, silently stood guard at the entrance to this passage. They were the only ones he had seen since entering the temple, but there had been others. Sentinels, all well concealed and tasked with keeping a constant and vigilant guard, had watched his every step. Despite his rank in the order, Kaseem's nerves filled his stomach. Sathanas, who had summoned him, was their grand master and was as powerful as he was terrifying.

No one was ever safe in his presence; he often sent servants to their next incarnation.

"I, Kaseem, beg audience with the great and holy Grand Master Sathanas," said Kaseem, his voice not revealing the apprehension he felt. "He has demanded my presence."

Without saying a word, both nodded, bowed to him, and let him pass. They knew of the summoning and therefore had expected his arrival. The passageway he entered was tight, but the ceiling remained well above his head. The air here was thick, heavily scented with the thick, rancid odor of the ghee lamps. The passage gradually curved to the left and, after about ten yards, came to a fork. Kaseem stopped and peered down the dark passage that led off to his left, remembering the many times he'd gone down there over the years. It was a terrible place, a place where condemned captives were held until their time of sacrifice, and their treatment was brutal.

Kaseem remembered the atrocities he'd witnessed and could faintly hear the water that fell from the mountain into the deep pit where the passage came to an end. He was still part of the world of men, and despite his love for the dark ones, he still failed in his heart. Someday he would come to live here and a certain change would set in. Kaseem shuddered; it must have been the cave's dampness.

As he turned to continue on his way along the passage to his right, he thought he heard a faint moan. He stopped and listened, once again peering down into the pitch darkness of the other passage. The stench of excrement and vomit drifted his way.

The floor of this passage began to rise up, soon becoming a steep slope. The walls closed in on him, and the ceiling angled downward, so much so that he had to bend over ever so slightly to keep from hitting his head. Soon he came to a wooden door whose frame filled the tight passage. Taking a deep breath, he knocked three times on the door and waited. It was tradition when called by the grand master to knock three times, only three, and then to wait for however long it took. Today his wait was very short.

"You may enter." The voice was low, deep with the rasping quality of old age, and yet there was strength in its timbre.

Kaseem pushed down on the latch and leaned into the door to open it. Once inside, he closed the heavy door behind him. The room he now stood in was large but not nearly as large as the first cavern he'd passed through. With eerie green light, lamps burnt on an altar to the old ones directly in the center of the room, its surface deeply stained by the numerous sacrifices that had been held there. Sathanas stood next to the altar and turned to acknowledge him. Kaseem knelt down on both knees and bowed his head, nearly touching the floor. Sathanas greeted him in a language that had been lost to time. It was not a human tongue and ill-suited to tongue and teeth.

"The glory of desire burns in brilliance and darkness," intoned the high priest.

"The black flame shall destroy even the stars of the heavens," replied Kaseem.

"You may rise, Kaseem," said Sathanas. Kaseem saw another fire burning in an iron grate carved into the wall at the back of the room. It was then he saw that they were not alone and watched as an acolyte carefully removed a pot from the grate and left through an opening next to the fire. The putrid smell of burnt flesh hung in the air.

Kaseem knew that Sathanas was old, but his true age was hard to guess. He wore a mask of yellow silk. The more modern and educated members of the order said that the mask maintained the illusion that their leader was deathless and with each new head taking the name of his predecessor. The superstitious members of the order claimed that Sathanas had greeted Alexander when his troops advanced into India. Kaseem felt his modernity fade away.

To Kaseem's knowledge, Sathanas rarely left this part of the cave. He was tall, almost skeletally thin, and wore dark robes similar to those of the guards Kaseem had passed. The sacred medallion hung from his neck. The dark-blue medallion showed the seven stars that the Englishmen called the Big Dipper. They were the center of the night sky, and all stars seemed to revolve around them. They were the heart of darkness. Sathanas's eyes were deeply sunken behind the pale mask. They reflected a strange black glow.

"It is good to see you, Kaseem, although I am disappointed at the progress of the mission you are leading. I trust my emissaries made my feelings on this point quite clear to you. It is my understanding," continued Sathanas, "that our partners have failed and that the first attempt on the painting was stopped by a mere security guard."

"That too is my understanding, Grand Master."

"This does not please me. The opportunity before us is too great for such incompetence to be allowed. Our partners promised us success, made commitments that they could handle such an endeavor. Perhaps they don't truly appreciate my level of tolerance for failure."

"I will move quickly to remind them of all that they are risking. My concern is that they may have an ulterior motive, some idea of why we seek this painting. Perhaps this apparent failure was not truly an accident."

"No, of that I am certain," answered Sathanas. He pondered this for a moment then shook his head in a dismissive gesture, sighed, and said, "They are like so many in the West, ignorant and greedy. No, all that motivates them is the promise of gold, which is what they mistakenly believe we are after."

Kaseem remained silent. To bring up the possibility of failure was something he dreaded, but he had little choice. Kaseem had no intention of being purified in some hell of Sathanas's choosing.

"Grand Master," Kaseem began, "please forgive my weakness and doubts, but once the painting is in our possession, we have no true way of knowing if it will lead us to that which we seek. What little we know comes from an old Scottish legend, and that legend has more than one version. Over the years, many have searched for the treasure and failed."

A rage that was never far from the surface flashed across Sathanas's eyes, and he glared down at his priest. The nervousness that filled Kaseem's stomach instantly turned to an icy fear. "Have we not been through this before? Why do you persist in asking the same questions over and over again? Perhaps I have placed my confidence with the wrong man. Perhaps your time in the West has weakened you, rendering you as useless as a whimpering woman."

Kaseem immediately dropped to the floor, prostrating himself before Sathanas. "Grand Master, I am completely devoted and ever faithful to our gods. I assure you on my sacred oaths that your trust in me is well placed."

"That which we seek is there," said Sathanas, the anger in his voice cut through the air like the edge of a dagger. "The djinn of smokeless fire has shown it to me in a vision. It rests in a coffin inside a vault. A sign has been carved on the vault, which keeps it free from my will, and within, a guardian has likewise been imprisoned."

With great effort, Sathanas mastered his temper. "Rise, Kaseem, but I remind you that I am and always will be better informed on the realities of the world of men than you."

"Yes, my lord," said Kaseem.

"I can see, Kaseem, that you are not like the other hands of the dark lord. The time you have spent in Western schools has taught you to seek the reason of why you do things. Curiosity was given to the humans by the demons to undermine the power of the one, so I shall honor yours. Have you read the books of the Hebrews?"

"My lord, what need have I of superstitions that serve the One?" asked Kaseem. It was a lie. He had read the Bible every time he had been stuck in an American hotel room. He found it quaint, misogynistic, and oddly prejudiced toward one Middle Eastern tribe.

"The witch of Endor provided Saul with true answers, yet she was condemned. Why would the one hate this?"

"I am not much on theology, Lord. Besides, it is a fable."

"It is not a fable! The creature called Lilith tried to free the human race from the yoke of the one by giving them perfect knowledge. The scrolls of Endor allow humans to ask intelligences far greater than their puny selves for perfect knowledge. The witch merely used them to bring back Samuel, who changed Hebrew history?"

"But why would Lilith have given this to her?"

"The lord and lady of darkness give knowledge to the most strong, the most ruthless."

Kaseem said, "I understand, my lord, as it is written, 'Might makes right!' But how is Lilith connected to this witch?"

"Lilith allowed the witch to channel her. As you know, most humans die because of this process, but her brain was so attuned as to become an instrument of great power."

"So the scrolls hold the ritual?"

"We seek more than the scrolls. We seek the witch's head. It has been preserved with certain herbs and enchantments to remain a communication link."

"So why is it in a Scottish vault?" asked Kaseem. Already he had begun to desire the head; the high priest knew desire would make him more ruthless. Later he would be dealt with.

"Centuries after the death of the witch, a stone coffin was found by a band of our followers. It had been buried on the plains of Shuman near the present city of Hifa. In the coffin was the talisman, the carefully wrapped head of the witch, and the scrolls. Think of it! The head once possessed by Lilith is within our grasp. At that time, they did not understand the power, the potential, but knew enough to keep them hidden. When Jerusalem fell to the Christians during the first crusade, the damned Templars discovered the scrolls and the head. They stole them and took them back to France. May their souls be consumed by the flames of torment throughout eternity."

Sathanas paced back and forth before the altar, struggling once again to keep his temper in check. "The ancient writings tell us that contained within the Scrolls of Endor are many powerful rituals, but the most powerful one, the one of the most significance to us, is the ritual of prophecy. And these rituals can only be accomplished by those who possess the head. It is fantastic! Think of the power that true prophecy would bring, lifting the vale away from our eyes and allowing us to see the future. It is limitless."

"Why didn't the Templars use the head and the ritual?"

"They made some use of it. The order grew very wealthy. When it was broken apart, the Portuguese branch of the knights became involved in navigation and, ultimately, provided information to Columbus and other explorers."

"But the Templars were destroyed, how could they fail?"

"They were too proud to ask the correct questions."

"Do we not already have in our possession ancient grimoires that can provide a way to see into the future?" asked Kaseem.

"No, Kaseem, there are only some that hint at prophecy. The scrolls are believed to be very detailed, much more so than any of the grimoires we know of, leading us in the ways to harness such power."

Kaseem was awed by this revelation. "With such power, we would become invincible."

Sathanas stopped his pacing and stared at Kaseem for a few moments. "Yes, but we cannot overlook the possibility that Rome may know of ways to protect against such power, although I have serious doubts. We must accept the possibility that the Templars may have made copies of the scrolls. There is no way to know. However, even if Rome does have copies of these writings in their possession, I question whether they have the intelligence to understand their potential. Rome grows more and more corrupt as time goes on."

Kaseem feared and respected Sathanas and wanted to believe him, but he was also painfully aware of the number of times that Rome had successfully intervened defeating their followers. He did not, however, think that it would be a good time to remind Sathanas of these facts. Nevertheless, whether Kaseem believed that the scrolls existed or if they had any chance of actually finding them didn't really matter. The responsibility to locate them and bring them to Sathanas was his, and he cursed his bad fortune to have been chosen for such a mission. He was all too familiar with the price of failure and knew that should he fail, there would be no hiding from his grand master; he would be found.

Sathanas interrupted his thoughts. "Go, Kaseem, and bring this revered relic and the Scrolls of Endor to me. All the resources of our order are at your disposal. I also want you to take Mukhtar with you. You will find his particular talents to be quite useful. Use our new partners to help you in your quest. But once your goal has been achieved, do not leave any of them alive. We do not want anyone to know that we have the scrolls in our possession." With that, Sathanas ended his audience with Kaseem, turning his back on him, facing the altar. Kaseem bowed to Sathanas and left quickly and quietly.

CHAPTER 5

MacBridan stretched out, settling back into the thick cushions of the deck chair with his feet up, his eyes closed, and his hands resting behind his head. Although the wind coming off the ocean had a cool touch to it, the sun more than made up for it, and MacBridan soon found himself half asleep as he lay listening to the soothing sounds of the ship and the ocean. They had disembarked Baltimore Harbor nearly two hours earlier; once everything had been loaded onto the ship and securely locked in the forward hold, he'd called Dolinski to report in.

"I trust everything went as planned," said Dolinski.

"No one even frowned in our direction. Of course, by the look of us, you'd have thought we were escorting the Scottish crown jewels. Between our security men in SUVs, the Virginia State Police escort, and the chopper that followed us, courtesy of the sheriff's department, we were one intimidating outfit," said MacBridan.

"Lord MacKinnon is not without political influence," said Dolinski, "but then, neither are we."

"Cori and her team supervised the loading of the ship without incident, and she has everything securely locked up." There hadn't been much for MacBridan to do while the ship was being loaded. So in an effort to not appear completely useless, he'd stood next to the moving vans, adapting different stances, looking as menacing as possible while eating two donuts and sipping a grande vanilla caffe latte from Starbucks.

"We also got a report from Dr. Van Dych," continued MacBridan.

"Good. What did he find?" asked Dolinski.

"At this point, precious little," said MacBridan. "He and two of our men met us at the dock. Van Dych already had the painting crated, and we have it on board with everything else. He told us that he, along with two specialists from the New York Metropolitan Museum of Art, thoroughly examined the painting."

"And?" asked Dolinski, somewhat impatiently.

"In short, they came up empty. There is not another painting, or anything else for that matter, hidden beneath it. They also examined it to determine if perhaps a more famous artist of the period, rather than the MacKinnon ancestor to whom everyone credits the painting, may actually have been the one to create this particular piece."

"I'm not too surprised that that didn't pan out," said Dolinski. "From my point of view, it certainly didn't appear to be a great deal of talent at work."

"No argument. They then proceeded to test the canvas, both sides, for secret writings, codes, and such but, once again, couldn't find anything. That left them with the frame. It didn't take them very long to confirm that it's as old as the painting, but is as solid as they come with no hidden compartments. The funny part is that the two specialists both agree that from a purely monetary standpoint, the frame is actually worth more than the picture."

"I appreciate their thoroughness, but there still has to be something we're missing," said Dolinski. "We know someone invested a great deal of money to steal that painting, a painting Lord MacKinnon would probably have just given them if they'd taken the time to ask him."

"At this point," said MacBridan, "if it weren't for the strong probability that it's Talon running the show, I'd say we might be giving our crooks a little too much credit."

"Perhaps, but we can't take that chance. Stay alert. If it's Talon, she won't give up easily, and it's obvious that she knows more about that painting than we do," cautioned Dolinski. "Contact me as soon as you dock in Glasgow."

As MacBridan lay there thinking about his talk with Dolinski, the warm sun and the gentle rocking of the sea began to take their toll, and it wasn't long before he began to drift off. Half asleep, he thought he heard a faint knocking sound far off in the distance. MacBridan shifted slightly into a more comfortable position, choosing to ignore it. But the knocking persisted, becoming louder and more frequent in its intensity.

Struggling to open his eyes, he managed to push himself up into a near sitting position, looked behind him, and said, "It's open."

Cori came in with her laptop in hand, passed through his cabin, and joined him on the balcony. "Well, I see that you're still working hard, almost as hard as you were back there on the dock. Next time, I want the job of standing around acting macho."

"It is obvious that you have no appreciation for the years of dedicated study that went into mastering such menacing intensity."

"You're right," said Cori. "I don't. How did your talk with Dolinski go?"

"As well as a talk with Dolinski can go. I updated him on Van Dych's findings, or lack thereof, and he's convinced that this has to be something more than just inept crooks."

"Isn't that what you were saying?"

"Yes, but now I'm not so sure. Let's just say my vote is split and could go either way. If it does turn out that it was Talon leading the team, then yes, we are clearly missing something.

But if it's not her, then we are more than likely dealing with some half-wits who have more muscles than brains."

"Let me settle the vote for you," said Cori. "The Virginia State Police came up with a partial print from the kitchen that panned out."

MacBridan opened one eye and looked at her. "Kitchen, panned out, not bad."

"No pun intended. It's not my style." Cori opened her laptop and got it running. "Twenty minutes ago, Ester King e-mailed me a report that just came in from Scotland Yard. I have it here if you'd like to see it. The print belongs to one Nicolette Cuvier, a.k.a. Talon."

MacBridan sighed and said, "I'm disappointed to hear that. It puts us back at square one. What is their interest in a worthless painting that even our client doesn't care for?"

"What if Talon is just a hired gun and knows the painting is worthless?" said Cori. "I remember when my grandmother died there was a big fight in my family over a dish towel."

"So your idea is that some rogue branch of the MacKinnon family is being sentimental in a deadly sort of way?"

"It's a theory, although not a great one." Cori smiled. "We should make port in Glasgow day after tomorrow, and the captain feels we'll arrive pretty early in the morning. In addition to the men and trucks that Lord MacKinnon will have there to meet us, there'll also be a man from our London office, Trevor Truecourt."

"Truecourt?"

"Yes," said Cori. "Former MI5, been with the Hawthorne Group for close to three years. He's been in touch with Lord MacKinnon's man, Marston Pierce, and is keeping him updated on all that we've learned."

"From what Dolinski was telling me, Pierce is a pretty tough, experienced guy. I'm glad he's on our side. As crazy as this case is starting to get, I'll be glad to get to the estate and turn all this over to him."

"Not me," said Cori. "I've never been to Scotland before, and I plan to take full advantage of the time we have. The MacKinnon estate is located far up into the highlands, just outside of Abbotsbury. The countryside is supposed to be bleak yet beautiful."

"It is," said MacBridan. "I've been to Scotland twice, and the land and the people are wonderful. Don't know if I've shared this little fun fact with you, but my ancestors are from the Isle of Skye."

"The amount of personal information that you have shared would fit on the cover of a matchbook."

"That's because I'm shy and timid."

"Then perhaps you're not a true Scotsman. I've been reading about the MacKinnon clan, and there's nothing shy or timid about them. In fact, as clans go, they have as violent and spooky a history as any out there. They not only survived the bloody clan wars but did well by them. One of the most interesting legends attached to the family states that at one time, the lord of the clan was thought to be an evil warlock."

"Please tell me you don't believe any of that stuff," said MacBridan, resuming his position on the deck chair, closing his eyes.

"Of course not, but the people who lived in the area sure did. They eventually rose up, attacked the manor house, and killed him," said Cori. "Still, whatever their beliefs were, this is going to be exciting. Ever since I was a little girl, I just loved Casper the ghost, and now I'm going to get to stay in a real haunted house."

MacBridan laughed at that and said, "Who are you, and what have you done with Cori? You make it sound like we're going to a big slumber party where we'll sit in the dark, hold hands, and perform a séance."

"The Scots love their ghost stories, and if you believe all you read, Scotland is loaded with ghosts, specters, and sinister spirits." MacBridan had experienced the dark side yet never courted it nor reached for it as an explanation of the world. Despite all that he'd personally experienced on a case years ago, he still had trouble accepting the possibility of the supernatural. Even though he possessed a mind grounded in empirical thought, he found himself still being haunted by the occasional nightmare stemming from those experiences. He gave little credence to things that shouldn't exist. The evil that men do is sufficient in itself.

Cori pulled up a different file on her laptop and said, "I'm not going to let you ruin this for me. Besides, you should look at this. It not only has some really amazing, photos of the house and the grounds, but also gives some pretty interesting details about the haunting. The MacKinnon family even has its own harbinger of death, the 'shadow people.'"

"Sounds more Irish than it does Scottish," said MacBridan. "You know banshees and all that." He was quiet for a few moments. "I usually don't dwell on the idea of ghosts, but I have to admit that that's at least original. Can't say as I've ever heard of shadow people before."

"I thought you were a history buff?" teased Cori. "Rather weak on this area I'd say. Scotland was steeled by people from Ireland, and the banshee, the clan spirit, is still believed by many modern-day Scots. I think we're going to have fun there and not just the usual 'defeat the bad guys' stuff."

"Need I remind you that we're not going to Scotland as tourists? That we have an assignment to complete, and that until we actually get all of this stuff loaded and delivered to the estate, that we happen to be the target of one of the best art thieves in the world?"

"Oh, I'm not worried about Talon," said Cori. "If she tries anything, I'll turn you loose and let you charm her into submission." MacBridan gave that some thought, smiled, and then happily drifted off to sleep.

Chapter 6

The sun had not yet started to brighten the morning sky as the tugboats slowly guided their ship into the Glasgow docks. It had rained most of the night, and a light drizzle continued to fall across the fog-covered harbor. Mac and Cori stood at the rail next to the gate where the gangplank would soon be placed. It was a little before five in the morning, and MacBridan knew they were in for a long and exhausting day. Both held steaming mugs of coffee in their hands.

"I'm going to need more than this coffee," said Cori. "It's freezing out here."

MacBridan smiled at her. "Well, I hate to be the one to say this, but get used to it. Scotland's not exactly known for its warm, sunny beaches. We're already pretty far north, and by the time we get to Abbotsbury, we'll be well into the highlands."

"I'm not worried," said Cori. "I've read all about the beautiful wool sweaters they make here, and I'm on expense account."

MacBridan sipped his coffee as the tugs expertly pushed the cargo ship up beside the pier. "If you get that past our accountants, I'll let you start doing my expense reports."

The heavy fog moved in waves, drifting across the docks in semitransparent vales. Men appeared out of the fog and began to coordinate with the ship's crew, securing the lines from the cargo ship. Once completed, they began to raise the gangplank up to the main deck.

"Good morning," said a voice behind them. They turned as the First Officer Henry Sherman joined them at the rail. He was a tall man and remarkably thin. Cori had remarked to MacBridan, after they'd first met him, as to how his uniform seemed to hang on him in such a way that it looked as if someone had carelessly draped him in uniform-styled material. If she didn't know better, she'd swear it belonged to his older, larger brother. "Looks like you're going to be in for a wet morning. This isn't expected to begin to blow out of here until sometime this afternoon."

"That's disappointing to hear," said Cori.

"You should see these docks in the winter. It's downright miserable," said Henry. "At least you won't have to wait long for your London contact. The harbor master let us know that he's been here waiting for over an hour."

Two of the ship's crew opened the gate and helped to guide the gangplank into position. As they bolted it to the ship, MacBridan pointed at a man walking along the pier heading toward the gangplank.

"Wonder if that could be our man?" said MacBridan.

From their vantage point, he didn't appear to be a very large man, yet there was no missing him. His pants were bright blue with the rest of him covered by an equally bright yellow rain slicker and matching rain hat. He reminded MacBridan of the guy he used to see as a kid on the box of Mrs. Paul's fish sticks. After a few words with one of the men on the pier, he started up the gangplank to join them.

"Well, we're certainly not going to lose him in the fog," said MacBridan.

"I don't care how it looks," said Cori, "if he's warm and dry, I'm taking that slicker away from him."

"Welcome to Scotland!" he called as he made his way up to them. As he got closer, they could see the full beard and mustache that were nearly as red as his cheeks. "I'm Trevor Truecourt."

First Officer Sherman took his ID and examined it before saying, "Welcome aboard, sir."

MacBridan estimated that under the slicker, the coat, and the hat, Truecourt was about five seven, five eight with a thick build to him, broad across the chest and shoulders. His nose had obviously been broken more than once, and there was some distinct scar tissue around his left eye.

"You must be Ms. Hopkins and Mr. MacBridan," said Truecourt, shaking their hands. "We got a wet one for you today, but I assure you that occasionally the sun does shine in Scotland."

Truecourt had a strong grip, but it was the heavy Cockney accent that most surprised MacBridan. Although not exactly sure why, this man wasn't what he'd expected, especially considering that Truecourt had been with MI5 for several years. Relying perhaps too much on stereotypes, MacBridan had expected him to sound and look more cultured, not like someone who actually belonged on the docks. On the other hand, he reasoned, the accent would probably have come in handy if he'd been involved in any undercover work in several of England's seedier criminal venues.

"Glad to hear it," said Cori. "I'm Cori, and this is James MacBridan."

"I'm familiar with your work, Mr. MacBridan. It is an honor to meet you."

"Good to meet you," said MacBridan. "Not to be too formal about this, but I'm afraid that we'll need to see your ID as well. Things have become rather sensitive."

"Of course, of course, not a problem," said Truecourt as he pulled out his wallet. "I was briefed on the attempted theft. We certainly don't want to lose any of Lord MacKinnon's family heirlooms."

MacBridan studied his passport and his Hawthorne Group identification papers. Once satisfied, he handed them to Cori. "I understand you also have some papers for us."

"More like a package of stuff actually. I left it in the car, so we'll be sure to go through it later. Customs will be coming along shortly, but I'm sure there won't be any problems." Truecourt then pulled out a leather portfolio from under his rain slicker and unzipped it. "What I do have are the inventory papers. If it's all right with you, I'd like to get started checking things in. Once I've finished, I'll review it with your list. Then, as we load the trucks, we'll do it all over again. I'm afraid it's quite a process."

"Nice portfolio," said MacBridan. "Is that new?"

"You've a keen eye, Mr. MacBridan. Only had it a week," answered Truecourt. "My wife gave it to me for my birthday."

Cori gave his identification back to him and said, "We'll let you get started. Mr. Sherman, could one of your men escort him to the forward hold?"

"Of course," said Sherman and motioned to one of his crew.

"Excellent," said Truecourt. "Once you clear customs, you can join me." With that, he turned and followed the crewman.

"He seems pretty efficient," said Cori.

"Yes, he does," said MacBridan. He watched Truecourt until he'd disappeared down the steps to the lower decks.

"Something wrong?" asked Cori.

"No, it's just that he's a complete one-eighty from how I pictured him. Even the accent seems somewhat out of character."

"He was a little hard to understand, perhaps, but I'm not sure I follow you. What were you expecting?"

"I don't know, but clearly, something a little more along the line of an Oxford grad, someone more polished."

Cori laughed at this. "More polished? You're one to talk. You look more like a thug than a highly trusted investigator for one of the most prestigious firms in America."

"True, but you're forgetting about my charming smile and my warm, cuddly side."

"Yes, you're just a teddy bear. I'll get my passport and our inventory manifest so we'll be ready. I'll be right back," said Cori, then stopped and asked, "Do you have yours?"

MacBridan patted his coat pocket. "Never leave the cabin without it."

Mac went and got a refill on his coffee and took up his post once again beside the gate. The moving trucks they'd spotted earlier hadn't moved, and he guessed they were waiting to hear from Truecourt. Three uniformed men started up the gangplank and made it to the gate just as Cori returned. First Officer Sherman greeted them and directed them to Cori and MacBridan. MacBridan was guessing that they were with Her Majesty's Revenue and Custom.

"Good morning," said the man wearing the captain's bars. Being of medium build, he bore an almost natural look of authority, with subtle graying beginning to take hold at temples, and a slight wrinkling around the watery blue-gray eyes. MacBridan guessed him to be in his early forties. "I'm Captain Cam Lawson, HMRC. I'll be checking you through customs, and my team will be supervising the unloading this morning. May I see your passports, please?" Once he checked them and made a couple of notes on the clipboard he was carrying, he handed them back.

"Here is a copy of our inventory," said Cori. "It's all primarily household items, along with several pieces of fine art, which we are escorting to the MacKinnon home in Abbotsbury."

Captain Lawson smiled and said, "Quite right. We are well aware that you are working for Lord MacKinnon, and we'll certainly do our best to expedite the process as efficiently as possible. We were also informed of the attempted theft back in Virginia. I have assigned extra men on the dock to ensure that all goes smoothly and securely."

"We appreciate that, Captain," said MacBridan. "Just so you'll know, a man from our London office is already on board.

He's currently below, going over the inventory, and he will be supervising the packing of the trucks, as well as being our guide for the drive north."

"I see, very well," said Lawson, preparing to make a note on his clipboard. "And what is his name so that I can inform my men?"

"Truecourt. Trevor Truecourt."

Captain Lawson paused, frowned slightly, and turned a couple of the pages back on his clipboard. "You say he's already aboard?"

"Yes," answered MacBridan. "Is there a problem?"

"It's just that I don't see how that's possible. Not twenty minutes ago, I left Mr. Truecourt in my office using the phone. He couldn't have possibly gotten on board ahead of us." Moving over to the rail, he carefully studied the dock. "Ah yes, I thought not. Here comes Truecourt now."

MacBridan and Cori moved quickly to the rail as another man started up the gangplank. Close to six feet tall, he was conservatively dressed, wearing a Burberry trench coat and rain hat.

"Captain, we may have a serious issue on our hands," said MacBridan.

The new Truecourt showed his ID to Mr. Sherman and then walked over to Captain Lawson. "I see you've met my colleagues," said Truecourt. "Ms. Hopkins, Mr. MacBridan, Trevor Truecourt at your service." His accent was very upper class, crisp, with each word well enunciated—Oxford.

"We need to move quickly, so I don't have much time to explain," said MacBridan. "But you are the second Truecourt to come aboard this morning." Mr. Sherman had moved up behind them and had already positioned two of his men at the gangplank.

"I don't understand," said Truecourt.

MacBridan quickly explained about the man who'd previously boarded and gave a detailed description of him. "His credentials were perfect. He even had a copy of the inventory."

"That's quite impossible, Mr. MacBridan," said Captain Lawson. "I personally increased the security on this pier and am confident that no one could have slipped through."

"Impossible or not, that's exactly what happened," said Mr. Sherman.

"Mac," said Cori, "I just hung up from our London office. This Truecourt matches their description. However, there's one thing I'd like to check out. Mr. Truecourt, would you please take your hat off?"

Truecourt stared at Cori for a moment, gave a small smile, and said, "Of course."

Cori turned his head to the left and looked behind his right ear. "The real Truecourt nearly lost this ear to a knife. There's the scar. Thank you."

"Cori, stay here with Sherman's men and make sure our impostor doesn't leave," said MacBridan. Turning to Sherman, he said, "Is this the only way off the ship?"

"Yes, at the moment anyway."

"Good. Truecourt, you're with me. Mr. Sherman, can you guide us to the hold?"

"This way," said Sherman and started off. Captain Lawson directed one of his men to also stay with Cori; then he and his other man quickly followed MacBridan.

Cargo ships are just that, giant vessels specifically designed to carry vast amounts of cargo to get the maximum possible profit from each voyage. They are not designed to get from one point on the ship to another in an expedient fashion. MacBridan's patience began to wear thin as he followed Mr. Sherman through a maze of passageways and tight, nearly vertical stairways. They finally reached the forward hold.

As they stepped into the massive interior of the hold, MacBridan quickly realized that this was not going to be as easy as he first thought. Piles of crates stacked as high as twenty feet filled the hold, creating several narrow avenues between them. Although the overhead lights were on, they were weak at best, leaving several areas of the hold deep in shadow. As his eyes adjusted, MacBridan tried to decide how to best organize their search when he spotted the lower half of a man's leg sticking out from behind a crate. "Mr. Sherman, over here," said MacBridan.

The man had been left lying up against a large crate. He was facedown and, at first glance, did not appear to be breathing. MacBridan knelt beside him, felt for a pulse, and was relieved to find that he was still alive. Together, they gently turned the man over. There was a large lump behind his right ear where he'd been hit. The wound had bled a little, matting the hair around it. The unconscious man was the sailor Sherman had sent with the fake Truecourt. MacBridan stood up and looked around. Stuffed behind a crate, he spotted the bright blue pants along with the yellow slicker the imposter had been wearing. As he picked them up, a fake beard and mustache hit the floor.

"Well, I guess we know what he doesn't look like," said MacBridan. "Mr. Sherman, I appreciate that this is your ship and that you're still in charge, but I have an idea as to how we should proceed."

"This is more your area than mine, MacBridan, but understand, when we catch this guy, he's mine."

MacBridan proceeded to quickly explain. "The man we're after is a pro, so we don't take it for granted that he's not armed," said MacBridan, speaking in a low tone so that they would not be overheard. "Normally, I'd suggest having Captain Lawson bring more of his men aboard to help us search. However, unless I miss my guess, our man knows he has very little to time to accomplish his goal. This gives us a very short window in which to stop him."

"You're giving him far too much credit, MacBridan," said Captain Lawson. "I hardly think a pro would allow himself to be cornered like this."

"I wish I could believe that he's cornered," said MacBridan, "but I'm not convinced. This man's obviously not working alone. His being able to slip past the security on the pier, to have impeccable credentials and even an exact copy of the manifest, speaks to the professionalism and planning that went into this. I think we can rest assure that a significant part of their plan is to get him out of here with whatever he's been sent to get."

"Does his outlandish disguise also make you think he's a pro? It's little more than a ridiculous clown's outfit, hardly a disguise a professional would use," argued Captain Lawson.

"The very fact that it is so ridiculous is why it worked. We have zero idea what this guy looks like, and that's after Cori, Mr. Sherman, and I all talked with him face-to-face. We were so focused on what he was wearing that we didn't focus on him. He made me think of Benny Hill rather than Professor Moriarty."

"What's our next step, MacBridan?" asked Mr. Sherman.

"We'll leave you here to watch the door and take care of this sailor. The three of us will spread out. Captain Lawson, if you and officer..."

"Officer Birkshire, sir," answered the young officer, easily in his early twenties, tall, and well built. MacBridan was glad to have him with them.

"You and Officer Birkshire will take opposite sides of the hold and work your way back. I'll head down the center aisle try to flush this guy out. The minute you see anything, call for help. Do not try to take him alone." Nodding their agreement, the men started to move as MacBridan added, "Captain Lawson makes a good point. This man may indeed be cornered. We really don't have any idea as to what their plan is for getting him off the ship, so take no chances. He'll be at his most lethal."

The men followed MacBridan's instructions and moved into position. At a nod from MacBridan, they began to move forward, immediately losing sight of each other. It was not a great plan; MacBridan knew that, but it was the best he could do on short notice. MacBridan moved forward as quietly as he could, listening for any sound that would give his adversary away. At each intersection created by the massive crates, he slowed down, carefully looking in all directions. As he crept along, he also kept a close watch behind him. Another problem was that there wasn't any way he could see on top of the crates. There was the chance that their man could try to escape by going over them, staying out of sight of everyone below until he came to the hold's door. MacBridan finally found what he was looking for a third of the way back. At one of the intersections, off to the left, a packing crate had been pulled out. Its side panel had been removed, broken pieces thrown across the floor. Due to the weak light, he couldn't see things too clearly. He listened for any sign of the thief but heard nothing other than the normal background noises that filled the hold. As carefully as possible, he started to move down the dimly lit passage. The crate was narrow and of a size that made it easy to guess that it had once held one of the paintings they were transporting. As he got closer, he could see that it was empty. He was about to yell out for everyone to head back to the door when his eye caught a glimpse of something flashing, partially hidden under the broken crate. Inching forward, he leaned over to get a better look. It was a cell phone.

Thwack! He heard the sap just before it made the dark hold lit up with bright yellow light. The blow to the back of his head caught him completely by surprise, sending him sprawling forward into the packing material. Instinct, more than anything, forced him to roll onto his back to try and ward off his attacker. The blow had not been hard enough to knock him unconscious, but he was having trouble focusing.

Fortunately, his assailant did not stick around to finish the job. MacBridan tried to sit up, but between the blow to his head and being tangled up in the broken crate, the best he could do was to raise himself up on one arm.

About eighteen feet away, he spotted someone, but his eyes refused to focus in on them. The man moved quickly into the intersection at the end of the passageway where the light was better, giving MacBridan a better look at him. Although his vision was still blurry, he could make out that the man was in uniform, identical to those worn by Lawson's men. Once again, MacBridan tried to get up, but the room began to spin, and he fell back on this side. MacBridan's fingers probed the back of his head. There was a good-sized welt forming, but the skin had not been broken. Continuing to examine the wound, he realized how lucky he'd been. He also realized how stupid he'd acted.

Once again, he struggled to get free of the broken crate. By rolling over on all fours and crawling backward, he managed to escape. He then sat down on the floor, leaned his head back ever so gently against a crate, and closed his eyes. The pain was intense. He needed time before trying to stand up, realizing that if he didn't, he'd just end up right back down on the floor. On the other hand, there was a thief to catch, one that he'd let get by him, so he didn't have the luxury of time. Opening his eyes, he was pleased to find that his vision was beginning to clear. It was then he saw the space between two other crates where the thief had been hiding. MacBridan looked closely and, with what little light there was, could see something leaning against one of the crates. MacBridan crawled over to get a better look and gave a grim smile. It was a painting, frame and all.

With the help of one of the taller crates, MacBridan pulled himself up to his feet. Once he was sure he wasn't going to topple over, he began to make his way back down the passageway to the door where they'd first entered the hold. It was slow going, but with each step, he grew more confident that his legs weren't going to fold up under him. As he reached the main passageway, he saw Mr. Sherman guarding the door. The sailor they'd found was sitting up but didn't look too good.

"You all right?" asked Sherman. He could see by the way he was moving that MacBridan was hurt.

"I'll be all right, but I may have to have my head examined," answered MacBridan, "for multiple reasons. Has anyone gone past you?"

"Just Lawson's man. He came at me at a run, said you had caught the thief, and he was going for help."

"How long ago was that?"

"Five, maybe seven minutes, why?"

"That was our thief. Is there any form of communication down here, an intercom or something?"

"No, not on this deck, but there is on the deck above us," said Mr. Sherman.

"I need you to hurry and alert Cori and the men with her to let no one, and I do mean no one, uniform or not, get off this ship."

MacBridan had no sooner finished talking when Cori, a sailor, and another of Lawson's men rushed into the hold. "Mac, we got your message. Where is he?" asked Cori.

"What message?" asked MacBridan.

"One of Lawson's men said that you'd caught the thief but that a couple of you had been injured. He's on the phone, calling for an ambulance and said that you wanted us down here as fast as possible," said Cori.

"That was our thief," said MacBridan. "You remember how ridiculous the first Truecourt looked? It was all a ruse. Under the slicker, the coat, and the bright blue pants was his ticket out here, a customs officer's uniform."

MacBridan explained to Cori and Mr. Sherman how he'd been jumped by the empty crate when Captain Lawson and his man returned. They heard enough of MacBridan's story to understand that their man had gotten away. Lawson quickly directed his officer to get back to the main deck and alert their men on the dock.

"The good news, if there is any, is that I don't believe he got what he came for."

"How's that?" asked Cori.

"Come with me, and I'll show you. I think we got to him quicker than they expected us to. If I'm right, he had to leave what he came for behind."

Cori, Mr. Sherman, and Captain Lawson followed MacBridan back down to the passageway where he'd found the broken crate. Reaching into the narrow opening, he pulled out the painting. They moved back to the intersection where they could all see better. "Unbelievable," said Cori.

"What's the matter?" asked Lawson.

"This is the same worthless painting they tried to steal in Virginia," said MacBridan. "What is it about this thing that could possibly be driving people to go to such lengths?"

Chapter 7

MacBridan spent the rest of his morning and the early part of the afternoon at a local infirmary. Immediately after he finished there, one of Captain Lawson's men drove him over for meetings with the HMRC along with the Glasgow police. Fortunately, Cori and Truecourt had been able to stay on board, giving their statements directly to Captain Lawson. The two of them then set about the task of supervising the off-loading of the ship and onto the moving trucks. Prior to loading, they were joined by a Lloyd's of London representative who worked with them in checking the inventory. By the time MacBridan returned, there was only about an hour's work left to get everything loaded and accounted for. Mac updated Cori with what little he knew and then stepped inside the harbor master's office to call Dolinski.

Cori had talked with Dolinski earlier that morning, letting him know of the fake Truecourt, the attempted theft, and MacBridan's run-in with the thief. "How's the head?" asked Dolinski—an ocean away, but his gruff, direct manner came across loud and clear.

"Didn't even break the skin," answered MacBridan. "Their best guess is that I was probably hit with a buckshot-filled sap. Fortunately for me, he was in too tight of quarters to get much oomph behind his swing. Perhaps adding murder to their crime list wasn't on the agenda."

"Cori said that you seemed to be okay, good to have it confirmed. That said, you're not going to be of much value to us if you keep leading with your chin, MacBridan. This is the second time they've gotten away from you. It would be nice to get to question someone in this gang further up the food chain, much further than they guy you caught at the MacKinnon farm."

"Yes, sir, I'm not too pleased with how things have turned out either. On the other hand, they've come at us twice now, and we have caused them to fail both times. What I find truly remarkable is that in both attempts, they went after the same worthless painting, and it's clear that these were professionally planned. It's also pretty obvious that they already had plan B well prepared in case they failed at the farm. The attempt on the ship could not have been pulled together in just a couple of days, especially when you consider all the documents they had to forge. We are clearly missing something about the significance of that picture."

"Your assessment of the professionalism involved in these attempts is spot on," said Dolinski. "Both have Talon's signature written all over them. After my talk with Cori this morning, I sent a note to Van Dych, updating him and letting him know that he needs to reevaluate his data. He and I will be meeting to discuss that later today."

"If memory serves me correctly, didn't Lord MacKinnon tell us that there were more of these paintings done by the same ancestor hanging at the main house in Scotland?" asked MacBridan.

"He did, four more to be precise."

"Then it might be a good idea for us to contact the estate's security man, Pierce, and have him secure the other paintings. Whatever the reason, someone has placed a very high value on the painting we're transporting, and they're not showing any signs of giving up. It stands to reason that the same people would be interested in the other paintings as well."

"I'll put a call into him right away," said Dolinski. "I've also been on the phone to our London Office. Truecourt is a good man with a good record. Although we have not been able to determine where the leak is, we have been able to rule out that it's not in our shop."

"That narrows it down to either the MacKinnon family or someone on their staff," mused MacBridan. "Disappointing to think that Lord MacKinnon has someone in the house working against us."

"Disappointing, but not surprising," said Dolinski. "Never forget, for the right motivation, people will do anything."

"Until we have something more definitive, I'm not going to share our suspicions about the family with Lord MacKinnon. While we're on the subject of who to trust, how do we handle Pierce? I know you respect the guy, but perhaps, I should keep him at arm's length as well, at least until we're more certain of where things stand."

"That won't be necessary, MacBridan. I know Pierce, and he'd sooner lose an arm than betray the people who have entrusted him. We'll see if the HMRC or the Glasgow police turn up anything. I already have another operative from our London office heading to Glasgow to ride point on this. I'll let you know as soon as we hear anything."

All in all, the call with Dolinski had gone well. MacBridan returned to the moving trucks in time to see the last few crates loaded. There were three large trucks in all with two man crews and a lead car that would be driven by Truecourt. Due to the latest attempt, it was decided that MacBridan would follow behind the procession in another car, guarding their flank. Truecourt also agreed to alter the routes he'd planned to use, even though those changes would end up taking them longer to get to the MacKinnon estate.

It was in the early evening when their small convoy finally pulled away from the docks. Cori rode with MacBridan as they slowly made their way out of Glasgow, heading north on their way to the Highlands. The roads were considerably narrower than MacBridan was used to, and he spent the first hour adjusting to driving on the wrong side of the road. It didn't help his concentration when Cori started to make fun of his driving, having just hit the curb for the fourth time.

The road north would take them up through Fort William, Inverness, and then past Achnasheen as they drove deep into the Scottish Highlands. Cori became enchanted by the rich beauty of the land and kept pointing out various sites as the rolling hills gradually became taller and even more alluring. "Scotland is absolutely beautiful. As soon as we stop, I'm getting my camera out."

"It's a magical land, and you won't believe the number of castles we'll see. The Scots were, and are, an amazing people," said MacBridan.

The radio that had been given by Truecourt to Cori beeped, and she pressed the talk button. "Everything all right, Trevor?"

"Oh, yes, quite lovely," said Truecourt. "There's an inn not too far up ahead, about a couple of kilometers or so, off to the right. We'll stop there for the night."

"Excellent. We're beginning to get a little hungry back here."

The inn was quaint, quite old and they were surprised as to how small the rooms were. Everyone but MacBridan sat down for dinner, as he took the first watch on the trucks. Truecourt and Hamish, one of the more burly drivers, relieved MacBridan so that he could get something to eat. Afterwards MacBridan joined Hamish, taking on the first watch. For MacBridan the hours passed slowly. He hated stakeouts and was relieved by Truecourt and another driver around 3:30 a.m. Fortunately the night passed without incident.

As they continued their trip north, both he and Cori we awed by the beauty of the highlands. As Cori put it, each curve presented another Kodak moment. The two lane roads kept their progress at a slow pace and the intermitant downpours didn't help any.

It was just after six that evening when Truecourt radioed to let them know that they'd soon be entering Abbotsbury. The MacKinnon estate was about twelve kilometers north of the small village. The road they followed kept them out of the village proper, and twenty minutes later, they came to the main gates of the estate.

The gatehouse was a moderately sized cottage built of stone, and MacBridan remembered reading that it was the "new" gatehouse, having been added sometime in the early eighteenth century. There were two security men working the gate, both tastefully dressed in hunting jackets, the perfect attire for country gentlemen. Truecourt handled everything with the security men, and they entered the estate. The wrought iron gates they passed through were easily fourteen feet tall, with gas lamps burning on both sides of the stone pillars that held them up all creating a charming atmosphere of times long past.

The drive to the main house was only about a car and a half wide and worked its way through thick trees. Cori silently prayed that they wouldn't meet anyone coming from the opposite direction. With the sun just having dropped below the horizon and the dense vegetation on both sides of the lane, they could see very little of the grounds. Finally, they emerged from the wood, and as the lane curved to the left, they got their first view of the MacKinnon manor house, proudly standing across a broad lawn.

The two-story structure was simply magnificent. All the lights were on in the great house, and they could see two wings emanating from the broad front entryway. Here, too gas lamps burned on either side of the main entrance, with multiple gas lamps on poles lining the drive as it curved around reminiscent of the days of Queen Victoria.

As soon as they pulled to a stop, the crews climbed out of their trucks but stayed next to them to keep watch. Even on the estate grounds, they were under orders to keep a close eye until everything had been unloaded. It was a cold, damp evening, but Cori and MacBridan didn't mind; it felt great to be out of the car. They joined Truecourt at the front door, which was opened by a man in what had to be a butler's livery. He was of medium height, somewhat heavyset, especially around the middle, with dark-brown hair. Upon closer examination, Cori could see that he practiced the art of the comb-over. She guessed him to be in his late forties, possibly early fifties.

"Good evening. Trevor Truecourt of the Hawthorne Group," said Truecourt, handing the man a business card. "Lord MacKinnon is expecting us."

"Of course, sir, please come in. Lord MacKinnon will be pleased to hear that you have arrived." He left them in the main foyer and disappeared into the left wing of the house.

"I didn't know people actually lived like this," said Cori, her voice filled with awe. Before them, in the center of the foyer, stood a grand staircase, which was easily fifteen feet across, rising majestically to the second floor. Hallways ran parallel to the staircase on both sides, leading deeper into the house. On either side of the front doors stood two full sets of armor, silent sentinels of power in full regalia. The walls were paneled with a dark, polished cherry wood, with crown moldings at least sixteen inches wide. Family portraits hung at perfectly spaced intervals, with two huge mirrors hanging directly across each other on either side of the foyer. Looking up, MacBridan gazed at the chandelier, which burned brightly and was the largest he'd ever seen. He wondered how much it weighed. More importantly, he wondered what was holding it up.

Lord MacKinnon soon joined them with the butler following close behind. Smiling ear to ear, he shook their hands, greeting each of them. "Mr. MacBridan, Ms. Hopkins, it is so good to see you again. And you must be Trevor Truecourt."

"Yes, sir, London office. I'm well acquainted with your career, sir, as well as all of the good works of the MacKinnon Trust. It is an honor to meet you," said Truecourt.

"Thank you. That is most kind," said Lord MacKinnon. Looking at MacBridan, he said, "I understand that there was some excitement at the docks. Have there been any other attempts?"

"Fortunately, no," answered MacBridan. "The trip north was happily uneventful. That said, I'll be glad to get that painting, as well as the other works of art, unloaded and safely secured inside."

"I think your qualifying that particular painting as a work of art is being most generous, wouldn't you say? However, Dolinski and Pierce agree that there's obviously more going on than we understand, so we've already increased the security here at the estate." Lord MacKinnon looked around and said, "That's odd, Marston should have been here by now. Fergus, would you please let Marston know that our guests have arrived?"

"Certainly, sir," said Fergus, leaving them once again.

"Welcome to my home," said Lord MacKinnon. "We have a late supper prepared and have been waiting for you. We would be very pleased for you to join us."

"Thank you. That is very nice," said Cori, "but before we eat, I'd like to talk with Marston and make sure we have everything well secured."

Lord MacKinnon smiled at Cori and said, "I see Ms. Hopkins is a most thorough and diligent taskmaster."

"You have no idea," said MacBridan.

"Excellent, excellent, I'll have Fergus inform the kitchen and the family that we'll be eating a little later."

Fergus had already returned and said, "Mr. Pierce is not answering his radio or the phone in his room, sir. His security team hasn't seen him either. Shall I search the house?"

"No, Fergus, that won't be necessary. I'll walk upstairs and get him. Marston likes to work in his room, likes the quiet of it actually, often with his radio turned down and the phone off the hook. It is odd, though," continued Lord MacKinnon. "Marston's the most punctual, schedule-driven person on the entire estate. If you'll excuse me, I'll be right back."

MacBridan's eyes met Cori's, and the silent communication between them registered loud and clear. Pierce's not being there was probably nothing; there'd been no scheduled time for their arrival. On the other hand, MacBridan knew that the men at the front gate would have alerted him of their arrival. Ever since they'd pulled away from the docks, they'd been waiting for the next attempt, watching for the slightest little thing that was out of place. Pierce's absence clearly qualified.

"If I may make a suggestion," said MacBridan. "Perhaps we could divide and conquer. There is a great deal of work that Cori and Trevor need to start on outside, so why don't I go with you to find Marston, and that'll free them up to get started."

"Very well," said Lord MacKinnon. "If you think that's best. It'll at least give me an opportunity to show you part of the house. Fergus, please see that the moving men have some refreshment."

"We'll be with the trucks," said Cori as she and Truecourt quickly stepped outside. Twice they had allowed the thieves to walk right by them. They were not going to be caught with their guard down a third time.

MacBridan followed Lord MacKinnon up the staircase. "Most of the house and grounds staff that live on the estate are quartered in a separate building behind the main house," explained Lord MacKinnon. It was a long stairway, and by the time they were halfway up, Lord MacKinnon's breathing became noticeably labored. MacBridan had observed during their first meeting that Lord MacKinnon was not in the best of shape. "Marston is the only one of my staff that has a room on the second floor. For that matter, the only other members of my staff that live in the main house are the Hendersons. You've already met Fergus. He's the head butler, and his wife Robena is the housekeeper. They're an interesting couple, polar opposites in personality, and they've been with us for close to fifteen years now. Robena runs every aspect of the house staff with a firm hand. Even Marston, that old warhorse, is careful when he's around her."

The top of the stairs ended at a broad intersection comprised of three separate hallways, one straight ahead and the other two heading off to the left and right respectively. The hallways were neatly furnished with wooden chairs and small tea tables. Straight ahead, standing at the far end of the hall in front of MacBridan was a large ornate grandfather clock. Here, too, he could see that the walls were adorned with paintings of what he guessed were family portraits, as well as other assorted subjects, a couple of which MacBridan recognized.

"Tomorrow I'll give you and Ms. Hopkins a proper tour of the manor," said Lord MacKinnon. "Until one becomes more familiar, it can appear to be a large and rambling structure. I have an aerial photo of the house downstairs in my study that I'll share with you. It really helps to get a better feel of the layout. The easiest way I've found to describe it is the joining of two letters from the alphabet, the letters *I* and *T*. Think of the letter *I* as the front of the house where you came in. If you then take the *I*, lay it on its side, the base of the *T* would intersect the *I* in the exact center. That is where we are presently standing."

"I see," said MacBridan. "So if I were to walk straight ahead down this hall to the grandfather clock, I'd find two more hallways, one to the left and one to the right."

"That's perfectly correct," said Lord MacKinnon. "We could house a small army here if we had to. Of course, back in the days of my ancestors, a small army was exactly what it took."

Lord MacKinnon turned and led the way, taking the hall to their left. This hallway only went a short distance before you came to an S curve, first turning to the left, then after a quick ten paces or so, back to the right. "Your room, along with Ms. Hopkins room, will be on the second floor," said Lord MacKinnon. "You might find it interesting to know that the room you'll be staying in once—"

At that moment, a woman's scream shattered the quiet of the hall. It was not a scream of pain but of pure abject terror. MacBridan reacted instantly, taking off at a run, quickly rounding the right hand turn of the hall. Dressed in a traditional maid's uniform, he saw her on her knees crumpled up against the wall halfway down the hall. She continued to scream, holding her face in her hands.

MacBridan knelt beside her on one knee, gently touching her shoulder. She was quite young, and MacBridan guessed her to be in her early twenties. She jerked away at his touch as he said, "What is it? Are you hurt?"

"It's him," she wailed. "I saw him!"

Out of breath and somewhat rattled, Lord MacKinnon trotted to a halt beside them. "Quiet, you silly girl. We can't understand a word you're saying. Who did you see?"

The maid had not taken her eyes off the door across them. "It was him! I saw him go in there. It was so terrible. The door slammed shut, and then I heard a man cry out for help." She hesitantly took eyes away from the door and looked up at Lord MacKinnon. Her voice, now barely above a whisper, said, "The gatherer's in there."

"Enough of that," barked Lord MacKinnon, struggling to calm his own nerves. "You're talking nonsense."

MacBridan stood up and looked behind him to see Fergus trotting down the hall. He then turned to the door she'd been staring at and tried to open it. "It's locked," he said. "Whose room is this?"

"Marston's," answered Fergus.

"Take care of her. I suspect she's in her cups," Lord MacKinnon directed Fergus as he moved to Marston's door and began to knock on it. "Marston, are you in there?" He too then tried to open the door, his face etched with concern. "Fergus, do you have your keys with you?"

"No, sir, but I can get them."

"There's no time for that. MacBridan, can you force the door open?" asked Lord MacKinnon.

"I can try," said MacBridan. He'd already been studying the door, which appeared to be more sturdy than most. Gripping the doorknob, he first tried to force the lock. He hadn't really expected that to work, but it had been worth the try. MacBridan then put his shoulder into the door and, still gripping the doorknob, lifted up and pushed as hard as he could, trying to see if there was any give at all. The door didn't budge an inch; its solid oak construction confirming for him that this was not going to be easy. Stepping back, he kicked the door directly above the doorknob, close to where he estimated the latch was. The door barely moved. Twice more he kicked it, putting as much force into the blows as he could. He then lowered his shoulder and slammed into the door, putting his full weight into it.

At last, the door gave way, making a faint cracking sound. Considering the pain searing through his right arm and shoulder, MacBridan couldn't tell if the cracking sound he'd heard had been his bone or the door. Again, he stepped back and rammed his shoulder full force into the door. With a loud splintering sound, the door burst open, taking part of the doorjamb with it.

The room was fairly large. From the look of the rolltop desk and the papers scattered across it, it was apparent that Marston used this as both his living quarters and his office. A small lamp sitting on the desk was the only light on, casting a dim light around the room. Two tall windows stood across MacBridan, with a large bed off to the left of the doorway. Two wingback chairs stood by one of the windows with a short rectangular table between them. A tray with a china teapot and a half-uneaten sandwich rested on the table.

At first glance, the room appeared to be empty. MacBridan moved to the center of the room and looked around. On the far side of the room, between the bed and the wall, MacBridan saw the legs of a man lying on the floor. As he approached the man, he saw that the body lay partially under the bed, most of it nearly hidden from sight. He quickly went over, pulled the man from beneath the bed, and began to look for signs of life, placing his hand on the man's neck. MacBridan could not find a pulse, the man's skin already cool to the touch.

"My god," said Lord MacKinnon. "Look at his face. What's happened to him?"

"Is this Marston?" asked MacBridan.

Lord MacKinnon did not immediately respond. His hand covered his mouth and MacBridan noticed that his breath was more laborious than when they'd climbed the stairs. His body slumped against the door, the knuckles of his hand white with force as his mind struggled with the sight before him. "Yes, poor man, that's Marston."

MacBridan stood up and walked back over to the door. "Fergus, we're going to need the police. See to it that no one comes into this room."

Lord MacKinnon had not moved and stood frozen to the floor, unable to look away from Marston's body. MacBridan walked back and stood next to the corpse, closely studying the man's face. Marston's eyes were wide open, almost bulging from the sockets. His lips were pulled back from his teeth in a ghastly grimace, which MacBridan guessed was the result of what had to have been intense pain. But it was the skin that MacBridan found the most troubling. Bright red blotches were spread across his face and neck, creating, in some areas, small open blisters.

"Had Marston been sick?" asked MacBridan.

Lord MacKinnon didn't respond at first, still staring at the body. "What?" He acted like a man coming out of a trance. "No, no, he wasn't sick, at least he hadn't said anything to me. Forgive me, it's just that I was talking with Marston not more than an hour ago, and he was fine. This is so very tragic."

"The maid said that the gatherer was in here. What did she mean?"

"Local superstition, sort of a bogey to scare children. It comes from the graveyard to take their souls away for Satan."

"Well, whatever this man saw, it didn't exactly fill him with delight."

MacBridan stepped in front of Lord MacKinnon, blocking his view, and gently guided him to the door. "I'll stay here and wait for the authorities," said MacBridan. "It would be a great help to me if you could let Cori know what has happened and be downstairs do direct the police when they get here."

"Of course," said Lord MacKinnon. "Yes, certainly, I'll do that."

MacBridan closed the door behind him. He wanted some time to look around before the local police got there and took over the crime scene. It was all supposition at this point, but MacBridan felt that there was a pretty good chance that Marston had not died from natural causes. He found that the bedroom door had been bolted shut from the inside. The windows were also securely bolted shut. MacBridan then went to the desk and, without touching anything, examined the papers that lay strewn across it. As best as he could determine, they all had to do with various aspects of the estate, covering items such as security schedules, reports, payroll, all in character with Marston's role.

He then went over to the body for a more thorough examination. The blotches made it difficult, but he could not find any signs of bruising or defensive wounds nor was there any blood on the floor. MacBridan studied the room for signs of a struggle, but here too he came up empty. He noticed that Marston's hands were tightly clenched, and MacBridan wondered if either of them held any evidence explaining the events leading to the man's death.

MacBridan stood up and walked over to the windows, trying to piece it all together. Although it looked like Marston had met his end alone, MacBridan wasn't buying it. Plus there was the maid who claimed to have seen someone enter the room just before Marston died. Why did his skin look the way it did? If someone had been in here, how had they been able to leave without being seen? MacBridan's gut told him that all of this was somehow tied into the painting they'd transported from the States. The stakes had just gone up.

Chapter 8

MacBridan decided that when the police did arrive, it would be best for him to be found waiting for them in the hall, outside the door to Marston's room. Based on experience, he knew they wouldn't want a civilian rummaging around the room and messing up their evidence. It was a courtesy they'd appreciate. Also, as an added bonus, he'd be able to attest that no one else other than he and Lord MacKinnon had gone in there, ensuring the integrity of the crime scene. Not too long after taking up his position in the hall, he heard the police tromping noisily down the hall. They were escorted by Lord MacKinnon who introduced them to MacBridan. They spoke with him briefly, looked at his identification, jotted down some notes, and asked him to wait downstairs for Inspector Wetmoore. MacBridan smiled to himself as he headed outside. Wetmoore. That was a fun name to have grown up with.

Once outside, MacBridan leaned against Truecourt's car, watching the beehive of activity unfold around him. It had taken the police less than twenty minutes to arrive, and they were soon followed by an ambulance, more police, and eventually the medical examiner.

"Have you met with Inspector Wetmoore?" asked Cori as she joined him. She'd stayed outside with Truecourt watching the trucks on the off chance that Marston's death had been a diversion, opening the way for the thieves to take another run at them. "I don't know if he's even here," answered MacBridan. "Lord MacKinnon introduced me to the two patrolmen who first arrived, and they asked me to wait for him. How did you know Wetmoore's name?"

"Fergus," said Cori. "Man's a fountain of information. We talked about Wetmoore, the police, his thoughts on Marston. I got the impression that he's not overly impressed with the inspector."

"Why's that?"

"Let me see, oh yes, his exact words were, 'Couldn't find a book in a library.'"

"Fergus said that?"

"As I said, man likes to talk. I also think he likes me."

"Have you been flirting again?" asked MacBridan, a smile spreading across his face.

"Of course not," said Cori with mock indignation. "I was just being nice. Never hurts to cultivate good relations with the natives."

"Well, I personally will be very interested to learn what Marston died from. I've never seen anything like it. It's as if his skin had been on fire but from the inside out, creating blotches of blisters, some had even burst. His face was contorted in such a way that he must have been in extreme pain."

"That sounds horrible. Were there any signs of a struggle?"

"No, at least none that I could see.

"I agree. The attempted thefts and his death are too coincidental."

"Yes, and you know how I feel about coincidence. Regarding the thieves, we already know that we're dealing with pros. So if I was in their shoes and my team had botched it twice, getting a man as experienced and resourceful as Marston out of the way would be a good next step."

"Which would not only be a significant escalation on their part but would further confirm their having close contact with someone in the MacKinnon household. They knew who to target and when."

"There's no doubt that someone on the inside is helping them. They've had all the details as to what was going on since day one in Virginia, and it doesn't appear to be any different here."

"Fergus told me that a maid saw someone going into Marston's room just before you got there."

"Hard to tell," said MacBridan. "She was hysterical when I got to her. She kept muttering something about seeing the gatherer."

"The gatherer? What does that mean?" asked Cori.

"The local version of Satan, or more precisely Satan's hired thug. Something scared her pretty badly, and I hope that we get to talk with her before the police. It would be nice to hear her side of things before she's influenced by them one way or the other. All I can tell you is that we had to literally break the door down, and there wasn't anyone in there but Marston."

"You remember the historical data on the MacKinnon family that I went over with you on the ship?" asked Cori.

"Oh, absolutely, I was mesmerized by every word."

"Well, had you been paying attention, you'd remember my telling you about one of Lord MacKinnon's ancestors who was not a nice person and was thought to have been in thick with Satan."

"Okay, yes, I do remember you mentioning that," said MacBridan. "Something about his dabbling in the black arts."

"You don't think..."

"Cori, we went down this road last night. Remember, you are in the Scottish Highlands, a land as soaked in superstition and folklore as it is in scotch. We need to talk with the maid, keep her on track, and try to get a much-clearer understanding of what actually happened. Some of these people are superstitious, but we can't be."

They turned as the two ambulance techs rolled their gurney out the front door placing the body in the back of the ambulance. Two other men followed them out, talking quietly to each other. One of them looked around, settled his gaze on MacBridan and Cori, and began to walk toward them. MacBridan noted that he looked young, thirty or so, with reddish blond hair that had not only started to thin out but was also deeply receding. As he got closer, MacBridan could see that he had the thick, firm build of an athlete. He was of medium height and wore a heavy wool overcoat, appropriate for the damp air.

"Good evening," he said as he approached them. "I'm Inspector Wetmoore." He had an infectious smile and appeared to be very much at ease.

"James MacBridan. This is my associate, Cori Hopkins."

They shook hands with Wetmoore. "The baron tells me that your firm has been retained to help the family coordinate their move back from America."

"That's right," said MacBridan. "Lord MacKinnon has been a client for some time, and we were retained to direct the move and provide security."

"It's good to meet you both. I'm only sorry that it's under these circumstances. Not that cheery of a welcome to Scotland is it?"

"Do you have any idea what Marston died from?" asked MacBridan.

"I was going to ask you the same thing," said Wetmoore. "Lord MacKinnon stated that you were with him and forced the door to Marston's room." Wetmoore smiled at this. "The doors in this house are made of solid oak. On my best day, I'm not sure I could have accomplished that."

"I'm sure I'll feel it in the morning," said MacBridan.

"Yes, of course. You got a good look at the victim, isn't that right?"

"Lord MacKinnon and I found Marston on the floor," said MacBridan. He reached into his pocket and gave Wetmoore one of his cards. "I'm with the investigative division of the Hawthorne Group. I quickly examined Marston, but he was already dead."

"I see, yes, Marston told me yesterday that there had been an attempted theft on some of the artwork at the farm in Virginia. He also told me that you and Ms. Hopkins were the ones who prevented the theft. I know he had been looking forward to having you here for a few days," said Wetmoore. He paused for a moment then said, "Ghastly business. What do you make of the markings on his face?"

MacBridan shook his head. "As I was telling Cori, I've never seen anything quite like that before. Considering that he'd been all right earlier in the evening, whatever it was hit him hard and fast. Based on the contortions on his face, I'd also guess that his end was pretty painful."

"The face was absolutely hideous, wasn't it?" said Wetmoore. "Extremely painful, interesting, my first thought was that he'd been terribly frightened by something."

"Did the coroner speculate on what might have happened?" asked Cori.

"No, no, not yet, but then he never does. What I mean is that Dr. Shepard is a rather conservative old chap and is not prone to speculation. How long will you be staying on?"

"We'd planned on being here for a couple of days while everything was unpacked and checked against the inventory," said Cori. "We're expecting a representative from Lloyd's to be arriving here tomorrow. Now, depending on Lord MacKinnon, that may change."

"How so?" asked Wetmoore.

"We had another attempt on the same painting at the docks in Glasgow," explained MacBridan. "In light of Marston's death,

Lord MacKinnon may want us to stay on for a few more days and work with him on the estate's security."

"Extraordinary! Another attempt on the same painting. It must be a remarkable piece," said Wetmoore.

"It is truly a one of a kind," said MacBridan.

"Well, I won't keep you any longer tonight. We'll talk more soon. I promised Lord MacKinnon that I'd be back out tomorrow to give him an update. I'm sure I'll see you then."

They shook hands with Inspector Wetmoore and watched him as he walked to the only remaining police car and drove away. "My guess is that he's far more competent than Fergus led you to believe," said MacBridan.

"He does come across as knowing his business."

"And gives little away. I can't recall any of our questions that he actually answered."

"Not too surprising if you think about it. He just met us, and at this point, we're all suspects to one degree or another."

Before Cori could respond, they heard Lord MacKinnon calling to them, "There you are," he said as he approached. He was closely followed by three other men. "These men worked for Marston." With his right hand he massaged his temple. "I still can't believe he's gone. Mr. MacBridan, what do you recommend we do next?"

By this time, Truecourt had also joined them. "It'd be best to get the valuable pieces of art, as well as many of the more valuable antiques, unloaded this evening. We can unload the rest in the morning. Considering all that's happened, I'll feel better once we have everything secured inside the house."

"We've arranged lodging for our drivers in Abbotsbury," said Truecourt. "We can have them back here first thing in the morning to complete the job."

"Very good," said Lord MacKinnon. "These men will help you and show you where you can put everything. Mr. MacBridan, I'd like a word with you."

"Why don't you and Ms. Hopkins go with the baron," offered Truecourt. "I can manage here."

"Excellent," said Lord MacKinnon. "If you need anything, just let Fergus know."

Lord MacKinnon turned and led them back into the house. They followed him through the foyer and down a cavernous hallway to a large dining room. Fergus was already there, setting dishes out on a serving table. "Dinner will be served shortly, sir."

"Thank you, Fergus. What about the rest of the family?"

"They know of Mr. Marston's passing and will be joining you here."

"Good. Please be sure to see that Mr. Truecourt has all that he needs. He's outside, supervising the unloading of the trucks."

"Certainly, sir," said Fergus and quietly left the room.

Lord MacKinnon sat down at the head of the table and leaned back against his chair, closing his eyes. MacBridan and Cori sat down on either side of him. "You never imagine things like this truly happening, especially in your own home." He was quiet for a moment then looked at MacBridan and said, "This may sound ridiculous, but I can't help but wonder if my family is at risk. I know I'm probably jumping to conclusions, but I'd like to know your thoughts on all these."

"Lord MacKinnon, you do not sound the least bit ridiculous," said MacBridan. "We don't yet know what Marston died of. The good news is that at this point there's no direct evidence that leads to anything other than some tragic reaction to something he came into contact with."

"But you don't think it's an accident," said Lord MacKinnon.

"I truly don't know. Hopefully, tomorrow, Inspector Wetmoore will have more information for us. However, we can't overlook the two attempts that have been made to steal the painting. Based on evidence recovered in Virginia, we do know that we are dealing with some talented and very expensive professionals. The two attempts and Marston's death are too close for comfort, and I have never believed in coincidence. Therefore, it is prudent that we do take the appropriate steps to secure the estate until we get things sorted out."

"Before your family joins us, this is probably a good to time to talk about another concern that we have," said Cori. "If it does turn out that Marston's death is not from natural causes—"

"You mean if we find out that he was murdered?" asked Lord MacKinnon.

"Yes, if we find out that he was murdered. At that point, we will have an entirely different situation on our hands and will need to start asking some tough questions," said Cori.

"What kind of tough questions?"

"The same questions the police will be asking. There have been two attempts made on the same painting. Both were well planned. They were intricate, detailed operations ran nearly back-to-back. It's pretty apparent that the thieves have someone helping them from within your household," said Cori.

"That's preposterous," said Lord MacKinnon.

"We appreciate you feeling that way," Cori continued, "but they've known too much, had too much insight into what we're doing, which unfortunately has kept them one step ahead and kept us on defense. It's not an easy thing to accept. I know that, but there's no other way that they could have gotten the information they had without having someone on the inside."

"Lord MacKinnon," said MacBridan, "we know how upsetting this is, but we have to let you know how things look, good or bad. This is one of the first items we'd planned to discuss with Marston after we'd unloaded."

"If there is someone on the inside helping the thieves, and I have strong doubts that there is, why would you have trusted Marston? Certainly you would have had to count him as an insider as well, wouldn't you?" asked Lord MacKinnon.

"Yes, usually we would have, and I did have concerns about Marston. In fact, he topped my list. He was not only in a prime position to know all the details surrounding the move but would have had experience with all of the security precautions that we were taking. Dolinski, you should know, dismissed those thoughts immediately. He was rather adamant about Marston's good character. If it does turn out that Marston was murdered, it will mean that whoever has been trying to get that painting has just taken things to the next level."

Lord MacKinnon slapped the tabletop with the palms of his hands, with the sound echoing loudly in the large room. "But the bloody painting is worthless!" he shouted. "There has to be more to it than just some cheap eyesore of an heirloom that my family has inexplicably held onto. I would have given the bloody thing away rather than have it cost a human life. Why would anybody do this? My family has no enemies."

"We agree that there's more to this than we know," said Cori, "but until we understand their motivation, our best way of finding them is to keep the painting secure and force them to try again."

Lord MacKinnon glared at Cori for a moment, and then his expression changed as the wind seemed to go out of him, and he slumped back in his chair. "My apologies for shouting. My temper sometimes gets the better of me. I had almost the same argument yesterday with Marston. He too was convinced that someone at the estate was helping the thieves, possibly even a member of the family."

"Did he say who he thought might be responsible?" asked MacBridan.

"No, but then he was not nearly so diplomatic as you have tried to be. You never got the chance to know Marston, but Dolinski will tell you that he was very direct and rarely minced words. He told me that it was most probably one of the people working at the estate, but that he couldn't rule out the possibility of it being a member of the family. I'm afraid I responded rather poorly."

"The maid we found in the hall before going into Marston's room, have the police talked to her?" asked MacBridan.

"They couldn't. Oh, they tried, but she was a mess. Mrs. Henderson had already given her a pretty potent sedative before the police arrived, so she wasn't too coherent."

"Mrs. Henderson?" asked Cori.

"Robena Henderson, Fergus's wife. She's the housekeeper," explained Lord MacKinnon.

"We'd like to talk with her as soon as we can, preferably before the police do," said MacBridan.

"I'll let Mrs. Henderson know. She'll see to it first thing in the morning, which brings me to what I wanted to discuss with you. I plan to talk this over with Dolinski, but I'd like for the two of you to stay on for a few days, at least until we can determine what's going on. If Marston was murdered, then I have a killer targeting my family and my home."

"I'm certain that Dolinski will not have a problem with that," said MacBridan. "We'd be happy to stay."

"Good, thank you. That means a great deal to me."

"Lord MacKinnon, what else can you tell us about the maid and what she might have seen?" asked Cori.

"I'm not sure there's anything more that I can add except that her name is Laria."

"Mac told me that even though she was terribly upset, she kept saying something about having seen the gatherer. Do you have any idea who she might have been referring to?"

Lord MacKinnon's face started to turn red again. "These people and their ridiculous superstitions! Since we've returned to Scotland, all I hear about is that bloody ghost. It's all a bunch of naive nonsense, and I'm tired of everyone obsessing over it." His voice continued to rise to a point that he was nearly shouting again.

"Now, now, Ronald, what are you going on about? I could hear you halfway down the hall." Standing in the doorway was an elderly woman with dark steel gray hair. She looked to be in her mid to late seventies, and even though she was scolding Lord MacKinnon, her eyes held great affection for him. The family resemblance in her face was easy to see. She was very thin and couldn't have been much over five feet tall. They all rose as she walked over to them.

"It has been a difficult evening, Aunt Jean. Ms. Hopkins, Mr. MacBridan, this is my aunt, Jean MacKinnon."

"I'm sure that Ronald has already said this, but welcome to our home. It is so good to have you here." Although she moved slowly, each step a deliberate act, there was strength in her voice and manner. "It is such a sad time for us. Mr. Marston was a noble man and will be missed." She looked at Lord MacKinnon, smiled, and said, "I sincerely hope you can help my nephew. He too is a good man but not as patient as he should be. I'm sorry to say he has his mother's foul temper, which obviously did not come from the MacKinnon side of the family."

"Behave," scolded Lord MacKinnon. "You don't want to be airing all the family's dirty laundry in one night."

Looking at Cori, Aunt Jean said, "As you now have little doubt, Ronald does not believe in ghosts. Unfortunately, many of the people who work here at the estate and live in the area do. We're credited with having several such creatures here at the manor, but we have one specter in particular that is especially famous." Her voice had taken on a quiet, mischievous tone, laced with conspiracy. She was clearly enjoying herself.

"Aunt Jean, must you?" sighed Lord MacKinnon.

"I take it that you do not share Lord MacKinnon's thoughts on the subject," said MacBridan.

"Goodness no, but I haven't given up on him. In my life, I've found that every time I think I know it all I'm proven wrong. Well, I hate being wrong, so I do my best to keep an open mind."

"There aren't many of those around here." The loud voice had come from one of the two younger men who'd just entered the dining room. He was a little taller than Lord MacKinnon, had the same stocky build, and had crossed the line from stocky to overweight. His hair was a mixture of dark red and brown hues, and he appeared to be in his early thirties. "If you want to stick around here for very long, you'll learn that differences of opinion are not tolerated."

Lord MacKinnon was obviously not amused by his comments. "May I introduce you to my son," he said. "Wallace, this is Mr. MacBridan and Ms. Hopkins."

"No need to be so formal, Father." Wallace gave Cori the once-over, then looked at MacBridan and said, "Must be nice to have your secretary travel with you, if you follow my meaning."

"For your sake, and out of respect for your father, I'll pretend I don't. Ms. Hopkins is my associate," said MacBridan.

Wallace either chose to ignore, or simply didn't hear, the warning from MacBridan. He moved to the bar at the end of the room and poured himself a drink. "Call it what you like, makes no difference to me."

"That'll be enough of that, Wallace," snapped Lord MacKinnon.

"It's all right," said Cori. "This evening's been hard on everyone. I'm sure we're all feeling the strain in one way or another."

"That's right. You're the Yanks moving our things. Well, we'll know who to blame if something's broken. We'd about given upon you tonight, thought you'd gotten lost." Wallace laughed at his own remark. Walking up to MacBridan, he said, "No hard feelings I hope," and extended his hand.

MacBridan accepted the gesture, but no sooner had he done so when Wallace tightly gripped MacBridan's hand squeezing as hard as he could. To Wallace's surprise, he found his grip greeted with equal pressure.

"No hard feelings at all. We're with the Hawthorne Group," said MacBridan, not releasing Wallace's hand. As he talked, he continued to steadily apply more pressure, the smile on his face not betraying the contest that was taking place. "We're helping to supervise all aspects of the move, as well as the security." Wallace grimaced and tried to pull away before MacBridan finally released his hand.

Wallace, not sure what to do, stared briefly at MacBridan before backing away. "You weren't telling them about the ghost, were you, Auntie? They've just arrived. We don't want to scare them away."

"I've known a lot of people in my time," said Aunt Jean. "They don't impress me as the kind that scares easily."

"I'm Barclay," said the other man. Close to Wallace in age, he was in his late twenties, roughly the same height but had a much trimmer build.

"Where is Kerr?" asked Lord MacKinnon.

"He's not back yet," answered Barclay. "He went into the village, but I'm not sure why."

"Barclay and Kerr are my nephews," explained Lord MacKinnon. "They work here at the estate. Barclay works closely with me, helping to manage the MacKinnon Trust."

"Welcome to Scotland," said Barclay as he shook hands with MacBridan. Looking at Cori, he said, "It is disappointing that your first evening with us is under such tragic circumstances. It's a horrible thing."

"We too are sorry. We've heard nothing but good things about Mr. Marston," said Cori.

"I enjoyed working with him," said Barclay. "He'd led a fascinating life, and some of the stories he shared were most remarkable."

Fergus came back into the dining room, wheeling in a small table covered with serving dishes. He was followed by a woman who appeared to be about his age, with dark hair and stern features. She had a sturdy build to her and was quick to direct Fergus as to the placement of everything. Aunt Jean explained to Cori that the woman was Robena Henderson, Fergus's wife. Cori had to fight to keep from laughing out loud as Aunt Jean whispered, "Don't let her intimidate you, my dear. It's just her nature to be the way she is. I don't believe she can help it."

They had just sat down for dinner when a young woman rushed into the dining room. She was very attractive with her auburn-colored hair pulled back, and although her features were much softer, MacBridan could see that she too was a blood relative. He couldn't help but notice the full, curvaceous figure that approached him. "I am so sorry, Uncle," she said as she kissed Lord MacKinnon on the cheek. "I'm afraid I lost all track of the time."

Lord MacKinnon did the introductions as she sat down next to MacBridan. "This is Faith, my niece," said Lord MacKinnon. "Faith's been living in London but has been visiting with us for a while."

Dinner passed quietly, and what little conversation there was concerned Marston and the family's recent return to Scotland. MacBridan noticed that with the exception of Wallace, each of them seemed to have had true affection for Marston. Wallace sat at the far end of the table, away from his father, and kept glaring at MacBridan. His silent challenge to MacBridan had backfired on him, and it amused MacBridan that Wallace actually looked like he was pouting.

After dinner, they left the dining room and walked down the hall toward the foyer, settling in the drawing room. The walls were filled with books, portraits, and collectables, illustrating the varied interests of generations of the MacKinnon clan. The two fireplaces, with their warmth and soft light, added to the comfortable atmosphere of the room. Drinks were served, Cori choosing a chardonnay while MacBridan joined Lord MacKinnon with a brandy.

Wallace, who was already two drinks ahead of everyone else, poured his own drink, a very healthy dose of scotch. He then walked over and leaned against the wall beside the larger fireplace and said, "Fergus was telling me that Laria got quite a fright, claims to have actually seen the dark lord."

"Please, Wallace, now don't start. It has been a very difficult evening, and that stuff is all nonsense, and you know it. Whatever it was that scared her, I assure you it wasn't a ghost," said Lord MacKinnon.

"Perhaps not, but the way she tells it, it was him all right, and he passed right through the door," persisted Wallace.

"Have you spoken with her?" demanded Lord MacKinnon.

"No, but—"

"I thought not. That's how these things start, taking on a life of their own. Someone tells a story claiming it to be the absolute truth. Then everyone who hears it has to add their own special twist until it becomes so outrageous and so far from the truth that it's not worth listening to."

"We're not arguing with you, Ronald," said Aunt Jean, her voice low and calming, "but the story is out, and you know these people as well as I do. They believe in this sort of thing. It'll be all over the village by tomorrow morning."

"Well, I can't help that. All I can say is that anyone who chooses to believe that kind of tripe is a fool," said Lord MacKinnon. He caught himself, realizing what he'd said and who it affected. He looked at his aunt Jean and said, "I'm sorry. That didn't come out the way I wanted it to. It's just that the whole situation has me at my wit's end. But I'll tell you now that Marston did not die at the hands of some cursed old spirit."

"How did he die, Uncle?" asked Faith.

Lord MacKinnon thought about it for a moment and then looked to MacBridan for help. "At this point, we're not certain," said MacBridan. "It appears that he may have had some kind of severe allergic reaction. Hopefully, we'll know more in the morning. I can tell you that his door and the windows in his room had all been locked from the inside, and there wasn't any sign of anyone else having been in there with him."

Wallace gave a small laugh filled with sarcasm. "I'm afraid that won't cut it. No one around here's going to believe a story like that. A man such as Marston doesn't suddenly just drop over from an allergic reaction."

"You don't know that, Wallace," said Faith. "Sadly, this sort of thing happens quite often. Allergies can be very tricky. One day you're mildly allergic to something, and then the very next time you're exposed, you can have a dramatically intense response."

"Faith is right. That kind of thing happens more often than you'd think. One good example is how some people can be affected by a bee sting," offered Cori.

"Exactly," said Faith, "that's a perfect example."

Wallace had finished his drink and was pouring another. "Myth or not, this even has Fergus rattled, and I don't remember the last time I saw him this upset."

"The sudden death of someone you're close to, someone you work with, is very upsetting for most people," said MacBridan. "It's not usually something you just shrug off and walk away from."

Fergus entered the drawing room to ask if they had all they needed. "We were just talking about you, Fergus," said Wallace.

"It was nothing, Fergus," said Lord MacKinnon, rising from his chair. Turning to his guests, he said, "It's been an exhausting evening, and if you'll excuse me, I'll see you all in the morning. Fergus, will you please ask Robena to show Ms. Hopkins and Mr. MacBridan to their rooms?"

"Certainly, sir," said Fergus.

Fergus followed Lord MacKinnon from the room. "It concerns me to see him so upset. You are right, Mr. MacBridan, this evening has put us all on edge. Laria claiming to have seen the dark lord just makes matters worse," said Aunt Jean.

"I told you earlier, my father will not listen to opinions other than his own, and he's not going to bend on this. Laria saw something. She'd have no reason to lie about it," insisted Wallace.

"You're too hard on him," said Barclay. "You know how talk of supernatural beings gets to him, but you insist on bringing it up."

"Oh, for heaven's sake, Barclay, give it a rest. He can't hear you now, so you can quit acting like you agree with every breath he takes. You're really rather pitiful," sneered Wallace. Barclay's face clouded over in anger, and he stood up, glaring at Wallace but held himself in check.

"The problem," said Aunt Jean, "started a couple of months ago when we arrived back here at the estate. As I was telling you earlier this evening, many believe our home to be haunted. On rare occasions, someone will see or hear something, and true or not, they blame it on a ghost, bolstering the stories. However, it's a little more serious due to our most infamous specter, one that to this day strikes fear into so many, the dark lord."

"I believe I read about him. According to legend, he lived several centuries ago and was accused of practicing the dark arts," said Cori.

"It is more than a legend I'm afraid. His name was Balgair MacKinnon, an evil soul if there ever was one," said Aunt Jean, her small frame nearly disappearing in the chair she was sitting. "He had gone off to join the crusades and, soon after, joined the Templars, but I assure you, he was anything but a Christian. He returned to Scotland just before the persecution of the Templars started, a coincidence that did not go unnoticed, especially by Lord Angus Mackinnon, the leader of the MacKinnon clan at the time."

"How long had he been away?" asked Barclay.

"It had been close to seven years, if I remember my family history correctly," said Aunt Jean. "At first, he was warmly welcomed home by the family and by the people of the village as a hero, and he had not returned empty-handed. It is said that he brought a king's ransom in gold, as well as some rather precious items, all trophies of the crusades. He also brought home a wife."

"I had read that he was married," said Faith, "but there doesn't seem to be much written about her. Where did she come from?"

"No one ever knew. Even now, her past remains completely shrouded in mystery. She was much older than him, small in stature, but fierce in temperament, and it is recorded that Angus had to talk with Balgair several times about her abusive treatment of the servants. There was one incident where she attacked a maid, nearly killing the poor girl."

"Despite our family's status, surely she wasn't above the law," said Faith.

"In those days, Angus was the law. Balgair and his wife created several problems for Angus. Had things continued on, Angus would have had to have either run them off or turn them over to the sheriff. Then, almost overnight, Angus became very ill. He was a strong man, no one could ever remember a time when he'd been sick. Rumors quickly spread across the countryside that Balgair's wife was a witch and that she had cast a spell on poor Angus. Witchcraft or not, in less than a month of taking ill, he died. Angus had been a good man and was widely loved. As devastating to the village as his passing was, the very next day, his only son and heir accidently drowned in the loch."

"Now there's a most interesting coincidence for you," said Wallace.

"Whatever it was, Balgair wasted no time. As the only remaining male heir, he stepped in and took the title of Baron MacKinnon," said Aunt Jean, her narrative completely captivating the room. "The next few years were terrible times for the estate and for the villagers. It was widely believed that

Balgair and his wife engaged in the dark arts worshiping the devil. The final straw came when young children started to disappear. Although no bodies were ever found, it was believed that they were being taken by Balgair and used as innocent sacrifices to Satan. True or not, the villagers rose up and stormed the estate. Balgair and his wife were captured, and their two young children were taken away."

"What became of the children?" asked Barclay.

"They were raised by the parson's family," answered Faith. She looked at her aunt and smiled. "I too have always been fascinated by this particular time in our family's history."

"Eventually, when the son came of age, he took over the estate, inheriting it and the title," continued Aunt Jean. "As for Balgair and his wife, she was immediately taken out and burned for being a witch. As the flames consumed her, she did not make a sound, not one scream, just stared at them with a maniacal grin on her face. With her dying breath, she cursed the villagers, telling them that they'd never be safe from Balgair's vengeance."

"The next day, there was a trial, of sorts, and Balgair was condemned, but it was to be a horrible death. The parson, the sheriff, and three other prominent members of the village buried Balgair alive in unhallowed ground, wrapping him and his coffin in blackthorn. But even going to these lengths was not enough. Despite their efforts to be rid of Balgair and the evil that had possessed him, the villagers still feared him. They were terrified that he was still alive, that the grave could not hold him. In order to quell the growing panic, the parson, along with several men, returned to the grave two days later to find that it had been opened. The coffin was in pieces, and Balgair was gone. Ever since then, there have been many who have claimed to have seen him at the estate. He comes to gather members of our family for hell. At other times, his wife shows up as a woman in black to punish the few good members of our evil line." Aunt Jean finished her tale, took a sip of wine, and closed her eyes. The only sound in the room was the crackling of logs in the fireplace.

"Now I understand why Laria was so terrified," said MacBridan. "If that's who she thinks she saw, that would just about do it for anyone."

"Come now, don't tell me you believe all this," scoffed Wallace. "That kind of talk will lose you my father's good graces quicker than you can imagine. It does beg the question, though. Tell us, do you believe in ghosts, Mr. MacBridan?"

MacBridan saw Aunt Jean looking at him waiting for his response. He smiled at Wallace and said, "Let's say that on very wise council, I'm keeping an open mind."

"Excuse me." It was Robena standing in the doorway. "If you're ready to retire, I'll show you to your rooms."

MacBridan and Cori both stood up. Cori said, "Thank you. That's very nice of you. I've not yet completely adjusted to the time difference, and I'm ready to call it a day."

"Where will they be staying?" asked Wallace.

"Lord MacKinnon asked that I put them in the south wing, not too far from your aunt. They'll be across the hall from each other with Mr. MacBridan in the Balmoral suite," answered Robena.

Wallace laughed at this and said, "Perhaps we'll get to test that open mind of yours after all. It may interest you to know that the Balmoral suite used to be Balgair's room. I do hope that won't keep you awake."

"I appreciate your concern," said MacBridan, "but don't worry. As tired as I am, unless he snores louder than I do, I'll be fine."

Chapter 9

Jean watched as MacBridan and Cori left the study with Mrs. Henderson leading the way. It had been a tragic day, terribly sad and difficult to understand. Yet Jean, for some strange reason, felt better than she had in several weeks. Ever since they had returned to the estate, tensions had been running high within the family, with the staff, everyone constantly on edge. It was the same kind of tension, that same nervousness one felt when waiting for an approaching storm to break, not knowing how bad it would be or if you'd be safe when it hit. This evening, that approaching storm had descended on them in all its fury, Marston being the first taken. Jean feared there'd be more.

In the past few weeks, she had seen too much, too many signs that the rest of the family was either oblivious to or refused to see, grounded in their own stubborn beliefs. It wasn't that her family didn't love her; they just wouldn't take her seriously. They were too quick to view her as a kind, gentle old woman with silly notions.

She knew her grandmother would have known what to do. Grandmother had died the month she landed in America. Over there, the strange events of her life were treated with therapy and pills, and by the time she returned to Scotland, she believed that her visions had been something called an Electra complex. But back in her family home, dreams and feelings began to warn her. Many foggy days she had visited Ramsay's grave, and many foggy nights she had read certain books in the manor library. Slowly her beliefs and worldview slipped from modernity.

If only Grandmother had lived! She had begun to expect to see a small woman dressed in black waiting outside the home. She tried to tell these things to Faith. Faith loved her, respected her, but certainly didn't believe her.

Grandmother had hinted that a gift was manifested in the female line of the family. It was not a gift from God but from Balgair's witch-wife. It could be used for good, but like a rifle over a fireplace, it could end the family when used in rage, fear, or greed.

The gift told her that MacBridan was not on the side of the witch-wife. It made her feel better, but she knew it would make Reznik angry.

Reznik, the spirit guide resident in her witch board, had told her and Faith that such a man was coming and that the fate of the MacKinnon family would hinge on his success or failure. Although Reznik was rarely wrong, too often his messages were enigmatic, hard to decipher, and lacked the clarity she desired.

She'd come to know of Reznik when she was a young child at her grandmother's knee, learning the secrets and methods of how to correctly use the witch board. Her grandmother had been quite patient in her teaching, wanting to be sure that she understood all its intricacies and would not forget. At times it had scared her, and she vividly remembered how much her mother had feared it.

In fairness, her mother had been correct; it was something to be feared. Their minister had most vehemently agreed with her mother, and growing up, she'd received several stern lectures from both of them regarding its use and the danger it represented. However, she'd never stopped turning to Reznik, especially in time of crisis. This ancient witch board had been with the family a long time and was a treasured heirloom. To the consternation of her nephew, she kept it set up in her room on display.

In its own way, it was quite beautiful. Made of polished wood, it displayed all the letters of the alphabet written in an ancient script, the numbers zero through nine, and several magical signs and symbols all in a delicate flowing pattern. The board was very sturdy and was stained with various shades of black, dark blues, deep reds, and purple blending together wonderfully. It was truly a work of art. Over the years, she'd learned to respect it and, in some ways, to fear it. After all, it was a portal to the spirit world and not to be taken lightly. Too many times, its warning of sickness and death had been accurate. Jean had learned that knowing of such coming events could be more frightening, more of a burden, than the events themselves. And too often she'd found herself helpless to prevent them from occurring.

But this time was different. Amidst the darkest of circumstances, Reznik had spoken to them of hope. St. Bridget was sending a warrior. In their short time together this evening, MacBridan had come across as being strong of character, confident in his actions, and not one to back away from danger. His being of Scottish heritage was all the proof she needed to know that he was the one. But Reznik had also forewarned of a malignant evil that was growing in strength, an ancient evil that was on the rise, one that could potentially consume this defender of her family. When Jean had asked what the outcome would be, Reznik had been vague, his words confusing.

"Aunt Jean, are you all right?"

"What?" said Aunt Jean, looking up to find Faith standing next to her. "Oh yes, certainly, why do you ask?"

"You were staring at the doorway so intently I thought there might be something wrong."

"Was I? No, just lost in thought I'm afraid. I'm feeling a bit worn-down."

"I've had it as well. I'm ready to call it a night if you are," said Faith. "Shall we go upstairs?"

"Yes," answered Aunt Jean. "That's an excellent idea. I believe that's what I'll do."

Aunt Jean said good night to Wallace and Barclay, and then she and Faith left the study, arm in arm, and started down the hall.

"What do you think of our guests?" asked Aunt Jean.

"I was actually rather impressed. They seem very knowledgeable, and Mr. MacBridan is awfully bold. It is so comforting to have them here with us, especially today."

Jean smiled at her niece and said, "Yes, I'm sure that it was his boldness that caught your eye."

Faith laughed. "Ah, now I see, it's matchmaking you're up to."

"I liked him, and you could do far worse. There's a rough edge about him, but I believe he is what your generation would call a hunk."

"Aunt Jean, you sly old girl. It sounds like you're the one after him."

"Take my word for it, he's a true man, and there aren't many around like him. He's very direct and a quick judge of character. He certainly put Wallace in his place straight off." She told Faith of their mild confrontation before dinner and of MacBridan defeating Wallace at his own game when they shook hands. "I've seen Wallace pull that stunt before. Well, tonight it backfired on him. The look on his face was priceless."

Faith laughed in delight. "It's what I get for not being on time. I would have loved to have watched that!"

Their pace up the staircase was slow but steady, with Aunt Jean holding onto the banister and Faith's arm. As of late, she'd found her balance to be a little off, a most frustrating ailment.

"Marston's passing is so sad. I'm worried about Ronald. I believe that having Mr. MacBridan and Ms. Hopkins here will be of great comfort to him. I'm frightened to think what it would have been like for him if he'd had to deal with all of this by himself," said Aunt Jean.

"Especially with Laria going to pieces and claiming to have seen the dark lord. For Uncle Ronald, that would have been the icing on a very nasty cake."

Having finally reached the top of the stairs, they proceeded down the long hallway, passing Cori's and MacBridan's rooms. "I'm not so sure she didn't see something. Hopefully, I'll be able to talk with them and let them know all that I'm worried about," said Aunt Jean.

"You're not referring to what we learned the other evening when we were using Reznik, are you?"

"Yes, of course, it may be helpful to them."

"Do you think that's wise?" asked Faith. She loved her aunt but didn't know how she actually felt about the witch board. She remembered the first time her aunt showed it to her and how to use it. It had been such fun, and growing up, she'd believed everything about it, its ability to tell the future and of the spirit Reznik who guided them. But now she knew that the board was merely Aunt Jean's way of accessing her subconscious, but to reveal such a superstition would make her look like an old fool. "Please don't take this the wrong way. Even though Mr. MacBridan says he has an open mind, I'm betting that he's more like Marston than we know. It might be asking too much for him to accept."

"Perhaps," said Aunt Jean, "but that's a chance I'm willing to risk. Marston was always fair with me about such things, and I believe that Mr. MacBridan and Ms. Hopkins are cut from the same cloth."

"I hope you're right. Heaven knows we need their help."

They'd come to the end of the hall where the grandfather clock stood intersecting with a shorter hall that branched out in both directions. Turning left, Aunt Jean's room was a short way down this smaller hallway. Faith's room was on the same side of the hall as her aunt's but in the opposite direction.

"I'll say good night to you here, my dear. Sleep well, and I'll see you in the morning."

"Don't you want me to walk you to your door?" asked Faith.

"That won't be necessary," said Aunt Jean, and she kissed her niece on the cheek. "I'll be just fine. Good night."

Jean took her time getting to her room. As she turned the knob, she looked back down the hallway to see Faith watching her. Her niece waved then turned to go to her own room. As Jean went in, she found the lamp beside her bed had been turned on and that the fire had recently been tended to. She smiled as she thought about Mrs. Henderson. Although the woman came across to everyone as a cold, hard taskmaster, Robena always saw to it that the house staff took especially good care of her, and she appreciated it.

As tired as she was, she wanted to spend a little time with her grandmother's diary. A few years ago, she had found it in a box of her grandmother's things. It helped her piece together the lore that her grandmother had wanted to give her, but it lacked the full picture. Her grandmother often wrote of Reznik and of the many predictions he'd shared with her through the witch board. She also wrote of dreadful things such as omens, evil spirits, and worst of all, the shadow people.

The diary broke off a few months before her grandmother's death when she had been stricken with fever shortly after seeing the shadow people. Jean shivered at the thought of those dreadful creatures. She'd seen them again; her most recent sighting having been just a few days ago. She feared that they were back and was all but certain that she'd seen them yesterday, just before Marston's death.

Jean kept the diary in the upper drawer of her dresser on top of her own journal. Getting them both out, she walked over and sat down in one of the chairs next to the fireplace.

The warmth from the fire greeted her face and hands as she settled down into the overstuffed chair. She'd update her own journal tomorrow, but tonight, she wanted to review some of her grandmother's passages. She soon found what she'd been looking for on the page dated October 10, 1941:

> They are definitely all around the house. My nerves are in a terrible state, and I can't sleep. Over the past few days, I've caught more and more glimpses of them on the grounds. They seem to be getting closer, bolder! It must have to do with the war. Thank heavens they've not entered the house. I must consult with Reznik.

At first, Jean hadn't been sure that they'd returned. But the fear she always felt for these demonic creatures nearly overtook her when she saw them on the staircase. That had been two days ago. There'd been three of them. Not only were they in the house, but she'd gotten a better look at them than normal. Grotesque in shape and size, they'd quickly darted out of sight, but the experience left her shaken.

Other than what she'd learned from her grandmother, Jean knew little about the shadow people, but she knew enough to fear them. They'd cursed the MacKinnon clan for centuries, and usually only the women saw them. They were roughly the size of people, but terribly formed, as if somehow they'd been mangled in some ghastly accident. Death was near, and the shadow people were on the prowl. She knew them to be death's servants, and that to see them meant that their master was not far away.

The next day, poor Marston died a most horrible death.

She wracked her mind over this. There had to be a way of protecting yourself from these evil creatures. She continued to scan the diary. She hadn't seen them today. Perhaps they were satisfied in taking Marston.

On the round tea table before her sat the witch board. She needed Reznik's guidance, needed him to advise her as to what to do, but she was too tired and was having trouble keeping her eyes open. Sinking deeper into the chair, she leaned her head back and closed her eyes. She had taken in a little more of the warmth from the fire, and then she retired. Tomorrow was another day.

The witch board's dark colors dimly reflected the light from the fire. The planchette rested in its place at the top of the board. The only sound in the room came from the wood crackling in the fire. Jean, her eyes closed, began to doze. Then, unseen by anyone, the planchette trembled ever so lightly, and its pointed end turned, just fractionally, toward Jean.

Chapter 10

The large grandfather clock at the end of the hall rang out, its deep, rolling baritone sounding abnormally loud. Announcing the eleventh hour, the clock's somber tones filled the quiet hallway as MacBridan and Cori followed Robena. She guided them to Cori's room, which like most of the rooms on the second floor was elegantly furnished. To Cori's delight, this particular room had a large canopy bed with two end tables on either side, a dresser and matching armoire, and a small writing table by the windows.

"This is absolutely charming," said Cori.

"It is one of my favorite rooms in the house," said Robena. "However, you may want to draw the curtains before retiring as you'll find this room catches the morning sun."

"Is there anything I need to know about the fireplace?" asked Cori. The fireplace stood across the foot of her bed, and the small fire that was still burning sat atop a bed of glowing coals, casting a soft light across the floor in front of it.

"Not really," said Robena. "There are more logs there in the bin if you wish to build it up. The house has central heating, so you'll be comfortable, but it never really gets what I call warm, especially on the days we have rain. So we keep the fireplaces going in the private rooms to take the dampness out of the air. However, I do need to let you know about our fire elf."

"Fire elf?" asked MacBridan, trying to keep from laughing, hoping he wasn't about to hear another wild tale like he'd just heard downstairs.

Robena's face gave way to a small smile but was quickly overpowered by her seemingly ever-present stern demeanor. "Well, that's how we refer to him. Early tomorrow morning, one of the house staff will come by and build up your fire to help take off the morning chill. They generally slip in around five thirty or so, so please don't be alarmed if you hear someone in your room."

"After the story we just heard, I appreciate you letting me know," said Cori.

"Is there anything else I can do for you this evening?" asked Robena.

"No, this is lovely. Thank you."

"Mr. MacBridan, if you'll please follow me, I'll show you to your room," said Robena.

"I'll be right there," said MacBridan as he watched Robena leave. Smiling at Cori, he said, "Try not to shoot the fire elf."

"Thank heavens she told us. I probably would have had a heart attack."

MacBridan laughed and said, "Sleep well. We have a great deal to do tomorrow. If you need me, I'm right across the hall. See you in the morning."

Robena was waiting for him at the door to his room. As they entered, he was surprised to find that it was much larger than Cori's. The bed was a tall, sturdy four-poster with a magnificent headboard. Like Cori's room, there was a fire burning in the fireplace, which was directly across the foot of his bed. A small oval table with two wingback chairs provided a comfortable sitting place directly in front of the fireplace. There was also a large dresser and an enormous armoire, the top of which nearly touched the ceiling. MacBridan saw that his luggage had been brought to his room and had been placed next to the door to his bathroom.

"Mr. Truecourt asked that we let you know that everything has been secured inside the house and that he and the movers will be back first thing in the morning. Will there be anything else this evening, sir?"

"No, this is fine. I have everything I need." As she turned to leave, MacBridan remembered the one thing he'd meant to ask her about. "Oh, yes, there is something you can help me with. Cori and I talked to Lord MacKinnon earlier this evening about our talking with Laria tomorrow morning. Did he mention that to you?"

"Yes, sir, she'll be available after breakfast."

"Excellent, that will work just fine. Thank you," said MacBridan.

Robena turned to leave, got to the door, and then hesitated for a moment. She appeared to be struggling with something, unsure of what to do next. Finally, having made up her mind, she looked at MacBridan and said, "This evening, they told you and Ms. Hopkins about Balgair MacKinnon. It's important for you to know that the years he lived here were a terrible time for the village, and they are remembered to this day as the cursed years. It was a time of terrible of suffering and terror. You're not from here, so I don't expect you to believe all that was said, but be careful to not make the same mistake that others have. No matter what you may believe, there is an ancient evil walking these grounds, and unfortunately, what Laria saw this evening was not the first incident that we've had."

"What can you tell me?" asked MacBridan.

"He's been seen by others around the estate, especially near the old chapel. They've also seen the dark ones here at the house and on the grounds."

"The dark ones?"

"They're known as the shadow people. They're hard to describe, for you rarely get more than a glimpse. They are like dark shadows but grotesque in their form. They get as close to you as they can, bringing a deep sense of dread. You know you're in danger, but you don't know why. They're almost as frightening as he is. The entire staff is on edge, and with Mr. Marston's death, it's going to make things even worse."

"Make things worse, how? Robena, we don't even know what he died from, but whatever it was, I assure you that he was not killed be anything supernatural."

"As you say, Mr. MacBridan, we don't know what he died from. You must understand, these kinds of sightings haven't happened for years. But now, ever since the family returned, they've started up again. And they're happening more and more often. Frankly, it is worse than I've ever experienced, and all of us are afraid for the sun to set."

"Do these sightings only happen at night?" asked MacBridan.

"No, but they do seem to be more frequent once the sun goes down. My husband and I have worked for Lord MacKinnon for several years. Like you, the baron doesn't believe in this either. I don't understand what's going on, Mr. MacBridan, but I'm not ashamed to say that I'm scared. The last time the dark lord made his presence known, nearly fifteen years before I arrived at the estate, two members of the MacKinnon family tragically met their deaths. Please do what you can to help them, to get Lord MacKinnon to listen to reason." She stopped as abruptly as she'd started, bowed her head, and stood there, staring at the floor. "Forgive me. I forget my place at times. Good night, sir."

Robena left, closing the door behind her before he could reply. MacBridan hadn't expected Robena to open up like that and was a little surprised that she had. True, he didn't believe the tale he'd heard downstairs. Scotland was full of such stories. But Robena's statement had been more revealing than anything else he'd heard. She and the rest of the staff not only believed in these ghostly creatures but were terrified that they actually could pose a physical threat.

MacBridan realized how this could only work to the thieves' advantage. For that matter, considering how everything else they'd done had been so well planned, he wouldn't be too surprised to find that they were the ones behind all of these ghostly sightings. Fear is a powerful weapon, and if "Balgair" wanted to steal a painting, he doubted that any of the staff would get in his way.

Had Marston been murdered? Like he and Cori, Marston believed the thieves had someone working for them on the inside. Had Marston gotten too close? Could it actually be one of the family behind all this? They were certainly an interesting assortment of characters! At this point, his mind hit overload, and he knew it was time for sleep.

Turning off the lamp, he collapsed onto the mattress. The fire had nearly burned itself out. Only a few small flames and the soft light from the coals were left. Turning on his side, he glanced at the windows and realized he'd not pulled the drapes. It didn't matter; he was too tired to get up and close them, and it wasn't long before he drifted off to sleep.

MacBridan's eyes flew open. He'd been in a deep sleep. Tired and confused, he took a couple of moments to remember where he was. Suddenly alert, he lay perfectly still, listening. He could feel his heart racing in his chest, his whole body tense. Although his eyes were open, it was so dark he couldn't see anything. He then realized that he'd somehow worked his way down under the blanket covering his head. He still couldn't hear anything, yet his nerves were on fire. Something was terribly wrong.

The creak of a floorboard, magnified by the surrounding silence, tightened the tension laced across his shoulders. Then he remembered the fire elf. That was it; it had to be. But why would that have startled him so? Lying on his stomach, he realized that his left wrist was near his face. In his haste to get to bed, he had not taken off his watch. Slowly he turned his wrist, ever so slightly, so that he could see the luminescent dial. It was 2:47 in the morning. Scratch the fire elf.

The tenseness that filled him quickly turned to fear, which made less sense. What was happening? Ghost stories never bothered him. A floorboard creaked—so what? Old houses make all kinds of noise, and this certainly qualified as an old house. Could he have been dreaming? Fear churned in his stomach, and he knew that this was more than just a reaction from a nightmare.

With his left hand, he slowly reached up, took hold of the comforter, and gradually pulled it back enough to where he could faintly see the window frame. The night sky was dark with very few stars visible. All remained quiet. Now that the comforter no longer covered his face, he was stunned by the intense cold that filled the room. The repugnant odor that accompanied it nearly made him gag. The fear in his stomach began to spread, threatening to take over as he quickly recognized the odor. It was the smell of otherness, the putrid, unmistakable scent of death and decay; he had smelled it before and prayed that he'd never encounter it again. MacBridan tried to focus, to get a grip on his frayed nerves. His mind groped for answers, anything to give him some idea as to what was happening. It was then, out of the corner of his eye, he saw a tall, dark figure glide past the window, a brief silhouette against the night sky. He was not alone.

MacBridan prepared to move. His only advantage was that he didn't think the intruder knew he was awake. Although the element of surprise would be on his side, he knew that it really wouldn't give him that much of an edge. Getting a tighter grip on the comforter, MacBridan got ready to move. Teetering on the edge of panic, he found himself nearly paralyzed. *What is wrong with me?*

Mustering his courage, MacBridan threw back the covers, bolting up in his bed, fists clenched. The room was so dark that he couldn't see very much, just vague outlines. The only light came from the few coals still glowing in the fireplace, but it was enough.

It stood at the foot of his bed, menacing and deadly still. MacBridan, on his knees, was face-to-face with it, unable to move. Blood roared in his ears; the cold numbing his senses.

It was tall, well over six feet, and appeared to be wearing a hooded robe, much like that of a monk's. Its features were completely masked by the hood and the darkness of the room, all except for the eyes. Where the eyes should have been were two dark red points, like molten steel piercing into MacBridan's soul. The palatable hatred of its gaze sent a physical pain through his chest. MacBridan fought for control against the panic screaming in his mind. The only coherent thought that he could pull together was to run. Something deep inside told him that to survive, he had to get away.

Acting on reflex more than anything else, MacBridan lunged backward, grasping in the darkness for the lamp next to his bed. Missing it, he slammed into the headboard. Frantically, he crawled toward the lamp, expecting to be attacked any second. In the darkness, his hand groped wildly, nearly knocking the lamp over, but was able to grab onto it before it could fall. Fumbling for the switch in what seemed like an eternity, he finally turned it on.

MacBridan whirled around to face his adversary, but it was gone. Frantically, his eyes swept the room, but it was nowhere in sight. In the same instant, the door to his room flew open and then slammed shut with tremendous force. Anger replaced the fear, and MacBridan jumped out of bed, continually scanning the room. He bolted to the door but couldn't get it open. It was jammed into the frame. Putting his weight into it, MacBridan gripped the knob and lifted up. The hinges screamed their protest as he yanked it open.

Cori, with her robe wrapped around her, stepped out of her room as he charged into the hall. "What's going on?" she asked MacBridan. "Did you hear that?"

MacBridan was breathing heavily as if he'd just run a race. Nearly breathless, he said, "I had company. Stay here, and keep watch. You see anyone, stop them." With that, he shot off down the hall toward the staircase. It never crossed his mind that all he was wearing was a pair of boxers. The hall was dark. Reaching the top of the stairs, he stopped to listen. The fact that he was still trying to get a grip on his own nerves didn't make it any easier. With his nerves strained to the breaking point, he jumped as the grandfather clock at the far end of the hall chimed three times.

The house was absolutely quiet, with no sign of life anywhere. He turned and started to walk back toward his room, constantly expecting the intruder to jump out at him. He saw Cori watching him as he walked back but had no idea what he was going to say to her. He couldn't explain what had just taken place in his own mind much less explain it to someone else. Someone or something—no, he refused to go there—someone had been in his room. How had they gotten away? The doors in this house were heavy and well-built. He'd learned that firsthand earlier in the evening. How could someone have opened the door so quickly and then slammed it shut with such force that it had become wedged into the frame?

"Mac, are you all right? Who was it?"

"I don't know. Come over here." They both crossed to the door of his room, which tilted downward at a slant as the hinge at the top had partially pulled away. "Stay here. I want to look around." This time, MacBridan made a thorough search of his room, under the bed, in the bathroom; he even moved the armoire enough to see if there was anything behind it.

"What are you looking for?" asked Cori.

"Someone is playing with us, and my bet is that it's Junior."

"Wallace? What happened?"

"I woke up to find someone standing at the foot of my bed. By the time I got the light on, they were gone."

"Did you get a look at them?"

"Not much, there wasn't any light in my room, but it looked like he was robed, you know, like what a priest or monk might wear. What I can't figure out is how they moved so quickly wearing such a costume. In the few seconds it took for me to get the light on, they were gone."

"What was that loud bang? I nearly jumped out of my skin."

"That was the sound of my door being slammed shut," said MacBridan as he went back to examine the doorframe. The wood around the top hinge had splintered, and the bottom hinge was slightly twisted.

Cori also examined it. "Do you have any idea how much force that took? They're going to have to replace the entire frame."

"Fire elf or not, going forward, I suggest we sleep with our doors locked. Tonight was designed to scare us. They won't get to play that card again."

"Tell me exactly what happened," said Cori. "What was it that woke you up? I mean, did you hear them?"

Finally having somewhat calmed down, he sighed and said, "I really don't know what woke me up." He then proceeded to tell her what had happened. The only part he left out was the burning eyes.

"So whoever it was, they were standing at the foot of your bed. You jumped up, confronted them, and then went for the light, which took...what...three, four seconds, and they were gone, right?"

"I'd say only about two or three seconds although it seemed longer."

"And it was then, once the light was on, that the door flew open and slammed shut."

"Yes."

"And you still didn't see anyone?"

"Quit talking to me like I'm the hysterical maid. That is what happened, and sadly, there just isn't any more to tell."

"Mac, I'm sorry, but where did they go? That's simply not enough time. These doors are too heavy. I'm not sure I could slam one of them hard enough to get it wedged into the frame. And even if I could, I have no idea how I'd go about doing that without being seen."

"Cori, I don't know what to tell you. I promise you this, though, we will figure it out."

Cori sat down in one of the chairs in front of the fireplace. She sat there quietly for a moment and said, "Mac, I'm not saying I believe this, and I know this will sound crazy, but you don't think that...I mean, this was supposedly Balgair's room."

"You're seriously asking me if I think a guy who's been dead for well over six hundred years is upset because I'm sleeping is his room. Cori, stories like the one we were told get more fantastic each time around, and there's rarely anything true about them. I do not doubt that the real Balgair, or whatever his name was, was probably a pretty nasty guy. I'm just saying that you can't put any stock into these wildly colorful tales. They are designed to entertain children and excite tourists."

"I know, the rational side of me is embarrassed, but the rest of me isn't so sure. Look, it's dark, I'm tired, and I guess I just got caught up in all of it."

"Don't worry about it," said MacBridan. He sat down in the chair across her. It was then that he noticed the slight trembling in his hands. Clasping them together, he said, "Just between us, whoever it was scared me to death. I didn't see this coming, I was just too worn out."

"Well, there's nothing more that we can do tonight. We'd better try and get some sleep," said Cori. "You want to stay in my room?"

MacBridan, putting his hand to his heart, gave a fake sigh and said, "If only you had said that like you meant it."

"Offer withdrawn. You're on your own," she said, got up, and walked to the door. As she started to leave, she stopped, looked back at MacBridan, and said, "I know they're just stories, but you'll understand if I sleep with a light on. Good night, Mac."

CHAPTER 11

For close to an hour after Cori left him, MacBridan sat and stared into the fire. He could not get the nightmarish image of the figure at the end of his bed out of his mind. The log he'd placed on top of the coals quickly started to burn, adding light and warmth to the room. The problem was that the more he thought about it, the less sense he could make of it.

While he certainly wasn't ready to subscribe to Cori's suggestion of having been visited by the dark lord of MacKinnon hall, he wasn't any closer to having a better explanation. The evening's events did, however, resolve the one working hypothesis that he'd been nursing before leaving Virginia. Not only was there someone on the inside working with the bad guys, he now had a name for that anonymous figure, Wallace. Although he didn't believe that Wallace was anywhere near sharp enough to have pulled all of this off by himself, he was pretty certain that he was somehow involved. At least he hoped he was. Wallace was easy to dislike.

What had caused him to wake up? How had the room become so bitterly cold? And the smell, where had that come from? But the most troubling piece of the entire incident was who had been in his room at the foot of his bed, and where had he gone? Clearly, the intent had been to scare him off, but how had they accomplished all those remarkable special effects?

The door could have been rigged to fall apart, potentially jamming as it had. But how did they manage to slam it shut, and why hadn't he seen anything? How had they gotten away so quickly? He finally calmed down enough to lean back in his chair and close his eyes. He rationalized that the goal behind every illusionist's trick was to fool the audience into believing the impossible to be true. Well, tonight he'd certainly been a good audience, but he wasn't willing to buy into it.

At about four in the morning, he managed to get up from his chair and lie back down on the bed. He was utterly worn out. He tried to sleep, but his nerves would not allow it. Each time he started to drop off, the least little sound would trigger his nerves, causing his eyes to pop open, dreading what might have returned. True to her word, Robena's fire elf slipped into the room about 5:30 a.m. The shattered hinges of his door made more noise than either of them anticipated. Mac pretended not to hear him, and he was soon gone.

MacBridan did manage to doze a little but finally gave up and by 7:00 a.m. was in the shower. Thirty minutes later, he left his room and lightly tapped on Cori's door. No answer. He waited a couple of moments then knocked a little louder. Finally, Cori opened the door, although just a crack. Her eyes were still closed.

"Good morning! It's seven thirty," said MacBridan, trying to make his voice sound as cheerful as possible. Cori hated cheerful people early in the morning. "Rise and shine. Up and at 'em."

"Keep chattering, and I'll get my gun."

"I'm afraid we have a rather full day in front of us."

She raised her face to glare at him, but it was a wasted effort as only one of her eyes would open. "Okay. Sure. I'll meet you downstairs," she mumbled and shut the door.

MacBridan smiled and headed off to the dining room. He'd worked with Cori on many assignments and knew that as good as she was at her job, she was anything but a morning person.

Add in a short night with broken sleep to the equation, he knew he was in for an interesting day with her.

Backtracking his way through the house, he soon made his way to the dining room. Breakfast was ready and waiting in serving trays on the buffet table, but more than anything, he needed coffee. The stimulating aroma from his cup started him on the road to recovery. Sipping the coffee, he found it to be far stronger than anything he was used to back home but just what the doctor ordered.

The view from the dining room looked out over beautifully manicured lawns and well-tended flower beds that ended at a line of trees off in the distance. The room faced east, but the morning sun was blocked by low clouds crowding the sky. As threatening as they appeared, it was not yet raining.

"Good morning, sir," said Fergus. "Mr. Truecourt is here to see you." Truecourt followed Fergus in, smiled, and went directly to the coffee urn. "You'll find breakfast on the table. Please help yourself. Is there anything else I can get for you, some tea perhaps?"

"I think I'll stay with coffee for now. Thank you," said MacBridan.

Truecourt came over and sat down next to MacBridan and said, "So how was your night at the manor?"

"A rare experience," answered MacBridan. "I think it would take some getting used to having servants around all the time."

"Perhaps, but I'd be willing to give it a try. We got here about thirty minutes ago, and the men are already unloading what's left in the trucks. Mrs. Henderson has taken over the operation. She is personally directing them as to where each piece is to be placed." He chuckled and said, "She'd make an excellent sergeant major."

"It looks like Cori and I will be staying on for a few more days than we'd planned," said MacBridan. "Lord MacKinnon has asked us to, and I'm sure that Dolinski will agree. Dolinski was a friend of Marston, had a great deal of respect for him. He'll have a personal interest in all this."

"You don't believe that Marston died of natural causes?"

"I'll be surprised if he did. This morning I'd like for you to stay with the movers and make sure that everything gets done. Cori and I are going to talk with the maid and then take a look around the estate. When the representative from Lloyd's gets here, give us a call. Cori will want to go through the manifest with them."

"Will you need me to stay on as well?" asked Truecourt.

"Not at this point, but we'll know more after our talk with Dolinski. If we do need help, you'll be the first one we call."

"Very good," said Truecourt. "We'll catch up later." Refilling his coffee, Truecourt left MacBridan alone in the room.

A few minutes later, Cori arrived. "Where did you get the coffee?" It was more of a demand than a question.

"Right over there." MacBridan pointed.

Cori made a beeline to the coffee urn and poured a cup, adding cream and honey. Her first taste caused her eyes to widen. "Wow, that's coffee."

"It's a little bit more potent here than what we get back at the office," said MacBridan.

"A little bit? Starbucks, move over. There's a new sheriff in town." She sat down next to MacBridan in the chair where Truecourt had been sitting. "After last night, I'm going to need an entire pot of this."

"I take it you didn't go back to sleep."

"After your freakish run in with an uninvited, nocturnal visitor, it was a little hard to relax. When I finally did drop off, the guy who slips in and builds up the fire—"

"The fire elf."

"Yes. Well, he picked that time to come into my room. It was embarrassing. What's so ridiculous about it is that I knew he was coming, knew he was supposed to be there. I still screamed.

Scared us both out of our wits. By the way, he's very nice, and his name is Tavis."

MacBridan couldn't keep from laughing. "The lengths you will go to flirt with men. Yesterday evening, you're making eyes with Fergus, this morning, it's the fire elf. You'd better be careful. They have a name for girls like you here in Scotland."

Cori gave MacBridan a withering stare. Changing the subject, she said, "I saw Truecourt in the lobby. He said he'd just talked with you."

"The lobby?"

"What?"

"You said you saw Truecourt in the lobby."

"Okay, foyer, my mistake, but this place is big enough to be a hotel."

"Did you mention to him what happened last night?" asked MacBridan.

"No, we just said hello, and he told me that he'd be giving us a call when the people from Lloyd's of London arrive. Why?"

"Good. For the time being, let's keep that little incident between us. I'll be interested to see if someone brings it up to us."

"All right, but someone is certainly going to mention the door to you room. It's wrecked."

"I'm going to say that I opened my window for some fresh air, stepped into the bathroom, and that the wind must have caught it slamming it shut. Even though I feel terrible about it, it was simply an unfortunate accident."

"That's pretty thin. We wouldn't believe a story like that."

"Of course not," said MacBridan, "but I'm going to play it that way. I'm much more interested in seeing who challenges my story. My money's on Junior, along with a much brighter accomplice of course."

Draining her cup, Cori got up to get more coffee. "So what are our plans for the day?"

Before he could answer, Lord MacKinnon came in, followed by Detective Sergeant Wetmoore and an older man dressed in a gray and blue pin-striped, double-breasted suit. His high forehead and gold wire-rimmed glasses gave him a studious look, much like a history professor MacBridan had once studied under years ago.

"Good morning," said Lord MacKinnon. "I trust you slept well. DS Wetmoore has an update for us regarding Marston. I've also let him know that you'll be staying on and helping out with the estate's security."

"May I introduce Dr. Rexford Weatherby, Scotland Yard. Dr. Weatherby heads their forensic science department in Glasgow. He'll be assisting us with the investigation. This is Ms. Hopkins and Mr. MacBridan."

"Good to meet both of you. I'm quite familiar with the Hawthorne Group and their excellent reputation."

"Please help yourself to some breakfast, and let's be seated," said Lord MacKinnon. "We're all anxious to hear what you've found."

Both men got some tea and joined them at the table. "That is why I have Dr. Weatherby with me. Dr. Shepard worked well into the night last night, but I'm afraid his findings were inconclusive. At this point, we really have no idea how Marston died. He appears to have been the victim of a very severe allergic reaction, which accounts for the blistering on the skin. It's interesting to note that the blistering covered most of his body. This allergic reaction culminated in a massive heart attack, which, at present, is the cause of death. The problem is that we haven't been able to determine what it was that he was reacting to or how it entered his system."

"That's where I come in," said Dr. Weatherby. "DS Wetmoore contacted the Yard last night due to Marston's SAS background. He also indicated that his death could potentially be tied to the attempted thefts you've recently experienced. I flew out at the crack of dawn this morning to personally review Dr. Shepard's findings."

"Do you agree with those findings?" asked Lord MacKinnon.

"At this point, yes. Dr. Shepard did a competent and thoroughly professional job. I'll be taking the body back to Glasgow with me for further examination. Our labs there are very well equipped."

"Do you have any idea what we might be dealing with?" asked Cori.

"Like Dr. Shepard, I don't like to speculate. That sort of thing tends to come back on you. However, one of my areas of specialization is poisons, more of a hobby actually," he said, smiling at Cori while winking at her. "I've spent a great many years studying them, both here at home and in Hong Kong. So it strikes me as being a bit odd that a man would suddenly end up and die from such a severe allergic reaction, and yet there isn't any mention in Marston's medical records of any kind of life-threatening allergies. Truth is, the man was healthy as a horse."

"Dr. Weatherby wanted to give Marston's room a once-over while we're here," said Wetmoore.

"We're not sure what we're looking for, but I can't take the chance of overlooking anything," said Dr. Weatherby.

"Of course, of course," said Lord MacKinnon. "We are happy to cooperate."

Fergus came into the room and was replacing the coffee urn with a full one. Wetmoore looked at him and said, "Fergus, the maid who was so frightened last night, is she up yet? I'd like for Dr. Weatherby to talk with her as well."

"I'm sorry, sir," said Fergus. "I'll check, but I believe she may still be asleep. She was so distraught after her incident that we had to give her a rather strong sedative."

"You have my number," said Wetmoore. "As soon as she wakes up, I'd appreciate it if you would give me a call."

"Of course, sir," said Fergus. "Lord MacKinnon, Robena asked me to remind you, especially while DS Wetmoore is here, that Major is still missing."

"Oh yes, I'm afraid that in light of everything else, I'd completely forgotten about him," said Lord MacKinnon.

"Someone is missing?" asked Wetmoore, his tone somewhat incredulous.

"Please, I haven't completely gone off my kettle. Major is our dog, a black mastiff, been with us for nine years. Two days ago, he didn't show up for dinner, which I assure you is completely out of character for him."

"I see. I'll make a note of that, Lord MacKinnon, and check with the station. Hopefully, he'll turn up soon," said Wetmoore.

"Has he ever gone off like this before?" asked MacBridan.

"Not that I can recall. He rarely wanders beyond the grounds and is more than punctual when it comes to meals. Watching him eat, you'd think we never fed the poor creature. Bit of a chowhound," said Lord MacKinnon.

"Now that I think of it, there have been two other dogs reported missing just this week," said Wetmoore. "And if memory serves, they too were black. There's an odd coincidence."

"Fergus," said Lord MacKinnon, "would you please show DS Wetmoore and Dr. Weatherby to Marston's room? They'd like to go over it once again."

After they left, Cori, MacBridan, and Lord MacKinnon sat down to breakfast. They let him know that they planned to call Dolinski later that morning. As Truecourt was supervising the movers, they were going to walk around the estate to become more familiar with the grounds.

"Well, I'd be sure to take a raincoat with you," said Lord MacKinnon. "It looks like today's going to be another wet one."

MacBridan and Cori left the dining room and went back upstairs to get their jackets. MacBridan was surprised to find two men already at work repairing the door to his room. Cori brought along a small umbrella, just in case. As they were coming down the main stairs into the foyer, they found Fergus waiting for them at the door.

"Mr. MacBridan," said Fergus, keeping his voice low, "the police are still examining Marston's room, but I wanted you to know that the moment Laria wakes up, I'll be sure to give you a call."

"I appreciate that," said MacBridan, looking at his watch. "When do you expect her to be available?"

"Normally she'd already be up and at her duties," explained Fergus, "but the pill we gave her last night was pretty strong for someone her size. I'm afraid that it may not be until around noon."

MacBridan smiled and said, "Getting that much sleep sounds pretty good. I'm sure Lord MacKinnon has given you my cell number, but here's my card just in case."

"Yes, sir, I have it," said Fergus. Looking at Cori, his expression softened, the trace of a smile danced at the corners of his mouth. "Any service I can provide, I'm only too happy to do so."

MacBridan and Cori stepped outside. MacBridan was grinning from ear to ear, doing his level best not to make eye contact with Cori. "Don't even go there," she warned him. "I'm not in the mood."

They followed a gravel path that led them around the west side of the house. Despite the dark gray sky, the manor house was breathtaking, its dark redbrick and ornate marble masonry bold and strong not betraying its true age.

"Any idea where this will take us?" asked Cori.

"Last night during dinner, Lord MacKinnon told me that this would guide us around the grounds to the various gardens. He also said that directly behind the house, we'd find another path that will veer off from this one taking us through the woods to the family chapel."

"Oh, I've been looking forward to seeing that," said Cori. "I read that the chapel is actually older than some parts of the main house." She grabbed MacBridan's arm and said, "Look at that gazebo. I don't believe it. Those roses are amazing."

Following the path, they left the house behind them and quickly approached the gazebo, Cori leading the way. Suddenly she stopped, almost midstride.

"Something wrong?" asked MacBridan.

"My camera's in my room. Why don't you wait for me here at the gazebo, and I'll go and get it."

"Cori, they're pretty, but I'm not really sure they're even roses. Besides, I'd really like for us to get a look at the grounds and the chapel before the Lloyd's of London people get here or the sky falls," said MacBridan, looking up at the dark clouds above them.

"Bite your tongue," said Cori. "Not only are those roses, but they happen to be extremely rare roses, usually only seen in China."

Walking up to the nearest bush, she bent over the oddly shaped blossom to fully experience its fragrance. MacBridan didn't know of Cori's avid interest in flowers, but she was obviously excited. Taking a closer look, MacBridan confirmed his earlier comment that these definitely didn't look anything like roses. The bottommost petals were white and slender, widely spaced, and almost symmetrical. Directly centered on top were more petals that were even more slender and longer, with a rose pink shade to them. On top of these were very short, darker reddish petals that curled up along the edges.

"This is the first time I've ever actually seen this species," said Cori. "I've got to talk to their gardener. You are looking at the *Epimedium sutchuenense*. Amazing!"

"What's amazing is that you can even pronounce that. I had no idea you knew this much about roses," said MacBridan. "Where did this come from?"

"Are you kidding? One of my dreams is to one day have my own flower garden filled with rare species. Living in a condo, along with my somewhat irregular work schedule, doesn't make that possible, at least for now. My mother loved flowers. She and I spent so much time together, working in the garden when I was growing up, and except for the bees, I came to love flowers as much as she did."

"An ace investigator and a budding horticulturist. What other passions lurk behind that invitingly demure demeanor?"

Cori gave an exasperated sigh, looked at MacBridan, and said, "Isn't it funny how the lives of people actually mirror that of a rose, beautiful blossoms surrounded by so many thorns. I'll be right back." With that, Cori turned and sprinted off toward the house, leaving MacBridan alone.

Considering the short night he'd had, MacBridan decided to take advantage of the situation and sit down on one of the benches in the gazebo. As he walked around to its entrance, he noticed another bench, nearly hidden behind a blanket of roses that climbed the lattice walls. Even more surprising was that the bench was occupied.

"Good morning to you, Mr. MacBridan," said the older gentleman, his brogue quite thick. "I've been looking forward to our meeting." Although he appeared to be somewhere in his late fifties, early sixties, his face was pale and worn. Despite this, it was a kind face but full of worry. His thinning hair was gray, conservatively cut, and he wore a green plaid jacket with black trousers. His ample stomach tested the buttons on his vest, which was off-white, and he almost looked as if he was in some kind of uniform.

"I'm sorry. We didn't see you sitting here. It's good to meet you, Mr...."

"My friends call me Dillon. I'm sorry that your first night here was so unpleasant, but then things here really aren't right, are they?"

MacBridan stared into the man's face, surprised by his comments. "I'm not sure I know what you're talking about."

Dillon chuckled, and when he smiled, his whole face brightened. "You'll find it's a small estate, Mr. MacBridan, and an even smaller village. You so much as sneeze around here, and you'll have three of us saying God bless you." His smile faded as he said, "It's a sad time, and I'm afraid the trouble's not over, no, not by a long way."

"Do you work here, Dillon?" asked MacBridan.

"Used to, but that was a long time ago. I'm close to the family, especially Ms. Jean. What a wonderful woman she is. She, too, likes these roses. She comes here quite often and just sits and thinks. It's a good place for sitting and thinking."

"Perhaps you can direct me. Assuming my friend ever comes back, we were on our way to the family chapel. I'm hoping that path over there is the right one."

"Yes, that will take you to the chapel. You haven't been here long, but I believe you to be a good man. Take care, Mr. MacBridan. Things are not as they seem, and you'll need to keep a wary eye. I'm especially concerned about Ms. Jean."

"And why is that?"

"You're right, you know, the man's death last night was no accident. Evil's a foot, Mr. MacBridan, an ancient evil, and I need your help. I can't watch over Ms. Jean like I'd like to all by myself," said Dillon.

"Dillon, the police are here now. They believe Marston died of a heart attack, nothing more. However, if there's something you'd like to tell me—" MacBridan heard someone calling to him, turned, and saw that it was Cori. She was motioning for him to join her. "Would you excuse me for just a moment? I'll be right back. I'd like for you to meet my associate."

"Ms. Jean, Mr. MacBridan, will you help me watch over her?" The man's tone had instantly changed, becoming far more intense than MacBridan would have thought possible from such a gentle being.

"Yes, of course, I'll be glad to help."

"Good. Thank you," said Dillon. He seemed genuinely relieved. "I'm afraid I'm keeping you."

"Not at all," said MacBridan. "Please wait here. I'll be right back."

MacBridan turned and made his way back toward Cori. She'd disappeared around the corner of the house, but he soon found her crouched over a small bush next the house. "What do you think of this?"

"It's a bush. What about it?"

"It's known as a Starlight rose. The blossoms only open in the evening and close before morning. I wonder where their greenhouse is. They have to have a greenhouse."

"We'll find it," said MacBridan, "but first, there's someone I want you to meet. He was sitting at the gazebo the whole time, and I didn't even notice him until you left."

"I didn't see anyone. Where was he sitting?"

"On a bench beside the entrance to the gazebo. It's almost completely hidden by the flowers," explained MacBridan. "Get this. He not only knew of the incident in my room last night but warned me that little goes on that isn't seen by everyone."

"Do you think he had something to do with it?"

"No, not at all, but it's a good thing to keep in mind. Not surprising, but clearly few secrets remain secrets here at the manor."

As they approached the gazebo, MacBridan couldn't see him. As they got closer, MacBridan realized that he'd left. "That's odd. I asked him to wait so that he could meet you. He asked me to help him with Ms. Jean, rather pointedly I might add, and said that he's very worried about her. I wonder why he didn't wait for us."

"Perhaps he's shy," said Cori.

"Well, like he said, it's a small estate. I'm sure we'll bump into him again. He did tell me that the path over there will take us to the chapel. Shall we?"

Twelve clicks of the camera later, and they were on their way. As they entered the woods, the landscape took MacBridan back to his childhood, reminding him of the forest he'd spent so much time exploring growing up in Kentucky. The path meandered through the trees, but like everything else they'd seen at the estate, it was well maintained. The clouds, however, not only kept the temperature on the cool side but blocked out a great deal of light, making it hard to see things not close to the trail. They hadn't gone too far when Cori stopped to take another picture zooming in on an oddly shaped flower she'd spotted way off in the trees. It was nearly hidden by the dim light and the thick foliage. Checking the view screen on her camera to make sure she'd gotten the shot she wanted, she quickened her pace to catch up with MacBridan.

As she walked on, something about the last picture started to bother her. There was something familiar about the blossom that wasn't right. Cori stopped to look at it again. She studied it briefly, then turned around, heading back down the trail to the spot where she'd taken the picture. It took her a moment or two to find the exact location. Looking through the lens, she once again zoomed in on the bulbous blossom, enlarging it as much as her camera would allow. Despite the surprise she'd experienced by some of the exotic roses back at the manor, this particular flower was definitely out of place.

"Cori," called MacBridan, "everything all right?"

"Mac, come here. I think you should see this."

It didn't take MacBridan long to make his way back to her. "Please tell me this isn't about another rare but exciting rose that I just have to see."

"Not exactly, but you're close. Look at this," she said, showing him the picture. "Ever seen that before?"

MacBridan studied the picture and said, "Yes, I have, if it's what I think it is. Where did you shoot this?"

Taking his arm, Cori pointed through the trees. "At first, I just caught a glimpse. It's pretty far off the path. With all the trees and the wind blowing the branches around, it makes it hard to spot. Look! There it is."

"That's some camera you've got there," said MacBridan, trying to see the flower more clearly. "From here, I never would have given it a second look. Let's walk over there and take a closer look."

"I'm no expert on Scottish horticulture, but I'm pretty sure it's not indigenous," said Cori as she plodded along, following MacBridan through the dense undergrowth. Despite the tangled vegetation, they soon made their way to a small clearing. Cori stood beside MacBridan, her eyes taking in the various plants in front of her.

"Well, there's your flower, and it's got friends. I'd say someone at the manor has a growing business that is in full bloom. And you're right, the opium poppy is not native to Scotland." There were at least three dozen poppies, their purple and pink blossoms topping the tall plants.

Cori stepped into the clearing for a better look, closely examining the other plants growing there. "This is amazing," she said. "Look at this. There's thorn apple, monkshood, belladonna, hemlock. It's like we've stumbled into nature's medicine cabinet."

"And unless I'm mistaken, that's mandrake growing over there behind you," said MacBridan.

"What an odd little garden. If I were the superstitious kind, I'd say we'd stumbled into a witch's garden."

"Let's not go there. They're already jumping at shadows back at the manor without us adding fuel to the fire," said MacBridan.

"Agreed, but I'd sure feel better, knowing who this belongs to. Every one of these plants can be used to kill, cure, or distort reality. There's more than one hallucinogen."

"I know," said MacBridan. "Most of these plants I'm familiar with, and you're right. They all can be rather potent in their own way. Dr. Weatherby would have an absolute field day," said MacBridan. As he studied the small garden, he looked at Cori and asked, "I'm curious. Why would you call it a witch's garden?"

"Timing, I suppose. A few months ago, I read a very interesting article on the healing power of plants. In that article, it talked about the fear people had years ago for those who knew the medicinal value of plants and how to use them, be it for good or evil. For centuries, particularly in Europe, women who knew the powers of these plants were often accused of being witches. Many died for that knowledge. The plants we have here, all gathered together into one neat little patch, would easily qualify as a witch's garden."

MacBridan looked around, but there was no sign of any clear path into the garden. He then walked the perimeter but still couldn't find any signs of anyone having recently been there. Then again, he knew that if someone was being careful, their leaving any kind of trail would be hard to spot.

"Take several pictures of this," said MacBridan. "This is something else we'll keep between us. If there was just one of these plants, like the poppies, I'd think someone was merely feeding their own habit. But to have all of these grouped together in one spot says the motive is broader than mere personal gratification. Good thing I sent you back for that camera."

"Isn't it?" said Cori, taking pictures of garden. "It's one of the things I admire the most about you. You're always one step ahead."

Chapter 12

The location of the old cottage had been forgotten by most that lived in the area, but it was nearly perfect for their needs. Set atop a small hill, it was completely isolated, resting just inside the tree line on the edge of a broad, overgrown pasture. The only access was via a long narrow dirt lane, which dead-ended at the cottage. Like the small structure, the road had not been maintained. Winding its way through the low hills, sections had nearly disappeared as nature encroached upon it from both sides. Eventually, it ran alongside the pasture, giving them a clear view of all who approached.

Built in the early 1900s, it was made of wood and field stone. Amazingly, it remained structurally sound, surviving years of harsh weather and neglect. Its peat roof was still in place, and so far, they'd found only two small leaks in the far corner of the back room. The cottage only had two rooms, their dirt floors hard packed, but they were of good size, each with its own fireplace.

Kaseem stood in the doorway, gazing at the thick clouds rolling across the sky. It had rained earlier, only a brief shower, but it had been enough to keep everything wet, sustaining the damp chill that to Kaseem seemed to constantly permeate the air. It was taking him longer than he thought it would to adjust to being someplace where it rained so much.

Mukhtar placed more wood in the grate, which quickly caught flame. Their guest had arrived a few minutes ago and was seated at the small table in the center of the room. As instructed, they had come alone. Although they'd talked by phone many times, this was their first time to meet.

"So good of you to find the time to visit with us today," said Kaseem, his voice heavily laced with sarcasm.

"It isn't a matter of time," snapped the visitor, "and you know that. We simply cannot risk our being seen together."

"Ah, I see. So then I guess that means you won't be inviting us to dine with you at the estate," said Kaseem, his mocking tone grating on the visitor's nerves.

"There's already more going on there than I'm comfortable with. Things should never have been allowed to get this far out of hand."

Kaseem watched them closely. He would never have chosen such a partner, someone so weak of character, so consumed by greed, but necessity had dictated otherwise. Ignoring their complaint, he said, "It is my understanding that the painting we are interested in has arrived."

"That's correct," confirmed the visitor, their fingers nervously tapping on the table. There was something about Kaseem that intimidated most of the people he came into contact with. He emanated an intensity that kept people on edge, his dark eyes missing nothing. And if he wasn't enough to bring tension into the room, there was Mukhtar.

Kaseem had heard of many incidents involving Mukhtar. He'd been a part of their order for many years, but he had never worked directly with him. His reputation was that of a cruel, pitiless individual, a trait that Sathanas had taken full advantage of in their labyrinth of caves. A huge, muscular man, his face bore many scars all clearly visible despite his full beard, which, surprisingly, he kept neatly trimmed. He rarely spoke, never smiled, and was fiercely loyal to their god.

Mukhtar had arrived in Abbotsbury a few days before Kaseem, preparing for his arrival. It was Mukhtar who had found the old house for them. Having tended to the fire, he leaned against the wall beside the door, making an obvious point of blocking the only way out.

"All of the household goods from America arrived yesterday evening," continued the visitor.

"Good. Then getting the painting should be fairly easy. How do you plan to achieve this?" asked Kaseem.

"Thanks to the ineptitude of your so-called professional, it will unfortunately be anything but easy."

Kaseem's eyes slightly narrowed. "Please explain."

"When they bungled their opportunity to take the painting in Virginia, it put everyone on alert. It was then that Marston, the estate's head of security, started to tighten things up, the thought being, they tried once, they'll try again. Which they did, on the docks in Glasgow, and they bloody well screwed that up also."

"May I remind you," said Kaseem, "that it was you who insisted on hiring a professional to do the job? If I remember correctly, you were quite pleased with the arrangement when we wired you the money in Paris to pay them. Our money, my friend, not yours."

"Don't you dare try blaming me for their incompetence. I hired them based on your recommendation. You told me she is one of the best in the business."

"And she is," said Kaseem, trying to keep his temper in check. People rarely talked to him in such a manner, especially someone so unworthy, so contemptible. Maintaining his composure, he said, "You still haven't told me what your concerns are."

"The second attempt to steal the painting not only confirmed everyone's fears that the thieves would keep trying but got Marston to thinking that the thieves might be getting inside help, possibly even from the family. The thieves obviously had access to too many details."

Kaseem shrugged. "The information you provided to Talon was quite detailed. I hope you weren't foolish enough to incriminate yourself."

"I'm not that stupid," said the visitor, "but then neither was Marston. He started to run checks on everyone, so I had to act."

"That was your doing?" asked Kaseem. "I heard of his death."

"I really didn't have much of a choice, did I? By getting rid of Marston, I thought I'd be rid of the one person who might be able to tie me in to this or might have a remote chance of standing in our way. I even staged it so that one of the maids would think she'd seen the ghost of the dark lord. It worked perfectly. It's rattled everyone at the estate. The servants are jumping at their own shadows."

"Then I don't understand what you're worried about. Getting the painting should be ridiculously simple."

"I'm worried about James MacBridan."

"MacBridan?" asked Kaseem.

"Yes, he's with a solicitor's firm called the Hawthorne Group. Lord MacKinnon has hired him and his associate to stay on at the estate and manage the security until a replacement for Marston can be found."

Kaseem laughed, but it was a laugh without mirth and had a sharp edge to it. "He is only one man. Mukhtar will take care of your MacBridan, won't you, Mukhtar?"

"It is my pleasure to serve," said Mukhtar, his voice low but full like a deep growl.

"All things considered, I would suggest that you do not underestimate him. Too many things have already gone wrong. A cautious, subtle approach would be much more appropriate," said the visitor, as if talking to a child. "It was MacBridan who stopped your professional both times. He knows what he's doing, and we can't afford to take anything for granted."

"As you seem to pride yourself as the expert here, what do you recommend?" asked Kaseem, disgusted by his visitor's whining, condescending tone. He looked forward to the day he no longer needed them, envisioning his dagger protruding from their throat, one less infidel.

"Think of me as you like, but the only part of this operation that has gone smoothly was my getting rid of Marston. I'll get the details of where the painting is being stored and the nature of the security protecting it. If you do decide to take MacBridan out, and it's probably something that will need doing, I would suggest using locals."

Kaseem grudgingly accepted the advice, although it galled him to admit that there was wisdom in their words. Taking a deep breath, he realized that he was letting his emotions get the better of him. Even Sathanas had commented on how poorly things had gone so far. He knew that a great deal of his anger was at himself for having allowed things to unravel. Going forward, he would take a more hands on approach, personally directing how things were done. "MacBridan has only one associate with him?"

"There are presently two, but the man will be heading back to London soon. The other is a woman, Cori Hopkins. Apparently, they've worked together before."

"Excellent. That doesn't seem to be too formidable a problem," said Kaseem. He paused as his thoughts went back to an earlier comment made by his visitor. "You said the servants are jumping at their own shadows. All this is because one stupid woman thinks she saw a ghost?"

"No, it is far more than that. MacKinnon hall is known in the area for being haunted, as well as for having the shadow creatures. It is they who are feared more than anything. They're supposedly some kind of curse that has followed the MacKinnon's for centuries ever since the dark lord was executed. They believe that to die at their hands is to lose your soul to the devil."

"And you don't believe things like the shadow creatures could possibly exist?"

The visitor looked down at the table for a moment and then said, "If you'd asked me, before the family arrived back from America, I'd have said no. But since they returned, things seem to have altered. It's hard to put into words, but it's like the atmosphere of the house has changed. Many of the servants have reported seeing things. There was one night on the staircase even I spotted something moving in the shadows, but when I looked, there was nothing there. I know I'm just getting caught up in a bunch of superstitious nonsense, but it does eat at your nerves."

Kaseem walked around the table, closer to their visitor, and then stopped to stand directly behind them. "So you completely dismiss the existence of the paranormal."

"Yes, I guess I do. It's just, well, I guess it's easy to let your imagination run wild. Besides, what difference does it make? So long as people are nervous, it is something we can use."

"Now I will give you some advice," said Kaseem. "It is best that you do not turn your nose up at things of which you have no understanding, especially the shadow creatures. My order is very old, and through the many blessings of the goddess Lilith, we serve the true god. As illustrated by your own Bible, his denizens walk the earth in many forms, some possessing great power. Believe me when I tell you, there is much that dwells in the twilight that people want to ignore, but that doesn't mean that those things don't exist."

"Our high priest is acutely aware of the being that inhabits the MacKinnon estate and the threat it represents," continued Kaseem. "He specifically warned me about it, to respect it. He also discussed potential ways in which to manipulate it, to use it to our advantage. It is this force, this entity that we have to be cautious of. If we do not handle it correctly, the danger to us all will be far more terrible than any silly fears you harbor about this MacBridan. Handling this is something that I will take care of, as well as MacBridan. I'm quite experienced."

"Are you serious? You're beginning to sound like one of those simple-minded servants. You're talking utter nonsense."

Mukhtar rose, pushed away from the wall, and started toward the visitor, but a look from Kaseem stopped him. Kaseem then clamped his right hand down hard on the visitor's shoulder, roughly gripping it. "You will never speak to me in that manner again," he said, his voice just above a whisper. It was all he could do to keep from murdering them on the spot.

"I'm sorry," stammered the visitor. The visitor struggled briefly but could not break the grip Kaseem had on their shoulder. "I didn't mean any offense."

"Before this is over, if you do exactly as I say, you might live to regret calling things you know nothing about nonsense. From this point forward, our only chance of success is for you to follow my instructions to the letter. There are dark forces involved here. As our side is gathering power, the other side will be choosing their champion. In this chess game, you are a small black pawn."

"What does that make you? The king?"

"A bishop perhaps, maybe only a knight. You are holding onto Western rationalism. Good for you. You are fated to see more. Blood will be spilt. The guardian was summoned with blood, bound with blood, and will release what is ours only with blood."

"Is there anything else you need from me? It's time I leave," the visitor stammered. "I must be getting back."

Kaseem released their shoulder but didn't move away, standing over them as he let his own temper cool. He regretted that he actually needed this fool, but there was no other way. He simply did not have the time to cultivate a new contact at the estate. He walked into the other room but soon returned with a small chest that he set on the table in front of them. He then opened the chest so that the visitor could see its deadly contents.

The visitor's shoulders slumped as they looked into the chest. "Is this still necessary? Surely there's some other way."

"After all you've already done, it is amusing to suddenly find you getting squeamish. Yes, in order for things to work our way, you must follow the plan that we have discussed. There is no other way. Besides, it is a small sacrifice. It's not like I'm asking you to give up your own life."

"I'm quite capable of killing. You've seen that, but not this person. They are innocent."

Once again, Kaseem stood behind them. Leaning over, he brought his lips near their ear. His voice was low but full of venom. "You will do as I say, without question, without hesitation. Do you hear me? There are reasons for this people like you cannot understand."

Closing the chest, the visitor nodded, took the chest, and stood up, preparing to leave.

"I'll expect to hear from you soon regarding the security arrangements surrounding the painting. We are close to our goal, and I will not let anything or anyone stand in our way. Is there anything else?"

"No," said the visitor, clearly shaken. "I will do as you say."

Kaseem's voice stopped them at the door. Although he despised them, he reminded himself again that he still needed their help and knew that he could not risk their doing something stupid out of fear or remorse. "You must trust me in this," he said. "The reward for both of us is great. We've told you this from the beginning, and I want to remind you again. While the price of failure is severe, all of the material wealth that we find, whatever gold or precious stones that are waiting for us, are yours. Those things are of no interest to us."

The visitor nodded, trying to mask their fear of these two men. "I understand. You'll hear from me soon."

The two men watched as their visitor got in their car and drove off. "You should not have stopped me," said Mukhtar. "They have no respect."

"Patience, my friend. Once they are no longer of any use to us, we will deal with them in a manner most fitting. Come, we have much to do."

Chapter 13

Leaving the garden of pharmaceutical delights behind, MacBridan and Cori made their way back to the path and continued on to the old chapel. The increasingly overcast skies made it darker than when they'd started out. But despite the chance of potentially being rained on, MacBridan was enjoying the walk. He loved any time he could spend in the woods. It was a quiet time of escape for him, each visit enhanced by the rich fragrance unique to the forest. Operating on too little sleep, he felt the familiar scents acting like a refreshing tonic.

The trail soon came to an end at a broad lane; its surface consisting of hard-packed clay and gravel. Being out of the trees, they could now clearly see the sky, and it did not look good. MacBridan hoped that it would hold off long enough for them to reach the chapel. They spotted the massive wall surrounding the churchyard to their left, a short ways down the lane.

As they approached the wall, Cori said, "Impressive. That has got to be close to twenty feet tall."

"Closer to twelve actually," said MacBridan. "I'll never understand why women are so challenged by spatial relations, but I thank heaven for it every day."

"What did you say?"

"Doesn't matter. You're right. It is very impressive. The Scots were wonderfully talented builders. It's important to note that when this wall was built, it was primarily for protection."

They soon came to the gates, two tall wrought ironworks of medieval art, each topped by what looked like multiple spearheads. Off in the distance, they could hear the faint rumble of thunder. MacBridan could smell the rain in the air and knew it wouldn't be long before the storm broke. "Here's hoping these aren't locked," he said.

Fortunately, the latch moved easily for him, and he pushed open one of the heavy gates far enough for them to enter. Before them lay the old churchyard, which was surprisingly large and utterly quiet. Many of the headstones were crowned with Celtic crosses or carved figurines, most leaning at odd angles, having settled into the earth. The chapel sat directly in the center and, like the wall that encircled them, looked to be very old and solidly built. There was a quaintly romantic air about it with its broad doors and arched windows. MacBridan guessed that the coat of arms carved into the stonework above the doors was that of the MacKinnon clan.

Cori immediately started taking pictures. "This is so beautiful," she said. "Mac, stand over here by the gate. No one's going to believe how large these are."

"As flattered as I am that you want to use me as a frame of reference, we are about to get drenched," said MacBridan. "In addition to that, there's lightning nearby, and I'm not going to stand next to anything with iron rods sticking up in the air. Let's see if we can get inside. Then, we'll do pictures."

"This place is so pretty that it almost doesn't look real. I mean, it's just so perfectly charming that it looks like something Disney did."

"It would be interesting to spend more time looking at these headstones," said MacBridan. Being a bit of a history buff, he'd spent a fair amount of time in graveyards doing research. "The generations of history just inside these walls could keep one occupied for months."

The path gently curved through the graves, leading up to the front doors of the chapel. Made of solid oak, the doors were banded with iron strips across them for added strength. MacBridan tried opening one of the doors just as more thunder echoed behind them. The storm was getting ready to break, the wind picking up.

MacBridan could not get the door to budge. "That's not good," he said. He then tried the other door. It briefly held but then, to his relief, opened easily.

They had no sooner stepped inside when large drops of rain began to pelt on the churchyard. "We couldn't have timed that much better," said Cori.

Although the chapel had tall stained glass windows running down both sides of the sanctuary, it was fairly dark inside. The center aisle was wide with pews on both sides leading to a mildly elevated altar. On the far wall directly behind and above the altar was another stained glass window, in a half moon shape, illustrating the ascension of Christ into heaven.

"Many of the windows," said Cori, "assuming that they're the originals, were brought over from France. This chapel happens to be one of the oldest Christian churches in northern Scotland and was built on the site of an old Celtic temple."

"You did your homework," said MacBridan.

"I did get a bit carried away. Once I read about the house, I became more and more intrigued by the whole area."

"We talked about this before, but what I find so amazing is that no matter what date in history you choose, you'll find that Scotland has a truly remarkable heritage," said MacBridan. "So many of the periods I've studied were as heroic and exciting as they were sad and violent." The rain outside, along with the wind, picked up in its intensity, pounding down on the roof and knocking against the windows.

"From the sound of that, we may as well take advantage of the time and look around," said Cori. "I'd say we're going to be here for a while."

MacBridan walked over to the right side of the church and began to examine the intricate carvings that he'd spotted between each of the windows. A mild shiver ran through him as he remembered his days as an altar boy. As he got closer to the wall, he could see that the stations of the cross had been sculpted into the stone, the detail of each one startling. Cori stayed more in the center, doing her best to get pictures of each of the windows, but the poor lighting was making that nearly impossible.

Maneuvering between two pews to get a better angle for her next shot, Cori caught something out of the corner of her eye moving up near the front of the chapel. She turned just in time to see one of the three small doors behind the altar silently swing open. A mild chill ran down her spine, and she turned to MacBridan to let him know what she'd just seen, but he too was already looking directly at the door.

Seeing the expression on Cori's face, MacBridan smiled and said, "Don't get excited. It's a very old building. We are in the middle of a storm, and the wind is pounding this place pretty good. These kinds of things happen all the time, even in new buildings."

MacBridan led the way to the altar and approached the open door. As he looked inside, he could feel a light, cool breeze coming from within and was surprised to find an old flight of stone steps leading down into the darkness.

Cori, a little behind him, said, "I certainly didn't expect to find a staircase in there. Where do you think that leads to?"

"Unless I miss my guess, I'd say we have found the MacKinnon family crypt. Let's take a look," said MacBridan and started to go down the stairs.

Cori grabbed his arm. "Are you crazy? I'm still not comfortable with the way that door opened all by itself. And if this is a crypt, I can't think of one good reason why I want to go down there."

MacBridan tried to keep the smile off his face. "Cori, this place is centuries old. What we saw was simply the wind catching a door that obviously had not been securely fastened causing it to open."

"But how do you know that? I didn't feel any breezes. Let's not forget the events of last night."

"You have nothing to worry about. Come on, heaven knows we have the time, and this should be pretty interesting."

MacBridan looked for a light switch but couldn't find one. Although he hadn't brought a flashlight with him, he started down the stairs and soon found what he was looking for. Small recessed alcoves built into the walls at regular intervals, each held a candle with small rectangular-shaped mirrored panels behind them. The alcoves were on both sides of the stairs, directly across each other. Using his lighter, he found that once the candles were lit, they put out an amazing amount of light. As they descended, an infinite army of reflections on their right and their left descended with them.

The stairs descended further than MacBridan anticipated, taking them deep underground. The stone walls were stained in places from moisture, and they discovered a couple of wet spots where water was seeping in. By the time they reached the bottom, MacBridan had lit five sets of candles clearly illuminating the staircase. As best he could tell in the dim light, the crypt was laid out in an inverted T shape, mirroring the manor. There were two rather short side passageways heading off to their left and right and a much longer passage lying directly in front of them. MacBridan quickly found more candles in other alcoves, and like the staircase, they had been placed along the full length of the passageway. Cori insisted that they light each one, and she took over this duty from MacBridan, taking his lighter from him. He had been right in his assessment; this was the family crypt, with graves dating back hundreds of years.

"You said that the chapel had been built on top of an old Celtic temple," mused MacBridan. "I wonder if they built it here because of this cave."

"Cave?"

"Yes, look up. The roof is natural rock. I'll bet you this cave played an important role in many of the Celtic rituals, a path to the underworld. Then, when the MacKinnons arrived, they found it to be a convenient and protected place to bury their patriarchs. You'll notice at the end of this passage the roof starts to slope downward."

"I would have missed that completely," said Cori.

"Well, you are a little distracted," said MacBridan, smiling at Cori. "I mean, if you light any more candles down here, I'm going to need to put on my sunglasses."

Cori chose to ignore his remark. "I can't get over how long this passage is. I wonder how far underground we actually are. We're clearly under the graves in the churchyard. The crypt is probably bigger than the chapel."

"I'll have to ask Lord MacKinnon, but it would be interesting to know if this is where the passage naturally ends or just where they decided to seal it off. Look, you'll notice that the stonework on the rear wall looks different from the other walls."

"I imagine that the passageway got too narrow to be practical for any—"

The explosion cut Cori off midsentence, and they both jumped. It was so loud that at first MacBridan thought they'd been shot at, the tight corridors of the crypt magnifying the sound. He ran down the passageway but slowed down just before reaching the base of the stairs. He didn't want to present himself as an easy target. Carefully moving along the wall, he looked up the stairs. Smiling, he sighed his relief, leaning against the nameplate on one of the graves. Looking at Cori, he said, "I appreciate that we had a short and eventful night, but we have got to get a grip. The loud bang was nothing more than your favorite door. Apparently, the same wind that opened the door got hold of it and slammed it shut."

The expression on Cori's face told MacBridan that she was not accepting his explanation. Pushing her way past him, she went up the stairs as quickly as she could without actually running. "Mac, it won't open," said Cori, struggling with the door. "Either we're locked in or someone's holding it, but it won't open." She leaned into the door, all the while trying to turn the doorknob.

Mac followed her up the stairs. "Here, let me give it a try." He tried turning the doorknob but couldn't get it to turn much at all. Using both hands, he applied a fair amount of pressure on the doorknob as he tried turning it, careful not to break it. Putting his shoulder to the door, he started to push but still could not get it to move.

"Mac, this isn't right. We should never have come down here," said Cori, her voice betraying the fear that ran through her. "We've got to get out of this place."

"Cori, it's okay. The door, for whatever reason, slammed shut a little harder than it should have and seems to be stuck. That's all. We'll get it open."

Mac backed down a couple of steps to get a better look at the door, trying to determine where it might have wedged against the frame. Stepping back up, he gripped the handle once again and started to methodically hit the door with his shoulder. Already sore from the previous night, he knew that bone and muscle was not a fair match against solid oak.

"Mac, stop!" said Cori, her voice strained, choking out the words. "Listen."

Standing perfectly still, they both listened to the silence that closed in around them. The only thing he could hear was their breathing. After a few moments, he started back to work on the door, but Cori grabbed his arm, stopping him.

"Don't," she hissed. "I know I heard something."

Again, he waited, listening as hard as he could but still couldn't hear anything unusual. Just as he was about to focus his attention back on the door, an odd sound floated up the stairs. It was faint, lasting but a few scant seconds, but something was down there. Neither of them moved. Hardly breathing, they once again waited as long, anxious moments passed in silence. Then, without warning, it started up again, this time much louder and more prolonged. It was a slow, grating sound that seemed to be coming from the far reaches of the crypt. Cori looked at Mac, her face completely pale. "What is that?"

The grating continued on, and after a few more moments, Mac realized what he was hearing. It was the sound of stone being pushed or drug across stone. Something down there was opening. He was about to share this with Cori when the noise abruptly stopped. Silence returned to the crypt. They both stood absolutely still, their eyes glued to the foot of the stairs waiting.

Suddenly, the air turned deathly cold, and the putrid smell that MacBridan had experienced in his room the night before nearly overwhelmed them. Not wanting to wait for the thing he'd seen in his room last night to reappear, Mac turned and lay into the door with everything he had, throwing his entire weight against it again and again.

"Mac, look, it's getting darker," cried Cori. "Oh my god, they're going out. Whatever's down there is coming toward us, and it's blowing out the candles."

Whatever it was, it wasn't moving quickly, but Cori was right. As it drew closer to them, it was slowly taking away their only source of light.

"Oh my Lord," whimpered Cori. "This can't be happening. Are you seeing this?"

Cori crowded up against Mac as the last candles in the passageway went out. She was close to panic, but there was little MacBridan could do, as he too felt the bitter chill of desperation. The cold grew in its intensity, numbing their senses. The odor had become so strong that breathing nearly caused them to choke. Cori cried out again, her back sliding down against the door, and she put her arms around her knees as she watched the first set of candles on the stairs blink out in the dark.

MacBridan didn't know if it was fear or an amazing surge of adrenaline, but this time when he hit the door, he felt it give a little. Preparing to hit the door again, he glanced back down the stairs just in time to see the next set of candles go out. He could now hear the sound of something scuffling across the stone steps but still couldn't see anything. Something inside told him that if he didn't get the door open soon, they would never get out. Gripping the knob with both hands, Mac lowered his shoulder level with the latch and threw his full weight into the door. With a loud, crackling screech, the door flew open, sending them tumbling into the sanctuary.

MacBridan sprang to his feet and pulled Cori away from the door and into the center aisle, placing himself between her and the splintered doorway. Breathing heavily, Mac waited to confront their tormentor. The rain was still coming down outside, but the wind had calmed down and was not blowing nearly as hard. Cori struggled to get to her feet. Both of them stood there, not knowing what to expect.

After a few moments, Cori said, "What are we waiting for? Rain or not, we've got to get out of here." With that, she began to back down the aisle toward the front of the chapel, never taking eyes off the doorway.

MacBridan had been shaken by the experience, but once again, his temper started to take over. They had done this to him last night in his room, and now they'd succeeded in scaring him again, this time in the chapel. His mind fought against the impulse to think that the things he'd experienced might be supernatural, but with even that thought dancing on the peripheral, he refused to leave. It was not in his nature to turn and run, especially from things he couldn't even see.

With his nerves having settled somewhat, MacBridan quickly went to the altar, grabbed a three-stick candleholder, and started back toward the steps. Cori watched this in stunned disbelief; she couldn't imagine that he'd even consider going back down there. MacBridan stood in the center of the doorway as he lit the candles, daring whatever it was to confront him.

Running back down the aisle, Cori grabbed his arm. "Mac, please, you can't do this. I don't know what just happened, but it's not something we're prepared to take on."

"Cori, you wait here and keep this door open. This shouldn't take long."

"This is ridiculous. You're acting foolish. Do you even have any idea what that was?"

"Cori, someone is trying to run us off, and I'm embarrassed to say it nearly worked. But now, we've got them cornered, and we're going to end this."

With the candles lit, MacBridan started back down the stairs. He found that the two sets of candles near the top of the staircase were still burning. When he reached the bottom of the stairs, he stopped to light more candles. All looked as it should, and he could not see any signs where something might have been moved. Taking a deep breath, he continued down the long passageway, studying the floor, looking for scrape marks. Reaching the end of the passage, he knelt down so that he could more closely examine the floor. He finally stood back up, frustrated. He had not been able to find anything, or anyone, that could explain what he and Cori had just experienced. Once again, his mind started to toy with the idea of supernatural explanations.

Reluctantly, MacBridan turned and walked back down the passageway, blowing out the candles as he went. Again, he found himself completely at a loss as to what they'd experienced and who was behind it. As a detective, his performance over the last twenty-four hours wasn't going to be winning him any awards.

Just as he started back up the stairs to join Cori, his mind took him back to a case he'd been on a little over a year ago in the small Massachusetts town of New Westminster. He remembered the terrible events of that case, and his hand reflexively went to the small crucifix he wore under his shirt. MacBridan was by no means a practicing Catholic; in fact, he rarely attended church of any faith. His wearing the crucifix had started while in New Westminster, oddly for protection. Despite the healing passage of time, he'd not been able to convince himself to stop wearing it. Touching the crucifix with his hand, he grimaced and muttered a brief prayer under his breath, "Not again, God, please, not again."

Chapter 14

Together, they thoroughly searched the chapel, every room, nook, and cranny to make sure they'd not missed anything. The only good news was that by the time they were ready to leave, the storm had passed. Although it was still raining, it was falling at a much gentler pace. The umbrellas they'd brought along would go a long way in keeping them dry. Having securely fastened the front door of the chapel, Cori held MacBridan's umbrella as he closed the tall gate.

"Cori, I can't explain what happened down inside that crypt, at least not yet, but I am not ready to start believing that there's some kind of demonic force out to get us. That's just a little too fantastic for me."

As they walked on through the rain, MacBridan waited for Cori to respond. Since their terrifying ordeal, she'd had trouble making eye contact with him. Still not looking directly at him, she finally broke her silence. "I'm not proud of my performance back there, but in all my life, I've never felt that way before. I was completely helpless, literally so scared I couldn't move."

MacBridan could sympathize with what she was going through; he'd been there before. He knew that her overriding concern was pretty basic. As a field operative, the last thing you can afford is to start questioning your own nerve.

"I appreciate what you're trying to do," continued Cori, "and I know you may not agree with me, but, Mac, we were not alone back there. Last night, after dinner, they told us that several of the people working at the estate have been experiencing strange events. All things considered, I'm not so sure how farfetched of a tale that was."

"Cori, I hear what you're saying, and I'm not dismissing your feelings or trying to argue with you, but that's exactly my point," answered MacBridan, "It's why I think we're being set up. We're being led to believe that there are unnatural forces at work here, but it's all falling into place a little too neatly."

"I'm not following that," said Cori.

"Yesterday evening, although I'm not entirely sure who first brought it up, we were told the incredible tale of the dark lord. Junior even makes a point of letting me know that I'll be staying in the dark lord's former room. And what happened? I had a visitor. Sorry, but that's just a little too much on the mark for me."

"Coincidental or not, it did happen. There's no denying that. We're no closer to understanding what occurred in your room last night than we are to understanding what we both just saw, or rather didn't see, down in that crypt. Mac, I could feel it. There was something at the bottom of those stairs. That horrible odor, the bitter cold. I'm no authority on ghosts or demons, but it matches up with everything I've ever read."

"Everything everyone's ever read, don't you see?" explained MacBridan. "Look, let's say that I want to scare you, make you think that this place is crawling with spooks. There's been enough written on the subject to let me know just what I'll need to do to get you to start believing you're experiencing supernatural forces. Cori, first they took Marston out of the picture, and now they're trying to scare us off. For whatever reason, it all comes back to that ridiculous painting, and we have to find out why."

"I still can't accept that what just happened back there was some kind of stunt or practical joke. No one's that good."

"It's no joke," said MacBridan. Silently, he agreed with her and knew that she was, unfortunately, bringing up the very points that were racing through his mind. "Marston was murdered, and if the scare tactics don't work on us, then I have no doubt that they'll be ready to take things up a notch. It is time we go on the offensive."

"What do you suggest? We haven't exactly been sitting idly by."

"True, but they've had us off balance. Think about it. In addition to our adjusting to the time change, the first task we faced when we docked, not counting our unexpected visitor, was the long drive north to the estate. The time change and the drive combined would be exhausting for anyone. But when we finally arrived, rather than getting to sit down, eat, and get some rest, we were faced with Marston's death, which was closely followed by the exciting activities in my room in the middle of the night. That little incident, along with what just happened, has been designed to further wear us down and send us off with our tails between our legs. We're not investigating. We are playing the part of spooked Americans. Well, I've had enough."

"I still think you're whistling in the dark to keep my courage up," said Cori. She thought about all that he was saying, shook her head, and said, "I hope you're right, but I'm having a hard time believing that what we just went through was staged."

They soon came to the place where the path to the manor house led off through the woods. Despite how wet things were, they left the road and set off into the trees. To keep from brushing up against the wet shrubbery, they walked single file, Cori leading the way. "We need to pick up where Marston left off," said MacBridan. "We need to get as much information as we can on the staff and the family, including Lord MacKinnon."

"Certainly you don't suspect him of being involved in this do you?" asked Cori.

"No, but I also don't want to chance our missing anything. If he's got a vulnerable spot, I want to know what it is. It's the only way we can protect him."

"I'll get to work on it this afternoon," said Cori. "I'll enlist Trevor to help."

"Who?"

"Trevor Truecourt, Hawthorne Group, our man in London."

"Isn't that sad? I'm more wiped out than I realized. I'd forgotten his first name. After lunch, we've got to call Dolinski, and then we'll get some rest. I'm not big on napping, but at this point, taking an hour or two out would be wonderful."

It wasn't too long before they reached the estate grounds leaving the woods behind. "Mac, I want to believe that everything that's happened so far has been due to human intervention. But there's a big piece of me that isn't convinced."

"Well, you'll never get me to admit it," said MacBridan, smiling at her, "but I'm not completely convinced either."

They entered the house through the front doors and went directly up to their rooms to change. Cori told MacBridan that she'd meet up with him downstairs for lunch and disappeared into her room. The workmen had completed the repair to MacBridan's door, and it looked good. His room had been straightened, the bed made, and more wood added to the bin. It didn't take him long to change, and he set off for the dining room.

Just as he reached the top of the staircase, he heard someone calling his name. He turned to find Faith coming toward him down the hall. "Mr. MacBridan, I'm so glad I caught you. Fergus asked that if I saw you to let you know that the trucks have been unloaded and that the inventory has been checked in as complete by Lloyd's of London. He also wanted me to tell you that Mr. Truecourt will be joining us for lunch before he leaves for London."

"Well, it's nice to get some good news for a change. I appreciate you letting me know."

"My uncle has the keys. Everything has been placed in the two rooms down the hall from yours," said Faith.

"That's good. With their being on the second floor, it makes them easier to secure," explained MacBridan.

"It's so terrible to think that these thieves might have had something to do with Marston's death."

"Hopefully, we'll soon know more about how he died," said MacBridan.

She took his arm and said, "I can't begin to tell you how pleased my aunt Jean and I are that you and Ms. Hopkins will be staying on with us. Our rooms are on the second floor also at the far end of the hall, mine's to the right of the grandfather clock and my aunt's is to the left. With all the madness going on around here, I know I'll be sleeping better, knowing that you're nearby."

MacBridan smiled and said, "Giving comfort is just one of the frills, and there's no charge. However, I hope I didn't wake you up last night. Inadvertently, I caused my door to slam just, and I'm afraid it made a pretty loud crashing sound."

Faith thought about it for a moment and said, "No, I don't remembering hearing anything. But then I'm usually a pretty deep sleeper. When you combine that with the thick walls of this house, it takes quite a bit to wake me up."

"You and your aunt seem to be very close," said MacBridan.

"Oh, we are. She's such a lovely lady. Up until lately, we haven't been able to spend too much time together, what with her living in America. It's so wonderful to have the family back here at the estate. Growing up, I used to visit them at the farm. I simply adore horses. In the evening, my aunt Jean would tell me these amazing stories about our family, all our dark secrets. It was so much fun."

"She shared one of those dark secrets last night."

"She certainly did. It's the one that's caused us the most trouble, and you only heard the half of it. Even without stories like that, it's easy to let yourself get spooked in this old house. The problem, as my aunt said last night, is that there are many in the village, and even on the staff, who believe that the dark lord still roams the grounds."

"Your aunt sounds like she might also fall into that category."

Faith's eyes flashed as she said, "My aunt is a wise, gentle woman, and she has experienced many things in her life firsthand. I don't know a great deal about ghostly things, but I will say this. I'm the first to side with her, especially when she reminds us that we are not omnipotent. The world isn't flat. It would do all of us good to listen to her more often."

Faith caught herself and took a deep breath, regaining her composure. "I'm sorry. I guess I'm a little touchy when it comes to people laughing at my aunt."

"Faith, I'm not making fun of your aunt in any way, shape, or form. I sincerely hope that I didn't come across that way."

"You didn't. I want you to know I appreciated your courtesy toward my aunt last night." They'd reached the top of the stairs and started down. Faith looked around to see if they were alone. "Mr. MacBridan, not to spring this on you, but I have some of my own concerns that I've discussed with my aunt and would like to talk to you about. In fact, I discussed these with Marston, which is why I think it's important I tell you, but I don't want to cause unnecessary trouble."

"Discretion is also included in our service," said MacBridan. "How can I help you?"

"I know that this will sound like petty family infighting, but it's really not. My uncle and aunt Jean have been absolutely wonderful to me, and I love them dearly. Without my uncle's help, I wouldn't have been able to finish school. He is so generous."

"Now I'm jealous. I've always wanted a rich uncle," said MacBridan.

"My parents are both gone. Uncle Ronald and my great-aunt stepped in to fill that void." She paused for a moment and once again looked around the foyer. "Do you mind if we step outside for a moment? I swear the walls truly do have ears."

The rain had all but stopped, but dark, brooding clouds stilled glared down at them. A slight breeze had picked up, and MacBridan was glad that he still had his jacket on. He couldn't be certain, but it felt like it had gotten cooler since they'd returned from the chapel.

"The mild display of friction that you saw last night between my uncle and Wallace is just the tip of a large and growing iceberg. Wallace is terribly spoiled, doesn't appreciate all that's been handed to him."

"Family dysfunction is pretty common, especially between children and their parents," said MacBridan.

"True, but it's more than that. I wouldn't be surprised to find that Wallace is behind the people trying to steal from us."

She was standing very close to him. Her soft green eyes were animated, looking deeply into his. *Under other circumstances*, thought MacBridan. "That's a pretty serious accusation. What is it that makes you think that?"

"Wallace, as you can imagine, grew up in the lap of luxury. He's never had to earn anything. Being an only child, he was terribly spoiled, especially being a son and the future Lord MacKinnon. My uncle and his wife tried having more children, two actually, both of which died in childbirth. My aunt never really recovered after the second baby died, and she passed away a couple of months after that. I'll always believe that it was from a broken heart. Anyway, as long as I can remember, Wallace has been nothing but a mean-spirited bully, lording his station over others as if he were heir to the throne itself."

"Faith, I'll agree with you that he doesn't make a great first impression, but that doesn't make him a thief, or potentially worse. As you say, he is the heir to the title and the estate. Why would he steal something that, for all intents and purposes, is already his?"

"The animosity between my uncle and Wallace runs deep and has become worse over the years. About three years ago, Wallace got into trouble over a girl in the village. I never learned the details, but my uncle returned from America, stepped in, and settled the problem. It was a situation that could have potentially put Wallace behind bars. For Uncle Ronald, it was the last straw. Ever since then, Wallace has been put on a mere pittance of an allowance. My uncle was very direct with him. Either he straightened up and went to work, even if it was working the family business, or he would go without. During Wallace's last visit to America, they had another big blow up. Aunt Jean said it was so bad that the threat of disinheritance was voiced."

"Wallace didn't live with the rest of the family in Virginia?" asked MacBridan.

"Heavens, no, Wallace hates the farm and anything to do with the business there. He was only too happy to stay here. He rather enjoyed having an ocean between him and his father, allowing him to play lord of the manor. It's very impressive to young women, especially naïve tourists."

"How well did that ride with the staff here at the estate?"

Faith laughed at this. "At times, it was fun to watch. Before the family returned, I didn't visit the estate that often, but when I did, it was almost comical. Mrs. Henderson all but ignored him, and when he did do anything too outrageous, Marston would step in and put him in his place."

"His confrontations with Marston, did any of them ever become physical?"

"Are you kidding, that spineless whelp? Wallace is a bully only over those weaker than him, which makes him nothing but a pathetic coward. I'll say this for him though, he at least had the good sense not to try pushing things with Marston. My uncle made it clear that Marston was in charge of the estate when he was away, and Wallace, frankly, was afraid of him."

"Interesting," said MacBridan. "It also helps to explain the exchange last night between Wallace and Barclay."

"Barclay is a sweet boy, and he works so hard, so does his brother Kerr, but he's not as sharp as Barclay, at least not in a business sense. Kerr is more the romantic lover of the family."

"Is there anything else about Wallace, other than his potential loss of his inheritance, that leads you to believe that he's behind all of this?"

"No, not really. I know he hangs around with some of the biggest losers in the area, drinking and causing trouble, but that's about it. Now that I think about it, I'm actually a little embarrassed that I told you. I know how all this must sound," said Faith.

"How did Marston respond to your concerns when you told him?"

"Not the way I wanted him to," answered Faith. "Marston knew almost as much about the kind of person Wallace is as I do. I'd hoped that he'd laugh it off, dismiss the idea as my being silly. Sadly, he took it quite seriously and thanked me. I don't believe he knew that Wallace was in jeopardy of losing everything."

"When did you and Marston talk?"

"The day before he died."

MacBridan thought things over then said, "Well, there's certainly no need to be embarrassed. I appreciate you sharing this."

Faith smiled and leaned into MacBridan, hugging his arm with her head on his shoulder. She looked up, and once again, their eyes met. She started to say something, stopped, and then shyly stepped away.

He followed Faith as they went back inside and met Cori coming down the stairs. "Please don't tell me I've missed lunch," she said. "I'm starving."

MacBridan was pleased to see that her normal composure had returned. Glancing at his watch, he saw that it was just after 1:00 p.m., which explained why his stomach was beginning to question whether or not his throat had been cut.

"Actually, you're right on time," said Faith. "Mr. MacBridan and I stepped out for just a bit of fresh air."

Faith preceded them down the hall. Cori looked at Faith for a moment and then smiled at MacBridan, raising her eyebrow questioningly. MacBridan shrugged his shoulders, gave a small smile, and put on the most innocent face he could muster.

Lord MacKinnon, Aunt Jean, and Barclay, along with Truecourt, were in the dining room when they arrived. Kerr was once again in town on business, and no one seemed to know where Wallace was. MacBridan wondered if he might still be at the chapel. During lunch, Truecourt reiterated the news that all of the family's possessions had successfully made the trip and had been verified and checked in by the representative from Lloyd's. Lord MacKinnon thanked them for a job well done, saying that he would express his thanks to Dolinski personally.

"We'd planned to put a call into him after lunch," said MacBridan. "Is there a speakerphone that we could use?"

"Certainly," answered Lord MacKinnon. "There's one in my office as well as in the library."

"No need to put you out," said Cori. "The library will work just fine."

"Very well," said Lord MacKinnon. "If there's anything you need, please let Fergus know. Also, I have a duplicate set of keys in my office to the rooms where everything's being stored. I want you to have them."

"That'll help a great deal," said MacBridan. "Cori and I want to look things over after our call."

As soon as lunch ended, MacBridan and Cori walked Truecourt to the door and out to his car. Cori told him that they she needed him to help her with background checks on the family, as well as the estate staff. "That's a tall order," said Truecourt. "I'll call the office once I'm on the road and get them started."

Fergus was waiting for them in foyer and led them to the library. After giving the storage room keys to MacBridan, he quickly showed them how to turn on the speaker feature on the phone. He then reminded them that if there was anything else he could do to just ask.

"I got to tell you," said Cori as she shut the door, "the service here is better than any hotel I've ever been to. It wouldn't take much for me to get used to having servants around."

"Well, Lady Hopkins, would you mind getting our boss on the phone, or shall I call Fergus back to have him dial the number for you?"

"I can manage. Thank you. And don't think I've forgotten about your 'bit of fresh air' with Faith," said Cori as she dialed the phone. "Either it was pretty cold outside or she was blushing."

"To be honest, she actually took me by surprise. We'll talk about that on the call, pretty interesting stuff."

"You'll tell us everything? Like why her cheeks were so red?"

"With my being a gentleman, I'm surprised you'd even ask. However, if I'm forced to go into all the details, you may have to leave the room. Man stuff. You know."

It didn't take long for the call to go through, and Ester King surprisingly answered on the second ring. It was late in the evening in New Your. "Ester, this is Cori and Mac. Is he available?"

"He's been expecting your call. I'll put you right through."

Dolinski's voice came across the speaker as bold as ever. "Good afternoon. You've had a difficult forty-eight hours. How are you?"

"Exhausted and mildly bruised, but otherwise okay," said MacBridan. "We're sorry about Marston. We know he was a friend."

"I appreciated the messages you left. I was absolutely shocked. Do we know what he died from?"

"Not yet," said Cori. "The local police are supposed to get back with us today, but we've yet to hear from them."

"Any ideas on your part?" asked Dolinski.

"Before the police arrived, I had an opportunity to examine the body. While I have no idea what killed him, I'm willing to bet that his death was from anything but natural causes."

"How tragic," said Dolinski. "We're pressing our contacts at Scotland Yard. As soon as I get the lab report, I'll get it out to you. Have there been any other developments?"

Both MacBridan and Cori brought Dolinski up to date, starting with when they'd arrived at the estate and MacBridan's breaking into Marston's room. They then told him about the incidents in MacBridan's room last night and at the chapel this morning, but they purposely left out any hint of conjecture regarding supernatural forces. MacBridan finished their narrative by telling Dolinski of his chat with Faith. Of everything that had occurred, it was interesting that Dolinski focused in on the garden they'd found in the woods.

"Based on what you saw, is there enough there to support a commercial venture?"

"You could clearly pick up some pretty good pocket change, but nothing in the way of a more significant amount," said MacBridan. "What's odd is the wide variety of plants that are growing there. It's like nature's own medicine cabinet. There's a little bit of everything. Thing is, unless you've had some training, most people wouldn't know how to extract the drugs from those plants."

"Perhaps your work with Truecourt on the background checks will turn up something that will help us out. I'm expecting Lord MacKinnon's call any time now, and I'll let him know that you'll be staying on. We can easily provide him with a security detail until he hires a new man, but I want you two there to dig into this and find the answers. With Marston, we've already got one potential murder on our hands, and I'm afraid that the body count has already gone up by one."

"How's that?" asked MacBridan.

"The fake Truecourt who boarded the ship in Glasgow was a well-known hood out of London by the name of Rans Cutler. He was identified by the first officer on your ship, as well as two laborers on the dock. His body was found floating in the harbor not too far from where you docked. He'd been executed, one shot to the back of the head."

"That's two killings almost at the same time, Marston and Cutler." MacBridan observed.

"If this is Talon's work, she's changed her style dramatically," said Dolinski.

"That or she's working with some pretty rough partners," said Cori.

"Either way, this changes things. I trust Truecourt gave you the package we had prepared for you?" asked Dolinski.

"He did. He gave us each a gun and the appropriate papers that allow us to carry them," said Cori.

"Good. Keep them close to you. I'm afraid that before this is over you may need them. When I talk to Lord MacKinnon, I'm going to let him know of Cutler's death. He needs to be clear as to how serious this business is."

MacBridan and Cori hung up. "Well, that certainly puts a new light on things," said MacBridan.

"Yes, it does," said Cori. Leaning back in her chair, she looked at MacBridan and said, "I'm not surprised to hear that Faith doesn't care much for Wallace, especially considering the relationship between her and her aunt. I wonder how Marston actually responded to her."

"Good question. Although it confirms what I already thought about Wallace, I'm still having trouble understanding the rest of it. I mean, he lives here. He doesn't have to hire a team of thieves to help him out. He could quietly carry out anything he wants any time he wanted to."

"True. And if what she told you is accurate," said Cori, "where would Wallace get the kind of money necessary to hire Talon? He'd have to have a partner."

"A partner who knows why that painting is worth stealing," said MacBridan. "That would make sense. By hiring a pro, Junior's hands remain clean. All he has to do is provide Talon with the inside information as to all that's going on. I like the partner angle, especially if they approached him with a large payoff. Wallace is not the sharpest tack in the highway. For the right offer, he'd probably buy into a hairbrained scheme like this, never questioning why they'd want such a worthless piece of canvas."

"For that matter, the same theory could hold true for any member of the family, if one of them does turn out to be involved in this," said Cori. She shook her head and said, "We've got to come up with something more solid and soon. We're operating on nothing but conjecture, and it's driving me nuts."

MacBridan got up and said, "Well, in the meantime, let's go have a look at the rooms we'll be protecting. I agree with Dolinski. The ground rules have changed, and we need to be armed at all times."

Chapter 15

Of the two rooms chosen by Marston to store the family valuables being brought back from the farm, MacBridan and Cori chose the one they considered to be the most secure to keep the artwork in. The other items such as the multiple pieces of antique furniture, the intricately detailed Persian rugs, and much of the Waterford crystal would be placed throughout the manor at Lord MacKinnon's discretion. They'd decided that none of these things were at risk as both attempts by the thieves had been targeted at only the one painting. However, to avoid taking any chances, all of the paintings and the other pieces of art would stay under lock and key for the time being. Additionally, it was decided to gather the other four paintings, done by the same ancestor, and put them in the safe room as well.

MacBridan left Cori upstairs, along with two of Marston's men, to move the artwork in and everything else out. Once completed, Cori would further secure the door and the windows with some of the equipment they already had at the estate. Interestingly, much of that equipment had belonged to Marston. Once finished, Cori planned to call Truecourt and have him overnight the additional equipment that she would need to complete the job.

Coming down the stairs, MacBridan saw Fergus crossing the foyer. "Fergus, I was wondering if I'd be able to speak to Laria now. Hopefully, she has recovered from last night's incident."

"She is doing better, sir. If you'll follow me, I believe she's in the kitchen with Robena."

They found Laria sitting at a small table nursing a cup of steaming tea. Fergus introduced MacBridan to her, and he sat down across her. She was a small girl with a pale complexion and dark circles under her eyes. In addition to the heavy sweater she was wearing, Robena came over and wrapped a shawl around her shoulders.

"I appreciate you talking with me," said MacBridan. "I'd like for you to tell me about last night. Exactly what did you see by Marston's room?"

"I saw him." Her voice almost too soft to hear. "The dark lord."

MacBridan nodded understandingly and asked, "Is there anything else you can tell me? What did he do? Did he say anything? Whatever you can remember will be helpful."

Laria looked at Robena as if asking permission. Robena nodded and Laria opened up. Unfortunately, what she had to say was of little use. Something had moved out of the corner of her eye, catching her attention. It looked like a monk, somewhat tattered, but she couldn't see a face. She started to get worked up again, so MacBridan brought the interview to an end. Thanking her for her help, he left the kitchen. Other than fueling the fires of superstitious fear, Laria wasn't going to be of any help.

MacBridan decided to return to the library. He needed to get a better feel for the house and the grounds. Fergus had laid out for him several diagrams of the house, the chapel, and the overall estate. Three of these had been done by Marston, and MacBridan found them to be very useful as they were amazingly detailed. There was also an assortment of architect's diagrams. Many of these had been done over the last sixty-five years as improvements were made to the house. Not surprisingly, he was drawn to the diagram of the chapel. The underground crypt was illustrated, but its dimensions were unclear. MacBridan had not yet had the chance to ask Lord MacKinnon about the crypt. He still wanted to know if, at one time, it had extended further than it does now.

The door opened, and MacBridan looked up to see Lord MacKinnon and DS Wetmoore enter the library. "Fergus said you were in here," said Lord MacKinnon. "I hope we're not interrupting."

MacBridan stood up and said, "Anything that takes me away from paperwork is always welcome."

"DS Wetmoore stopped by with an update, and I wanted you to hear what he had to say," explained Lord MacKinnon. Looking at Wetmoore, he said, "I'll share a little good news with you. Mr. MacBridan and Ms. Hopkins will be staying on with us for a few days. I've asked them to tighten things up around here and keep an eye out until I can bring on a new chief of security."

"That is good news," said Wetmoore. "It will make me feel better knowing that you're here."

"Please, gentlemen, sit down," said Lord MacKinnon. "So what do you have for us?"

"The report from Scotland Yard is being sent to me, but from what I've been told, it pretty well mirrors that of our coroner, Dr. Shepard. At this point in time, Mr. Marston's cause of death is being listed as a massive coronary infraction."

"A heart attack," said Lord MacKinnon. "I must say I am surprised and relieved, all in the same breath." He shook his head and said, "Sometimes things just don't make sense, do they? Marston was in better shape than any of us, stayed away from junk food, and didn't smoke. I think his only vice was the occasional scotch. How sad."

"You said, 'At this point in time.' I take it they're not finished with their investigation," said MacBridan.

"Scotland Yard is, Dr. Weatherby isn't," said Wetmoore. "Heart attacks are certainly not uncommon and take people of all ages every day. However, because he was in such good condition, Dr. Weatherby isn't convinced. He believes that there are still too many unanswered questions. For instance, he's still trying to determine what could have brought on such a massive heart attack. The autopsy, unfortunately, didn't give any obvious answers. As to the blistering on Marston's skin or why his face was so contorted, he has no idea what could have possibly caused that, but he's convinced they're connected."

"Wouldn't the incredible pain he experienced account for his face?" asked Lord MacKinnon.

"It may, but it's unlikely. Many people die in tremendous pain, but when they pass, the muscles in their face relax. Dr. Weatherby hates unanswered questions and is not yet ready to let this one go."

"I'm guessing that not all of the toxin screenings came back negative," said MacBridan.

"For the most part, they did. However, Dr. Weatherby did find one small irregularity with the blood, but it is my understanding that it wasn't anything significant nor is it something that they've been able to identify. There was only a trace element found, and frankly, it was almost missed. Were it not for Dr. Weatherby's passion for poisons, it might have been completely overlooked."

"Then that doesn't make sense," said Lord MacKinnon. "Why list a man's death as being of natural causes if there's so much uncertainty?"

"I wanted you to know all that I know," said Wetmoore. "This is now considered to be a closed case in the eyes of Scotland Yard. Dr. Weatherby is alone regarding his concern over that trace element."

Lord MacKinnon looked at MacBridan and said, "So where does that leave us? Do we have a killer on the prowl or not?" His face reflected the worry and exasperation he felt.

"For now, I would recommend that we go with what we know," answered MacBridan. "Until someone tells us otherwise, Marston died of natural causes, no murderer and no ghostly creature preying on the living. This will be good in that it will hopefully take some of the tension off the shoulders of everyone here. On the other hand, our thieves are alive and doing well. We will still take every precaution we can regarding the painting and the rest of the artwork."

"Very well," said Lord MacKinnon, nodding in agreement. "Marston was well liked, and as sad as his passing has been, knowing that it was from natural causes will make it a little easier. I'll let everyone know at dinner tonight."

"Mr. MacBridan," said Wetmoore, "when I said that I was glad to hear that you and Ms. Hopkins are staying on, I meant it. I'll be the first to admit that I do not have a great deal of experience with international art thieves."

"I appreciate that," said MacBridan, "but we'll still need all the help you can give us, especially now. As you said, with Scotland Yard viewing Marston's death as a closed case, no one is going to be paying much attention to what goes on up here."

"I am not without influence," said Lord MacKinnon. "If I need to make some calls and get them back on this, just say the word."

"Just between us," said MacBridan. "I'm afraid that my opinion lines up more with that of Dr. Weatherby. I'm having trouble buying into the idea of a simple heart attack. Let's let Dr. Weatherby continue his work before we play that card, Lord MacKinnon. If I see the need to push our friends at Scotland Yard, I'll ask you to make the call."

Lord MacKinnon stood up and said, "We'll let you go, Sergeant. We appreciate you making the trip out here to talk with us. I have some other business that I have to attend to, and I'm sure you do too."

As Wetmoore started to get up, MacBridan said, "Actually, there are one or two other items I'd like to discuss with the sergeant if he has the time."

"Of course," said Wetmoore.

"Very well," said Lord MacKinnon, "I'll leave you to it."

Once Lord MacKinnon left, MacBridan leaned back in his chair and studied Wetmoore. "Well, Sergeant, what do you really think of all this?"

"I believe he was killed. The problem is, I don't have a shred of evidence to support it."

"How soon do you expect you'll hear back from Weatherby?"

"Not until he knows something, one way or the other. For him, it's not a question of right or wrong. It's a matter of filling in the blanks. He's a pretty tenacious guy. I'd guess around a day or two."

"Our art thieves are still at large, and we're pretty confident that they're getting inside help."

"Inside help?" said Wetmoore. "Do you mean the staff? Certainly you don't suspect the family."

"These people are pros. There's no doubt. But in order for them to have tried what they did at the farm and then on the docks in Glasgow, they needed someone on the inside giving them all the details of our plans." MacBridan proceeded to bring Wetmoore up to speed on all the details surrounding both of the attempted thefts. "It's not much help, but we've narrowed it down to either a full-time member of the staff or one of the family."

"Have you shared this with Lord MacKinnon?"

"We have."

"How did he react?"

"Not well."

"I'll bet he didn't," said Wetmoore, a broad smile across his face.

"Fortunately, it was Cori who raised this concern with him. She's far more diplomatic than I am. Turns out Marston had the same suspicions."

"How can I help?" asked Wetmoore.

"We're in the process of working up background checks on everyone here. Being a local, I was hoping you could give me what you know about the staff, the family, all the scuttlebutt that our research isn't going to reveal."

"In other words, the local gossip. I understand," said Wetmoore. He thought about it for a few moments then added, "I'm afraid I don't have too much to tell you. I guess if it were up to me, I'd have to focus on the Hendersons."

"The Hendersons? Do you mean Fergus and Robena? I sincerely hope they're not involved."

"Why?" asked Wetmoore.

"You don't know Dolinski."

"Who's that?"

"He's the man I report to. I can't call him from a secluded Lord's estate set deep in the Highlands of northern Scotland and tell him the butler did it."

"I see your point," said Wetmoore, "but I was actually referring more to Robena's son. He's from her first marriage and has given them nothing but trouble, constantly getting mixed up in things. If I'm remembering this correctly, he served time for robbery a few years back."

"Where is he now?" asked MacBridan.

"Good question. I'll get back to you on that."

"Anything else?"

Wetmoore shook his head. "Perhaps the groundskeeper, Barth Lackland, but that would be a stretch. It's a small village so people talk, but the word is that he's living beyond his means."

MacBridan laughed at that. "Who isn't?"

"True," said Wetmoore, "but the reason it's made for good pub conversation is that he's been known to visit some local brothels, one in particular I'm told over by Kinlochewe. But like I said, nothing that really points to collusion with international thieves."

Wetmoore stood up to leave. "As soon as I get the report from Scotland Yard, I'll let you take a look at it. I'll also follow up with you on the whereabouts of Robena's son. For now, I'm going to find Fergus and see if I can spend some time with the maid who was so badly shaken up last night."

"I hope that goes well. I do appreciate all the cooperation," said MacBridan.

"Lord MacKinnon's a very important man, a good man. I'll do all I can to help protect him and his family."

As he started out the door, MacBridan called out to him, "Sergeant, one more thing. I meant to bring this up when Lord MacKinnon was with us. Any update on Major?"

"We haven't found him yet, but we have received reports on three more dogs that have gone missing."

"Were they black too?"

"Yes, come to think of it, they were," said Wetmoore. "Is that significant?"

"Probably not, but I thought you had mentioned that the last time when you told us about the other dogs that had been reported missing. I was just wondering if it might all be connected."

"Who would be out stealing black dogs?"

"Hard to tell," said MacBridan. "There are a lot of crazies out there."

MacBridan tried to refocus on the diagrams, but other thoughts were now racing through his mind. His primary focus was supposed to be protecting the estate from the thieves. Neither he nor Cori had any doubt that they'd try again. But now another line of thought was beginning to eat away at him.

The circumstances surrounding Marston's death were not yet clear. For that matter, the findings left enough open items on the table that they were still being investigated by a top forensic specialist. When MacBridan combined the odd nature of Marston's death with the intruder in his room and added to it the unexplainable event that he and Cori experienced in the crypt, one's mind started to trend in a direction he didn't want to go. Add in a backdrop of black dogs disappearing, a weak, superstitious mind could start seeing the dark lord behind every tree.

MacBridan shook his head, rubbed his hands through his hair, got up, and looked out the window. He had to stop that. He was being ridiculous and decided that he needed a break. A cup of strong Scottish tea would get him back on course. On his way to the dining room, he made a mental note to himself. On the next call with Dolinski, leave out all theories that point to the butler having done it or to anything vaguely supernatural. Such theories would not be constructive nor do anything to further enhance his career.

Fergus had let him known that they kept a tea service laid out in the dining room all day along with different breads and cakes. Lord MacKinnon was already there fixing himself a cup of tea as MacBridan entered the room. "How was your talk with Wetmoore?"

"Just fine. He comes across as being a good man."

"I agree," said Lord MacKinnon. "He's young and a little innocent, but that probably has more to do with a lack of experience than anything else."

"Life will fill in the blanks there," said MacBridan.

"A Scotsman and a philosopher?" said Lord MacKinnon, smiling at MacBridan. "A fine combination."

"Not really," laughed MacBridan. "Just the voice of a man who has been repeatedly abused by experience."

Lord MacKinnon chuckled at that. "Not to change the subject, but I just got off the phone with a gentleman who will be joining us for dinner this evening," said Lord MacKinnon. "He called to confirm his arrival, along with that of a colleague of his. This was all arranged several weeks ago, but I hadn't heard from him in some time. They'll be guests here at the estate for the next few days."

"They'll be staying here at the manor?"

"No, I offered, but they declined. They'll be staying in town. This really isn't all that uncommon. The estate has been here for many centuries, and although the exact boundaries have shifted somewhat, it consistently draws the attention of many historians. Our guests have asked permission to examine some of the early period art pieces that we have as well as some of the older parts of the house. They also expressed a strong interest in examining the chapel."

"Do you know these men or know of them by reputation?"

"We've never met, but I assure you their credentials are impeccable. Naturally, I'll want you to talk with them and let me know if you have any apprehensions. I doubt that they'll be in the way."

With that, Lord MacKinnon left to return to his office. MacBridan started to return to the library but then decided to further examine the cakes that had been set out. He too was a guest and didn't want to be rude by ignoring such hospitality.

His thoughts went to the two men joining them for dinner. A smile formed on his face regarding their wanting to examine the chapel. Considering his lone experience there, he laughed and thought, *Good luck with that.*

Chapter 16

The view from Aunt Jean's bedroom looked out over one of the largest flower beds on the estate. She loved the gently curving white gravel paths that led to several beautifully designed fountains and shaded sitting areas. Beyond the flower garden lay the broad manicured lawn, stopping abruptly at the edge of the woods. On clear days, she could see the Celtic cross proudly standing atop the spire on the family chapel rising well above the tree line. Jean had always felt secure and comfortable here, resting on her favorite chair next to the window. Many were the times she had dozed off in this chair, her afternoon nap now a daily event. But today, she was having trouble relaxing.

The weather remained much too wet, and she decided against taking her usual stroll through the gardens after lunch, so she returned to her room. Taking advantage of her quiet time alone, she sat down next to the witch board, trying to coax the answers she so desperately needed from Reznik. However, the only answers he would give were to questions that hadn't been asked, at least not out loud. Could he read her thoughts? She trembled at the idea that this could be possible.

Aunt Jean glared at the board. Reznik, the board's spirit guide, was acting like most men today and not listening to her questions. She decided to take one more run at it.

Placing her hands lightly on the planchette, she asked, "Was Marston's death an accident?"

The planchette moved quickly, spelling out the following: *The darkness is growing in strength.*

"Is the family at risk?"

A dark legacy will demand justice.

"Why won't you answer my questions?" demanded Aunt Jean, her anger rising in lockstep with her fears.

Your time of trial is upon you.

Aunt Jean pushed back from the board and walked away from it. Surprisingly, she found her breath had become labored, her heart racing. She'd never known Reznik to act in this way, and it scared her. She decided they both needed a break.

On the small table in front of the fireplace sat a tea service, along with some sweet breads, that Laria had brought up to her a few minutes ago. Although Laria seemed to have recovered from the shock, the haunted look in her eyes was still there, a nervousness that had not quite gone away. Laria had actually seen the dark lord leaving Marston's room the night Mr. MacBridan arrived. Poor child! Just the thought of it caused Aunt Jean to grip the arms of her chair. That's an experience one wouldn't get over too easily.

A light tapping at her door startled her. "Yes?"

"Aunt Jean, it's me," said Faith, barely opening the door. "Are you busy?"

"No, my dear," she called. "Please join me."

Faith came in, shut the door behind her, and walked over to the window. As she passed by, she glanced at the witch board, many of its symbols still a mystery to her, sitting on the table next to the fireplace. The planchette had been left in the middle of the board. "I see you've been talking with Reznik. Any good news?"

"How did you...oh, did I leave the planchette on the board again?"

"You did. He'll think you're ignoring him."

"Yes, well, the feeling's mutual. I can't remember a time when he's been more obtuse! I don't understand what's wrong."

"I'm sure this will pass," said Faith reassuringly. "Didn't you tell me that this once happened with your grandmother?"

"Not exactly," said Aunt Jean. "I really don't know what happened back then, but it's funny you should mention her. This afternoon, I've been going through the last few letters she sent to me as well as reading through her journal again. I'm afraid it's all been quite unsettling."

"How so?"

"As you know, my mother never approved of the witch board, and my grandmother never told her anything about Reznik. The whole idea scared her. Letting her know that there was actually a spirit guide communicating from the other side would have been too much. I now appreciate her feelings more than ever."

"Hasn't it been in the family for a long time?"

"Oh yes, for many generations, but it's not something we brag about or share with people outside of the family. It was brought over by Balgair's wife."

"You're joking," said an astonished Faith. "This belonged to her? Didn't people believe that she was a witch?"

"Yes, and I still marvel that it wasn't tossed in the fire and destroyed with her when they burned her at the stake. Somehow, it escaped the wrath of the villagers. But then I don't believe that was by accident."

"I'm not sure I understand what you're saying."

"We'll talk about it later. It doesn't matter at the moment. The board is ancient and has remained with the MacKinnon family for hundreds of years, being passed down generation to generation and almost always to a MacKinnon woman."

"Because of the gift, the second sight you've told me about," said Faith.

"Yes," answered Aunt Jean. She wanted to tell Faith that she'd seen signs of the gift in her, but now was not the time.

"As you know," Aunt Jean continued, "my grandmother used it a great deal and taught me how to use it. Several years after she passed, I had it shipped to me in the United States. Your uncle Ronald sees it as so much women's nonsense. No one else really minded that I had it sent over. In one of her last letters to my father, she asked that I be the one to look after it. Once my mother and father had passed on, I kept it set up out in the open."

"She must have loved you very much."

"She and I were kindred spirits," said Aunt Jean. "That said, I'm at a loss to understand what could have happened to have changed her way of thinking so dramatically."

"What happened?" asked Faith.

"A week or so before we sailed to America, her whole attitude changed. She stopped using it altogether, not with me, not with my sister, not with anyone. She kept it set up in her room but wouldn't go near it and wouldn't let us."

"Did she write anything about it in her journal?"

"No. Her last several entries were all about how scared she'd become. She wrote about several instances of where she saw the shadow people on the grounds and eventually in the house. She was convinced that her time was near and that they were coming for her," said Aunt Jean.

"How dreadful," said Faith. "That is so sad."

"A few weeks after this change of heart that she died. We, of course, were in America by then. All of us agonized over her having died alone. The idea had been for her to regain her strength and then join us. I still miss her so."

"What did she die of?"

"She was found early one morning still in her bed. The doctor said she passed in her sleep, apparently from a heart attack. What's interesting is that the servant who found her said that the planchette was on the floor, not far from her bed."

"That's odd," said Faith. "Did they know how it got there?"

"There was no way of telling, but I've always believed that she tried talking with Reznik one last time. Whether she did it before she went to bed or got up in the middle of the night, I don't think it went well. I believe she felt the same frustration with the board that I'm feeling and chucked the bloody planchette across the room."

Faith smiled at this. "It's becoming more and more obvious that the famous MacKinnon temper is not reserved for just the males in this family."

"No, it isn't," Aunt Jean agreed. Faith had taken the chair across her, and they both sat quietly, looking out the window. Faith studied her aunt for a few moments, then said, "Aunt Jean, please don't misunderstand me, but perhaps it's not Reznik that's the problem."

"Really. What do you think it is?"

"So much has been going on, especially the last couple of days, which have been absolutely dreadful. The threat of thieves stalking the grounds, Laria claiming to have seen a ghost, all climaxing with poor Marston's death, everyone is off their game."

"Reznik has always been there for me before," said Aunt Jean, "in good times or bad. Why would things be any different now?"

"You've always taught me that to effectively communicate with him, it is important for me to clear my mind, relax, and focus on the board. I think the stress we've all been under has kept you from being able to do that."

"I see your point, but I'm not so sure," mused Aunt Jean. "In some of my darkest moments, I've never experienced this. Reznik has never failed me. Faith, it's as if he's as frightened by the evil in this house as we are."

"Aunt Jean, please," said Faith, coming to her feet. "Reznik is not a real person! It's just a name your grandmother made up to influence a little girl, no different than you did with me. I know that you believe in the board and that you believe you are truly communicating with a helpful spirit. I understand. But now it's upsetting you, and you have to start putting things in a rational perspective." Faith caught herself before she went any further, suddenly feeling terrible at the hurt and disappointment she could see in her aunt's eyes.

"I'm sorry, Aunt Jean," said Faith, sitting back down. "I'm not angry with you. I'm just afraid of this making you sick."

Aunt Jean looked away and didn't say anything. She sat quietly with her hands folded in her lap, staring at the sky. She had known for some time that Faith doubted Reznik and the board, but she so needed her to believe, now more than ever. Without Faith, she'd be absolutely alone with no one to share her thoughts, her concerns.

"Aunt Jean, I'm so sorry. I didn't mean to hurt your feelings."

Aunt Jean closed her eyes, fighting back the tears, and bowed her head. For the life of her, she simply could not find the words that would make her niece see that she was wrong, that Reznik and the witch board were real. The silence between them was terrible.

Faith leaned forward in her chair, bringing herself closer to her aunt. "Aunt Jean, please, let's put this beh—" The light, scratching sound behind them broke the silence of the room, making them both look behind them. Faith stood up and turned around to see what was there. Aunt Jean turned in her chair, trying to see what was going on. They both stared at the empty room.

Aunt Jean scanned the room, and it took her a few moments for her to realize what had happened. A grim smile of satisfaction spread across her face.

"Faith, look at the planchette."

"What?"

"The planchette, Faith, look at it."

The planchette, sitting on the witch board, was moving on its own, slowly, scratching out the sound they'd heard. Faith couldn't believe her eyes. It was moving, and no one was near it! Faith cautiously walked over and peered down at it but wouldn't touch it.

"How is this happening?" asked Faith, her voice just above a whisper.

"Follow it, Faith. What is it saying?"

Faith watched as the planchette now seemed to pick up speed, barely giving her time to keep up. *Marston's blood will spread to you, death following death.*

"No!" shouted Faith, swatting at the planchette, knocking it to the floor.

"What is it, Faith?" asked Aunt Jean. "What did it say?"

Faith backed up, getting away from it, and leaned against the bed. Her face had grown pale, and her hand trembled as she touched her face. She couldn't take her eyes away from the board. Finally she looked at her Aunt. "Oh my god, this can't be."

Aunt Jean held her hand out to her. "Don't be afraid, my child. Come. Sit back down. We have much to talk about."

Chapter 17

MacBridan casually checked his watch as he looked across the room. It was 7:30 p.m., and the entire family, with the exception of Lord MacKinnon, had gathered together in the study to enjoy their predinner cocktails, all patiently waiting for their guests to arrive. Kerr, Lord MacKinnon's other nephew, was also in attendance this evening, and for MacBridan, it was the first time he'd gotten to meet him. Jokingly, he'd bet Cori ten dollars that Kerr really didn't exist. The bet was that Barclay didn't have a brother and that Kerr was completely imaginary, another eccentricity of this remarkably colorful family.

The mood, for a change, was happily lighthearted, and MacBridan was glad to see it. The family had been through the mill. Of course there hadn't been an attempted theft, a ghost sighting, or a murder in the last twenty-four hours, so it wasn't all that surprising that everyone was feeling better. Upon reflection, MacBridan acknowledged that life at the manor hadn't been a picnic for Cori and him either.

It also helped that Lord MacKinnon had created a distraction for the family, which was getting a great deal of attention. There was quite a stir regarding the mystery dinner guests who would soon be joining them. Lord MacKinnon had not shared a great deal of detail with anyone as to who they were or why they would be there.

"Mr. MacBridan," said the young man, "I'm Kerr MacKinnon, Barclay's brother. I've heard some interesting things about you, and I'm pleased to finally get to meet you." Kerr looked a great deal like Barclay, only trimmer in his overall build but had the same reddish-brown hair and the obvious MacKinnon features.

MacBridan smiled at the young man as he extended his hand to Kerr. "It's good to finally meet you too, and please, I go by either Mac or James. Frankly, Cori and I were beginning to think that they were keeping you locked up in the dungeon."

Kerr reached out to shake hands with MacBridan then stopped, slightly pulling his hand back. "I need to be careful about this. Aunt Jean told me that shaking hands with you can be a painful experience."

MacBridan laughed. "I guess that little incident didn't go unnoticed after all."

Kerr smiled broadly as they shook hands and said, "Aunt Jean's a sharp old bird. She doesn't miss much. I'm just waiting for the right opportunity to bring it up to Wallace. I understand the arrogant prig had it coming."

"The conversation seemed to be getting a little out of hand, and it was the best way I could think of to get folks settled down. The way things were going, it was either that or Wallace and I would have started marking our territory, which would have been embarrassing for both of us."

They laughed at this just as Aunt Jean and Cori joined them. "I see you two have met," said Aunt Jean, "and if I know anything about men at all, especially from the tone of that laughter, we just missed a joke that I'm sure neither Ms. Hopkins nor I would have appreciated."

"Do you see what I mean?" asked Kerr. "It wasn't actually all that bad, Aunt Jean. Ms. Hopkins, it's good to meet you as well."

"It's Cori, and I'm pleased to meet you also. We weren't sure if you were ever going to turn up."

"So I understand," said Kerr.

Aunt Jean looked at MacBridan and said, "You two have had a rather full day and a half with us. I do hope you'll find sometime soon to sit down and relax."

"It has been somewhat nonstop," acknowledged MacBridan.

"Fergus was telling me that you and Cori braved our wet skies to visit the chapel," he continued.

"That's right. We went there early this morning and were fortunate to get there just before the really hard rain hit us," answered Cori. "The chapel is just beautiful."

"It was an experience I'll never forget," said MacBridan. Aunt Jean looked at Mac thoughtfully but didn't say anything.

"Personally speaking, I think you're terribly brave," said Kerr, looking at MacBridan.

"How's that?" asked MacBridan.

"Of all the rooms that we have in this sprawling house, they have you staying in the very room that once belonged to the dark lord. I don't care how silly it may sound. You couldn't pay me to sleep there. That takes far more courage than I have."

"Now, Kerr, don't start in on all that," scolded Aunt Jean. "We put Mr. MacBridan through enough of our family's dreadful history yesterday evening. I'm sure he's heard all he wants to hear on the subject."

As Aunt Jean changed the subject, MacBridan noticed that Wallace and Faith were still deep in conversation, sitting across each other by the fireplace. Fortunately, it appeared to be pleasant. Faith smiled sweetly at Fergus as he freshened their drinks.

Lord MacKinnon cleared his throat as he entered the study. He was followed by Robena and two Catholic priests. All conversation stopped. Faith and Wallace stood up to greet their guests. Barclay, who'd been tending to one of the fires, put the poker down and walked over to stand next to Faith. MacBridan hadn't seen Father Collin in a couple of years since the bad business in New Westminster. It was there they'd first met. If Father Collin was here, MacBridan's hopes for a normal crime were gone.

"I'd like to introduce all of you to our guests this evening," said Lord MacKinnon. "This is Father Novak Krizova and Father Collin Sherry. Both have traveled from Rome to be here with us this evening. These two gentlemen are both historians from the Vatican. They are here to study parts of the house, the chapel, and several of the works of art our family has been fortunate to have acquired over the years. Unfortunately, I couldn't convince them to stay here at the manor. They have taken rooms in the village and will be visiting with us over the next few days." Turning to the two priests, he said, "We are honored to have you with us and want you to know that you are most welcome as our guests."

"Thank you," said Father Collin, the fine Irish lilt in his voice came out strong and clear. "We are most appreciative of your hospitality to have opened your beautiful home to us. We will do our best not to be in the way."

Cori shot MacBridan a questioning glance as Lord MacKinnon started around the room making individual introductions. MacBridan nodded once slowly at her and then turned his attention back to the two priests. Father Novak was a small, frail-looking man, maybe an inch or two over five feet tall, with a gray thinning tonsure donning his head. He appeared to be in his late sixties and wore glasses with some of the thickest lenses that MacBridan had ever seen outside of a Jerry Lewis comedy.

Father Collin, on the other hand, hadn't changed much at all since MacBridan had last seen him. In his early fifties, Father Collin was a large, robust figure of a man, well over six feet tall with broad shoulders. Thick salt-and-pepper hair ringed the top of his bald head, making him look a little older than he was. Perhaps his most differentiating feature was his sharp, penetrating eyes. MacBridan felt they had the ability to peer into one's very soul. To MacBridan, Father Collin had always looked more like an aging athlete than a priest.

Finally, MacBridan made eye contact with Father Collin, but there was absolutely no sign of recognition from him at all. MacBridan didn't understand but decided that until he knew more; it would be best to play along.

"This is James MacBridan of the Hawthorne Group and his associate Cori Hopkins," said Lord MacKinnon. "I told Father Novak and Father Collin of Marston's passing and how graciously you volunteered to step in and manage our security for the time being."

"It is good to meet both of you," said Father Novak. His accent was thick and obviously Slavic, but MacBridan couldn't pinpoint it any further than that. "Your being here at such a tragic time was clearly God's hand at work. I will pray for Mr. Marston's soul."

"An unexpected death is always such a sad and difficult thing to deal with," said Father Collin. "Lord MacKinnon expressed his gratitude for all of the help that you have given to him and his family. As Father Novak so correctly pointed out, a blessing from God, I'm sure."

"They have been a great comfort to everyone," added Lord MacKinnon.

"The Hawthorne Group," said Father Collin. "I can't say I'm familiar with it. Is it an American firm?"

"You're quite right, Father," answered Lord MacKinnon. "It is a law firm based in the United States, although they do have offices in London. My family has done business with them for many years. Ms. Hopkins and Mr. MacBridan are with their investigative division. During our move back from America, they provided the security for the very artwork that you're here to study."

"How fortuitous that you arrived when you did," said Father Collin. MacBridan heard irony in the adjective and returned in kind.

"It was, wasn't it?" said MacBridan. "The way things happen around here, one could almost start believing in coincidence."

Father Collin continued on, ignoring MacBridan's remark. "As you're now in charge of the security for the estate, perhaps I could spend some time with you after dinner and more fully discuss our plans. We certainly don't want our presence to cause any difficulties."

"I'd be happy to, Father," said MacBridan. "Cori and I have become intimately familiar with the MacKinnon's collection, and I'd like to know exactly what your interests are. That way, we might be able to make things easier for you."

"Excellent, then it's all settled," said Lord MacKinnon. "Shall we proceed on into the dining room? I'm sure we're all ready for the excellent meal that Robena has prepared for us."

Once they were all seated, with Lord MacKinnon's permission, Father Novak gave the blessing. During dinner, Father Collin sat between Lord MacKinnon and Cori, rarely looking across the table at MacBridan. Once again, Wallace positioned himself at the opposite end of the long table away from his father but seemed to be in a more pleasant mood than usual. Based on what MacBridan had seen and heard about Wallace, this was almost out of character for him. MacBridan sat between Faith and Father Novak. Although Father Novak spent most of his time in intense conversation with Aunt Jean regarding mostly religious matters, MacBridan did learn that he was from Romania. From what little he could overhear, it sounded as if Father Novak had had some harrowing experiences during the Cold War. However, it was hard for MacBridan to pay much attention to the small priest as Faith occupied most of his time.

After dinner, the family returned to the study to enjoy the comfort of the fireplaces, relaxing with brandy and port.

Father Novak declined the meeting with MacBridan and Cori, choosing to remain with the family. Lord MacKinnon reminded them to take jackets if they were going to take a walk outside. While Mac and Cori were getting their coats from their rooms, Fergus brought Father Collin's overcoat to him.

Stepping outside, Father Collin immediately said, "I thought we'd first take a wee bit of a stroll to fully enjoy the beauty and quiet of the night sky. I always find the Scottish Highlands to be so enchanting."

Several moments of silence passed between them as they walked down the lane at a leisurely pace. Finally, MacBridan couldn't hold back any longer and said, "And we're to believe that you're here, at this particular point in time, to study artwork," said MacBridan.

Father Collin smiled and said, "In addition to parts of the manor, especially the chapel. Please, let's continue our walk and enjoy the evening a bit more before we talk." Looking at Cori, he said, "In case you're wondering, that wonderfully rich scent drifting through the air is from the loam on the forest floor. Several deep breaths of that and you'll find yourself with far less stress."

"At dinner, you told me that the best cure for stress was good, strong Irish whisky."

"That I did, that I did," Father Collin agreed, "but it's not always available. Therefore, it is important that we be aware of God's other gifts, which he gives to us in abundance, when Irish whiskey's not within our reach. This evening, it is the gift of this magnificent forest."

They walked on in silence. The cool evening air made them most appreciative of Lord MacKinnon's advice to bring along their jackets. As they approached the tree line, Father Collin said, "I'd say we're a safe enough distance from the house. It is good to see you, James, you look well."

The last time they'd seen each other, MacBridan had been seriously wounded. His recovery had been a long and painful process. "So do you, Father. I can't begin to tell you how completely taken by surprise I was when you walked into that study this evening."

"I had hoped you'd be pleased to see me."

"Don't misunderstand me, I am," said MacBridan. "It's just that I don't know whether to be happy to have you here or start looking around for the flying monkeys."

Father Collins chuckled at this. Looking at Cori, he said, "I don't know how much James has shared with you, but when we first met, it was during some extraordinary events."

"He shares very little about anything," said Cori.

"Still, your being here at this particular time is rather remarkable," pressed MacBridan. "Here we are up against one of the top professional art thieves in the world with a murderer on the loose, and you just happen to pick this particular time to drop in and study art. Now that is absolutely amazing, wouldn't you say Father?"

"Coincidence happens only when God chooses to remain anonymous," said Father Collin. "No, if I had to label the timing regarding my being here, I'd say it's more along the lines of synchronicity."

"Synchronicity?" asked Cori.

"I often see it in play. Although I haven't read a great deal of psychology, the psychologist Carl Jung and the physicist Wolfgang Pauli developed a theory of meaningful coincidences. Pauli won the Noble Prize by the way. He believed that the universe is held together in two ways. Firstly, by cause and effect. Secondly, by events that seem to be separate but are actually edges of a larger five-dimensional event. We all taste it at times. For example, you are thinking of a certain song and your best friend walks in the room humming it."

"Five-dimensional?" asked Cori.

"Something a little bigger than the three dimensions of space and the fourth dimension of time."

"But you're not here to discuss philosophy and physics," prompted MacBridan.

"No, and I'm afraid that this evening, our time is limited. I do not want anyone to get suspicious. It is critical that you fully understand why Father Novak and I are here. We're well aware of the attempted thefts on the family's artwork, but you have much worse trouble on your hands. You are up against a far more dangerous adversary than you realize. Hopefully, we can help."

"What can you tell us?" asked MacBridan, not surprised at Father Collin being well informed as to all that was going on.

"How much do you know about the dark lord of the MacKinnon clan?"

"Not a great deal," said MacBridan. "In his day, he was the local bad boy, got cross ways with the villagers, and was killed for his trouble. Also, supposedly, I'm bunking in his old room."

"I ran across him in my research before we left for Scotland," said Cori. "His name was Balgair MacKinnon and was supposed to have been a Knight Templar. He returned to the MacKinnon home around the same time as the demise of the Templars, bringing a wife and some retainers along with him. He was not home very long before the reigning Lord MacKinnon and his son both died, making him the legal heir. Legend has it, he practiced the dark arts and that his wife was a witch, and eventually the villagers rose up against them. He is also credited with haunting the manor house to this day."

"How wonderfully concise you are," said Father Collin. "I've heard so much about you, Ms. Hopkins, and it is an absolute delight to finally get to spend time with you."

"You're here because of a legend?" asked MacBridan. "You should stick with your first story about studying art. It's much more believable."

Father Collin gave a tight smile. "I'm afraid Balgair's role in this is more than just legend. We believe this does tie into the Templars, and the church obviously has a tremendous amount of knowledge regarding them. I'll keep this as brief as I can. There was a Knight Templar living in France in the early 1300s by the name of Esquiu de Florian. History does not paint him in a very positive light. Over the years, Florian worked his way up in the Templar ranks to become the prior of the Templar preceptory of Montfaucon in the region of Perigueux. However, for some unknown reason, he was removed from his position and returned to the rank and file."

"Florian, yes, I remember hearing about him in a documentary," said MacBridan. An avid history buff, MacBridan enjoyed anything dealing with the Templars. "If I remember correctly, he did all that he could to get the provincial master to return him to his position, but the master wouldn't do it. Failing that, Florian then went after his former superior and stabbed him to death, effectively sealing his own fate. He then escaped into Spain and eventually conspired with Philip against the Templars."

"That's exactly right," said Father Collin.

"I certainly don't know that much about the Templars," said Cori, "but it is my understanding that they were extremely loyal to their order. What would have motivated this knight to turn against them so terribly? Was it just simple revenge?"

"Revenge certainly played a role, but it was more a terrible lust for power," answered Father Collin.

"How would his conspiring with Philip have helped him to gain power?" asked MacBridan. "The Templars, due in part to his efforts, were destroyed, and despite his help to the king, he wouldn't have been trusted by anyone."

"We believe that two men with totally separate agendas, King Philip and Florian, came together rather fortuitously. It is important to keep in mind all that was going on at the time. France was nearly broke, and Philip greatly coveted the Templars' wealth but didn't have a reason that he could use to go after them. However, Philip did know how easy it was to accuse someone of heresy and make it stick. This was also the time of the Inquisition. Philip was close to a Dominican brother named Guillaume Imbert, who happened to be the grand inquisitor for the inquisition in France. Imbert was not only Philip's friend but was his personal confessor and very loyal to him. It was well known that Imbert benefited financially from his relationship with the king."

"So the stage was set, but Philip still didn't have anything that he could use to go after the Templars," said MacBridan.

"And that's where Florian enters the picture. His testimony, so to speak, charging the Templars with heresy provided Philip with an inside witness and a signed statement, more than enough to allow him to move forward. Whether or not any of what Florian said was true didn't matter to Philip at all," explained Father Collin. "As to Florian, he needed money and knew that his own life was in jeopardy. The Templars were after him for the murder of his master. His siding with Philip was as much an act of self-preservation as anything else. By working with Philip, he would be handsomely rewarded and, at the same time, would effectively remove his own death sentence."

"Did it work? What happened to him?" asked Cori.

"No one ever knew. Florian seemed to just disappear from the pages of history. For the longest time, it was believed that though he'd been instrumental to Philip's success, the king had Florian arrested and executed, thus securing his silence forever. Then, about nine months ago, the church came into possession of some old letters sent by one of Florian's retainers to his father in France letting him know that he was all right. The letters explained that he was with Florian, and they'd escaped the Templar purge. He told his father that they were on their way to the north of Scotland to hide as Florian had family there."

"The MacKinnon clan," said Cori.

"That's what we believe," said Father Collin. "We believe that Balgair had changed his name years back when he first joined the Templars. A man with a false name and a false past is hard to find, especially if he ever had to disappear in a hurry. The two most compelling reasons for believing that they are one and the same are the physical descriptions of both men, along with the date of Balgair's arrival in Scotland."

"The date of his arrival?" asked Cori.

"Balgair's return to the clan closely coincided with that of the downfall of the Templars. The timing of his return supports our theory."

"So if you're right," said MacBridan, "the wealth Balgair brought with him was probably stolen from the Templars, in addition to whatever he was paid by Philip. Then by doing away with the current Lord MacKinnon and son, he attained all that he sought, power and status."

"Precisely, but it was more than just gold that he stole form the Templars." Looking at Cori, Father Collin said, "His testimony against the Templars was about their heresy, their worship of the devil. Sadly, we believe he was actually projecting his own behavior, along with that of his followers. Balgair did practice the dark arts, and we believe that his wife, so to speak, was most proficient. Judging from that which has been written about her, we also believe that she was possessed."

"You don't think that they were married?" asked MacBridan.

"No, but it was the easiest way for him to explain her presence once he returned to Scotland. There is a pattern to these rites. It requires a male, the magus, and a female, the scarlet woman. She provides power, and he provides focus," said Father Collin.

"In my college dorm, my roommate was into that stuff," said Cori. "Didn't Aleister Crowley call his wives and mistresses scarlet women?"

"Yes," said Father Collin. "In fact, after the devil talked to him in Cairo, he returned to his estate of Boleskine on Loch Ness. He probably was looking for the relic that Balgair found. He even named his daughter after Lilith. He had good references, but frankly, the Vatican has more."

"Stop," said Cori. "Father, no offense, but if you really expect us to believe that this guy was some kind of warlock, then you have a problem because that is patently ridiculous. Balgair may indeed have worshiped the devil, and I can believe that he did some pretty bad things to the people who lived around here. But the idea that he was successfully conjuring up demonic creatures to do his evil bidding is preposterous. In the world of reality, that stuff doesn't exist."

Father Collin smiled. "I have often found that reality all depends on who's defining it. Ms. Hopkins, I do know how all this must sound to you, I truly do, but please bear with me a little bit longer."

Cori looked to MacBridan for support, but rather than shaking his head in scornful disbelief, he appeared to be deep in thought. Was he actually buying into all of these nonsense? Past relationship or not, why wasn't he challenging this priest? Typically Mac was one of the strongest skeptics she knew, especially when it came to anything supernatural. His apparent silent agreement with this was completely out of character.

"Assuming Florian and Balgair are the same man, how did he know of all that had been discovered in Jerusalem? To this day, there's still a great deal of speculation as to what they might have actually found. Numerous books have been written regarding this, but the Templars kept that as one of their most tightly guarded secrets, even from the majority of their own order," said MacBridan.

"When Jerusalem fell to the Christians during the first crusade," explained Father Collin, "the Templars took possession of Temple rock. It was there, after an exhaustive search, that they found many things hidden in deep underground passageways. Most of what they found was treasure in the form of gold, silver, and precious gemstones, but they also discovered hundreds of scrolls and several ancient artifacts. All of these were removed, brought back to France, and stored at the preceptory at Montfaucon."

"Now the light comes on," said MacBridan. "Florian became the prior of Montfaucon and therefore had access to all of those scrolls. But over the years, many men had preceded him in that position. How is it that he was so negatively influenced?" asked MacBridan.

"Priorities change," said Father Collin, "and it wasn't until Florian's time that any serious effort to translate the scrolls was made. Florian was given the assignment to translate the scrolls, study all that had been found, and make a report on his findings directly to the Templar grand master."

"Once again implementing a plan designed to maintain the utmost secrecy, keeping the knowledge they'd found within a very tight circle," commented MacBridan.

"He first took stock of the treasure, updating the balance of the wealth that was there. It is at this time that we believe he set some aside for himself. Then the translation of the scrolls began. The knights working for him found that some of the scrolls contained ancient grimoires. Florian was entranced by the power these ancient rites promised and quickly issued a stern ruling. If any knights translating the scrolls came across one containing grimoires, they were to immediately give it to him. He then would personally take charge of it, all in an effort to 'protect' the hearts and souls of his brethren."

"How noble," said MacBridan. "At the same time increasing his own knowledge and keeping everyone else from fully understanding what he was amassing."

"Grimoires," said Cori. "Now I remember. That's what you came across during your investigation in New Westminster when you first met Father Collin. What exactly is a grimoire?"

"Most of the more potent grimoires we know of are quite old, dating back well before the time of Christ," explained Father Collin. "For all practical purposes, they are a set of directions regarding the words and actions necessary for casting spells and invoking demons, usually for the practice of necromancy."

"Bringing the dead back from the grave," said Cori. "Surely you don't believe that nonsense is real, do you?" asked Cori. "I mean, I know people can talk themselves into believing almost anything, but at the end of the day, this is all fantasy."

"Ms. Hopkins, the Bible speaks to us directly about all of these. There are many passages that tell of demons, witchcraft, possession, and of those who worship Satan. There are sacraments of evil as well as of good. You would be quite surprised if I told you how many exorcisms the church performed just last year."

"Father, I believe in God, do not think otherwise. But this other stuff is all man-made to influence weak minds. I'm sorry, but that's where I have to draw the line," said Cori.

Father Collin nodded and said, "It is difficult to grasp, I'll grant you that, especially in our science-driven culture. We live in an age where nothing is real unless it can be empirically proven, and yet the unexplainable continues to confront us every day. Despite what you may think of this, I urge you to take care. Not believing that something exists doesn't mean it isn't real." Father Collin stopped and looked at his watch. "I continue to distract us. We'll have time tomorrow to further debate this, but tonight, there is more that I need to share with you, and we're tight on time. Are either of you familiar with Lilith from the old Hebrew scriptures?"

"I trust we're not talking about Frasier's wife from the television sitcom," said MacBridan.

Father Collin smiled at that. "We're not. The Lilith I'm referring to figures very prominently in Hebrew legend and mythology. In brief, she was supposed to have been Adam's first wife, but unlike Eve, she was made totally separate from Adam. She was equal to Adam, not from Adam. Lilith was perhaps the first feminist and chose to turn away from God and follow Satan. Over the centuries, there have been many cults who have worshiped Lilith, and she is seen as a strong demonic force."

"How does she tie into all of this?" asked MacBridan.

"There is an old and very dangerous sect," explained Father Collin, "based deep in the mountains of Pakistan, close to the Afghan border. They have been in existence beyond memory. To this day, it has many devoted followers. Just as a priest of the Catholic Church can act *in persona Christi*, Lilith can act as the persona of the devil, creating demonic offspring, producing psychic gifts in bloodlines, even giving literal birth to monsters."

"Please, you two are jumping all over the place. What does any of this have to do with Balgair and the Templars?" asked Cori.

"And right you are to rein us in," said Father Collin. "In 1 Samuel 28, Saul goes to a witch, contrary to God's command, to learn of his fate. The Bible tells us that he went to the witch of Endor and that she raised Samuel's spirit. For all his trouble, Saul did not receive good news. Nevertheless, it is believed by many who follow Satan that the witch of Endor was possessed by the demon Lilith, briefly taking human form. Not long after her meeting with Saul, she was beheaded, but her followers rescued the head, and it was taken to Jerusalem. The head was one of the artifacts the Templars found, encased in a jeweled casket, and took it back to France. Balgair, through his study of the scrolls, realized whose head it was and that an extremely powerful talisman had fallen into his lap. When the time came to escape, we believe that he took a hefty amount of gold along with the head and the scrolls containing grimoires."

"So that's what you're here to find," said MacBridan. "You're not interested in the gold. You're after the head and the scrolls."

"Precisely, and we're not the only ones," said Father Collin. "No one knows where Balgair built his crypt or what became of his treasure. Over the centuries, many have searched. We're pretty certain that Balgair built his crypt somewhere on the family grounds, but we've no idea where. When the villagers rose up in defense against the atrocities he and his wife were committing, they were both quickly captured. His wife was immediately taken out and burned at the stake, cursing her executioners and the MacKinnon clan. The villagers then went to great lengths to destroy the evil in Balgair, burying him alive in unhallowed ground. His retainers rescued him, but he was nearly gone and too weak to flee.

"Following his instructions, a hand-selected group of five retainers took him to his crypt where he'd already placed the gold, the scrolls, and most importantly, the head. Based on some writings the local priest recovered from the manor, we know that Balgair had also built a shrine to Lilith in the crypt where they actively worshiped her and their lord Satan. His five retainers took their position in the crypt and committed suicide in front of him. Already dying from his ordeal with the villagers, Balgair then committed suicide and lies in a coffin in the center of a pentagram. His five retainers lie in coffins at the five points, most probably following instructions from one of the grimoires he found in the scrolls. Balgair believed that even in death, this would give him tremendous power."

"Temporarily dismissing my utter skepticism toward all of this, how do you know what Balgair did?" asked Cori.

"A fair and reasonable question," said Father Collin. "Balgair was meticulous in keeping notes on all that he was doing and all that he had translated from the scrolls. He'd laid out a plan, even rehearsed it with his men, as to what they were to do in the event of his death. As I stated a moment ago, there was a local priest who came with the villagers, and he took charge of all of Balgair's papers that were found in the house. At that time, the priest was one of the very few people in the area who could read."

"Didn't his plan include taking his wife with him?" asked Cori.

"He wouldn't have needed her anymore," said MacBridan. "If trouble arose, she would be the perfect distraction for the villagers' wrath while he made his escape."

"Sounds like a great guy," said Cori. "That part, I can believe."

"The few retainers he left behind were put to the sword. He was a thoroughly evil man," said Father Collin. "Come, we best be getting back. It's getting late."

"So you've come to not only warn us about this fanatical sect, who also wants the artifacts, but to find them before they do," said MacBridan.

"These people are cruel and ruthless and usually leave a trail of death wherever they go. I suspect one of their most sadistic priests, a man named Kaseem, has been sent to retrieve the scrolls and the head. I seriously doubt he cares anything for any gold that may be there."

"The thieves that we're up against have been targeting one painting in particular. We're pretty sure that their leader is a woman named Talon. She is one of the top art thieves out there. What doesn't make any sense is that the painting they're after is all but worthless. It was painted by a member of the MacKinnon family a long time ago and has zero value in the art world. Could this tie into what you're looking for?" asked MacBridan.

"Kaseem has many resources, and it is very likely that he has information that we don't. I want Father Novak to examine this painting tomorrow."

"This guy must be something if you're this worried about him. Have you run into him before?" asked MacBridan.

"Once, and it cost the life of a very dear friend. I had just been ordained and didn't know all that I needed to know about Kaseem or his sect. Make no mistake, he is without mercy and is as cruel as he is effective, effective as a skilled human criminal and as a sorcerer. He may be able to raise certain demonic forces to his aid."

"Sure," said Cori, rolling her eyes. "Still, he's just one man. Does he work with a team?"

"We don't know if he has brought any other followers with him. In the past, he has typically recruited local thugs to do his dirty work. Mac, be careful. These people have absolutely no qualms when it comes to killing," said Father Collin.

"I appreciate the warning," said MacBridan, "and again, I'm very glad you're here."

"I have to confess," said Father Collin, "when I learned you were working with the MacKinnon family, I made sure that you weren't told I was coming. That was one reaction I didn't want to miss out on, and you did surprisingly well. Remind me never to play poker with you."

They were getting close to the house now. "Is Ubel here with you?" asked MacBridan.

"Yes, he's here. Considering who the players are, I thought he'd be very useful to have around." Ubel Obermann, definitely not a priest, was associated with Father Collin's order. Having narrowly escaped the police and death years ago, Ubel had been nursed back to health at a monastery in France. During the weeks he spent recuperating at the monastery, he'd supposedly turned his life around and now put his unique talents to work for the church.

MacBridan, however, doubted Ubel's true motives. Up until his miraculous conversion, Ubel had racked up a long criminal record, primarily killing for a living. MacBridan believed that professional killers lived without conscience or any level of moral code. It had been his experience that people like Ubel didn't change.

"When can we expect to see you tomorrow?" asked Cori.

"We've planned to arrive close to 8:00 a.m. I'd like to have a look around and then lay out a strategy with you on how we'll proceed."

"I trust that Father Novak knows everything you've shared with us," said MacBridan.

"Of course. You'll find that he's a very talented man in many ways. He's also a brother in my order. I have a great deal of affection for him. On the other hand, you'll find that Father Novak can be annoyingly clever at times."

"Then tomorrow, I'll bring you up to date on everything that's been going on here at the estate. There are one or two items I'd like to get your thoughts on," said MacBridan.

"That would be splendid," said Father Collin. He moved closer to Cori, placing his hand gently on her shoulder. "Our first meeting has been difficult, I understand. I also know how much first impressions can mean. Over the next few days, I'm sure we'll have the time to get to know each other much better, but for your own safekeeping, all I ask is that you keep an open mind. If it's any consolation, Mac and I first met under very trying times, and things happened so fast that neither of us had time for explanations."

Cori smiled at the priest and said, "I've heard nothing but good about you, Father, so I'm confident that we'll come to a meeting of the minds. However, for my own sanity, I'm praying you're wrong regarding the supernatural elements. If those things truly do exist, I'm not sure I'll be able to handle it."

Father Collin laughed, gently squeezing her shoulder. "Now you're beginning to understand why the Irish depend so much on their whiskey. It helps."

Chapter 18

Upon their return to the manor, Father Collin, Cori, and MacBridan joined the rest of the family in the study. Aunt Jean, accompanied by Faith, had retired for the evening a few minutes earlier. Lord MacKinnon offered Father Collin a nightcap, but he refused, explaining that he and Father Novak had an early morning and wanted to get settled into their rooms.

"I completely understand," said Lord MacKinnon. "As it turns out, I too have an early start. Something came up this afternoon that I must attend to. Unfortunately, I'm afraid that because of this, I'll have to be away for the next few days. In my absence, regarding the security here at the estate, Mr. MacBridan will be acting with my full authority." Wallace's head snapped around at this and glared at his father. To his credit, he didn't say anything in front of their guests.

Turning to Father Collin and Father Novak, Lord MacKinnon said, "Between MacBridan and the Hendersons, I'm confident that you'll be well taken care of. I do apologize for having to run off like this, but it is a rather urgent matter."

"There's no need for apologies," said Father Novak, "but I'm not sure who the Hendersons are."

Lord MacKinnon smiled at the older priest and said, "Fergus and Robena. You met them earlier this evening. They run the manor for me."

"Oh yes," said Father Novak, "of course. I'm afraid my memory isn't as sharp as it once was."

"And yet the trivia the man remembers can drive one to distraction." Father Collin chuckled. "Lord MacKinnon, thank you again for opening your lovely home to us."

Lord MacKinnon, Cori, and MacBridan walked with the two priests to the front door where they were met by Fergus. He helped Father Novak on with his coat, and they all bid good night. As they watched the two men leave, Lord MacKinnon turned and said, "May I have a word with you and Cori?"

"Certainly," said MacBridan. They followed him to the library where Cori was pleased to find a fire burning in the fireplace. She immediately went over and stood in front of it, still chilled from the night air.

"May I offer either of you some brandy?" asked Lord MacKinnon. "Nothing works better to warm one up after an evening walk around the grounds." Cori passed, but MacBridan gladly accepted.

"It was a little colder outside this evening than I expected," said MacBridan.

"It's the dampness, gets to you every time," said Lord MacKinnon. "You were gone for quite a while. I trust everything is in order?"

"Father Collin is a bit of a talker," said Cori. "I think he was pleased to have a fresh audience to discuss his work with. He has some very interesting ideas regarding the influence of culture and the art produced during the same period, which is why they are excited to be able to study your family's collection. I'm looking forward to spending more time with them."

"With all that has been going on, I nearly canceled their visit," said Lord MacKinnon. "But I didn't think they'd be in the way. In fact, I'm rather hoping that their presence will help to lighten the tension around here."

As Lord MacKinnon handed him his drink, MacBridan asked, "How long do you expect to be away?"

"That's why I asked you to join me," said Lord MacKinnon, walking over to an open briefcase sitting on the long table. "I'll be leaving for Paris first thing in the morning. Here are the numbers where I can be reached. Of course, you have my wireless number, but I don't expect you'll need it. I shouldn't be away for more than three or four days."

The door to the library burst open, and Wallace stormed into the room. His face and eyes were red from too much drink. He glared at his father and MacBridan, ignoring Cori. "What is the meaning of this?" demanded Wallace. MacBridan guessed that he was trying to sound menacing, but his words were slightly slurred.

Lord MacKinnon sighed and said, "As usual, you've had too much to drink. Whatever are you babbling about?"

"I'm talking about MacBridan acting with your full authority," said Wallace, nearly shouting at this father. "In your absence, estate matters come to me. He will act only when I give him the authority. No unknown hired hand from America is going to come in here and take that away from me."

"Don't you dare bark at me," growled Lord MacKinnon. "Look at you! You can't even manage your own sobriety much less the estate. I won't have this conversation again, especially now. When you decide to sober up and demonstrate some level of maturity, we'll see what responsibilities you can handle."

Wallace's face darkened, and he moved toward his father, both fists clenched. MacBridan quickly stepped in, placing himself between the two men. Wallace stopped, hate etched across his face. "You don't scare me," said Wallace, unconsciously backing up a step. "Get out of my way, or I'll knock you on your ass."

"You need to learn where your strengths are and where they're not," said MacBridan, his eyes locked on Wallace's.

"We are here at your father's request to protect the family and to manage the security of the estate until Marston can be replaced." His voice was low, his words measured, trying to get Wallace to calm down and not do something stupid. "It is what we do, and we're very good. It's also a skill set that you do not have. Learn to let others do what they're trained to do."

Lord MacKinnon came up and stood beside MacBridan. "You're making a fool of yourself. Now get out of here."

Some of the fight had gone out of Wallace, but the bitterness raged within him. Pointing at MacBridan, he said, "You think you're such a hotshot. Well, I got news for you. Your day's coming, I know, and it's sooner than you think." With that, Wallace turned and stomped out of the room, slamming the door as he went out.

"My apologies to both of you," said Lord MacKinnon, embarrassed by the incident. "I can only guess at what you must be thinking. Wallace does have his good qualities, but there have been problems. I'm afraid most of it is my fault. The boy has been too pampered, never really forced to take on responsibility, and now he's having trouble stepping up to being a man. There are so many things I should have done differently."

"I'm not so sure you're being fair to yourself," said MacBridan. "Each person determines their own path, and at some point, everyone has to take responsibility for their actions. I'm sure, in time, Wallace will find his way."

"From your lips to God's ear," muttered Lord MacKinnon.

Not wanting to prolong the moment, Cori left her spot by the fire and walked toward the two men. "I'm going to check the security arrangements on the room where we have the art stored and then turn in. It has been a full day. I'll see you upstairs, Mac." As she turned to leave, she looked at Lord MacKinnon. "Have a safe trip. We'll keep an eye on things here."

"Thank you," said Lord MacKinnon. He watched her leave and said, "She's a very remarkable woman. You're fortunate to have her as part of your team. Have the two of you worked together for very long?"

"Yes, for close to six years. She's one of the best."

"And most attractive."

"There's that too," said MacBridan, smiling at Lord MacKinnon. "Although if you were to listen to her and had never had the opportunity to meet her, you'd think she was one of the ugly duckling's siblings."

Lord MacKinnon chuckled at that. "So many women are that way. Well, I have a couple more things that I need to do this evening. Be sure to let me know if anything should happen."

"We most certainly will," said MacBridan. "There is one more item I wanted to ask you about. Since we arrived, we've been tied to the estate. It's time that we take more of a proactive approach, so tomorrow, I plan to go into the village. I wanted to get your opinion as to who would be good for me to talk with, someone who would know what's going on in the area, you know, the local gossip. I need to know if there's been anyone new hanging around, strangers in town, get the lowdown on people, especially those working at the estate. We don't believe our thieves have called it quits. By tapping into the pulse of the community, it could give us some insight that we otherwise wouldn't have." In light of all that Father Collin had just shared with them, this took on even more importance.

Lord MacKinnon turned his nose up at this. "I'm not sure I see how that sort of thing can be helpful. Personally, I have no time for gossipers."

"With all that's been going on, Marston's death, the sightings of the dark lord, you know that the village is alive with talk. I want to know who's listening, who's asking questions. The people we're after have to be somewhere, and I'm counting on the chance that someone has seen or heard more than they realize."

"I'm not sure that I'm the best one you should be asking," said Lord MacKinnon, closing up his briefcase. He stopped, thought for a couple of moments, and said, "If it were me, I'd talk with Shaw Gordon. He's a lowlander by birth, but otherwise a good man, been here most of his life. If there's one person in the whole village who'll have what you're looking for, it's him. He's the proprietor of a pub called The Hanging Man."

"Not too inviting of a name," commented MacBridan.

"On the contrary, the pub's been there for a long time and is quite popular with the locals. It's on the south side of the village and stands near the crossroads where the gallows used to be. There was a time when you could have your favorite ale and enjoy the spectacle of a good execution all at the same time. Things were different then. I still drop in occasionally. Shaw serves a good lunch."

"Sounds like he's exactly whom I want to talk to. I'll see you when you get back," said MacBridan. Leaving the library, MacBridan headed upstairs. Only then did he realize just how tired he was. Cori was only half right. It hadn't only been a full day; it had been a nonstop marathon since they'd arrived. Maybe he ought to change rooms with Cori tonight and let her play with the ghost.

Walking down the hall, MacBridan passed a maid he didn't recognize. "Good evening, sir," she said. The accent was different, and MacBridan couldn't place it. He began to wonder just how large the staff was.

"Good evening," said MacBridan and then spotted Cori leaving the room next to his where they'd stored the artwork.

She waited for him by her door. "How's Lord MacKinnon doing?"

"He's fine. Sadly, I think he's used to Wallace playing the part of the buffoon," said MacBridan as they went into her room. Cori had added some logs to the fire, and they both sat down in the wingback chairs facing it.

"The guy's a jerk. It was wrong of me, but I was kind of hoping he'd be dense enough to take a swing at you. Getting knocked down a couple of times would probably do him some good."

MacBridan smiled and said, "Now, what I have told you about beating up the clients. No matter how well intentioned, it just doesn't go over well."

"I'll try to keep that in mind, but I'm not making any promises. So what are our plans for tomorrow?"

"I'd like for you to stay close to Father Collin and Father Novak. One, for appearances sake, and two, if they do learn anything, I want us to know what it is. We already know that the painting by itself is virtually worthless, but if it is somehow connected to some missing treasure, then things would finally start to make sense."

"How could it be connected?" asked Cori. "Dr. Van Dych took that painting apart, and there's nothing there, no secret writing, nothing painted over, nothing hidden in the frame."

"Agreed, but there's still something we're missing. The sect that Father Collin described would certainly have the means to bankroll someone of Talon's ilk. Although I doubt it, the thefts could even be just a distraction. It sounds like the real goal is to find the treasure or, more likely, the artifacts."

"Why do you doubt that? Using the painting as a distraction certainly is plausible," said Cori.

"A couple of things. Father Collin told us that Kaseem usually hires local talent. That would have been far cheaper for him than bringing in someone as high-end as Talon and, frankly, would have achieved exactly the same thing were it all just a ploy to get us to look the other way. Also, the painting they've targeted is what bothers me the most."

"Why?"

"If it truly was meant to be a distraction, I believe they would have gone after one of the more valuable pieces. That would have made us, the police, and especially Lloyd's of London far more vigilant on guarding the art. They've targeted some minor family heirloom. At this point, besides you and me, who really cares if that particular painting is stolen or not?"

"I see your point, but I still can't figure out how that painting ties in to anything," said Cori.

"Neither do I, but that's what I'm betting on. There's no other reason to go after it. I'm afraid that we're still desperately light on facts and strong on speculation."

"Okay, I'll stay close and continue to monitor the security here at the estate. What are your plans?" asked Cori.

"Lord MacKinnon told me of a pub in town called The Hanging Man."

"Charming."

"I thought so," said MacBridan. "The proprietor is a man named Shaw Gordon. I plan to start with him and see what the locals are saying. Hopefully, we'll get a lead or two on either the thieves or this Kaseem guy."

"Watch your back. Marston's death makes it pretty clear how far they're willing to go. If Kaseem is behind this, he may decide to take a run at you while you're away from the estate."

"That wouldn't be all bad. I would like to get my hands on one of them."

"There's something else I want to talk to you about," said Cori. "I do like Father Collin. He seems to be as kind and as sharp as you described him, and I know that he helped you on a previous case."

"But..."

"But I can't help believing that he's perhaps a little bit off upstairs, black magic, possession, witches. I'm sorry, but I stopped believing in that stuff when I was twelve. And furthermore, why didn't you say anything? I kept waiting for you to either burst out laughing or help me reel him back in."

"Cori, I've had some experiences that no matter how hard I try, I can't explain. Father Collin was with me for some of those.

Several weeks after those incidents, he and I talked and even now, even though I was there and saw everything with my own eyes, I still don't know what to think."

"Are you telling me that you believe all these?"

"No, I'm not. Let me ask you a couple of questions. What was it that confronted me in my room in the middle of the night and had enough strength to splinter the door? What did we experience down in the crypt earlier today?"

"I don't know, but despite my earlier thoughts, in the light of day I'm not convinced that it was anything supernatural."

"Exactly, we don't know. All I'm saying is that based on what I've been through, I realize there are things out there. Some of my absolutes may not be so certain after all. So until I do fully understand, I try keeping an open mind."

Cori sat quietly for a few moments, staring into the fire. "What I felt at the chapel was a level of fear I didn't think was possible. It's crazy, but I could feel something was there, something terrible that we had to escape from. As hard as I've tried, I can't get it out of my mind. I can't explain what happened, but at the same time, I can't let myself believe that it is something as bizarre as what we've talked about. That kind of thing leads to madness."

MacBridan reached over and held her hand. "Look, before you have Father Collin and me both committed, let's give it a little time. In all probability, we're going to find that it's someone trying to scare us off, just like we thought. All I ask is that you listen to Father Collin. He is very knowledgeable on things I've never heard of. He's a great ally, and we can't dismiss his ideas on things just because we don't believe them to be possible. I made that mistake before, and it nearly got me killed."

"I remember, that was a bad time, and too many people died," said Cori. "All right, but I'm warning you. If it turns out that he's right, I'm on the first plane out of here."

Chapter 19

"Sir, Father Collin and Father Novak," said Fergus, announcing their arrival to MacBridan. The two priests entered the dining room, thanking Fergus for his help. Fergus had already taken their overcoats, and MacBridan noticed that Father Novak was wearing a thick sweater in addition to his jacket. MacBridan, Cori, and Faith were already eating from a buffet that included kippers, oatcakes, sliced sausage, and fried bread as the two priests joined them.

"Good morning," said Faith, dressed in a rather snug-fitting light blue sweat suit. "We have a full breakfast buffet already set out. What can we get you?"

"Thank you, but I believe I'll just have some tea," said Father Collin. "Brother Novak?"

"I'll have some tea as well," answered Father Novak, "with honey and cinnamon if it's not too much trouble."

As Fergus was getting their tea, Father Collin said, "We had a bite to eat in the village before coming out, but thank you for offering."

"I trust your rooms are comfortable?" asked Cori.

"Oh yes, they are splendid," said Father Collin. "Father Novak and I are well rested and rearing to go."

"Cori will show you where we have the art stored," said MacBridan. "In light of the recent attempts, we've been keeping the collection under lock and key. We've also locked up the other paintings done by the same ancestor whose painting the thieves have targeted. The light's not the best in that room, but we can move any pieces you want to examine to the library."

"You won't be joining us?" asked Father Collin.

"I have a couple of errands that I need to take care of in town," said MacBridan. As he was talking, Wallace and Barclay entered the dining room.

"Good morning," said Barclay. "Mr. MacBridan, I couldn't help but overhear. I'll be leaving for the village in a few minutes and would be glad to give you a lift."

"I was going to ask Fergus, but if it's no trouble, I'll take you up on that," said MacBridan. Wallace didn't say anything to anyone. He quietly got something to eat and sat down at the far end of the table. His eyes were bloodshot, and his face looked tired.

"I'm sure we'll see you when you get back," said Father Collin. "Perhaps later in the day either you or Cori could show me where the chapel is. I've read so much about it."

Cori and MacBridan glanced at each other, and both remarkably managed to smile. "I'm sure one of us will be available," said MacBridan. "I know Cori especially enjoyed our visit there yesterday and is anxious to go back again." Although she continued to smile, the look Cori gave to MacBridan was unmistakable.

The Hanging Man was about as quaint as could be, and MacBridan was confident that its picture graced the pages of several travel guides with the purpose of bringing tourists to Abbotsbury. The building looked very old, largely made of stone, with what appeared to be wooden shingles on the steep-sloping roof. The shingles were deeply weathered, many covered with moss, all adding to the building's charm.

MacBridan entered through the broad front door at the corner at the building. Once inside, he followed a small walkway of sorts against the right side of the pub. The left wall of the walkway was only waist high, enabling him to see the many tables in the main dining room. At the end of the walkway, one could either veer to the left and find a table or go directly to the bar, which stretched across the back of the pub. As best as he could tell, he was alone.

The dining room was filled with heavy wooden tables, some with chairs, others with benches. The ceiling was off-white in color, supported by several thick wooden beams running from one end of the pub to the other blackened by time. The front of the pub had four large windows, which allowed a surprising amount of light; each window made up of several small, diamond-shaped panes of glass. MacBridan guessed that many of the panes were old as they offered a mildly distorted view, common in old glass. A fireplace big enough to sit in graced the far side of the dining room, and a fire was already burning.

The bar itself was a work of art, highly polished with each of the lower panels carved with scenes of men hunting boar and deer. Shelves of steins lined the wall behind the bar along with multiple bottles of liquor. MacBridan leaned against it just as a man emerged from a doorway behind the bar.

"Afraid we're not quite open yet, but we will be in about thirty minutes," said the man. "You're welcome to take a seat and wait here if you like." Well into his sixties, the man was of average height and thick in build. His hair was dark, as were his eyes, and he had long sideburns connecting to his thick, full mustache. The sideburns and the mustache were sprinkled with gray, giving the man a very distinguished look. MacBridan had to listen to him carefully as his brogue was as thick as any he'd encountered since their arrival.

"I'm guessing that you're Shaw Gordon. My name's James MacBridan."

"James MacBridan, now why does that name sound familiar," said Shaw, setting up a tray of clean glasses at one end of the bar. "Ah yes, now I recall. You're one of the Americans staying at the manor. Been a bit of excitement there lately, I should say, what with Marston dying and that bloody ghost at the heart of it all. Can't say I'd be comfortable lying my head down to rest there."

MacBridan's smile grew larger. "Lord MacKinnon was right. You are the man I want to talk to."

"Lord MacKinnon? Good man, don't see him that often, but then, he's a busy gentleman. I understand that. Now what is it that Lord MacKinnon said that would make you want to talk with me?"

"Just yesterday, I asked him who in the village would be the keenest observer, the most knowledgeable person regarding the local area. Without a moment's hesitation, he recommended you, was quite emphatic about it. Also said that you serve a good lunch," said MacBridan.

"Well, that's awfully nice of him, awfully nice," said Shaw, coming out from behind the bar. Picking up a rag, he moved into the dining room and began to wipe down tables. "I keep my eyes open. In this business, you have to. You being a detective of sorts, you know what I'm talking about. We share that, you and I, keeping our ear to the ground, watching people, and picking up on things. What would you like to talk about?"

"Up until today, I haven't had the opportunity to come into the village and look around. In light of all that's happened, I thought it would be a good idea to get some local insight from someone such as you," said MacBridan. "Mr. Gordon this—"

"Call me Shaw."

"Of course, Shaw. Now all that we discuss must remain confidential. I trust we can keep this conversation between us?"

"You can ask my old friend Fergus at the manor or anyone here in the village, my word is my bond," answered Shaw.

"Good, I appreciate that," said MacBridan, smiling to himself. Despite Shaw's strong assurance of his absolute discretion, he was pretty certain that everything they said would soon become the main dish served at the pub to any who would listen. In truth, it was exactly what he was counting on. While his plan was to get as much information out of the pub keeper as he could, getting misinformation out across the countryside wouldn't hurt either. "In the past few weeks, have you noticed any new arrivals here in Abbotsbury? Anyone who seemed out of place or perhaps asked a lot of questions, overly interested regarding the MacKinnon estate?"

Shaw stopped and thought about that for a moment. "This sounds like it's going to be thirsty work. If you like, I'd be happy to pour you a pint."

"Too early for me, but if you have any coffee, I'd like that even more."

Shaw chuckled as he returned to the bar. "Americans and my wife, you all love your coffee. She's not American, mind you, but she watches a great deal of American television, and I think that's where she gets it. For my peace of mind, she drinks a little too much of it, but there's certainly no telling her, if you know what I mean," he said, winking at MacBridan. Shaw looked under the bar, frowned, then pulled down a large, heavy stein off the shelf. "Haven't brought the tea and coffee mugs out yet, so I'll pour you a tall one in this. Would you like milk or sugar?"

"No, thank you," said MacBridan, picking up the steaming drink. "Black is just fine."

Shaw went back into the dining room and continued to clean. "Now that I think about it, I can't say that anyone in particular stands out. Past few days, it's been mostly my regulars. Many of the staff from the manor comes in here now and then, but no one new that I've seen."

"What about the MacKinnons? Do you see much of them?"

"Now and then." He paused for a moment, unsure of what he should say. "I don't want to sound like a whining, gossipy old woman, especially in light of Lord MacKinnon's kind words, but as much as I like and respect the family, I don't have anything good to say about that son of his. The boy is worthless. He drinks too much, tries to throw his weight around, and generally causes problems. He knows that if he gets into any trouble, his dad will pull him out of it. It's a bloody shame actually. I mean, he's nothing like his father, and his behavior reflects badly on the whole family."

"Does he get into trouble often?" asked MacBridan.

"Not like he used to. He's just a loud-mouthed moron with a very high opinion of himself. For a while, he hung around with the wrong crowd. If it weren't for the way people respect Lord MacKinnon and all that he's done for people around here, someone would knocked that boy's head off a long time ago."

"What about the rest of the family?"

"The two nephews are good lads. They work hard and are like most people, you know, down to earth, never putting on airs. Kerr likes to throw darts, but frankly, he's a miserable player. It's not unusual for him to be paying for a round of drinks due to his losses." Shaw stopped his cleaning, backed up a step, and looked out the window. He squinted to get a better look and said, "Now there's a prime example for you of the very kind of lowlives I was referring to. Actually, been a while since this one's been around here."

MacBridan got up and joined him at the window. "Is that someone Wallace used to hang around with?"

"No," grunted Shaw. "That one's too mean for Wallace, but he's the same worthless sort. That's Carl Meyer, and he's a mean one, picks on those weaker than himself and is always looking to start trouble. And he's never alone, always has one or two blokes backing him up. One-on-one, he's a bloody coward.

Comes from bad stock, he does. Every constable around here knows Carl."

"Bad stock?" asked MacBridan.

"His dad came over from Germany not too long after the war, Gerhard Meyer. For a time, there was suspicion that Gerhard was a Nazi that his father was Kurt Meyer of the SS. But no one could prove anything, and what was known was mostly rumor. Eight years later, he married a girl from Glasgow and brought her home with him to the Highlands. Their only son, Carl, came late in their marriage. Naming the boy Carl got the rumors going again. Kurt Meyer was infamous as an SS officer, known for his cruelty and, unfortunately for the boy, still well remembered."

"And Carl Meyer and Kurt Meyer sounded too close for comfort for everyone," suggested MacBridan.

"The locals thought that it was a slap in the face naming the boy after such a monster of a man. Whether the people were right or wrong about his heritage, the boy was in and out of trouble almost from the day he was born."

MacBridan looked at the man standing across and down the street from the pub. He looked tall, six one or two, and MacBridan guessed that he weighed in at around 260 pounds. Wearing an army jacket and boots, he looked to be in his late thirties with dark hair, which was deeply receding. There were two other men with him similarly dressed, wearing work clothes as if they'd just come off of a construction site. They were standing at a roundabout and appeared to be waiting on someone. "Does he live here in Abbotsbury?"

"Heavens no, I believe he lives close to Achnasheen. He's definitely someone you don't want to turn your back on. The police have arrested him a few times for assault, and there was a story last year about him molesting a young boy. DS Wetmoore went after him as hard as he could but couldn't make it stick. Story is the police were all over it, but he and his gang threatened the mom, she's wasn't married at the time, and the charges were dropped. He's pure scum."

"And you say Wallace used to hang out with people like that?"

"At heart, Wallace has no backbone and never really carries through on anything. First sign of real trouble, and he runs, usually to daddy if it's real bad. Unfortunately, I can't say the same for Laine Henderson."

"Any relation to the Hendersons who work at the manor?"

"He's their son. He and Wallace knew each other and hung around together for a time, but Laine wasn't as lucky as Wallace, or at least not as protected. He stole things, started as a child, and eventually was sent to prison for three robberies. My heart went out to Fergus and Robena. It's always toughest on the parents, I'm sure, but all the same his being sent to prison was good riddance if you ask me."

By this time, two other men had joined Carl. They talked for a moment, and Carl motioned toward the pub, but they stayed where they were. He was clearly the leader. Carl kept checking his watch every few seconds.

Shaw walked back to the window and looked out. "I don't like the looks of that. I wonder what they're doing."

No sooner had he asked when a black Mercedes with heavily tinted windows pulled up. The driver's window went down, but from his position inside the pub, MacBridan could not see who was driving. Meyer leaned over to talk to the driver, and the other men crowded around. They talked for a couple of minutes, and then the car drove off.

Meyer spoke briefly with his men, slapping one of them on the back in a good-natured way, and together they headed toward the pub. Shaw looked at MacBridan. All of the color had left his face. "This isn't good. Do you think it might be you they're coming for?"

"They got their instructions from whomever was driving that car, which makes them the hired help. If they are coming to talk with me, I'd like to know who sent them."

"Mr. MacBridan," said Shaw, his voice tinged with panic, "Carl's not a big talker, doesn't have the brains for it. If it's you they're after, this will get pretty rough. Come with me, quickly."

Shaw rapidly made his way through the dining area and went back behind the bar. As he started to go through the door he'd emerged from earlier, he glanced back over his shoulder to find that MacBridan wasn't with him. MacBridan was standing back at the bar with his coffee.

"Are you not coming, man?"

"If I leave, I won't find out what he wants or who sent him. Who knows? Perhaps they just want to buy me a drink and welcome me to the village."

"This is no time for jokes," said Shaw. He wanted to get out of there, but he wasn't the kind of man to abandon a guest, no matter how crazy he might be acting.

"Fill this up with a little more of that coffee, and then you'd better leave. If I am their quarry, I don't want to get you mixed up in this," said MacBridan. "It's okay. I do this for a living."

Shaw hesitated for a moment and then did as he asked, his hand visibly shaking as he topped off MacBridan's stein with the hot coffee. "I'm going for help," he said and dashed out the back.

MacBridan stood at the center of the bar. Leaning against it, he waited for Meyer to come in. He didn't have to wait long. The front door burst open, and Carl and his men poured into the pub.

Being up close didn't help Carl at all from a first impression standpoint. His face was very thin, his features sharp and narrow, almost birdlike. As he strode down the walkway, his eyes honed in on MacBridan. His smile was crooked, favoring one side of his face, his expression triumphal. His prey was cornered.

Carl swaggered into the dining room and stopped about ten feet in front of MacBridan along with one of his men. The man with him was a few inches shorter than Carl and stood a step behind. Mimicking his leader, he coldly smiled at MacBridan. He wore an overcoat that was too big for him, and it gave him an off-balanced look. His teeth had to have been the most crooked set of molars MacBridan had ever seen. *No*, MacBridan thought, *not true.* He remembered having seen a barracuda once with teeth that had been even more crooked, but it was close.

The tallest of Carl's troops stopped at the end of the walkway and leaned against the wall, effectively blocking the way out. MacBridan estimated his weight to be close to Carl's, but unlike Carl, he looked to be in pretty good shape. The man's conservative dress reminded MacBridan of some of the finance guys back in New York, but there was something about the eyes, a manic sort of expression that gave an edge to his demeanor.

The other two men walked into the bar area and took up positions on either side of MacBridan, both of them leaving about eight feet of space between themselves and the trapped man. The one to MacBridan's left was of average height and heavily tattooed, the most prominent being a spider's web covering most of his throat. MacBridan guessed that these were to draw the focus away from his rapidly thinning hair. This guy was clearly employing the comb over.

The man to his right was the smallest of the five but looked the worst, with an eye patch over is right eye, his face badly scarred. But his most intimidating feature was his body odor. The guy smelled like he'd slept in a septic tank partially filled with rotting seafood.

MacBridan calmly faced Carl, the small of his back resting against the bar. His overall stance was casual, holding his coffee in his right hand. His eyes never left Carl's. If MacBridan was worried about being outnumbered, it didn't show. His expression was almost one of mild amusement, like someone watching a pet do a trick.

"You smell that, lads?" asked Carl, his voice too loud, clearly enjoying being center stage. "That's what a queer from America smells like." His men laughed at this, joining in on Carl's fun. "He's a real man's man, if you know what I mean." They waited for MacBridan to respond, but instead, he simply stood there, sipping his coffee.

"You know, Carl," said tattooed throat, "I think the big man's too scared to say anything."

"I think you're right," said Carl. "The big American has an even bigger yellow stripe down his back. Speaking of yellow, I just hope he doesn't wet himself. He'd smell worse than he already does." Once again, laughter filled the pub as the men laughed at their leader's amazing wit.

A small smile played at MacBridan's lips. Looking at Carl, he said, "My mother, you forgot about my mother."

The room went totally silent. Carl's men glanced at one another, then at Carl, not sure what to do. The crooked smile he'd been sporting when he entered the pub left his face, and Carl seemed truly baffled. "What?" he said, looking at MacBridan as if he'd been speaking Greek.

MacBridan, who was still leaning against the bar, mildly adjusted his stance, putting most of his weight on his right leg. He smiled at Carl and said, "I didn't mean to interrupt. I was just trying to be helpful."

"Helpful with what?" answered Carl, nearly yelling.

"You're trying to come across as a real bad guy, tough, scary, that sort of thing," said MacBridan. "With all of the insults you're throwing at me, my guess is that you're trying to provoke me into doing something. I was just trying to help you by letting you know that you'd forgotten to say anything bad about my mother. I mean, let's face it, nobody backs away from an insult against their mother. Am I right?"

Carl slowly shook his head as if he couldn't believe what he was hearing. "MacBridan, you're an arrogant ass. I'm going to enjoy cutting you up into little pieces."

MacBridan looked around at Carl's men. "Now there's no need to be embarrassed in front of the boys. I'm pretty sure it's not the first time they've seen you screw up. Look, if you want to start over, it's okay with me."

Rage coursed through Carl's body. He clenched his fists so tightly that the white around the knuckles was visible. His face had turned red, and just as he started to move toward MacBridan, the door to the pub opened, and Father Collin walked in, closely followed by Ubel. "God bless all here," he said loudly, pushing his way past the tall man and went up to the bar, standing between MacBridan and tattooed throat.

Ubel stopped by the tall man, placing himself between him and the door. He lightly leaned against the wall and began to stare at the man, his face neutral of all expression. Ubel's pale, piercing blue eyes were cold, his stare penetrating, which was enough to unnerve most men. Standing a couple of inches over six feet, Ubel had a trim, athletic build. Of Slavish heritage, his pale features were accented by his long ash-blond hair that he wore in a short ponytail.

"The pub's closed, Father," said Carl, barely controlling his temper. "Time for you to leave."

"Nonsense," said Father Collin, smiling broadly. "The Hanging Man is always open at this time of day, and I'm in need of refreshment. Barkeep!" said Father Collin, leaning over the bar and looking to see if someone was there.

"I don't know if you're daft or just hard of hearing, but I'm telling you to get out. This is a private matter. Do you understand?" said Carl, spitting his words out.

Father Collin looked at MacBridan then turned around and scanned the faces of the other men in the pub. "Son, it's never a good idea to come between a man and his drink, especially an Irishman. Why don't you join me in a pint?"

"Irish," said Carl, slowly nodding his head, "never cared much for the Irish. This is going to be fun." With that, he motioned to the man standing with him a signal that had obviously been prearranged. The man instantly rushed toward MacBridan. The stein MacBridan was holding was still nearly full of steaming, hot coffee, and he flung it into the man's face. Screaming, the man stopped, grabbing his face with both hands.

In one fluid motion, MacBridan then brought the stein around in a hard, arcing swing to the right. The heavy mug smashed into the side of the scarred man's head, as he too rushed in toward MacBridan. The man didn't make a sound. Staggering first into the bar, he crumpled to the floor.

Tattooed man charged at MacBridan from the other side. MacBridan's back was to him and didn't see him coming. Father Collin reached out and grabbed the front of tattooed man's jacket with both hands. Using the man's own momentum, he spun him into the bar. Stunned by the impact, he staggered back, and Father Collin caught him with a left cross, putting him down.

MacBridan brought his focus back to the man he'd thrown the coffee at. Stepping in close, he delivered a hard right jab into the man's hands, which were still holding his face. The blow landed squarely just below the man's nose, sending him backward over one of the tables.

In all the commotion, the tall man had not dared to take his eyes off Ubel. He couldn't. Ubel's eyes bore into him. Then a trace of a smile suddenly appeared on Ubel's expressionless features, his face taking on an almost demonic look. In an effort to escape, the tall man started to take a step back away from Ubel, but it was too late. Ubel lashed out, driving the knuckles of his right hand into the side of the man's neck. It was a vicious blow and delivered so quickly that the tall man didn't even see it coming. As the man's knees started to fold, Ubel landed a left upper cut on his chin, sending him flying into the bar area.

The entire fight was over in mere seconds.

Carl couldn't believe his eyes and desperately looked for a way out. In the batting of an eye, things had taken a dreadful turn, and he suddenly found himself very much alone. The inside of the pub was absolutely quiet.

MacBridan advanced on Carl. "Now that that's over, it's time for us to talk."

Carl's face paled, and he tried to hold MacBridan off but to no avail. MacBridan gripped his jacket by the collar, drug him across the floor, and easily pinned him against the wall next to the fireplace. Father Collin stayed at the bar, keeping watch over Carl's fallen comrades while Ubel joined MacBridan standing just to his left.

"Please, we weren't going to hurt you. We were just supposed to push you around a little, scare you. That's all," said Carl, his voice cracking in fear, his eyes darting back and forth between the two men.

MacBridan slapped him hard across the face with an open hand. "You don't even lie well. Now listen to me closely. For the first time in your ill-begotten life, you're going to tell the truth. Who sent you, and what exactly were your instructions?"

"I don't know who the ugly Paki was," stammered Carl. "Really. It's like I told you. He just wanted us to push you around a little and tell you to leave Abbotsbury."

MacBridan slapped him again. "Carl, you really don't have any comprehension just how far out of your league you are. Lie to me one more time, and this is going to become very unpleasant."

A loud clicking sound broke the silence, and a knife appeared in Ubel's hand, its six-inch blade long and narrow. "You're too soft, MacBridan. Give him to me. He'll talk. I promise."

Carl's eyes bulged out looking at the knife. "No, please," he begged on the verge of tears. "I've told you what I know."

"Last chance. Who hired you, and what were you supposed to do?" repeated MacBridan. Carl's legs were no longer doing their job, and MacBridan found that he was holding the man up.

"I'm not real clear on his name, I swear. It's odd sounding. He's a foreigner, hard to understand with dark skin, black eyes. He told me that he'd pay us a lot of money to take care of you real good."

"When do you get your money?" asked MacBridan.

"I don't know. He gave me a little of it already and said if we did this right, he'd pay us the rest and have another job waiting for us."

"Where do you go to collect?" pressed MacBridan.

"I don't know, really. Somehow he got my cell number, I think from a guy I worked for before. Anyway, he called me yesterday, told me what he needed, and said he'd call, to be ready at any time. This morning, I got a call telling me to be at the roundabout down from The Hanging Man in thirty minutes. I barely made it. He showed up, gave me your name, and you know the rest."

MacBridan gave an exasperated sigh. "The money, Carl, how do you get the rest of your money?"

"He's to call me today and tell me where to meet him. I won't know until then."

Ubel stepped in closer. "He's lying. My turn."

Tears rolled down Carl's face. "No! I swear to you, I'm not lying."

"Here's what you're going to do, Carl. The man's name who hired you is Kaseem. He's not a nice person. When he calls, you let him know that you not only failed miserably, but that I'm coming after him. You got that?" MacBridan raised Carl up and pulled him in closer. "And if I ever see you again, I will turn you over to my friend."

MacBridan released Carl and shoved him toward the door. Carl looked around, not sure of what might be coming next. "Run, son, run," said Father Collin, his voice almost a whisper. Carl wasted no time, leaping over one of his men and running out the door. In the distance, police sirens filled the air.

"We need to leave," said Father Collin. "Are you going to wait for the police?"

"Yes, I want to let Wetmoore know what's going on. Getting his help in finding Kaseem will help to put more pressure on him. By the way, how did you two know where I was?"

Father Collin smiled at MacBridan. "It was the luck of the Irish as well as Ubel's sharp eyes. We'll catch up at the manor. We have things to discuss."

MacBridan looked at Ubel. "All things considered, never thought the day would come when I'd be happy to see you. Thank you."

Ubel nodded at MacBridan. He and Father Collin quickly left out the back. MacBridan sat down on one of the bar stools and looked around the pub. Kaseem had made his first direct run at him and had depended too much on amateurs. Kaseem would not make that mistake again. Although today's failure wouldn't stop him, it would make things more difficult for him. At that, MacBridan leaned back and smiled.

The doors to The Hanging Man swung open, and Wetmoore, followed by two burly officers, rushed in. They were closely followed by Shaw. Each of the officers held batons. They surveyed the damage, looked at the four men lying on the floor, and then looked at MacBridan, comfortably sitting at the bar.

MacBridan smiled at Shaw and said, "I need to apologize. I'm afraid I broke that stein you gave me."

Chapter 20

MacBridan spent the next couple of hours with DS Wetmoore, providing him a slightly altered version of the truth regarding all that had taken place at The Hanging Man. Meyer's men kept shouting that MacBridan was lying, that he had been joined by two other men just before the fight started, and that they had been the ones defending themselves. Shaw Gordon broke the tie, loudly and adamantly professing that when Meyer and his gang headed toward the pub, MacBridan not only forced him to leave but was definitely quite alone. All four men were charged and locked up, the credibility factor going to Shaw and MacBridan.

"Of course, you know you'll never be able to buy a drink in The Hanging Man from now on," said Wetmoore as he drove MacBridan back to the estate. "You are, or soon will be, the village's new hero."

"Good to be appreciated in one's own time," quipped MacBridan, trying to find a comfortable position for his large frame in the cramped squad car. "Shaw's a good man. He tried his best to get me out of there and was reluctant to leave me."

"The vast majority of the people in Abbotsbury feel the same way as Shaw does about Meyer and his cronies. Come to think of it, I can't say I've ever met anyone who actually likes him. Yet he always seems to weasel out of things. This time, things are different, and we're all anxious to track him down.

We'll finally be able to put him behind bars where he belongs. Actually, I'm more than a little disappointed you let him go."

"I had to. The man behind Marston's murder, as well as the attempted thefts, is the same man who sent Meyer to get me out of the way. My little altercation confirms for us that he's still in the area and hasn't given up," said MacBridan.

"May I remind you that Marston's death has not yet been ruled a homicide," corrected Wetmoore.

MacBridan looked at Wetmoore. "If Cori and I are right about who this guy is, you'll need to watch your back as well. It's our understanding he won't hesitate to kill anyone, police included, if it will get him what he's after."

"And you have a credible secret source giving you the information as to who this person is."

"The source is a man I've worked with before. He's unlike many of the sources you or I would cultivate. He's actually one of the good guys and went to some length to get hold of me. He wanted to warn me, to let me know that he'd received information about who is behind all of this. I have no reason to doubt him."

"Kaseem," confirmed Wetmoore.

"Yes," confirmed MacBridan.

"Does Kaseem have a last name?"

"All I've been given is Kaseem," said MacBridan, "and we're not sure he's working alone. Kaseem made an error in judgment today using Meyer for his wet work, but he won't make that mistake again. It's important to note that if he does have his men with him, they won't go down near as easy as Meyer did. Like Kaseem, they're pros, and this is not their first rodeo. I can't encourage you enough to have your officers use extreme caution if they do find him."

Wetmoore slowed down to turn into the estate, the security men waving them through. "It still doesn't make any sense that this guy, whoever he is, would target a painting that has so little market value."

"From the start, there's been a big piece that we keep missing, and I'm still not clear where to look. That said, Kaseem wants that painting for some reason, and he's going to great lengths to get it. With Meyer failing to take me out of the picture, I'm hoping it will flush Kaseem out into the open."

"Be careful what you wish for," said Wetmoore. "Not to change the subject, but I understand there are two additional guests visiting the manor but staying in the village."

"Two priests," answered MacBridan, "from the Vatican. Art history experts sent to study the MacKinnon's extensive collection, which is what Lord MacKinnon told me. Apparently their visit had been arranged weeks ago."

"Perhaps you should let them have a go at that painting."

"Cori suggested just that, but I'm not holding my breath. We had the canvas, the frame, every part of that painting thoroughly examined before we set sail."

The gravel on the lane leading to the manor crunched as Wetmoore brought the car to a halt. "I'm still amazed at how well you did against five men. I know you're a big guy and obviously in good shape, but that's still an almost impossible turn of events. You're sure there isn't anything else I should know?"

MacBridan smiled at Wetmoore as he climbed out of the car. "If I wasn't such a hard-nosed, uncaring ruffian, my feelings would be hurt by your complete lack of confidence in my abilities. Clearly you doubt my athletic prowess."

"What I doubt is that you're telling me the whole truth. Having someone like Kaseem lurking about is bad enough, and as much as I appreciate the help you're giving the MacKinnons, I won't allow you or anyone else to go rogue cowboy on me. Does the American reference make what I'm saying clear for you?"

"Crystal," said MacBridan. "I'm just pitching in and doing my small part to help local law enforcement."

"Don't start flexing for me, MacBridan. It won't get you anywhere. Just know that I'm still not buying into all of this, but for the time being, the end result more than makes up for it. When we do catch up with your new friend Carl, it'll be interesting to see what he has to say."

"He and his friends are used to outnumbering their victims and bullying them around. Having seen their performance this morning firsthand, I'm pretty sure they've never dealt with a pro before. Let's just say that they were unprepared. Thanks for the ride back."

"I'll be in touch," said Wetmoore. "You need any help, you let me know. We'll get here as fast as we can."

Wetmoore pulled away, and MacBridan turned to find Fergus waiting for him at the door. "Ms. Hopkins asked that I let you know that she is with the two priests in the library."

"Thank you Fergus."

"Is there anything I can get for you, sir?"

"I'm good, thank you."

"Very well, sir, lunch will be served at one."

MacBridan went straight to the library. As he entered, he saw that all five of the paintings done by the MacKinnon ancestor had been brought down from the storage room and were lined up near the windows where the light was the best. Father Novak, sitting in a chair, was examining one of them with a magnifying glass while Cori and Father Collin looked on.

"Glad to see you're still in one piece," said Cori. "Father Collin filled us in on what happened."

"How did it go with the police?" asked Father Collin.

MacBridan joined them by the windows, took off his jacket, and sat down in one of the overstuffed chairs. "I didn't like having to lie to Wetmoore, but I'm pleased to report that he saw through it and doesn't completely believe my story. In fact, he's confident that I'm holding something out on him. It's not like he's mad or anything. I'd say it's more his being curious. Anyway, as to the rest of the police, they're ecstatic that they have those four goons locked up and a solid reason to go collect Meyer."

"They better find him in a hurry if they want him alive," said Father Collin. "Kaseem does not tolerate failure very well."

"So Wetmoore didn't believe that you accomplished holding off five thugs all on your own," teased Cori, smiling at MacBridan. "Smart man, I'm starting to like him more and more."

MacBridan leaned back in his chair. "It also didn't help any that the four men they arrested kept contradicting my story. Had it not been for Shaw Gordon's sworn statement that I was alone, I might still be there."

"Did any of them mention that one of your guardian angels happened to be a priest?" asked Father Collin.

"Your being a priest didn't seem to have registered with them, but then they didn't impress me as the church-going type," said MacBridan. "For whatever reason, they never brought that up, and it's a good thing they didn't. Wetmoore knows you're here. He even asked about you and Father Novak. Had one of them blurted that out, I'm positive Wetmoore would have connected the dots."

"I'm sure he would have," agreed Cori.

"Not to sound ungrateful, but how did you know where I was and that I was in need of assistance?"

"You'll need to thank Ubel for that," said Father Collin. "He'd stayed in town to continue working on a couple of items for me. Not too long after you left the estate, he called to let me know that he'd spotted one of Kaseem's men, a giant of a man named Mukhtar. Ubel didn't know what he was up to but found him sitting in a car, not too far from The Hanging Man, watching the pub. Around the bend from where Mukhtar was parked, Ubel also noticed some men gathered at the roundabout. Knowing your plans, I decided to join him. Ubel was to wait for me if he could, but either way, he was to back you up."

"I don't remember telling you where I was going, other than to say that I was heading into the village."

"I told him," said Cori. "Father Collin told me that Ubel was nearby, and so I shared your plans with him."

MacBridan gave a grim smile and said, "You and Ubel have my undying gratitude, but I wonder why Mukhtar didn't go in with them?"

"It's like I said yesterday evening, that's not how Kaseem operates. Mukhtar was waiting where the men he'd hired couldn't see him. Once you arrived, he drove over to them and gave them their final instructions. Mukhtar is brutal, pig of a man, and while I'm confident that the money was good, you can be sure that he let Carl and the boys know what would happen to them if they failed."

"Which they did," said MacBridan.

"Which they did," said Father Collin. "Which is why I think the next time we see Carl, we'll need a broom and a pail to pick up the pieces."

Cori looked at MacBridan. "They were expecting you."

"So it would seem," agreed MacBridan.

"Ubel was just getting ready to go into the pub when I got there, so we went in together."

"You'll probably see Ubel before I do," said MacBridan, "and although I never thought I'd say this, please tell him I owe him one."

A voice filled with frustration, and not a little anger interrupted their conversation. "You and Father Collin may have thwarted Kaseem in the village this morning, but I'm afraid I haven't been very successful here," said Father Novak, his glasses off as he rubbed his eyes. "Kaseem never does anything without a reason. Therefore there has to be something he needs in this miserable painting or in the whole series. If there wasn't, he wouldn't be interested."

"Father Novak thought it would be good to examine the entire series of paintings," said Cori. "So I had them all brought to the library."

They joined Father Novak as he adjusted his glasses and continued to gaze at the five landscapes. "They all have the same theme. In each one, the artist shows us that his perspective was from inside the house, actually illustrating portions of items that I'm assuming were in his bedroom. The primary focus, though, is centered on the grounds of the estate as seen through his window. Other than that completely simplistic observation, I'm at a loss." With that, Father Novak got up from his chair and began to pace back and forth in front of them, briskly rubbing his hands together to warm them up.

"He'd never tell you, so I'll let you know. In addition to his knowledge of art, Father Novak is actually one of the foremost talented cryptologists in the world. Over the years, he's become an expert at breaking codes and discerning secret writing," said Father Collin.

Father Novak barely smiled at Father Collin's remark, never taking his focus away from the task at hand. "You're very kind, Father, but you do tend to exaggerate," he murmured.

Cori, who had been studying the pictures with Father Novak, said, "On the small table to the left of the window, it looks like there are a couple of letters and maybe a number printed on a tablet or a box. This seems to be in all the pictures, but the letters and numbers are different. What is that?"

"It's hard to say. With the subtle shadowing the artist attempted, and completely failed to accomplish I might add, it would appear to possibly be a magazine or maybe even a book. He was not good at clearly illustrating dimensions. For the most part, the other objects on the table vary picture by picture," answered Father Novak.

"Not to change the subject, but I'm afraid I have some more news regarding Kaseem, and it's not good," said Father Collin. "While we were enjoying dinner with you and the family yesterday evening, Ubel took a look around the estate grounds."

"None of the security men reported seeing him," said Cori.

"I hardly find that surprising. I'm sure you'd agree that unless someone literally knocks on their door, the security here is somewhat passive. Nevertheless, at dinner last night, I learned from Lord MacKinnon that the family dog is missing."

"That's right," said MacBridan. "It's a large black mastiff named Major. Wetmoore stated that recently they'd had several dogs, all black, reported missing."

Father Collin sadly shook his head. "I was afraid of that."

"What is it?" asked Cori.

"Ubel found the mutilated remains of three dogs, all of them black, one a mastiff. They had been ritually sacrificed," said Father Collin.

"You're telling me that Kaseem has been stealing dogs so that he could just butcher them for some ritual," said MacBridan, his temper starting to get the better of him. "To what end? There's no point in it."

"It's part of an old satanic ritual. Kaseem is using this to help him locate the artifacts he's after by preparing the way for the spirit of the dark lord," explained Father Collin. "He is opening a portal to whatever evil may lurk here. In many cultures, dogs are sacrificed to be guardians in the underworld, but Satanist transforms them into the yeh hounds, the hounds of hell."

Cori rolled her eyes. "Here we go again."

"Kaseem will do anything he has to in order to find these artifacts. Like us, it is obvious that he believes that they are a part of treasure Balgair brought with him and are supposedly hidden in his tomb. To his cult, these artifacts, especially the head, are beyond priceless. Over the years, many have searched and failed to find the tomb, including various members of the

MacKinnon family. Father Novak and I discussed this at some length last night, and the fact that he's done this scares us. By taking the lives of those animals, he's beckoning the dark forces of the spirit world. If he can't get at the painting to find the clues hidden there, he'll try to find the tomb another way."

"Putting his deranged beliefs aside, killing those poor creatures is pretty sick and serves absolutely no practical purpose," said MacBridan.

"Finally," said Cori under her breath, backing up MacBridan, all too willing to challenge Father Collin on what she perceived as pure nonsense.

"If I may," said Father Novak, inserting himself between them. "Father Collin shared your skepticism with me. I completely understand. A long time ago, I too once believed as you do. However, over the years, I've experienced too many things that fly in the face of logic, some that even challenge one's sanity. Because of all that I've seen, I now know that I can't just dismiss something because it doesn't fit in with my perception of reality, no matter how fantastic it may seem. Sadly, what we're telling you is real, and all we're asking is for you to trust us on this, if for nothing more than your own protection."

The room turned quiet except for the crackling of the wood burning in the fireplace. "Please continue, Father," said Father Collin.

"The ritual we are talking about is one of desecration. The way in which the dogs were sacrificed plays an important part of the ritual. Kaseem is preparing the way so that the portals of evil can erupt. There is already substantial evidence that a strong evil inhabits these grounds and has lingered here for generations. Last night, Aunt Jean told me of her fears concerning the shadow people," said Father Novak.

"Yes, I plan to visit with her today to talk more about that," said Father Collin. "It's our understanding that this resident evil, if you will, has primarily focused on the MacKinnon women for many generations."

"Father, Aunt Jean is a sweet, kindly old woman," said Cori. "I think she's wonderful, and I like her a great deal, but I'm sure that if we look, we'll find a logical explanation behind the things she believes she's seeing."

Father Novak chuckled, then reached out and touched Cori's hand. "My apologies, I'm truly not laughing at you, but it's funny how some things never change. Young people consistently believe that their elders are feeble minded while older people continually look down on the young as being completely ignorant and without experience."

"It's why I want to spend more time with her," explained Father Collin. "I want to listen to her and learn, in detail, what it is that she believes is happening. Cori, to your point, it may just be the result of an overactive imagination. But in light of everything that's going on, it also may be something more, something we can't afford to overlook."

MacBridan appreciated how Cori felt. But he also knew that they'd personally experienced a couple of out of the ordinary events since they'd arrived. It was time they put all of their cards on the table. "We haven't had much of an opportunity to bring you up to speed on our activities, but now's as probably a good a time as any to do that."

Cori's eyes locked onto Mac's for a couple of moments and then nodded her agreement. Walking over to the door, she checked the hallway to see if there was anyone there before closing it. "Someone within the MacKinnon household has been feeding information to the bad guys," she said, explaining why she'd checked the hall. "Unfortunately, we've come up short as to who it is and why they're helping them."

They all moved to the large table and sat down, Father Novak claiming one of the chairs closest to the fire. Taking turns in the narrative, Mac and Cori brought the two priests up-to-date on all that had happened, starting with the attempt on the painting in Virginia, to the fake Truecourt on the docks, and ending with the events surrounding Marston's death.

"Considering whom you've been up against, you've been very fortunate," said Father Novak.

"It also explains the incident at the pub a little more. You've gotten in the way too many times," said Father Collin. "Kaseem wants—no—*needs* you dead."

"I plan to discuss that with him face-to-face," said MacBridan.

"There's more," said Cori, "but I hesitate to tell you about it. I know you're going to read more into it than there is."

"Please," said Father Collin, "we're fighting a common enemy. Everything is important."

"Someone has been trying to scare us off," said Cori.

The two priests waited, and when no one said anything else, Father Collin asked, "How so?"

MacBridan looked at Cori and said, "I'll take the lead on this."

"We haven't shared this with Wetmoore, but someone has planted their own little garden of pharmaceutical delights in the woods not too far from the house. The police haven't determined what killed Marston yet, but I'm betting that his death, brought on by an apparent severe allergic reaction, was possibly induced by the harvesting of some of those plants."

"Exactly which plants did you find there?" asked Father Novak. Cori ran through the list of the ones they were able to identify.

"I have pictures of all of them," said Cori. "I'll show them to you after lunch."

"Whoever did this knows what they're doing," said MacBridan. "It makes me wonder if Cori and I may also have been the victim of some of these plants using some kind of hallucinogen to enhance what we experienced."

Father Collin smiled broadly and tried to keep from laughing. "Now I'm really looking forward to hearing this.

To get all these disclaimers out before you even begin to tell us what happened, lets me know that it must be something truly remarkable." Looking at Cori, he said, "I'm guessing that it falls right in line with the kind of things I've been talking about, and you're having trouble admitting it, even to yourself."

Cori held Father Collin's gaze for a couple of moments and then looked down at her hands clasped tightly in her lap. "So I see that priests also practice the fine art of 'I told you so.' Go on, Mac, they need to know."

MacBridan then told them of the thing he saw in his bedroom, how the room's temperature had plummeted, the almost overpowering stench and its nearly impossible exit from the room, destroying the heavy wooden door.

"Have you seen it since then?" asked Father Collin.

"No, not since that first night," answered MacBridan.

"Remarkable," murmured Father Novak.

"As Mac told you, all this took place in the middle of the night. Their second attempt was later that day," said Cori. "If you consider how worn down we were and add in the possible use of drugs, it's easy to understand how we were fooled."

"Ms. Hopkins, you are delightfully obstinate," said Father Novak. "Please, tell us of the second incident."

Once again, MacBridan took the lead, giving the narrative, with Cori adding comments as the story went along. He provided as much detail as he could remember regarding the chapel and was especially detailed on what they saw and heard in the crypt.

Father Collin gazed at both of them. "You've been up against it almost day and night from the beginning. I can't begin to tell you how impressed I am on how well you've held things together."

"Don't patronize us, Father," snapped Cori.

"Not in the slightest," said Father Collin. "I am impressed. Not many could have held up under all of that as well as you have." Looking at MacBridan, he said "Seems like old times."

MacBridan shook his head. "I believe this time's different, Father. Our adversaries are flesh and blood, and we will stop them. I'm not yet ready to believe it's more than that."

Before either of the priests could respond, a light tapping at the door interrupted them. It startled Cori, and she jumped up, facing the door. Fergus stuck his head in, announcing that lunch would be served shortly. They thanked him, and he closed the door.

"Ready to believe or not," said Father Collin, rising from his chair, "there's more at work here than meets the eye. We'll talk more later today, but please, both of you, be careful. We are up against dark forces of unimaginable power."

Chapter 21

Once lunch was over, MacBridan, Cori, and the two priests made their way back to the library. Fergus and Robena served a thick lamb stew full of carrots and potatoes followed by a custard called a spotted dick. It was all MacBridan could do to keep from making a poor joke. Aunt Jean, Faith, and Wallace had joined them, but Kerr and Barclay had not yet returned to the estate. Wallace scowled at MacBridan.

"Junior has definitely not forgiven you," said Cori.

"True. It's tough on a guy when his own game backfires on him in front of others. Then have Lord MacKinnon make a point of leaving me in charge of the estate instead of him, and you effectively pour salt into an open wound."

"It was the right move. He's not ready for that kind of responsibility," said Cori, putting her jacket on the back of a chair near the fireplace. "That has to worry Lord MacKinnon."

"You really think so?" asked MacBridan.

"It would me," answered Cori. "Depending on how the will is written, Wallace is most probably the next baron to walk the streets of Abbotsbury. Sadly, he's got a lot of growing up to do before he can fill those shoes."

Father Novak immediately went back to his study of the five paintings, effectively shutting out everything else around him. Father Collin watched him for a moment and then walked over to Mac and Cori. "So may I ask what your plans are for this afternoon?"

"I thought I'd stay here with Father Novak," said Cori, "see if I can be of any help. Also, Truecourt called while we were at lunch, so I need to get back with him."

"I'm going to make use of Lord MacKinnon's office for a few minutes," said MacBridan. "I want to call Dolinski and bring him up-to-date. He's going to want to know as much as I can tell him about Kaseem."

Father Collin nodded his head. "Yes, I imagine so. It will be difficult to find out much about him using conventional means. Over the years, his cult has done a frighteningly good job of staying under the radar. Interpol tracks criminals that they can understand. The cults of the shadow commit crimes that don't register, except for the occasional human sacrifice."

"As soon as Dolinski and I are finished, I'm going to once again check the security systems we've installed in the bedroom that we're using for storage. There's an idea I've been toying with, but to determine if it's really practical, I need to look at that room again," said MacBridan. "How about you?"

"Ubel's busy looking into a few things for me, and frankly, I'm not sure when I'll hear from him. Originally, I'd planned to visit the chapel this afternoon. After hearing of your experience there, I'm anxious to see it. However, things have changed, and I plan to talk with Aunt Jean. At lunch, I asked if I could visit with her this afternoon, and she was most open to my spending time with her."

"Did you think she'd have a problem talking with you?" asked Cori.

"You never know," answered Father Collin. "She didn't grow up Catholic, and though it may sound odd, sometimes people feel uncomfortable around a priest."

"That's only true with you, Father Collin," Father Novak interjected, not even looking up as he examined the third painting with a magnifying glass. "Only you."

Father Collin gave a small laugh. "I never know when he's listening." Looking at MacBridan, he said, "Come, I'll walk with you."

Leaving the library, they walked down the hall and entered the foyer, but rather than going up the stairs to find Aunt Jean, Father Collin said, "There's something else I wanted to talk with you about. Father Novak and I thought it might be best if I spoke to you alone."

"Because of Cori?" asked MacBridan.

"Frankly, yes, but please don't take this the wrong way. She's a delightful young lady and is obviously very competent. We trust her, but she's already struggling with some disturbing concepts that are outside of her normal sphere. We felt that with what I have to tell you, it would only serve to upset her even more."

MacBridan looked around, and they appeared to be alone. "I understand but don't underestimate her. She's smart, and she's tough."

"If it becomes necessary, I assure you, we'll certainly share this with her." Father Collin also looked to see if anyone else was nearby. "In talking with the house staff, it appears that the incidents of a haunting started up again a couple of weeks after the family returned to the estate, after Aunt Jean's return in particular."

"What are you saying?"

"Aunt Jean appears to be the catalyst for many of the things that are happening. We cannot forget that she is a female relative, a direct descendant of Balgair and his wife. That one fact is very significant. Remember, the people in the area at that time thought Balgair's wife to be a witch. We understand why as we believe that she was possessed by a strong demon. On the night that the villagers rose up against Balgair, as soon as they caught her, they drug her from the house and burned her at the stake. Her dying words were used to curse the MacKinnon clan. Ever since then, the women of the MacKinnon line have been extraordinarily sensitive, possessing almost a sixth sense, if you will. Some have referred to it as the curse, others have not viewed it so negatively. Because of her heritage, of being a direct bloodline back to Balgair's wife, Aunt Jean has what is called demon strain. It's in her blood. It doesn't mean she's evil. It means that she is related to the watchers, the beings in Genesis born of the mating of humans and fallen angels. I thought this might be a bit much for Ms. Cori."

MacBridan smiled at the priest. "I agree. Demon strain, are you saying that Aunt Jean may have some kind of disease?"

"In a manner of speaking, she most certainly does. Are you familiar with Father Gabriele Amorth?" asked Father Collin.

"No, I can't say I am."

"Father Gabriele is a cardinal and, over the years, has been a mentor to me. He played a strong influence in my life when I first came to God and is the primary reason that I sought to join my order. I have learned so much from him. So that you'll know, Father Gabriele is the Vatican's chief exorcist. The things that he has seen, that he's experienced firsthand would leave you seeing the world from a totally different perspective."

"How does this tie into Aunt Jean?"

"In the early days of the Christianity, two apocryphal books were written called the *Books of Enoch*. They tell of the genetic interference from the other side. You and I and all humans are tempted by things of the senses. For example, I just gave into the sin of gluttony with the marvelous lamb stew. But imagine if you had even more senses to be tempted by, perhaps a sense of the future or the power to know a person's hidden thoughts or to be able to make someone well or sick by your whim. By introducing these kinds of abilities, people are lured into doing sins that most people would never dream of. This demon strain can turn the kindest of people."

"I understand chemical dependencies and how they can be hereditary, but this is pretty far out there," said MacBridan.

"Mac, only because of your past experiences, I know that you have more of an open mind. Nevertheless, this is serious. Because of this strain, Aunt Jean is more susceptible to a demon's influence. Due to the blood that flows within her, it is likely that she has been a recipient of the MacKinnon curse and may indeed have some level of second sight."

"Meaning, she might be able to see or experience things that others around her can't," said MacBridan. "If true, then this could lead her family to think of her as being either crazy, senile, or all of the above."

"Very possible," answered Father Collin. "Imagine seeing a whole world that no one else sees. When you are young, you learn to keep your mouth shut, but as you become older, you let things slip. Innocent old women start talking about demons, and they are sent to the stake."

"Are you sure she's innocent? I mean, her temptations must be enormous. She's old and is seeing the world pass her by. Maybe she is influencing events from a bitter place," said MacBridan. He knew all too well that more power meant greater potential for evil as well as good.

"Which is exactly why I want to talk with her. I want to know more, know what it is that she's seeing and hearing. Of course, sadly, there is the possibility that it may just be the ravages of old age."

"But you don't think so."

"No. No, I believe she and the evil that inhabits this place are feeding off each other. This presence, whatever it is, is drawn to her, and with all that Kaseem is doing to stir things up, she could be in real danger."

"Father, to be honest, this is a bit of a stretch even for me," said MacBridan.

"I understand, but whether you believe it or not doesn't alter the reality of what is happening. She could easily turn out to be a victim in all this before it's over. Mac, I'd like for you and Cori to help me keep an eye on her as much as is possible."

"That's the second request I've had along those lines. A couple of days ago, I met one of the house staff...what was his name? Oh yes, Dillon. He too expressed his strong concern for Aunt Jean. In truth, he was most emphatic, almost demanding that I commit to protecting her."

"Did he say what was worrying him?"

"No, on that, he was rather vague. I'm not sure that he knows."

"Interesting," said Father Collin. "Once I've finished talking with her, I'll let you know what I've learned."

"Come in," said Aunt Jean in response to the light tapping on her door. As the door opened, she said, "Father Collin, I've been waiting for you. Please, do sit down, join me."

Father Collin found her sitting by the fire and took the chair across her. Her room was warmer than any other he'd been in since they'd arrived at the estate. Father Novak, who was always chilled no matter where they were, would be jealous. "I'm so glad that we could spend some time together this afternoon."

"It's so nice having you visit us. I spent some time yesterday evening with Father Novak, a very charming man and so interesting. He's led such an extraordinary life."

"We're happy to be here, but I wish it were under better circumstances. Mr. MacBridan told me about the threat of theft that's been hanging over the estate and the tragic passing of Mr. Marston."

"I still find it hard to believe he's gone."

"He also told me that one of the house staff believes that she saw the ghost of Balgair," continued Father Collin. "For that matter, I've found much of the staff to be on edge because of the many strange things going on at the estate. They truly believe in this ghost, and worse, they fear it."

Aunt Jean looked at Father Collin for a couple of moments, closely studying his face before responding, "I can only imagine how all of this must sound to you."

"If you mean that it might sound strange or ridiculous to me, then you'd be mistaken. Due to my calling, I've personally seen and experienced several inexplicable things, some which not only defied all explanation but were terrifying. I've also found that these particular occurrences were most often manifestations of the enemy."

"The enemy?" asked Aunt Jean.

"Too often we forget that there is a never-ending battle being waged for our souls," answered Father Collin. "We must always be vigilant, for we are in a constant struggle of spiritual warfare where the prize for second place is spiritual damnation."

"I don't find your words to be very comforting, Father," said Aunt Jean, sighing deeply. "I don't know what to do. For the last few weeks, I've lived in a state of growing fear that is eating away at me piece by piece. I'm afraid that your talk of damnation has made it even worse, giving voice to my deepest fear."

"Please believe me when I tell you that that is not my intent. Father Novak shared with me his concerns for you and urged me to talk with you as soon as I could. My reason for visiting this afternoon is to help you face whatever it is that's frightening you. I believe I can help, but first, you have to tell me what it is."

Aunt Jean looked very tired, almost drained. She closed her eyes, leaning her head back against her chair. She stayed that way for quite a while until Father Collin began to wonder if perhaps she'd fallen asleep. "There's not really anyone here that I've been able to open up to," said Aunt Jean, her eyes still closed. "To Ronald, it's all nonsense. Wallace is consumed with Wallace, and Faith, my dear Faith, wants to believe, but for the most part, she's just going along with things to humor me."

"Wants to believe what?" asked Father Collin.

"Like me, the gift, or curse, depending on your point of view, is in her. She's fighting it because it doesn't fit in her world, but there's no denying that it's within her."

"Tell me more about the gift."

Aunt Jean finally opened her eyes and looked at him. "How silly of me," she said. "Here I am prattling along, and you don't even know what I'm talking about. Let me tell you how it all began." Aunt Jean then launched into the tale of Balgair and his wife, their violent end, and the curse on all MacKinnon women, screamed by his witch of a wife as the flames consumed her. Much of what she said confirmed what he already knew, but Aunt Jean added details he hadn't heard before. The gift gave the MacKinnon women the ability to see spirits. It also enabled them, to some degree, to see into the future. But the worst of it was their ability to see the shadow people. To see them was to see death and know that it lurked nearby.

She told Father Collin how her grandmother had encouraged her to use the gift, to see it as a special talent. It had never really posed a problem for her while growing up and had only become one since their return to the estate. Over the years, she'd found it amusing, sometimes even comforting. She had known that her family would survive the war. "There's soon going to be a death in the family, and I'm terrified that it's me. I've recently seen the shadow people, and they are becoming bolder, coming closer and closer. I think that I've seen them in the house once or twice."

"What are the shadow people?"

"They are absolutely featureless, although sometimes I think I can see their eyes. These harbingers of death look like shadows people would cast on a sunny day, only very, very dark and frighteningly grotesque in their shape. Each time I see them, an almost uncontrollable fear takes over, nearly overwhelming me. Instinctively, I know that I can't let them touch me. They are the essence of hate and decay, and when they're close enough, I swear I can feel the terrible anger they hold for me."

"Why do you think they want to hurt you?"

"Because I'm alive, and they envy that. They are condemned to the darkness and prey on the living for whatever temporary release it may give them. If they can touch a living being at the moment of death, the life force runs through them. They're addicts of life, and they certainly don't want to move onto the fires of hell. It was the same for my grandmother. I have her diary, and as her end approached, she too saw them and knew that they were coming for her. She feared them as much as I do. Father, I'm scared out of my mind. I believe in God, I truly do, but I'm so afraid that He's turned away from me. I feel if I were in grace, they couldn't menace me."

Father Collin shook his head and said, "God is always with us," his tone calm and assuring. "He will never forsake you. Tell me, do you believe in our Lord Jesus Christ? Have you accepted Christ as your savior?"

"Yes, yes," said Aunt Jean, her voice filled with agony, silent tears streaming down her face. "Yes, I have, but when I see those creatures, it's like hell itself is personally coming for me."

Father Collin sat quietly, getting his thoughts together. "You said that your grandmother encouraged you to use the gift. How?"

"Growing up, I spent a great deal of time with her. We were very close. In her room, she had an old family heirloom that has been handed down for generations, and she kept it out on an end table. My mother called it a witch board, but I never really thought of it as being anything more than a game. My grandmother used it all the time and showed me how to make it work. Some days, it worked better than others, but we enjoyed it, and it answered many of our questions. Grandmother believed that it could tell the future. All in all, it was great fun."

"Needless to say, my mother absolutely hated it. She did not want us near it. It scared her. She was not a MacKinnon by birth, unlike my grandmother, which made it hard for me to talk to her about such things. So when I began to feel the gift, I turned to my grandmother for answers. I did mention these feelings to my mother a time or two, but those talks didn't go very well. Frankly, more than once she insinuated that Grandmother was a little off and that we shouldn't believe any of the nonsense she told us."

"Us?"

"My sister and I. Colina was younger than me, Faith's grandmother."

"I see," said Father Collin.

"Eventually, things came to a head, and Mother forbade us from playing with the witch board. That, of course, did not stop Grandmother. She would simply shut the door to her room, and it became our secret. It being a secret made it all the more fun and not just a little wicked. I'm pretty sure, looking back on it now, that mother knew what was going on, but there wasn't much she could do. Grandmother was rather strong willed."

"What became of this witch board?"

"You do know what I'm talking about, don't you? Today they're quite different in design and are called Ouija boards, but they're really much the same thing," explained Aunt Jean.

"Yes, I do. I've seen them in toy stores. But as far as true witch boards, the old ones like you're describing, I've read about them but have never seen one."

"If you'd like to look at it, it's behind you on the end table there by the bookcase. When Grandmother died, not too long after we moved to America, she willed it to me."

Father Collin turned in his chair as far as he could but was having difficulty seeing it. "May I?"

"Please do. It's quite beautiful."

The table sat in the shadows, and as Father Collin got closer, he got a good look at the witch board. He froze, not daring to move forward, as a sudden pang of fear shot through him. He couldn't believe his eyes, easily recognizing that which lay before him. The board was at least an inch and a half thick and obviously quite old. To his knowledge, if this was truly an original, there were only two others like it in existence. It was believed that only nine of the Neculai boards had ever been made, most having disappeared through the centuries.

The boards were constructed in such a way that they acted as a prison for a demon trapped inside by a human sorcerer. The human's voice tormented it to reveal information it possessed. Demons are different than humans; they can see the world of pure thought, what Plato called the world of forms. What such an instrument could reveal to one with the gift, like Aunt Jean, was disastrous.

"It's an antique," said Aunt Jean, "and beautifully done. The craftsmanship is amazing! Many of the symbols are so very odd. I can't imagine where the craftsman got the idea for them, but Grandmother taught me their meaning. In fact, depending on the order in which they come up, each one can have several different meanings. I've been working with Faith, and she's getting there, but in fairness, it is a bit complicated."

Father Collin studied the board carefully, unsure of his next move. This was no toy. The planchette was shaped like a crescent moon with intricately carved characters running across it. He wasn't able to read Enochian, but had seen the alphabet in the Vatican secret library. At its center, a dark red crystal, probably garnet, had been deeply embedded, piercing through to the other side. The twenty-four facets of a trapezohedron had created all sorts of occult lore, from the twenty-four runes to the number of years Faust sold himself to the devil. Father Collin had never thought he would see such an item. Summoning his own courage, he moved closer, positioning himself between Aunt Jean and the board. He stood there, dreading what he had to do next as he didn't know what would happen.

"If you'd like, you can bring it over here."

"That all right," said Father Collin. "I wouldn't want to risk dropping it."

Aunt Jean chuckled, remembering times past when the board had been subject to some pretty rough treatment. "I doubt you could hurt it even if you wanted to."

More true than she knows, thought Father Collin. Neculai boards were reported to be protected by several dark charms. Leaning over, he carefully reached out for the planchette. He stopped, quickly pulling his hand back. The planchette had slightly trembled at the approach of his hand. Taking a deep breath, he reached for it again. Just as his hand got within a couple of inches of touching it, the planchette flew across the board away from him. He straightened up so quickly, stepping back from it, that he nearly tripped himself. He remembered Father Amorth's dictum, "Fear of the devil is no sin, but giving into that fear will always lead to sin." He quickly crossed himself.

Father Collin stared at his hand. He hadn't felt any pain, and yet his hand had gone completely numb, his fingers incapable of moving. He hadn't even touched the planchette, but it radiated enough force to give him spiritual pain. How did the old lady use it? She wasn't as human as he. Fear filled his stomach, and his hands trembled at the revelation. If he didn't act at his best and the Lord didn't act with grace, Aunt Jean's soul was hell bound.

Trying to mask the thoughts and feelings racing through him, he returned to his chair. It was the first time in a long time that he found himself in the position of not knowing what to do or say. Discovering a Neculai had been completely unexpected. This was the stuff for the big boys.

"Is everything all right, Father?" asked Aunt Jean. Father Collin didn't respond but started into the fire as if she hadn't spoken. "Father?"

"What?" he said, looking up at her. "Oh, yes, everything's just fine. I'm just a little awed by its presence."

"I've never really thought of it that way, but you're right. It does have a certain bearing to it."

"I'm sure Father Novak will take a keen interest in it as well. Art is his passion," said Father Collin. "I'd like to go back to what we were talking about earlier. You said you feared that God has turned away from you. He hasn't, and over the next couple of days, if you'll work with me, I'll show you that He hasn't."

"Oh, Father, you don't know what that would mean to me."

Reaching into his coat pocket, he brought out a rosary with white beads and a silver cross. Then, reaching into his inside coat pocket, he pulled out a small glass bottle and set it on the oval table between them. "As Christians, we are all God's children, the cross of Christ uniting us as one." He leaned over and gave the rosary to Aunt Jean. "Keep this with you at all times. Every time you pray, hold the cross tightly. Will you pray with me now?"

Her eyes brimmed with tears. "Yes," she almost whispered, "I would like that."

Father Collin rose from his chair, picked up the bottle he'd placed on the table, and prayed silently. Then, looking at Aunt Jean, he said, "This bottle contains holy water. I wish to place the sign of the cross on you."

Aunt Jean nodded her consent, shut her eyes, and slightly bowed her head. Father Collin placed holy water on his index finger and made the sign of the cross on her forehead. She flinched at his touch but remained silent.

"In the name of the Father, of the Son, and—"

A loud clattering sound broke the silence, and they both looked toward the table that held the witch board. Father

Collin could see that the planchette had slammed against wall landing on the floor.

"What happened?" asked Aunt Jean.

"In a moment," answered Father Collin, not betraying the tension he felt, "let us finish. In the name of the Father, of the Son, and of the Holy Spirit, I commend Jean MacKinnon to your keeping oh, Father, for now and forever. Amen."

Father Collin placed the holy water back inside his coat pocket and sat back down. "I'm afraid that was my fault. When I was looking at the witch board, I must have left the planchette too close to the edge. It certainly picked an unfortunate time to fall."

"Not to worry. I'm sure it's okay," said Aunt Jean. "I promise you that it's not the first time it's been dropped." She was quiet for a moment and then said, "Father, the liquid you used to make the sign of the cross on my face, you said that it's holy water."

"That's right. This particular bottle has been prayed over by the Holy Father himself."

"Can you tell me what's in it?" asked Aunt Jean.

The oddity of the question took him by surprise. "I'm not sure I understand what you're asking."

"I was just curious," said Aunt Jean. "When you first touched me, it stung, and I was wondering if there's something other than water in there. I'm not Catholic. I don't know what herbs and so forth you add to it. Probably something I am allergic to."

A chill ran down Father Collin's back. "I guess I must have picked up some static electricity off the carpet, which ended up stinging you a little," he lied, not daring to share the truth with her.

Aunt Jean chuckled at that. "I'm sure that was it. I feel so much better, so relieved. Thank you, Father."

"Over the next few days, I'd like for us to spend some more time talking, and if it's okay with you, I'd like to have Father

Novak join us. I believe that together, we can keep the shadow people at bay."

"Then you believe me," said Aunt Jean, incredulous that she'd actually found an ally.

"Every word," said Father Collin, "but I'm going to need your help. Anywhere you go, anywhere, you must promise me that you'll keep the cross I gave you with you. Will you do that for me?"

"Father, I must be honest with you. I don't even know how to use a rosary," said Aunt Jean.

"That's not important," explained Father Collin. "The cross of Christ is stronger than the shadow people. Let Christ be your shield."

"Am I interrupting?" said a voice from behind them. Looking up, they saw Faith standing in the doorway.

"Faith, no, not at all," said Aunt Jean.

"I came by to see if you'd like to go for a walk with me in the garden." Faith stopped as she spotted the cursor lying on the floor. "What happened here?" she asked, picking it up and placing it back on the board.

"I'm afraid I was a bit careless when I was looking at it," said Father Collin. "After I sat back down, we heard it fall."

Faith frowned ever so slightly as she looked at the wall next to the table on which the board rested. "Odd. Something has put a gash in the wall here."

"That is odd," said Father Collin.

"Now let's not make a mountain out of a mole hill," said Aunt Jean. "Father Collin and I have had a very nice talk. Father, would you care to join us on our walk?"

"That is most kind, but no. If you don't mind, I'd like to just sit here and enjoy your fire for a few more minutes."

"You want to stay here?" asked Faith, her voice betraying her disapproval.

"Yes," said Father Collin. "If that's all right?"

"Of course, Father, stay as long as you like," said Aunt Jean who took a thick wool sweater from the armoire and put it on. "We'll see you at dinner this evening." As she left the room, Faith followed her, but it was clear that she was not comfortable leaving the priest in her aunt's room.

Father Collin sat and waited, listening to them walk away. After a couple of minutes, he got up and moved to the door, looking out into the hall to make sure they were gone. As quietly as he could, he moved to where the hall intersected and carefully peered around the corner. Aunt Jean and Faith were about halfway down the hall, heading toward the staircase.

He quickly went back to Aunt Jean's room and closed the door. Looking at the witch board, he decided to keep his distance. It would have to be dealt with, but he was not prepared to do so now. Once again, he brought out the holy water and also a small container that held the scared host. Moving to the windows, he prayed then sprinkled the window frames with the holy water. He then placed a piece of the host above each window. He then did the same thing to the frame around the bedroom door. Finally, kneeling in the center of the room, Father Collin prayed one last time and left.

He hurried down the hall as quickly as he could, anxious to confer with Father Novak on what he'd found, but first, he had to find MacBridan. The stakes had just been raised, and he knew that he was going to need his help.

Chapter 22

"You're certain that it is a Neculai?"

"I was shocked, Father, and not a little intimidated. It is about the last thing I expected to find when I went to see her," said Father Collin.

MacBridan walked into the library and joined the two priests. "What seems to be the problem? Your text message seemed pretty urgent."

"I'm glad you got here so quickly," said Father Collin. "I knocked on the door to the storage room but didn't get any answer. Thinking you might not be able to hear me, I tried to open it, but it was locked, so I decided I'd better text you."

"Dolinski and I just finished talking. Like us, he's concerned about Kaseem and wants to know more. If necessary, he's ready to send a team to back us up from our London office, all we have to do is ask. Cori is in the office now, going over some documents with Truecourt that he faxed to her."

"I'm glad to hear that help is standing by. It just may come to that," said Father Collin. "My apologies. I'm still a little rattled from my talk with Aunt Jean."

MacBridan smiled at this. "Do you mean to say that sweet, harmless, little old lady rattled you? That's probably not something you'll want to share with your buddies back at the Vatican."

"The concern is centered more on what Father Collin found in her room rather than the talk itself," explained Father Novak.

"Mac," said Father Collin, "I know that you're a bit of a history buff. Do you know what an Ouija board is or the history behind them?"

"My best friend growing up had one. We played with it now and then. Why?"

"The idea for Ouija boards is quite old. When William Fuld made his commercial board, he happened to have heard of a medieval legend of the Neculai boards. He liked the idea of a board and planchette that two people could play with. It was a big hit early on, mainly for dating couples. You sat knee-to-knee and asked naughty questions for the spirits to answer. What Fuld didn't know was that the legend had a factual and dark basis," explained Father Novak. "It seems that Father Collin has made a rather disturbing discovery."

"What would that be?" asked MacBridan.

"It seems that one of the MacKinnon family heirlooms," said Father Collin, "is a Neculai board. I can only imagine how they got their hands on it."

MacBridan shrugged and plopped down into one of the chairs. "I'm guessing that's an old-fashioned Ouija board. Lots of families have them, although my parents didn't seem to like me playing with them all that much."

"The original witch boards were very different from the Ouija boards that are sold in toy stores today. They were very rare and only used by practitioners of the dark arts. Typically, warlocks possessed them," said Father Novak.

"Warlocks?" asked MacBridan.

"It means a *loch singer* in Scottish, men who could undo the locks between the worlds. Ironically, when Anton LaVey founded the Church of Satan, he dug up this old and ugly term," said Father Collin.

Father Novak placed his hand on Father Collin's shoulder and beckoned him to sit down. "During the fifteenth century, there was a powerful warlock who lived in Romania by the name of Neculai. He was greatly feared and had a great deal of influence as he was also an advisor and confident to the ruler Vlad Dracul."

MacBridan groaned, slumping down in his chair. "Dracula? Please tell me you're not about to give me a vampire story."

"No, we're not," said Father Novak, "but you are correct in that it was Vlad Dracul who did inspire Bram Stoker when he created the Dracula character. Truth is Vlad, in real life, was far worse than any vampire whoever graced the pages of fiction. As I'm sure you know, he is remembered for his extreme cruelty for impaling thousands of people and watching them as they slowly died. It is said that he once even feasted in the midst of their torment. It is believed that his terrible acts of torture were, to some extent, due to the influence of Neculai, who advised him that by doing these horrific acts, he would defeat his enemies."

"Vlad was very successful. He held out against both the Ottoman Empire and Genghis Khan," continued Father Novak. "It is believed that Neculai had tremendous knowledge of the dark arts and was constantly searching for a way to directly communicate with Satan. Neculai imprisoned nine demons of the Order of the Cherubim into the boards. The demons are forced to speak the truth."

"Well, if it's the truth," said MacBridan, "then no harm can come of it."

Father Collin said, "Don't be foolish, man! Think of these truths, exactly how much torture it will take to break a man so that he will betray his king, the art of spreading small pox on the battlefield. All of these things are truths."

"But what you are telling me is all legend, right?" asked MacBridan.

Father Collin nodded. "Neculai did exist. That is fact, and yes, much of this is mostly legend. Little is known about Neculai as he only appears in a few old manuscripts from that period. Most of the writings about him come from a young monk who was in his teens during Neculai's reign of influence."

"It is important that you know the rest of this," said Father Novak. "Neculai built nine of these witch boards, but there was still a critical piece that he was missing. Somehow, he found a way to trap nine demons, imprisoning them in nine separate garnets that would hold them forever. These garnets he embedded in the planchettes. The demons trapped in the garnets were easily outwilled by men like Neculai and Vlad, who had an unbending intent for power. They could easily dupe ordinary humans."

"So you are telling me that Aunt Jean has been drawn in by this thing and could potentially be a tool for evil? I'm afraid I'll have trouble buying into that."

"The board will be happy enough to take her soul, but I doubt that she'll be raising armies against Christendom," said Father Collin.

"How could a sweet, slightly dotty old lady own the one ring from Mordor?"

"As I said, it is a family heirloom that has been with the MacKinnon's for a long time. It has been passed down through generations and was given to her when she was quite young. It was her grandmother who taught her how to use it, to correctly interpret the symbols on the board. Aunt Jean's grandmother, just before she died, willed the board to her," said Father Collin, his voice revealing the weakness he felt.

"So if one buys into the whole legend, then she has been damned without knowing it," said MacBridan. "Do you believe all these?"

"James, as you know, my order is charged with fighting this kind of corruption. Father Gabriele Amorth, who we talked about before, plays an important role with my order and the education that we are given. They taught me about Neculai and his witch boards in the event I ever came across one."

"Okay, but how can you be sure that it's authentic?" asked MacBridan. "Like so many ancient artifacts, it could be a forgery."

"A valid argument," agreed Father Collin. "Just last year, someone tried to pass off two such forgeries to a collector of religious artifacts."

"It might have worked if he'd just tried to pass off one," said Father Novak. "He was too greedy."

"This collector knew how rare they were, so he called in his local priest to help authenticate them. The priest then called my bishop, and he determined them to be fraudulent."

"But you're convinced that this one is real," said MacBridan.

"When you see it, you'll understand. They are magnificent works of art," said Father Collin. "Because I am a priest, a servant of the Lord Jesus Christ, I am the natural enemy of the forces embedded in these boards. I won't go into the detail around that, but when I reached out to touch the cursor, it moved away from me, shunning my touch. But the evil within the board struck back, causing my hand to instantly go numb, and it stayed that way for several minutes." He looked tired; the incident had obviously shaken him. "If I hadn't personally experienced it, I'd have trouble believing it myself."

"How did Aunt Jean react to all of these?" asked MacBridan.

"She didn't see any of it. I intentionally positioned my body between her and the board."

"There is more, though," said Father Novak. "Tell him."

"Aunt Jean shared with me her perspective on the curse that Balgair's wife placed on the MacKinnon women. She told me she's seen the shadow people, recently and more than once. She desperately fears for her soul."

"Does she know about the supposed dangers of this board she owns? Did the two of you talk about that?"

"Heavens no! That would have put her completely over the edge. What I did do is give her a rosary and asked her to keep it with her at all times. I then asked if we could pray together, and she was quick to agree. Using holy water, I placed the sign of the cross on her forehead. Two things happened when I did this, neither of which is good."

"Please, Father, continue," prompted Father Novak.

"The holy water actually hurt her. She said that it stung, and I felt her flinch when I touched her. Also, in the middle of our prayer, the planchette flew off the board and slammed into the wall. The word of God enraged it, and it tried to strike out, to distract us from completing the prayer. Demons feel great pain in the presence of the Lord's grace because they remember losing that grace millions of years ago. You cannot underestimate how old and alien these beings are."

The room went silent. Finally MacBridan said, "Father, I'm not sure how I can help here. Spiritual matters are clearly your area of expertise. I'm not saying that I doubt you, but it's going to take me a little time to digest all that you've just told me."

"I understand. If I hadn't witnessed the cursor moving away from me and had my hand rendered useless, I too would be questioning what really happened. We're all skeptics, Mac, we have to be."

"Would you like for me to take the board somewhere and destroy it?" asked MacBridan.

"No!" said both men, Father Novak coming out of his chair. "That could be disastrous," he continued. "It is a prison of a very angry demon. Demons hate the race of men. What would you do if some human had kept you in a cell the size of a walnut for over several hundred years when previously you had all of space and time to fly about in?"

"Then what would you like for me to do?"

"We agree that Kaseem has been getting help from someone here at the estate. Have you or Cori determined who that might be?" asked Father Collin.

"I have my guesses, but unfortunately, we're no closer than we were. That said, Truecourt has gone in and done background checks on everyone. That's what he and Cori are going over now. Hopefully, he would have found something that will help to point the way."

"Very well," said Father Collin. "Then I'd like for you and Cori to take a look at Aunt Jean's room. See if you can find any listening devices, anything that would indicate that someone is trying to keep an eye on her or maybe even trying to scare her."

"All right, we'll have a look around, but what could possibly be their motive for doing any of this? She's certainly not going to inherit the title and, as far as I can tell, has very little, if any, influence over family matters."

"I'm convinced this is tied in to all that's been going on, but I don't have anything to back that up. It's just a gut feeling," answered Father Collin.

MacBridan smiled at this. "My gut is where half my hunches come from, so that's good enough for me. Is Aunt Jean in her room?"

"Not at the moment, so now would be the perfect time. Faith came by while we were talking, and they've gone for a walk on the grounds."

MacBridan stood up, stretched, and headed for the door. "I'm not sure how long Cori will be on the phone, but if you see her, please ask her to join me."

"Certainly," said Father Collin, "and, James, thank you."

MacBridan looked at the priest and nodded. He found it interesting that whenever Dolinski, and now Father Collin, needed him to do something they saw as a personal request, they both used his Christian name.

"Mr. MacBridan," said Father Novak. "While in her room, you will be in the presence of great evil. Do not touch that board. You will be tempted."

Walking down the hall, MacBridan passed by his and Cori's rooms, the room they were using for storage, and finally came to the tall grandfather's clock at the end of the hall. It was nearly 3:30 p.m. Not seeing anyone, he turned left and stopped at the door to Aunt Jean's room.

MacBridan knocked and waited. Not hearing anything, he knocked again then tried the doorknob, partially opening the door. "Ms. MacKinnon, it's James MacBridan."

Silence answered his call as he pushed the door wide open. Standing in the doorway, he looked around, making sure that he was alone. To be extra careful, he backtracked down the short hall to where it intersected and checked to make sure that no one was coming. Quickly returning to Aunt Jean's room, he shut the door and considered where to begin his search. He immediately spotted the witch board on a table in the corner and walked over to it for a better look.

It was indeed a work of art, the colors deep and rich, although darkened with age. Many of the symbols on the board were unique in their design, all meaningless to him. Unlike a Ouija board, it seemed to be set up in quadrants surrounding a circular area in the center of the board, each filled with various signs and symbols. The garnet in the planchette seemed to give off light, some trick of optics. MacBridan realized how stupid he was to listen to the priests, such medieval thinking. If you let people like that run the show, there would be no penicillin, no electric light. Heck, he could just take the board from the old lady, get rid of it, and do them all a favor. He strode over to pick it up and froze.

Where had those thoughts come from? Father Collin had saved his life once. Father Novak seemed a learned man. And stealing from his client's family seemed like a bad career move.

Knock it off, he thought to himself. *You're starting to sound as crazy as they do.* They'd warned him not to touch it. Unfortunately, and he'd been this way most of his life, telling him no not to do something was the equivalent to waving a red flag in front of a bull.

MacBridan studied the board. Try as he might, neither the board nor the planchette looked threatening to him in any way. Remembering Father Collin's experience, he decided that it only made sense to move cautiously. So extending the index finger of his right hand, he slowly reached out, lightly touching the planchette. He barely touched it then jerked his hand back.

He waited. Nothing happened.

Feeling a little ridiculous, he reached out and touched it again, this time leaving his finger on the cursor.

Again, he waited. Still, nothing happened.

Pleased that no one had witnessed his shameful performance, he stepped up to the board and picked the cursor up to get a better look. *This place is really starting to eat away at me*, he thought, shaking his head. Surprisingly, the cursor was much heavier than it looked. The deep, intricate carvings on the top side were continued on the bottom. The garnet, he noticed, came to a sharp point. The trapezoid-shaped facets were so interesting, so fascinating, light seemed to dance across them. A clock chimed in the manor, breaking in on this reverie. How long had he just been staring at the stone?

Regretfully, he set it back down; he knew he had to get started. He needed to hurry because he had no idea how much time he actually had. Starting with the bookcase, he began to look for hidden listening devices. The room was quiet except for the occasional sounds coming from dying embers in the fireplace.

At first, it was very faint, almost a whisper, but a soft giggle echoed behind him.

Looking over his shoulder, he glanced to see who was there. The room was empty. He was still very much alone. Had the sound come from outside? Turning back to the bookcase, he resumed his search. The room smelled of old woman and wood smoke, like his own great-aunt's room.

This time, the giggle was a little louder, a little more prolonged, and sounded almost like a small child in its high pitch.

Jerking his head around, he thought he caught movement out of the corner of his eye by the dresser across him. Was someone hiding from him? All senses primed, he carefully walked toward the large antique dresser.

The mahogany dresser was about waist high with a tall oval mirror, and it stood on four thick legs carved to look like the paws of a lion. There was nothing under the dresser, and it simply wasn't possible that anyone could be behind it. He knew he'd heard something, but what? The oddest thoughts kept sneaking into his brain—*the name* Reznick *is Czech for* butcher.

The giggle burst out again, and this time he saw it, or at least saw something.

He'd been looking at the mirror atop the dresser and had seen the curtains on the left hand side of the windows move. MacBridan turned and studied the curtains carefully. Smiling, he noticed the slight bulge giving away the person concealed behind them. Got you!

"Games up," said MacBridan, crossing the room. "You can come out now. I don't bite."

MacBridan patiently waited, standing next to the bed. Taking nothing for granted, he reached behind him under his sports jacket, making sure his gun was ready if needed. Whomever it was, they remained absolutely still.

Stepping up to the curtains, MacBridan yanked them away. There was no one there. Turning around, he quickly scanned the room, his eyes alert for any movement. He let go of the curtains, letting them fall back into place. The telltale bulge that had so plainly been there before was gone.

Once again, the soft, childlike giggle filled the room, mocking him. A floorboard creaked, and the door to the bedroom silently but quickly swung open. MacBridan dashed around the bed, out the door, and into the hallway. Not seeing anyone, he took off toward the grandfather clock, pulling his gun.

Rounding the corner, he nearly collided with Cori, each grabbing one another by the arms. Startled, Cori said, "You all right?"

MacBridan looked past her down the hall, but it was completely empty. "Did you see anyone just now?"

"No. What's going on?"

At that moment, the door to Aunt Jean's room slammed shut. Spinning around, Mac and Cori sprinted the short distance to her door. MacBridan tried the doorknob but could not get it to turn. Keeping the pressure on the doorknob, MacBridan rammed the door twice more with his full weight, but it wouldn't budge.

The light, soft giggle sounded again, this time all around them. MacBridan stopped what he was doing and looked at Cori. "Tell me you heard that."

"What was it?"

MacBridan rubbed his shoulder. "I don't know, but it's really beginning to make me angry."

"Is someone in there?"

"There shouldn't be, but at this point, it's hard to say. I was in there, searching her room when all this started. I'm positive that when I went in there, I was alone," said MacBridan.

"When all what started?"

"Father Collin asked me if you and I would take a look in Aunt Jean's room, see if anyone was spying on her or perhaps trying to scare her. I hadn't been in there too long when—"

Without warning, the door to Aunt Jean's room slowly opened.

MacBridan and Cori watched the door as it swung all the way back. They looked at each other, and then MacBridan stepped forward. "Block the door."

Cori's gun seemed to appear in her hand out of nowhere. "Got it."

MacBridan thoroughly searched the room. As before, he came up empty. "I really hate it when Father Collin is right."

Stepping into the room but still blocking the door, Cori asked, "Right about what?"

MacBridan quickly filled her in on his talk with the two priests. He then told her how rather than leave it alone, he'd examined the planchette. Not long after he put it back down, strange things started happening with the giggler who wasn't there. "I swear, Cori, I kept thinking the weirdest thoughts. I really thought about just stealing the board."

"That doesn't sound like you at all. I don't like the way this case seems to be affecting you."

"Cori, I didn't get good at my job by not being open to impressions."

"If your clerical friends are right, maybe you shouldn't be too open to impressions."

"I think someone, some real flesh and blood, is out to get Aunt Jean." MacBridan almost added "and me too."

"Someone's just pulling your chain," said Cori, noticing the witch board. "I'm sure that whatever happened, it had nothing to do with that thing." Despite her very vocal attitude, Cori stayed away from the witch board.

"I'm all for that theory," said MacBridan. "Just tell me how they did it."

"Kind of like what happened at the chapel, isn't it?"

MacBridan let the question go unanswered. "I'll take this side of the room. You take that side. We search everything, but let's first look for a hidden doorway."

"As in secret passage hidden doorway?"

"I appreciate that it sounds a little bit like late night TV, but there's got to be a logical solution to all this, and I'm not leaving here until we find it."

Together, they attacked the room with professional efficiency, leaving no possibility unchallenged. After twenty minutes, they'd completed their search. "Mac, that thing in your room, the incident in the chapel, now this. What's going on?"

MacBridan was standing by the window, deep in thought. Looking out, he saw Faith and Aunt Jean as they walked across the lawn. "I wish I knew. Father Collin believes that Aunt Jean is tied up in all of it, but even he isn't sure how."

"And he wants us to keep an eye on her."

MacBridan nodded. "I know we didn't find anything, but it might not be a bad idea to put one of our own listening devices in here. Do you have any equipment left?"

"No, but I could take one from the storage room and put it in here if you think it's that important."

"At this point, I'm not sure what to think," answered MacBridan.

"Do I have the time to do it now?"

Pointing out the window, he said, "There's Aunt Jean and Faith. I'm guessing you've still got a least thirty minutes."

Cori joined him at the window and looked out at the two women. "It doesn't make sense why anyone would be targeting her. She's an old woman without any money and less influence."

They stood there watching the two women in silence. Finally MacBridan turned away, and Cori followed him. Just before he got to the door, he stopped abruptly, causing Cori to nearly trip over him.

"What's wrong?" she asked.

MacBridan didn't say anything. He turned around and rushed back to the window.

"Mac, what is it?"

"I don't believe it," he muttered. "Cori, come here and look at this, look at them."

Joining him back at the window, she carefully watched the two women as they walked along. "They look fine to me. What am I missing?"

"Look closely. What do you see?" said MacBridan, the intensity in his voice alarming her.

Cori slowly shook her head. "Mac, I'm sorry. I don't see anything out of place."

"There are only two of them. Look at the ground behind them."

Suddenly Cori's eyes widened. "Two of them, three shadows. How can that be?"

"No idea," said MacBridan. "But whatever is going on, it appears to be right behind them. Come on!"

MacBridan ran out the front door, veered sharply to his right, and took off, trying to catch up with the two women as quickly as he could. Cori was right on his heels. Brushing past the corner of the house, he saw that they had almost reached the tree line.

"Wait! Hold it!" he shouted.

Aunt Jean and Faith turned to look at him. He didn't know if they'd understood what he'd said, but he'd at least gotten their attention. He slowed down but only slightly, trying to see if he could spot anyone else. As he got closer, the look on Faith's face seemed to be one of anger, but that quickly changed to curiosity.

"Mr. MacBridan, whatever is the matter?" asked Aunt Jean. "You've given us quite a start."

By that time, Cori had also joined them. Mildly out of breath, MacBridan said, "I certainly didn't mean to startle you, but it's starting to get dark, and I saw you heading toward the woods."

"I'm not sure I understand the problem," said Faith, obviously unhappy with the interruption. "My aunt and I take walks here all the time. We're quite all right."

"Of course," said MacBridan, glancing at Cori. "It's just that, well, you see, Cori and I were talking, and she just got a weather alert on her cell phone."

"Oh, I see," said Aunt Jean. "Not good news, I'm guessing."

"I'm afraid not," said MacBridan. "There's some pretty heavy rain not too far from us, and it appears to be heading this way. We noticed that you weren't carrying an umbrella, and we didn't want you getting caught out in the storm."

"That is most kind of you," said Aunt Jean. "I guess we should turn back. A good soaking wouldn't do either of us any good."

"It certainly wouldn't," agreed Faith. Taking her aunt's arm, they started back to the house. "Thank you." Faith shot MacBridan a look; she wasn't buying his story but conceded to his wishes.

MacBridan and Cori followed but stayed about twenty paces behind them. They looked around, but there wasn't anyone else in sight. The third shadow was gone.

"For being such an accomplished fibber, that was pretty weak," said Cori, laughing at MacBridan. "No umbrella? Is that the best you could do? What happens if it doesn't rain?"

"It's late spring, and we are in the northern Highlands of Scotland. Trust me, it's going to rain."

Kaseem's phone rarely rang and he immediately answered it. By looking at it he couldn't tell who was calling. "Yes," he answered.

"What is being done about MacBridan? He's continuing to dig into things and given the time he's going to figure out that I'm helping you." The near paniced voice was that of Kaseem's contact at the estate and his anger at their calling him was immediate.

He despised them for their weakness and especially for challenging his authority. "MacBridan will be dealt with, it is out of your hands. Do as you're told and do not call me again, I will contact you."

"But what if I need to reach you? What if I have something important that you need to know?"

"Enough! If MacBridan figures out your part in all this it will be because you gave yourself away," snapped Kaseem, ending the call. Looking at Mukhtar he said, "We may need to move on MacBridan sooner than we planned. Unfortunately, we may need to remove our own asset at the same time."

Chapter 23

When they got back to the house, Aunt Jean thanked them again for their concern. Both women then headed to their rooms to prepare for dinner. MacBridan and Cori watched them as they carefully went up the long staircase.

"I don't think they bought our story about the rain," said MacBridan.

"Our story?" said Cori. "What happened to you out there? For the man who's renowned for his works of pure creative genius when passing off expense reports, the best you could do was to lie about the weather? I'm guessing 'the dog ate my homework' was big for you as a kid."

MacBridan smiled. "Admittedly, it wasn't all that convincing of a story. Come on, I want to talk with Father Collin. My run in with the giggler is really bothering me."

"Don't forget. I heard it too," said Cori, her face clouding over. "This is all so unreal, so impossible. It's like being stuck in an episode of the *Twilight Zone*. I'd give anything to be able to change the channel. You know how lame this will sound later when we tell people we were menaced by the giggler."

They found the priests still in the library, both seated by the fire. Father Novak had nodded off while Father Collin sat quietly reading. "As you can see, we're taking a break."

"I hate to wake him," said MacBridan, "but he'll probably want to hear this."

Father Collin gently nudged the sleeping priest, and he immediately woke up. "Excuse me, Father," he said. "I hope I wasn't snoring."

"Nothing of the kind," Father Collin assured him. "Mac and Cori are back, and they want to talk with us."

Bringing two more chairs over by the fire, they sat down on either side of the priests.

"Were you able to find anything in her room?" asked Father Collin.

Mac shook his head. "Nothing that we were looking for, but something certainly seems to have found us."

MacBridan quickly told them what he experienced in Aunt Jean's room, him and Cori being temporarily shut out in the hall, and then the extra shadow tracking Faith and Aunt Jean as they strolled across the lawn."

"The two of you have got to start trusting us! We know what we're talking about," scolded Father Novak. "I don't care how crazy we may sound at times. There's a malignant evil stalking this place, and it's dangerous. We warned you not to touch that board! Does one of you have to get hurt before you'll finally believe us?"

"Father," said MacBridan, "my touching the witch board may have set off what happened. I just couldn't see it as being dangerous."

"The creature imprisoned in the witch board is simply a little more desperate," said Father Novak. "I'm glad that it scared you. I'm sure that you and Cori have already come up with a hundred reasons that can explain what happened to you, all without any demonic culprits."

"I'm willing to concede there are things at work here that I don't understand. But at the same time, I cannot forget about the human factor involved. There are some very bad people targeting this family, and we'll do what we have to in order to protect them."

"We are fighting the same enemy," said Father Collin. "It's all tied together, and that's how we need to view things."

Taking a deep breath, MacBridan tried to calm down, gripping the arms of his chair. "Okay, so here's where all this leaves us. Someone at the estate has teamed up with Kaseem to help them find the treasure Balgair brought back with him. Whoever it is, they need Kaseem to either help figure out where it is hidden or they simply do not have the resources to act alone. It's obvious that the paintings done by the MacKinnon seafaring relative hold clues to its whereabouts."

"So then all five hold parts of the answer," said Father Novak, nodding his head. "With any one of them missing, the hidden message would be incomplete."

"What I'm still having trouble understanding is how someone like Kaseem or Talon even got involved in this," said Cori.

"I'm sure we'll find out, but remember, Kaseem doesn't care about the treasure," said Father Collin. "They're after power, power that can be gained by getting the artifacts his sect believes Balgair stole from the Templars. That is his goal, nothing else."

"Regarding Talon, I'm not all that concerned about her. She's merely a means to an end," said MacBridan. "She was brought in to get them the painting, nothing more."

"Are you defending her?" asked Cori. "Are you forgetting about Molan Sullivan, the lowlife who impersonated Truecourt on the docks? He failed, and for that, ended up facedown in the bay. Don't be taken in by this curvaceous little French tart. In my book, she's as much of a killer as Kaseem."

"Perhaps, but I'm still not sure. It doesn't fit in with how she's operated in the past," said MacBridan.

"I have to agree with Mac," said Father Collin. "Indiscriminate killing is Kaseem's style. We cannot allow him to walk away from this. Given any chance, he is to be shot on sight."

Cori was as surprised by this as she was with MacBridan's defense of Talon. "Did you just suggest that we kill this guy in coldblood? Not that I disagree, but doesn't that go against one of the ten big rules you guys are supposed to be out there advocating?"

"Cori, you cannot reason with a rabid dog," said Father Collin, "and Kaseem is far, far worse. He has tortured and killed many people in his time, and it was on his orders that those men were sent to attack Mac at the pub. If necessary, he'll do whatever it takes to achieve the goal that he's been assigned."

"Please, please," said Father Novak, "we continue to bicker among ourselves when our energies should be focused on the ones who threaten us." Looking at Mac and Cori, he said, "What do you plan to do next?"

Mac smiled at the elderly priest. "With everything that's been going on around here, I guess we're all a little on edge." He paused for a moment before continuing, "One of our people, Truecourt, did background checks on everyone here, trying to help us determine who the bad guy is. If we can figure that out, we can isolate them and at least cut off communications to Kaseem from inside the estate," said MacBridan.

"That's the information he called me with while we were at lunch," said Cori. "It gives us a lot more to think about, but I'm not sure it helps to narrow the field." Cori got up and walked over to a pile of papers she'd placed on the table before joining Mac in Aunt Jean's room. Getting what she needed, she returned to her chair. "Everyone ready?"

"Fire away," said MacBridan.

"As it turns out, both of the nephews, Kerr and Barclay, are broke."

"I thought they both worked for the estate," said Father Novak. "Surely, Lord MacKinnon pays them a fair wage."

"He most certainly does," said Cori, "and it comes with room and board here at the estate. In fact, it would be called a generous wage, but Kerr has a gambling problem, which got him into serious trouble with a loan shark in Edinburgh about a year ago. Lord MacKinnon bailed him out, but it wasn't cheap."

"Does Truecourt think that the lack of funds is because Kerr is paying Lord MacKinnon back?" asked MacBridan.

"That's what it looks like," said Cori. "There hasn't been any upward progress with any of his bank accounts in some time."

Father Collin gave a small laugh and said, "These background checks are obviously most thorough."

"What's the story on Barclay?" asked MacBridan.

"Barclay really likes the ladies," said Cori. "Two years ago, he was arrested in Inverness for soliciting carnal acts from an undercover officer. Locally, he's known for his overactive libido and his eagerness to, how shall I say this, enjoy life to the fullest. He'll spend in excess on whichever lady he takes a fancy, too, married or single."

"Discreetly stated," commented Father Novak approvingly.

"Faith is a student, premed, and has taken time from her studies to be here with her aunt," continued Cori. "Both of her parents are dead. Her father passed away when she was a child, her mother when she was seventeen. Unlike Kerr and Barclay, she does have some money as her father left her a comfortable nest egg."

"Anything on the servants?" asked Father Collin.

"There sure is," answered Cori. "The Henderson's have been with the family for many years and, from all we could gather, are trustworthy. It's their son, Laine, who is the problem."

"That fits with what Shaw Gordon was telling me at The Hanging Man," said MacBridan.

"Laine has quite a record and is currently out on parole. Truecourt checked with his parole officer and learned that he's hit or miss with his check-ins. He doesn't seem to have any kind of steady work but always has money."

"Never a good sign," muttered Father Novak.

"The rest of the house staff are pretty benign, but as for the groundsmen, three are new to the estate, having been hired in the last four months. Considering what we know about Talon, it's worth pointing out that all three are French." Cori paused and looked directly at MacBridan, waiting to see if he was going to once again rise to Talon's defense.

MacBridan met her stare for a moment then raised his eyebrows, putting on his most innocent face.

Rolling her eyes and frowning at him, Cori continued her report, "The gardener is also relatively new, having started just over five months ago. What's significant about him is that he may be an acquaintance of the Hendersons' son, but Truecourt hasn't been able to confirm that."

MacBridan leaned back in his chair, looking up at the ceiling. "Terrific. Rather than helping us to hone in on the guilty party, we've got more suspects than we started with. You left out Junior."

She shrugged and said, "There's not a great deal to talk about. Wallace has had some local trouble, nothing too serious, and has a pretty poor reputation in the village, where he's lovingly known as the spoiled boy king."

"Well," said MacBridan, "at least he lives up to his billing."

"We don't appear to be any closer than we were." Father Novak observed.

"Perhaps," said MacBridan. "But it's good information to have. Need time to give it a little more thought."

There was a knock at the door, and they all turned as Fergus entered the library. "Dinner will be served shortly," he said.

"Thank you, Fergus," said Cori, flashing him a big smile. "We appreciate you coming to get us. I am so ready to eat."

"It is my pleasure," he said, returning her smile. He then quietly left, shutting the door behind him.

"You continue to throw yourself at that man," teased MacBridan.

"Don't even go there," said Cori, casting him a withering look.

The two priests started to get up, but MacBridan stopped them. "We've been playing defense ever since this case started. It's time that we turn things around and go on the offensive. Before we join the family, I'd like to tell you what I have in mind because I'll need your help." He quickly took them through his plan.

"I'm not disagreeing with your plan," said Father Novak, "but will you be giving them enough time to respond?"

"That's the idea," said MacBridan. "We'll tell them the case is breaking. They will have to act quickly, and I hope stupidly."

Dinner with the family went well, and surprisingly, it was Aunt Jean who teased MacBridan about the weather story he'd given them earlier. Not only had it not rained, but the clouds had partially cleared. Everyone joined in, except Wallace, and the mood was happily light and upbeat.

"While we have everyone here, there's an announcement I need to make," said MacBridan. Fergus, who had been attending to the buffet table, started to leave. "Fergus, you need to hear this also. I'm sure the staff will be interested."

"Very good, sir," he said and stood by the door.

"When Cori and I first arrived, many of you met Trevor Truecourt. Well, he called us just before dinner, and I'm pleased to announce that our London office, in coordination with Scotland Yard, have arrested two men in Inverness whom we believe have been behind the attempted thefts."

This welcome news was met with smiles and even some light applause. "Do you know if they had anything to do with Marston's death?" asked Barclay.

"Not at this point," answered Cori.

"Cori and I will be leaving right after dinner to drive to Inverness to join in on the questioning of these men. I've already talked with Marston's men. They'll continue to keep a sharp lookout until we're sure that we have the right guys. The painting, which has been at the center of all of this from the start, is safely locked away in the storage room. We're confident that the security systems we've put in place will protect it if it turns out that these men are not the ones we've been looking for."

"Will you be gone long?" asked Aunt Jean.

"Just this evening and part of tomorrow. If all goes well, we expect to be back by this time tomorrow night. While I'm gone, it is only reasonable that Wallace should oversee the home," MacBridan added with a smile. Anger and relief played across Wallace's weak features like clouds scuttling across the Scottish sky.

There was another round of well-wishing as they excused themselves and left the dining room. Fergus followed them out. "If you will give me just a few moments, I'll bring a car around for you to use."

As he scurried off, Father Collin joined them in the foyer. "A word before you go," he said, ushering them outside. His face was grim. "I've just heard from Ubel, and he'll be waiting."

"What is it?" asked MacBridan.

"Ubel found Carl Meyer, or at least what's left of him."

"Left of him?" asked Cori.

"Just north of town, tied upside down to a tree. He was disemboweled. He didn't die quickly. It was clearly a ritual killing."

"Kaseem?" asked MacBridan.

"Considering the method of his death, we're all but certain."

At that moment, Fergus pulled up in a small green Citroen. "The tank is full, sir. It shouldn't give you any trouble."

"Sorry to spring this on you, Fergus, but as you can imagine, we're anxious to get going," said Cori.

MacBridan took the wheel, and the two of them drove away. "I sincerely hope they have the right men," said Fergus. "The family needs to get this behind them."

"God willing," said Father Collin as the car's taillights disappeared into the trees. "God willing."

Night quietly settled over the estate. Before the grandfather clock at the end of the hall had struck twelve, all lights were out; the household retired. The night sky was partly overcast, the wind buffeting through the upper branches of the trees. The nearly full moon made itself known, casting its silvery light across the grounds through breaks in the broken clouds. Apart from the night sounds coming from the woods, all was quiet.

Upon leaving the estate grounds, MacBridan and Cori soon came upon Ubel about two miles down the road waiting for them. Taking over the driving, Ubel soon turned off onto a narrow, overgrown lane that he'd found, which ran parallel to the MacKinnon estate.

"How in the world did you come across this?" asked MacBridan as the car slowly made its way through the woods.

"A couple of nights ago, I followed one of the security men," said Ubel. "He left his post and came here to drink."

"He may not be much of a guard, but at least, he's provided some value, no matter how inadvertent it may have been," said Cori.

"Father Collin said you found Carl," said MacBridan.

Ubel nodded. "He died hard." He left it at that, not giving any other details. Soon he brought the car to a stop in a small clearing. They got out, and he began to lead them through the woods, back to the estate. It was slow going as they couldn't use flashlights. Even when the moon's light was able to break through, it barely penetrated the thick cover of trees.

"I'll be nearby," said Ubel. He turned and disappeared back into the trees.

Hugging the shadows, they made their way back to the house. Father Collin had left one of the windows in the library unlocked, and they were soon back inside. As quickly and quietly as they could, they made their way upstairs, Cori taking up position in her room, MacBridan locking himself into the storage room.

Settling down for what could be a long wait, MacBridan eased into a comfortable chair on the far side of the room deep in the shadows. The picture they'd been protecting rested on a pedestal in the center of the room, draped by a white cloth. It was 12:30 a.m., and the vigil began.

The night crawled along, time seeming to make little progress. MacBridan soon found himself struggling to stay awake. Maybe Father Novak had been right; maybe the people they were after wouldn't go for their ruse. More than once, he caught himself dozing off. Then, just before 4:00 a.m., a sound at the window caught his attention. Not daring to move, he watched as a dark figure outside expertly manipulated the latch and raised the window. Trying to peer through the darkness, he could just make out the rope the intruder had used to lower themselves from the roof. The whole performance was impressive, especially considering that his nocturnal visitor had successfully bypassed the alarms Cori had installed on the windows. Clearly they'd used an electronic override system to do this, a system that did not come cheap, but was impressive nevertheless.

Once inside, the thief made sure that the window was securely propped open then stood perfectly still. The thief then tiptoed to the pedestal in the center of the room. Clouds swallowed the moon at that moment. MacBridan could barely make out the thief's shadow.

Carefully the thief removed the cloth covering the painting, letting it drop to the floor. Then, producing a small penlight, the thief turned it on to examine the canvass. Rather than finding the landscape done by the MacKinnon ancestor, the light revealed a white canvass with a MacBridan original—a circle with a smiley face.

"I admit it's lite on depth of style, but it clearly communicates how happy I am to see you," said MacBridan, simultaneously turning on a powerful flashlight.

The thief whirled around, using the penlight to see who was there. "Easy," warned MacBridan. "Move very slowly, and keep those hands where I can see them." MacBridan lifted his gun so that the thief saw what he held in his right hand.

The thief wore a monk's robe, cinched at the waist that looked old and tattered, complete with hooded cowl. The outfit made the thief look like Balgair's ghost. Although the hood had fallen back, a black ski mask prevented MacBridan from seeing its face.

"Do as I say, and you'll probably make it through this in one piece," said MacBridan. "Now, with your left hand, carefully remove the ski mask."

The thief didn't respond at first but looked around as if weighing his options. Finally, using his left hand as instructed, it pulled off the mask. MacBridan smiled to himself, not surprised at who stood before him.

"Good evening, Mr. MacBridan. I tried to tell them that this was a setup," said Talon. "But rather than listen to an experienced professional, they continue to base their decisions on the opinions of their informant. How brilliantly stupid."

"Good evening, Talon," said MacBridan, lowering the flashlight some so that she wasn't blinded by the light, "or should I say Ms. Cuvier?"

"Where's the painting, MacBridan?"

"What? No 'hello'? No 'I've missed you'? A less secure man would be hurt."

"I'm not here for playful banter. Where is it?"

"You can't seriously be asking me that while I have a gun trained on you. Kaseem must be a pretty brutal task master. Or is it you? Either way, you're racking up quite a body count."

"No matter what you may think, MacBridan, I'm not a killer. You may know Kaseem's name, but you have no clue as to what you're up against. Take my advice. Give me the painting, leave Scotland, and go hide before he starts hunting you."

"That's not how it's going to go. Cooperate with us, and we'll do all that we can to help you, but as things stand right now, even if you're not a murderer, you're going down as an accomplice."

Talon slowly shook her head. "MacBridan, you are without a doubt the biggest douleur dans le arese I've ever met."

"Nice try, but flirting with me now really isn't going to help you. Who's the inside guy, Talon? Who's been feeding you all this wonderful information?"

Talon bowed her head for a moment then looked up directly at MacBridan. Her right hand brushed up against her face, moving some strands of hair out of her eyes. It had all been very natural, very smooth, but it had also been the distraction she needed. Her left hand came up holding a small but lethal automatic.

"You didn't impress me as the kind of girl who accessorizes."

"Shut up, MacBridan. For all the trouble you've caused me, I should shoot you right here and now."

MacBridan's smile grew bigger. "Gun or no gun, there's no getting out of here."

Talon sighed. "We both keep making the same mistake. We continue to underestimate each other." Raising the gun slightly, she asked, "Now where's the painting?"

"Where it should be," he answered. "Away from here, and out of your reach."

"You're not going to win. These people are absolutely ruthless. I've watched them. They literally will stop at nothing. Giving me the painting is the only chance you have of staying alive."

"Talon, you're not thinking this through. I too have seen how Kaseem rewards failure. Put down the gun, help us, and we'll protect you."

She burst out laughing. It was a genuine laugh, but it was tinged with fear. "If only that were true. When Kaseem's patience finally runs out, and that won't be much longer, you won't be able to protect yourself, much less anyone else. No, I think I'll stay where I am for now."

As she finished speaking, she dropped a small cylindrical object on the floor that rolled toward MacBridan. By the time he saw it and realized what it was, it was too late. The object went off, filling the room with a blinding flash of light. MacBridan's hands flew to his face as he hit the floor, stunned and unable to see. His gun and flashlight went flying, his gun discharging as it hit the floor.

Chapter 24

Cori kept her door cracked wide enough to give her a good view of the hall while she waited. As the night stretched on, it became a battle just to stay awake, much less alert. Fortunately, the grandfather clock chimed its musical cords every fifteen minutes, which at least helped her to keep track of the time. The problem came when Cori realized that she'd not heard the chimes ring between 3:00 and 3:45 a.m. She had definitely dozed off. Standing up, she silently did some stretches, doing her best to find any smidgen of energy left in her.

A little after 4:00 a.m., she thought she heard voices, but they were faint, so faint that she wasn't sure if her mind was playing tricks on her. Trying to keep the hinges on her door from creaking, she carefully opened it a little bit wider to see if she could hear any better. Although muffled, she could definitely hear people talking. Listening again, she was pretty certain that it was coming from the storage room. Gun in hand, Cori stepped into the hall, which was nearly pitch-black. Pressed against the wall, she began to slowly work her way toward the storage room, all the while doing her best not to make any noise. She was still about fifteen feet away when a small explosion went off, light from the blast shooting out from under the storage room door, followed by a gunshot.

"Mac!"

Snapping her flashlight on, she rushed to the door, but it was still locked. The flashlight dropped to the floor as she dug into her pocket, her fingers fumbling for the key. "Mac! Mac, open the door!"

Seconds, which felt like hours, dragged on before she was able to get the door open. Cori stepped in, gun leveled, quickly taking in the whole room. The window across her was wide open. The painting and its pedestal had been knocked over, and MacBridan was on his knees, trying to get up off the floor, his hands rubbing his eyes. "Are you all right?"

"I will be," he said as she helped him to his feet. He staggered slightly then managed to regain his balance, reorienting himself with his surroundings. "It was Talon. I had her. She was here in this room, and I managed to let her get away. Again!"

"Flash grenade?"

"Yes, a small one, but it did the job," answered MacBridan. "At the moment, all I'm seeing are large blackish blue dots."

Cori went to the open window and looked out. The rope was still there, swaying with the wind. "How did she get past the alarm?"

"No idea. It was all pretty impressive to watch, but then that's why she gets the big bucks."

Cori couldn't understand how Talon could have accomplished this. She'd already started to study the wiring she'd run on the window frame when a high pitched scream came from down the hall. "Aunt Jean?" asked Cori, looking at MacBridan.

"I still can't see well enough to do anything. Go to her, and do not leave her for any reason," directed MacBridan. Although his vision had started to clear, he knew at this point he'd be more in the way than anything. Helplessness was perhaps the feeling he hated the most.

Retrieving her flashlight, Cori left MacBridan and ran down the hall. Remembering her experience with the giggler the last time she'd been to Aunt Jean's room sent a chill through her body. Just as she reached for the doorknob, a pitiful wail of absolute terror erupted from inside. Cori pushed the door open and burst into the room.

MacBridan moved to the window, but his vision had not completely cleared. Squinting seemed to help and luck tilted in MacBridan's direction as he spotted Talon running across the lawn toward the tree line. The monk's costume appeared to be slowing her down. He didn't hear any other sounds coming from Aunt Jean's room and knew that Cori could take care of herself. Grabbing the rope, he began to lower himself to the ground.

Still shaken from the flash grenade, his descent went far faster than he'd intended, and he hit the ground pretty hard. Through the faint light from the moon he glimpsed Talon as she darted into the woods. Unless he was mistaken, Talon was following the same path that they'd used when they'd walked to the chapel. His chances of catching her were slim; he knew that, but the thought of her slipping through his fingers yet again was intolerable.

Aunt Jean lay on the floor in a crumpled mass, her back up against the wall farthest away from the windows. Her skin was frighteningly pale in the light from Cori's flashlight. Kneeling beside her, Cori could see that she was trembling uncontrollably. Aunt Jean flinched at her touch then looked up at her, her eyes locking on to Cori's.

"Help me," she whimpered, "please, they're after me."

As Cori helped her up from the floor, she looked around again, confirming that they were indeed alone. "It's all right," said Cori. "There's no one else here."

There was absolutely no strength left in Aunt Jean. Cori carefully maneuvered her into a chair next to the bed. Aunt Jean frantically pointed toward the window. "Over there," she said, her voice filled with desperation. "They stood on air outside the window. They've come for me. I know it."

"I want you to sit still," said Cori. "Everything's okay. There's no one here but us. I'm going to look around."

Cori turned her flashlight off. While she waited for her eyes to adjust to the dark room, she stayed beside Aunt Jean, her hand gently resting on the old woman's shoulder.

"Why did you turn your light off?"

Cori could hear the panic in Aunt Jean's voice. She sounded like a small child. "If someone is still out there, I don't want them to see me. It looks like the moon may give me all the light I'll need."

"You sit tight. I'm just going over to the window."

"No!" said Aunt Jean, gripping Cori's hand as tightly as she could. "Please don't leave me. They'll take you too."

Cori gently pulled away from Aunt Jean. "You have to let me see who's there. I want to know who's doing this to you so that I can stop them. I promise I'm not leaving you."

Crossing the room, Cori stood to the side of the window. The moon cast its gentle glow across the landscape, providing enough light for her to have a good look at the grounds below. Although some areas remained lost in the shadows, nothing out of the ordinary caught her attention. Just to be sure, Cori tried opening each of the windows. They were locked tight. Looking directly down, Cori estimated that they were easily a good twenty to twenty-five feet off the ground. The old woman's mind must be slipping. No one needs to deal with murder and crime in their last days. Cori said a prayer for the old woman, and as though she had heard it, she stopped whimpering.

She went back, and once again knelt down beside the frail woman. Cori pulled a quilt from the foot of the bed and wrapped it around her shoulders, hoping that the added warmth would help to calm her. "I didn't see anyone. Whoever it was, they're gone now," she said, doing her best to calm her down.

Without warning, Aunt Jean's entire body stiffened, her nails burying into Cori's arm. Her eyes grew wide, and she tried to speak but was having trouble catching her breath. "They're back," she choked out. "Look! Oh my god, they're back!"

Coming to her feet, Cori whirled around to look at the window. The nightmarish scene before her hit with the impact of a physical blow. She froze, completely unable to move. Cori could not believe what she was seeing. An almost unbearable fear shot through her body; she could hear the blood racing in her ears. Standing outside the window, a window that was close to two and a half stories above the ground, were the silhouettes of dozens of people. Cori's mind rebelled, the whole scene terribly perverted. These couldn't be people; it was all wrong. Their bodies were twisted, mangled. The creatures keep surging toward the windows. They moved like liquid, a tide of darkness that made them lose their individual shapes. Despite the moonlight, Cori couldn't make out any of their features; they were utterly black. But she could see their eyes, small sickly green pinpoints emanating pure hatred.

Cori fought hard to keep from panicking. She knew she had to do something to somehow get her and Aunt Jean out of there, but her body refused to respond, like a dream that doesn't let you run. Panic threatened to take her over when Aunt Jean screamed and tried to get out of her chair. Her scream snapped Cori out of it. Turning to Aunt Jean, she briefly struggled with her, forcing the old woman back down into her chair.

"No," she shouted, pulling her gun. "If they do get in, I want you out of my line of fire." She whipped back around, ready to do all that she could to protect her.

The window was empty, the creatures inexplicably gone. Cori quickly moved to the bed and turned the lamp on. Precious light flooded the room, helping her to get a better grip on her nerves. Looking at Aunt Jean, she motioned for her to be quiet. She moved to the door and carefully checked the hall. It was dark and mercifully empty.

Coming back into the room, she shut the door and fastened the dead bolt. Glancing at the window, she checked to see if they'd returned. They had not returned. She knew she had to check the window out to see if they were somehow lurking outside, but her nerves wouldn't let her. For the moment, she just couldn't bring herself to do that.

Turning on two more lamps, she went back over to Aunt Jean. The woman sat there with her head down, silently crying. She looked so small, so helpless. "It's all my fault," she sobbed. "It's the curse. It is my time, and they've come for me."

"Listen to me," said Cori, her voice loud and stern. "You're okay. No one's coming for you, not as long as I'm here. Do you understand?"

Aunt Jean looked up at her, slightly nodding her head. Tears covered her face; Cori realized that the old woman had taken her teeth out. Cori took her in both arms and hugged her. She held the frail old woman for a few moments. Aunt Jean was so light, like Cori's grandmother had been in her last trip to the hospital.

"There's one more thing I have to do."

Taking a deep breath, she crossed to the windows. The moon displayed the grounds below in a ghostly white light, but all looked as it should. Moving closer to the glass, she tried to look straight down. Nothing. Cori shut the curtains and went back to Aunt Jean, bringing a chair with her.

"Did you hurt yourself when you fell?" she asked.

Aunt Jean didn't respond. Cori wasn't sure she'd heard her.

"Aunt Jean? Did you hurt yourself anywhere?" she asked again.

Finally Aunt Jean looked at her and shook her head. "I don't think so. I never let people see me without my teeth," she added sheepishly.

"We're going to have the doctor check you out anyway," said Cori. "I've taken some pretty good falls in my time, and you can't be too careful." Cori went to the fireplace and piled some of the smaller logs in the bin onto the bed of coals that was still glowing. It didn't take long before small flames began to appear.

"We'll get the fire going again and get some heat in here," said Cori, the sound of her own voice felt reassuring.

"You saved my life," said Aunt Jean. "Maybe more than that."

Cori helped her out of the chair, and bringing the quilt with them, she supported Aunt Jean as they moved to the chairs in front of the fire. "We're here to protect you, MacBridan, Father Collin, all of us. They're busy at the moment, but I'm not going to leave your side. If you'd like to lie down, you let me know, and we'll get you into bed."

"I want to stay here by the fire. I'll be fine," said Aunt Jean.

Cori sat down next to her. Now that things seemed to be calming down, worry began to replace the fear. Where was MacBridan? Had those things gone after him? It was her first moment to actually catch her breath and reflect over all that she'd just gone through. She breathed in deeply, trying to let go of the fear that still lingered within her. She was surprised to find that her hands still trembled. At that moment, a terrible realization washed over her. Either they were up against unimaginable demonic forces, which would mean that the two priests had been right all along, or, and this was more probable, she was losing her mind. All things considered, she prayed that it was her mind letting go of its grip on reality.

Chapter 25

Running at full tilt, MacBridan plunged into the woods, doing his best to close the gap between him and Talon. He panted in the smell of forest loam, his breath fogging the air. His last glimpse of her had showed that she was still struggling with the monk's robes. He hoped this might give him an edge slowing her down. The thick canopy of leaves that arched above him filtered out any of the moonlight that had been lighting the way, forcing him to turn on his flashlight. Its strong beam lit up the path but, at the same time, gave away his position to anyone who might be watching.

The flashlight created shadows from the trees and bushes around him, jumping and moving as he ran by, keeping his nerves on edge as he raced down the trail. At any moment, he expected one of Talon's accomplices to jump at him out of the darkness. He had no way of telling if she'd continued her escape through the woods or had taken refuge in the dense undergrowth. Although he remembered the path being reasonably straight and not all that long, tonight it seemed to stretch on forever.

Up ahead, he could see a dim light breaking through the trees and knew he was getting close to trail's end. Slowing down, but only slightly, he watched as closely as he could to make sure no one was waiting to ambush him. MacBridan stopped at the edge of the lane, turning his flashlight off. He stayed close to the tree line, not wishing to reveal himself in the bright moonlight. Trying to catch his breath, he looked up and down the lane, listening, hunting for any sign that would lead him to where Talon had gone. The night was still; the sound of his own blood pounding in his ears was like kettle drums. The spots had almost left his eyes. The only movement came from the treetops swaying in the wind.

"You must be very careful tonight, Mr. MacBridan."

The man's voice had materialized out of nowhere, causing MacBridan to jump. It came from behind him, so close that he could almost feel the man's breath on his neck. MacBridan whirled around, leveling his gun at the man standing not five feet away from him.

"The one you're chasing ran through the gates to the kirk," said the older man, pointing the way with his left arm. MacBridan immediately recognized him. It was the servant he'd met by the roses that day he'd been waiting for Cori. Taking a deep breath, MacBridan lowered his gun, trying to rein in his shaky nerves.

"What in the—," started MacBridan, his temper rising to the surface. "You almost got yourself shot! What the devil are you doing out here?" It was all he could do to keep from shouting.

"I've been having trouble resting," answered Dillon.

"Well, you're definitely in the wrong place at the wrong time," said MacBridan. "You need to get out of here and head back to the house."

"Don't follow him into the churchyard, Mr. MacBridan. What waits there is far too dangerous."

"It's follow her, not him, and I'm a little dangerous myself."

Dillon's face clearly showed his concern, his voice filled with urgency. "You don't understand. The gatherer walks tonight. Something has called to him. You will be placing your mortal soul in danger."

MacBridan impatiently shook his head. "I don't have the time for this, Dillon. Go home. This could get pretty rough, and I don't want you getting hurt." With that, MacBridan turned and ran down the lane toward the chapel.

The moon held true, lighting his way. When MacBridan reached the gates, he found one of them was already slightly open, leaving a space about two feet wide. Not wanting to give himself away, MacBridan knew better than to trust the old hinges to be quiet. Carefully he squeezed his large frame through the opening without moving the gate. At first glance, the churchyard appeared to be devoid of life. He noticed that the wind had begun to pick up a little as leaves swirled around the base of the headstones.

MacBridan inched forward, watching, listening, using the taller monuments as cover. The sudden sound of a latch catching behind him, metal on metal, stopped him. He quickly turned back around, ready to face his attacker. The heavy iron gate that he'd just worked his way through had closed. Staying in the shadow of a tall stone angel, he intently studied the area around the gates, looking for whoever had closed it. Had Dillon followed him in? Was he still trying to help? None of the gravestones near the gate were large enough to hide anyone. Could the wind have done that with such a heavy gate? It didn't seem possible, but it was the only explanation he could stomach.

Turning back around, he continued to make his way around the graves, looking for his quarry. The chapel loomed ahead of him. House of God or not, based on his previous experience there, it was definitely not a welcoming sight.

MacBridan stopped, dropped to one knee, and froze. Out of the corner of his eye, he'd caught something moving. Peering into the darkness, he watched and waited. Then, well off to the right of the chapel, MacBridan spotted her as she cautiously moved deeper into the churchyard. Talon was also trying to hide behind the larger tombstones and kept looking behind her to see if she were being pursued. She still had a good forty to fifty yards before she'd be at the rear wall of the enclosure. *Talon, you've finally run out of places to hide*, MacBridan thought to himself. He would look forward to telling this story, capturing an international art thief single-handedly. A broad grin spread on his face.

Then, unexpectedly, MacBridan spotted a second figure much farther back. He watched as this other figure rose up above the graves looming over them, impossibly tall. MacBridan reasoned that it was some sort of an optical illusion, for it appeared to be close to seven feet tall. An all too familiar fear that he remembered from his last visit to the chapel began to fill his stomach. The figure started to move, not walk but glide. The thing glided around and through the graves, heading directly for Talon. She too had stopped, crouched behind a bulky monument. MacBridan was pretty sure that she was completely unaware of the thing moving in her direction. Like her, the creature was hooded, with long flowing robes. MacBridan watched in fascinated awe as it closed in on her.

"Talon, behind you!" shouted MacBridan. "Watch out!"

MacBridan started toward her as fast as he could, doing his best to keep an eye on the creature while at the same time trying to keep from tripping over any of the smaller grave markers. Talon saw MacBridan and briefly hesitated. She then turned around, finally catching sight of the thing bearing down on her. It was close to her, too close.

"Talon, move, get out of there," yelled MacBridan. He stopped and, taking quick aim, fired two shots into the upper torso of the advancing creature. Both shots must have missed as he heard them ricochet off the far wall of the churchyard.

Although the shots missed, they did motivate Talon into action. Turning away from it, she started to run, but it was too late. The creature fell on her, completely enveloping her in its robes, taking her to the ground. A terrible shriek of pain and terror ripped through the night then abruptly stopped.

All was quiet. Nothing moved, just the pounding of the blood in his ears.

MacBridan held his ground, not sure as to what he should do. For that matter, he wasn't even sure about what had just happened. His sense of self-preservation screamed at him to run, but he couldn't leave Talon behind. Remembering his flashlight, he reached for it and aimed the powerful beam at the spot where she'd gone down. At first, he couldn't see either of them. Then the dark cloaked figure rose up over the motionless form lying on the ground. It stood perfectly still, looking down on its kill. The hood covered its face, but as the wind blew, the robes moved enough to where MacBridan could see the faint outlines of a dark red cross spread across a dirty white tunic.

MacBridan couldn't move. Then, at the same moment as the creature began to move toward him, thick clouds covered the moon, blocking out its light and casting a deep, impenetrable blanket of darkness across the churchyard. The effect was devastatingly claustrophobic.

MacBridan fired two more shots. He knew that at that range, he couldn't miss. But as before, they seemed to pass through the thing with absolutely no effect, and it continued to glide toward him. Looking in both directions, he realized that the chapel was closer than the gates, so he took off for the chapel doors.

As he turned toward it, his left hand smashed against a waist-high monument, shattering his flashlight. He struggled on, the faint silhouette of the chapel guiding him. Thick clouds continued to blot out the moon. The wind suddenly picked up, violently tossing the trees back and forth. He'd lost track of the creature when something snagged his foot sending him stumbling forward, but he somehow managed to keep from crashing into ground. He kept going. A wailing moan swelled up behind him. The creature was moving fast; he could feel it and knew that one more wrong step would mean his death.

Not more than ten steps in front of the creature, MacBridan lunged for the chapel doors. The one on the left was locked. MacBridan reached for the other door, but it too was bolted shut. He turned to face the creature, pressing his back up against the chapel doors.

The creature hovered directly before him.

Its face was lost in the dark folds of the hood that covered its head, the long robes hanging down nearly touching the ground unaffected by strong wind. The cross MacBridan had glimpsed earlier on its chest was now clearly visible. The creature's waist was cinched with a broad belt, and MacBridan saw a scabbard hanging from it.

The apparition radiated a deep cold. He tried to reach for his gun, but his arm wouldn't respond as numbness quickly spread throughout his body. The finger that had touched the planchette throbbed. The creature glared at him, lost interest, then glided away. MacBridan watched, unable to take his eyes away as it moved through the graveyard. It soon entered the deep shadows near the wall, and although he couldn't be sure, it appeared to pass through the tall stone wall.

Still leaning with his back to the door, MacBridan found that he was surprisingly out of breath. He could still feel the presence of the creature, and his stomach rebelled. MacBridan slowly slid to the ground, his legs splayed in front of him resting on the steps leading into the chapel. The same wailing moan that he'd heard before cried out again, only now it was far away. For a moment, he thought he was going to be sick.

MacBridan sat there, pulling his shattered nerves back together. His mind raced, trying desperately to grasp what had just happened, unable to even hazard a guess at what he'd just witnessed. He was pretty sure that Talon was dead. But why was he alive? The thing had come at him, caught him, but had left him alive. Why? His mind went back to Cori at the estate. Had that thing been waiting for her in Aunt Jean's room? He cursed himself for not having gone with her, angry that he'd let his pride get in the way. He silently prayed that she was all right and that help would come with the morning.

Chapter 26

What little remained of the night passed slowly. The wind ushered in a light rain, steadily soaking everything. MacBridan was miserable. Not too long after the creature left, MacBridan once again tried to get into the chapel, but the doors were securely bolted. Without his flashlight, he could see very little but knew he had to get to Talon. If by some miracle, she was still alive, he was the only one in a position to help.

Still shaken, MacBridan's nerves slowly settled down, and he found himself getting colder and angrier by the moment. He reached into his jacket pocket for his cell phone, but it was gone, hard to tell where he'd lost it. It had been close to twenty minutes since he'd last seen or heard anything from the thing that had attacked them. Stepping away from the relative safety of the chapel, he set out to find her. He was more upset with himself than anything. He didn't know what else he could have done, but in the end, he'd failed to save her. Worst of all, he couldn't stop thinking about Cori. If anything had happened to her, he knew he'd never be able to forgive himself.

As he made his way toward Talon, something crunched underfoot, and he realized that he was walking on his ruined flashlight. The eastern sky finally began to lighten with the coming dawn, but the heavy ceiling of rain clouds dominating the sky hampered the sun's efforts. MacBridan kept walking, somewhat unsteadily, constantly watching for the creature to return. Talon's crumpled form lay about twenty feet in front of him. Again, guilt washed over him. Logically he knew he was being ridiculous, but for some reason, he continued to heap the blame on his shoulders.

Talon was lying facedown on the ground, the monk's hood and robe completely covering her. As he got closer, MacBridan looked for any sign of life. It was then he realized that something was wrong. The body on the ground looked to be too big to be Talon's. MacBridan knelt down for a closer look. There was enough light now where he could see most of the churchyard. Once again, he checked to make sure that they were alone. There was no sign of the creature. Leaning over, he gently turned the body over and pulled the hood back. Mud and grass matted down the hair in places and streaked across the face. MacBridan could not have been more surprised. The dead fleshy face of Wallace stared up at him, the eyes wide open silently expressing the stark terror that had been Wallace's last earthly experience.

Without warning, the gates to the churchyard creaked in protest as they opened. MacBridan's reflexes took over, and in one fluid motion, he spun around, gun in hand, taking aim at the man standing just inside the gates.

"I heard shots. What happened?"

It was Ubel.

"Took you long enough to get here. Where have you been?" asked MacBridan.

"Near the front gates of the estate. If they got past you, I was to stop them there," said Ubel as he walked through the churchyard. He seemed calm, as if he were having a leisurely stroll through the gardens, oblivious to the rain.

"It's Wallace," said MacBridan.

Ubel barely nodded. "You killed him?"

"No, something else beat me to it. Do you have your cell phone with you?"

Ubel nodded, taking it out of his pocket.

"I need for Father Collin to check on Cori and Aunt Jean. I'm guessing they're in Aunt Jean's room. It's been rather a full night."

Cori looked over at Aunt Jean and then at her watch. As best she could tell, Aunt Jean had finally dozed off. Cori got up, adjusted the blue and cream quilt covering the old woman, and put two more logs on the fire. The fire crackled as the well-seasoned oak yielded its heat. She tried calling MacBridan again, but he still wasn't answering. She wanted to go and look for him, but knew she couldn't leave Aunt Jean unprotected. Some time ago she'd heard shots, or at least she thought they'd been shots. The sound had been faint, yet in many ways unmistakable.

A light tapping at Aunt Jean's door startled her. She pulled her gun and silently went to the door. "Who's there?" she asked.

"It's Father Collin."

Unbolting the door, she opened it to find Father Collin standing there, his face displaying his concern. "Are you all right?"

"Yes. I've lost my mind, but other than that, I'm doing just great."

He and Father Novak entered the room, closing the door behind them. Father Novak went directly to Aunt Jean.

"I think she's okay," said Cori, "but we'll need a doctor to check her out. I found her on the floor beside her bed."

"What happened?" asked Father Collin.

Cori shook her head. "I'm not sure what happened, but it was horrible. Something, some things that is, tried to attack her. There were several of them." Again, she shook her head, trying to escape the memory while at the same time trying to put into words what she saw. "They were horrible. I've never seen anything like them."

Father Collin put his hands on Cori's shoulders. "Are you sure you're okay?"

Cori stared into his eyes for a moment. "I didn't know what to do," she whispered. "I felt so helpless, so completely terrified that I couldn't even think straight."

"It's okay. We're here with you. We'll help," said Father Collin. "Where's MacBridan?"

"I don't know. I can't reach him. We split up. He went after the thief, and I rushed over here to help her. About thirty minutes ago, I thought I heard shots. He's not answering his phone."

Father Collin nodded. "We heard them too. Father Novak?"

Father Novak was standing beside Aunt Jean. "She's fine, just sleeping."

Cori heard a low, buzzing sound and looked around, trying to find its source. "That's me," said Father Collin, reaching into his pocket. He quickly glanced at his phone then answered it. "I see," he said after listening for a moment. "She and Aunt Jean are fine. Father Novak and I are with them now. Stay there, and I'll join you."

"What is it?" asked Cori, gripping Father Collin's arm.

"That was Ubel. He's with Mac. He's okay, but we have another body. I'm going to join them at the chapel. We need for you to call DS Wetmoore."

"I'm coming with you," said Cori.

"Cori, we need you here," said Father Collin. "Father Novak and you need to stay with Aunt Jean. She's obviously being targeted, and they may come back for her. Together, I'm confident that the two of you can guard her against anything the dark side may throw at us."

Cori hesitated briefly. "And you're sure Mac's okay?"

"Yes, he's doing just fine. Please stay here. We'll be back as soon as we can."

It took longer than he wanted, but Father Collin finally made it to the chapel. He quickly spotted MacBridan and Ubel and walked over to them. In the distance, they could faintly hear sirens heading their way. Father Collin stood next to the two men, breathing heavily.

MacBridan looked at the priest. "You talked with Cori?"

"Yes," answered Father Collin. "I didn't get much in the way of details from her, but she had quite a night. Apparently, they came after Aunt Jean."

"Why?" asked MacBridan. "That doesn't make sense."

Father Collin leaned against a tall headstone and tried to regulate his breathing. "Is everything all right, Father? Do you need to sit down?" asked Ubel.

"I'm fine, sorry," muttered Father Collin impatiently. "I'm just getting too old for all of this."

"Or you're getting sedate in your ways in addition to having too much scotch too often. The sin of gluttony, Father," said MacBridan, smiling at him.

Father Collin chose to ignore him and stared down at the body. "What happened here?"

"As we hoped, they took the bait and came after the painting," said MacBridan.

"Talon?" asked Ubel.

"Yes. However, she used a small flash grenade that I didn't see coming and, I'm embarrassed to say, got away. By the time my eyes had cleared, I caught sight of her running across the grounds toward the woods. It was then that we heard Aunt Jean cry out, so Cori went to help her, and I took off after Talon."

Father Collin walked over and looked down at the body. "This is Wallace. Are you trying to tell me that Wallace was Talon?"

"Not unless he's an absolute master of disguise," said MacBridan. "Apparently, Wallace was helping Talon and somewhere traded places with her as she was making her escape. Dillon helped with the misdirection, and I followed the person whom I thought was Talon into the churchyard."

"Did he attack you?" asked Father Collin.

"He didn't get the chance," said MacBridan. He looked back at the gate. The sirens were much clearer now, and they'd soon have company. "I'll tell you more about it later, but this thing attacked him and killed him."

"A thing?" said Father Collin.

"Yeah, that's all I've got. I have no idea what it was, but it moved quickly and brought him down."

Father Collin knelt down next to Wallace, bowed his head in prayer, and then with his forefinger, drew the sign of the cross on Wallace's forehead.

Two cruisers crunched to a stop on the gravel outside the gates. MacBridan turned to face them and found that Ubel was gone. DS Wetmoore came in followed by three of his men. Two of them stopped, taking up position on each side of the gate.

"Morning, Sergeant," said MacBridan. He glanced back at Father Collin in time to see the priest quickly remove something from around Wallace's neck and discreetly slip it into his pocket.

Father Collin stood up. "I've given him last rights. He's in God's hands now."

"Wallace," said Wetmoore. He turned to his officer to call for an ambulance. "How did this happen?"

"We had a break in at the estate last night," explained MacBridan. "It's a long story, but the short version is that the thief went for the painting, failed, then got away from me. I gave chase. Somewhere along the way, Wallace took their place and ran in here to hide. At least, I guess that's why he ran in here."

"Did you kill him?" asked Wetmoore.

"No. Someone else did."

"Who?"

"I don't know. I saw them, tried to stop them, but they got away."

"Sounds like getting away from you is pretty easy, doesn't it?" said Wetmoore.

"My professionalism is awe-inspiring."

"Once we finish up here, I'm going to want the long version. Are you carrying?"

"Yes."

Wetmoore nodded. "Give the officer your weapon." MacBridan did. "What are you doing here, Father?"

"The break in at the house left us all pretty shaken. Ms. Hopkins let me know that Mr. MacBridan had gone after the thief. I went looking for him and found him here."

"And you just happened to come to the chapel," commented Wetmoore.

Father Collin gave a small smile and shrugged. "Here on the grounds, there are only so many places to look. It's not really all that remarkable."

"I'd like for you two to go back to the house with this officer and wait for me in the library."

"You and I need to talk before you contact Lord MacKinnon," said MacBridan. "As bad as this is going to be for him, I want to spare him as much unnecessary pain as I can."

Wetmoore considered MacBridan's request then nodded. "Very well, we'll talk before I call him."

By this time, another car had arrived, and MacBridan recognized Dr. Shepard as he entered the churchyard. *It's pretty bad when you've been some place for only a few days and you already know the local coroner by sight,* thought MacBridan.

Wetmoore had been examining MacBridan's gun. "This has been recently fired. You sure you didn't shoot Wallace?"

"Positive. I shot at his assailant."

"Where were you standing when you shot at this mystery person?"

MacBridan pointed to a gravestone whose top rose up in the middle with a large stone vase resting on it. "I may be off a little bit but roughly right over there."

"Then you were reasonably close," said Wetmoore.

"I suppose so."

"Did you hit them?"

"It didn't look that way."

"Nice shooting."

"Did I mention that it was dark?"

Dr. Shepard knelt down next to Wallace's body and began to examine him.

"Father, MacBridan, I'll see you back at the house," said Wetmoore and turned his attention to Dr. Shepard. Accompanied by the officer, Father Collin and MacBridan left.

MacBridan, using Father Collin's phone, called Cori while they were walking back to the house. They all agreed that Wallace's death would be kept quiet until they talked with Wetmoore.

Faith soon joined Father Novak in Aunt Jean's room, relieving Cori who quickly headed off to join MacBridan and Father Collin in the library. With the coming of dawn Cori, felt that Aunt Jean would be reasonably safe. Faith called her aunt's doctor, and he promised to get there as soon as he could. Cori passed Fergus on the stairs on her way down. He was bringing tea and oatmeal to Aunt Jean's room.

Cori passed the officer standing in the hall as she went into the library. MacBridan, who had been drying out by the fire, went to her as the stress from the previous night finally broke through to the surface, and she fell into his arms. He gently held her as she cried. He'd only seen Cori cry once before.

"Thank God you're all right," she said as the tears slowed down. "I'm sorry. I know I'm being silly, but it was so horrible. These things, they were hideous. I don't know what they were, but they were after Aunt Jean. I know now that some of the stuff the priests have been talking about is real. Unfortunately, tonight my world has gotten a little less real."

"It's okay, Cori," said MacBridan. "I never should have left you."

Fergus had also been kind enough to bring oatmeal, coffee, and tea to library. Father Collin poured Cori a cup of hot tea. "Sit her down over here by the fire," he directed. "We need to talk before Wetmoore joins us." Cori gratefully accepted the tea. MacBridan stayed next to her.

"I'll start," said MacBridan, knowing they had very little time. "While we did succeed in drawing them out, I'm afraid things have gone from bad to worse." MacBridan proceeded to relate the string of events that had occurred that night, including Dillon's being where he shouldn't have been. The end results were not good and the disappointment he felt was easy to see on his face.

"Dillon?" asked Father Collin.

"Yes, he's one of the servants here at the estate. I met him the day Cori and I went to the chapel."

"Oh yes," said Father Collin, "you mentioned him. He's the one that you told me is so concerned about Aunt Jean."

"What was he doing out there so late at night?" asked Cori. Her eyes were red, her voice steady.

"He said he was having trouble sleeping or something like that. He'll never know how close he came to permanently going to sleep."

"I'd like to talk to him," said Father Collin. "There's a coincidence Wetmoore will never believe."

"Not sure I do either, Father, but it wasn't the right time to press him. But here's where it starts to get even stranger. Dillon warned me. He knew about that thing in the churchyard and told me that I'd be risking my soul to go in there. He called it the gatherer."

"The gatherer?" asked Cori.

MacBridan nodded and continued his narrative, giving as much detail as he could up to his examination of the body and discovering that it was actually Wallace.

"Oh my god," said Cori. "You sure you didn't kill him?"

"You're the third person to ask that. Why does everyone immediately jump to the conclusion that I had anything to do with his death?" said MacBridan. "Okay, the guy was a pampered, immature jerk, but I usually need a little more motivation than that to actually kill someone."

Father Collin seemed to be lost in thought, staring intently into the fireplace. "It will be interesting to learn from Wetmoore what Wallace actually died from."

"Father, what was that thing? As sure as I'm standing here, I watched it kill Wallace, and it wasn't a pleasant death. It smothered him in darkness as it fell on him, drowning out his scream."

Father Collin looked at MacBridan, checking his watch. "We'll come back to that," he said. "I want to hear what happened with Aunt Jean and Cori before the good sergeant joins us."

"I kept trying to call you," said Cori.

"Somewhere along the way, I lost my phone. I'll look for it later."

"Cori," said Father Collin, "we need to know everything that happened, each tiny detail. As hard as it may be, please don't leave anything out."

"I don't plan to," she said. "You'll want to have me committed after I'm finished, but at this point, I really don't care. It was worse than a nightmare because there was no waking up, no way to escape. As unbelievable as this will sound, I swear to you it's what happened. That's what terrifies me the most."

"Did you not just hear what I went through with Wallace in the churchyard?" asked MacBridan. "Did that not sound crazy to you? Frankly, you're going to have to work pretty hard to outcrazy my story."

When she finished telling them what had happened, MacBridan gently squeezed her shoulder and said, "Well, as stories go, we'll call it a draw."

"I was almost as scared as Aunt Jean, but I can't tell you why," said Cori. "Also, I'm pretty sure she knew what those things were. Personally, I've never believed in ghosts, but now I don't know what to think."

"They weren't ghosts," said Father Collin, shaking his head. "I'm afraid they were something far worse."

Cori looked up at him. "Good, that makes me feel better. You know what those things are?"

"I have a pretty good idea," said Father Collin. "We're going to have to keep a close watch on Aunt—"

He stopped as the library door opened, and Wetmoore came in, taking off his raincoat and hanging it on the coat rack by the door. "I was only out there for an hour or so, and I'm chilled to the bone. Can I have a cup?"

"We've a whole pot," answered Father Collin.

Wetmoore poured himself a cup and joined them by the fire. "As you all seem to have played some role in last night's activities, I'm glad to have you here with me. MacBridan, I'd like to start with you. And please, let's make this story a little more complete than the one you gave to me about your adventures at the Hanging Man."

MacBridan smiled at the young sergeant. "I've always been nothing but completely honest with you."

"Of course you have," said Wetmoore. "Now I'd like the long version of what happened last night."

"Okay. Cori and I decided that the only way to catch the thieves that had been targeting the painting here at the estate was to find a way to flush them out into the open. As you and I discussed, we were pretty certain that the thieves had an inside source. So we set a trap. We let the entire household know that we had to leave for the evening but would return, hopefully, twenty-four hours later."

"I see. The idea being that the inside man would then contact his cohorts, and they'd try to once again steal the painting. Very theatrical. I believe I saw that in a Charlie Chan movie," said Wetmoore.

MacBridan, undaunted, continued on. "Seeing as how we didn't give them too much advance notice, we were also hoping that the short notice would cause them to make a mistake. We knew it was a long shot going in, but they went for it. It was Talon who broke in. I thwarted her efforts to steal the painting, but she escaped using a flash grenade."

"Thwarted her efforts?" said Cori, rolling her eyes.

"What's wrong with that?" asked MacBridan.

"Where did this happen?" asked Wetmoore.

"Upstairs in a room we've been using to house the artwork we brought back from Virginia."

"I'd like to see the room when we're finished here," said Wetmoore.

MacBridan nodded. "Cori had been down the hall, and when the flash grenade went off, she used a key she had to get into the room. It took a few moments for my sight to return. It was then that we heard Aunt Jean cry out. Cori went to help her, and once my vision cleared, I went after Talon. From the window, I spotted her running toward the woods."

"Why did Aunt Jean cry out?" asked Wetmoore.

"The noise must have startled her awake," explained Cori. "The whole family has been on edge, and she didn't know what was going on. I did my best to comfort her."

Wetmoore considered that for a moment, then looked back at MacBridan. "Go on."

"I chased Talon, or at least I thought it was Talon, through the woods. For whatever reason she, or he, as it turns out, ran into the churchyard. I followed and soon caught sight of them heading toward the back of the churchyard. As I was moving in on Talon, I spotted a third party coming up behind her."

"How much of a description can you give me?" asked Wetmoore. "Of course, considering you can't tell the difference between a beautiful French girl and an overweight Scotsman..."

"Again, it was dark," said MacBridan. "The clouds blocked the light from the moon, and I shattered my flashlight almost as soon as I entered the churchyard. He was tall and appeared to be in good shape."

"Why do you say that?"

"Because of the way he moved. He was very quick and agile and, I'd also say, very strong. He brought Wallace down without much of a struggle."

"My men found marks on the wall that surrounds the churchyard where your bullets struck. I do find it rather amazing that you missed with all four shots. I'd bet a fair amount of my wages that you're actually pretty good with a gun."

"It was a judgment call. I needed Talon alive to give me the answers as to who was paying her and why. When I saw this other person attacking her, excuse me, him, I tried to stop them, but Talon was in my line of fire. In the dark, I didn't want to risk shooting everyone, so I had to aim a little wide."

Wetmoore was silent for a few moments and then took a sip of tea. He carefully looked at the three of them. "Once again, your story is plausible, and yet I know I'm not getting the whole picture. That said, I'm reasonably sure you didn't kill Wallace, or at least you didn't shoot him. Dr. Shepard couldn't find a mark on him."

"Then what did he die from?" asked Father Collin.

"At this point, we have no idea. There was no bruising that we could find, no obvious puncture wounds, nothing. Hopefully, we'll know when Dr. Shepard completes his examination."

Wetmoore then addressed Father Collin. "How is it that you were the one that went looking for MacBridan this morning and not Ms. Hopkins?"

"I can answer that, Sergeant," said Cori. "I ended up staying with Aunt Jean the rest of the night. While she was glad to learn that we really hadn't left the estate, the break-in completely unnerved her. This worked out well because her room is just down the hall from the storage room. Leaving her door open, I was able to keep watch in the event anyone else came to take the painting. Later, I heard the shots. When Mac didn't return, I tried calling him but couldn't reach him."

"It seems that in all the excitement, I dropped my phone somewhere," said MacBridan.

"Amazing," said Wetmoore, "absolutely amazing. Bad guys continually slip through your fingers, you can't shoot straight, and in an emergency situation, you lose your equipment. Thank heavens, you're on our side."

Cori continued on, "As Father Collin and Father Novak were new to the estate, we were reasonably sure that they weren't tied into the thefts. Nevertheless, we checked them out, and the Vatican completely vouched for their authenticity. We let them know what we were doing and asked them to stay here in the library last night to help keep watch. We didn't know if the thieves would take the bait or not, but the windows from the library gave a good view of the front lawn. We needed all the eyes we could get."

"What were they supposed to do if they saw someone?" asked Wetmoore.

"Nothing at all," said Cori. "We had each other's cell numbers. If they saw something, they were to let me know. When I couldn't reach Mac, I called Father Collin and asked them to join me in Aunt Jean's room. Because the thieves had tried again, I couldn't leave. So I asked Father Collin if he'd look for Mac at the chapel. It was the direction he'd headed, and it was really the only other place I could think of."

Father Collin smiled at her. "Well said. There's really very little I can add to that. Until Cori called, it had been a quiet night for us. I'm just glad that I was there to pray over that poor boy's body. God rest his soul."

DS Wetmoore did not look satisfied, but their stories matched the facts as he knew them. "We need to call Lord MacKinnon."

"If it's okay with you, I'd like to be the one to talk with him," said MacBridan. "There's no easy way to do this, but I feel that it should be me. He left me in charge, and I'm afraid I've more than let him down."

"I wouldn't be too hard on yourself, MacBridan," said Wetmoore. "Wallace was in and out of trouble most of his life. Although I have no idea why he'd help some thieves try to steal a painting, I can't say it's completely out of character for him. I don't think you killed him. What little evidence there is says you tried to stop whoever did."

MacBridan gave a small smile. "I appreciate that, but he died on my watch."

Wetmoore stood up and placed his teacup on the table. "I'd like to see the storage room, and then we'll give him a call."

"Okay, Sergeant," said MacBridan. "I appreciate your trust."

Wetmoore gave a grim smile. "Don't get too carried away. I still believe that for some reason, you're not telling me everything, but yeah, I guess I do trust that in your own stumbling way, you're on the baron's side. Now let's take a look at that storage room."

Chapter 27

The next few hours were busy for everyone. Cori stayed close to Aunt Jean, as did Faith, and was with her when the doctor arrived. Fortunately, his examination did not uncover any serious injuries, but she'd clearly received quite a bruising from hitting the floor. Despite his findings, he scheduled her to come by his clinic right after lunch. To be safe, a series of X-rays and tests were ordered to ensure that nothing had been missed. Cori volunteered to come with them; she had begun to feel protective of Aunt Jean.

After examining the storage room, MacBridan and DS Wetmoore made their way toward Lord MacKinnon's office. Wetmoore had been amazed by the scorch marks left on the rug by the flash grenade. "It's amazing you weren't hurt more seriously," said Wetmoore as they walked down the hall.

"True, but I really don't think that was her goal," said MacBridan.

"Why do you say that?"

"All she needed was a distraction in order to get away. The more I think about last night, the more I'm convinced that they wanted me to go after her. We now know that it was Wallace whom I eventually ended up chasing. Kaseem wanted me to go after him and had already directed Wallace to lead me to the churchyard. We may never know the truth, but I'm willing to bet that Wallace was told by Kaseem that his men would take good care of me once I followed him in there."

"Then you believe that Kaseem meant to kill him?" asked Wetmoore.

"I'm pretty sure Wallace was the backup plan in the event that Talon didn't get the painting."

"I'm not sure I'm following you on this," said Wetmoore.

"Our ruse was intended to lure them in so that we could catch one of them. Talon wasn't fooled, but remember, she's not calling the shots, Kaseem is and forced her to take a run at it just in case. Once she confirmed that it was a setup, she only temporarily took me out of the picture. They planned to substitute Wallace at some point, allowing her to get away. However, at the same time, they knew that the last thing they could afford was for me to get my hands on Wallace."

"Because he'd talk."

"Louder than an off-key opera singer. Wallace would be a major weak link in any chain. And yet by killing him, they would potentially accomplish a couple of goals. The most obvious is that once dead, he wouldn't be able to tell us what he knew, which I imagine was'nt much, but still enough to be damaging. Second, was to get us to believe that Wallace had been their inside man."

"And you don't think he was," said Wetmoore.

"Do you?" asked MacBridan. "Wallace was too dim-witted, too arrogant to ever pull off anything like this. No, ultimately he would have given them away. As it turns out, our plan certainly didn't go the way we hoped, but neither did theirs. I'm not buying into their deceptions."

"What you say makes sense," agreed Wetmoore. "No one who knew Wallace for more than five minutes would ever trust him with anything sensitive, or especially anything that would need to be kept secret. The really bad news is that the situation has escalated. By killing him, they've now taken things to the next level."

"Perhaps," said MacBridan, "but that's only assuming that Marston's death was by natural causes. I never have believed that. Don't forget what I've told you about Kaseem. He'll do anything, kill anyone, to get what he's after. For him, the stakes are that high."

MacBridan opened the door to the office, and they both went in. Wetmoore had agreed to let MacBridan take the lead on the call with Lord MacKinnon. Using one of the numbers Lord MacKinnon had given him before he left, MacBridan had no trouble in reaching him.

To say the least, it was a terribly difficult call. MacBridan carefully detailed all that had happened, tragically leading up to Wallace's death. He delivered the news as gently as he could, but there was no easy way to break this kind of tragedy to a parent. The phone went silent on Lord MacKinnon's end.

"How did he die?"

"We do not yet know the cause of death," answered MacBridan. "I can tell you that it was quick. Lord MacKinnon, I tried to stop them, but I failed."

Lord MacKinnon took a moment then cleared his throat. "I'm sure you did all you possibly could. What could he have been thinking? What could have driven him to turn against me like this?"

"Sir, we don't believe that Wallace was working with them against you. Worse case, we think he may have been doing this to discredit me. They were using him, and at this point, we believe that he was set up."

"MacBridan, I appreciate you're trying to spare my feelings, but things certainly appear to be pretty clear to me."

"These people are pros," said MacBridan. "It's hard to say what they told Wallace. I believe that they probably positioned the whole thing as some sort of prank on Cori and me. However they did it, short of his acting as a decoy for them, we have no other evidence that he's been helping them."

"Wetmoore still there?"

"Right here, Lord MacKinnon," said Wetmoore.

"I'll want to talk with you as soon as I return," said Lord MacKinnon. "I'll start to tend to the arrangements right away." Finally, his voice cracked, and the strong front he'd been putting on crumbled. "Why did this happen?" he cried, his voice choked with emotion. "Had they just asked me I'd have given them the bloody painting!"

"There's much more to this it than just the painting," said MacBridan. "We're pretty certain as to who's behind all of this. The painting may simply have been the means to achieve what they actually want. Even if you had given them the painting, what they're after is most likely hidden somewhere here at the estate. We have every reason to believe that either way, people still would have been hurt."

"Find the man behind this, MacBridan," growled Lord MacKinnon. "Find him, and kill him, or I will."

"We'll find him," said MacBridan.

Lord MacKinnon let him know that he'd get back to the estate as quickly as he could, but that it may not be until late that evening or early the following morning. With that, Lord MacKinnon hung up.

"Those conversations are never easy," said Wetmoore. "Thank heavens, I haven't had to do too many of them. They're absolutely dreadful."

MacBridan's demeanor had darkened to one of barely contained rage. He was angry at the circumstances and his seemingly impotent ability to alter them. Despite their best efforts, they really hadn't accomplished a great deal since all this had started back in Virginia.

He wanted his chance at Kaseem. He hated how Kaseem used people and his total disregard for those he killed. But most of all, MacBridan was angry at himself. His gut had told him from the beginning that Marston had been murdered, and now, on his watch, he'd allowed his client's son to be murdered.

He walked with Wetmoore to the door who promised to let MacBridan know whatever information he and his team turned up. MacBridan then found Fergus and asked him to gather the family together in the study. Twenty minutes later, with the exception of Aunt Jean, they were all waiting for him. Father Collin joined MacBridan as he told them all that had occurred the previous night. Wallace's death hit them pretty hard, but MacBridan noticed that no tears were shed.

Shortly after lunch, Cori went with Faith and Aunt Jean as they prepared to leave for the clinic. MacBridan went back to the library with Father Collin, and they sat down by the fireplace. "As bad as things are, now's not the time to give up. This business is far from being over," said Father Collin. "For all his bad traits, Kaseem is anything but a quitter."

"Neither am I," said MacBridan, his voice quiet yet intense, his blue eyes blazing looking for anything to vent his anger on.

"Mac, you need to keep in mind that your presence here is the only thing keeping Kaseem from kicking in the front door and taking whatever it is that he wants. You stopped him in Virginia, you stopped him on the docks in Glasgow, and when he tried to get rid of you in the village, the team he sent in failed," said Father Collin.

"Thanks to you and Ubel."

Father Collin shook his head. "You're missing my point. Blaming yourself for all that's been going on, including Wallace's death, is a waste of time. It was Wallace who put himself in jeopardy, not you. You have frustrated Kaseem's plans several times, and you did it again last night."

"Well, it sure doesn't feel that way."

"And who says only the Irish are slaves to their emotions?" chided Father Collin.

The door to the library opened, and Father Novak came in. Nodding at Father Collin, he said, "All finished. I've hidden it in Mr. MacBridan's room."

"You've hidden what in my room?"

"Why the witch board, of course. While you were addressing the family, I went in and got it. Now I need to get a few things from my case, and then I'll go back to her room and make other preparations," said Father Novak.

MacBridan raised an eyebrow in question. "Preparations? By the way, how did you get into my room?"

"The preparations that Father Novak is referring to are part of the rites of exorcism," explained Father Collin. "Father Novak will do all he can to cleanse the room of the evil that's been living there. These rites will also help to ward off the shadow people that attacked Cori and Aunt Jean last night. Considering all that has happened, we've had to move quickly. This will help to protect Aunt Jean in the event they decide to return."

"I found it to be quite interesting that I chose the same hiding place as you did," said Father Novak. He smiled as he told Father Collin, "Mr. MacBridan hid the painting that the thieves are after under his bed."

Father Collin chuckled at this. "Most ingenious! Who would ever think to look there?"

MacBridan tried to glare at the two priests but failed to pull it off. "Look, last night when we slipped back into the house, it was already pretty late. I'd left the real painting in the storage room. I had to so that when I showed Fergus how the alarms worked and gave him the key to keep while we were away, he'd be sure to see that it was actually in there. Fergus is a talker. I was pretty certain that he'd tell everyone what he saw, which would help us to draw in the bad guys. Nevertheless, I didn't have a lot of time to be creative, so I rammed it under the bed." Both priests continued to smile at him. "And one more thing, did I mention it was dark?"

"Yes, that explains it," said Father Collin.

"Not to change the subject, but Aunt Jean agreed to your taking the witch board from her room?" asked MacBridan. "It was my understanding that she's rather attached to that thing."

"After last night, she was more than agreeable," said Father Collin. "Still, it was very hard for her. She told me that starting when she was a small child, she came to depend on it to give her direction. In fact, she even shared with me that Reznik is the name of the spirit guide that she communicates with. It is interesting to note that Reznik means butcher."

MacBridan had heard that among his crazy thoughts in Aunt Jean's room. He didn't want the witch board hidden in his room. He especially didn't want to sleep over it!

"Actually it seemed to bother Faith more than it did Aunt Jean," commented Father Novak. "She acted as if we were trying to hurt her aunt."

"She is very protective," noted Father Collin.

"Speaking of things that tend to bother one, that reminds me, what was it that you took off Wallace in the churchyard just as Wetmoore showed up?" asked MacBridan.

"You saw that?" said Father Collin. "I must be slowing down." Reaching into his pocket, he pulled out a chain with an oval-shaped medallion attached to it. There appeared to be letters, of a sort, etched in silver on a black background. "What do you make of this, Father Novak?"

The other priest took the medallion, briefly studied it, and then sadly shook his head. "He never had a chance."

"You recognize that?" asked MacBridan.

"I most certainly do," said Father Novak. "In fact, in many circles, it would be greatly prized and considered to be of great value. This piece is very old. I'm guessing, judging by the craftsmanship, that it predates the coming of Christ."

"That's what I thought," confirmed Father Collin.

MacBridan took the medallion and looked closely at the etchings on its face. While the lettering resembled runes, they were quite different in the angling of their design. The weight of the medallion surprised him. "I've seen something similar to this before," he muttered almost to himself, trying to remember where. "What exactly is it?"

"It's a curse, in a manner of speaking, used by members of the cult of Lilith," said Father Novak. "This is used to mark someone for death. The individual being targeted by this little trinket wouldn't have any idea of the significance of what they were being given. By wearing it, they would inadvertently be inviting the forces of darkness to come after them. Cult members, through specific incantations, would draw on the dark forces to possess and kill the person wearing this. It's like drawing a bull's eye on their forehead."

"Putting the curse stuff aside for a moment, why would Wallace ever wear such a thing?" asked MacBridan.

"I imagine it was all a part of the setup," said Father Collin. "They got him to dress up as Talon to draw you in. This was probably given to him to wear under the guise of being part of the costume. Instead, it targeted him, drawing in the specter that killed him."

"Which would explain why Mr. MacBridan was passed over," said Father Novak. "He wasn't marked."

"You're not saying that Kaseem controls that thing are you?" asked MacBridan.

"It's not exactly control. These things prey on human life. By giving Wallace the medallion was almost like giving the creature a hunting license. Kaseem told Wallace to run to the churchyard, so when he was taken, you would see it and be terrified. Kaseem would have to have been near the churchyard last night, performing the incantations, in order to summon that creature to do his bidding."

"I don't understand what happened last night, but this kind of thing can't be possible," said MacBridan, but there was no conviction in his voice.

"Surely, by this time, we're beyond that," said Father Collin.

MacBridan sat silently, taking all this in. "Wait a minute, now I remember. When I was searching Aunt Jean's room for bugs, I saw a medallion on her dresser, right next to the lamp. It was very similar to that one. At that time, I thought it was something Celtic."

"No, this is far from being anything remotely Celtic," said Father Collin. Looking at Father Novak, he said, "We'll have to get that medallion from Aunt Jean also."

"Agreed. I'll be anxious to learn where she got it," said Father Novak.

Suddenly, MacBridan sat up straight, as if he'd heard something. He got up and quickly walked over to the where they had the paintings lined up, studying each of them one at a time. "It couldn't be that simple," he muttered.

The two priests joined him. "What is it, Mac?" asked Father Collin.

"Are these paintings supposed to be in any specific order?" asked MacBridan.

"I'm not sure I know what you're asking," said Father Novak.

"Do we have any way of telling which painting he did first? We need to line these up in order from first to last. Can we do that?"

"Yes, I think so," said Father Novak, looking at the back of one of them. "Here it is. I remembered seeing this earlier. He dated them. Why? How does it make a difference?"

"Bear with me. Finally, we may have something in all this that makes sense. I'm going to go get the painting that's in my room. Father Novak, while I'm gone, I'd appreciate you putting these in the order in which they were painted. Father Collin, please find us the biggest map of Scotland that you can."

MacBridan rushed down the hall to the staircase, taking the steps two at a time as he hurried to his room. Surprisingly, he found that the door to his room was locked. Although he was pretty sure that he'd left it that way, when Father Novak had told him that he'd hidden the witch board in there, he'd begun to have doubts. MacBridan smiled to himself as he unlocked the door, realizing that Father Novak had picked the lock. *Good thing he and Father Collin work for a very forgiving boss*, thought MacBridan. *The two of them sure do tend to bend the rules.*

Getting down on the floor, he slid the painting out from under the bed. He quickly looked at it, confirming his theory as a smile spread across his face. Relocking his door, he returned to the library.

MacBridan brought the painting over to Father Novak. "Where does this one go, Father?"

Father Novak examined the date. "Place it third over from the right."

MacBridan placed it where he'd been directed, stepped back, and studied all five. His smile stayed in place.

"Finally," he said, "we are a step ahead."

"I'm afraid I'm missing it," said Father Collin. "What are you seeing that we're not?"

"Let's wait until Cori gets back," said MacBridan. "We're all going to have to move on this quickly if we are to beat Kaseem."

They waited nearly an hour and a half before Cori, Aunt Jean, and Faith returned from the clinic. The tests had gone well, but Aunt Jean was exhausted, her face a tired shade of gray.

While they'd been waiting, MacBridan and Father Novak took advantage of the time. Together, they went back upstairs to Aunt Jean's room to get the medallion, leaving Father Collin to watch over the paintings. It seemed silly to MacBridan, but the priests had insisted on having one of them with him to handle it. Thirty minutes later, they gave up their search. MacBridan was positive that it'd been there, but it was nowhere to be found.

Rather than return to the library, MacBridan kept watch for Cori in the foyer, stepping outside to meet them when they pulled up. Fergus helped Faith to take her Aunt upstairs to her room for some overdue rest. Cori followed MacBridan down the hall to the library. Once inside, MacBridan fastened the dead bolt, ensuring that they wouldn't be disturbed or overheard.

"What's going on?" asked Cori. "Did I miss something?"

"You'll need to ask him," said Father Novak. "He refused to say a word until you returned."

MacBridan smiled at his audience. "I want you to come over here by the paintings. I may be wrong about this, but I don't think so." Father Novak, as requested, had the paintings lined up facing the windows to make the most of the afternoon light. He sat down in a chair by one of the windows, facing the paintings, and Father Collin stood next to him. Cori, feeling the strain from their long night, sat down in the other chair next to Father Novak.

"The whole idea of a treasure of some sort being hidden here at the estate seemed rather far-fetched to me," said MacBridan. "The legend, as we all know, had Balgair bringing stolen Templar treasure, along with some valuable artifacts, with him to Scotland. But that's all I thought it was, a legend, as did most people.

"However, years ago when the MacKinnon ancestor who painted these pictures returned from the sea, he stirred the legend of the treasure up all over again. He claimed that he had learned of its secret location, which, not surprisingly, quickly endeared him to the family, many of whom he'd never been that close to. Unfortunately, he became deathly ill before he could lay his hands on it. Due in part to his shady reputation, his boasting of this secret location was believed by most of the people here at the estate."

"After he passed, many searched for the treasure, but all came up empty. Then recently, someone here guessed that this nefarious ancestor may have concealed the treasure's location in the paintings themselves. This makes sense because he had to have believed that he'd eventually get better. The problem he faced was that his sickness often brought on a high fever, thrusting him in to a state of delirium, which negatively affected his memory. This frightened him. He couldn't risk forgetting the location, and there was no one he could trust with the secret. So the paintings were his solution, a clever as well as a safe place to write the location down."

"So he did use some kind of secret writing," said Cori. "How is that possible? Dr. Van Dych had a team of experts closely examine this painting, the canvass, the frame, everything and couldn't find any evidence of secret writings."

"He didn't do anything near so elaborate," said MacBridan. "Our painter was sick and probably not that well educated, so any kind of secret writing would probably have been beyond him. He simply used what he had, the things that were around him. Father Collin, it was something you said that put me on the right track."

"Glad that I was able to help," said Father Collin, "but I'm afraid I'm at a loss as to what that may have been."

"When we were talking about the witch board that Father Novak took from Aunt Jean's room, you said that she had depended on it over the years to give her direction," answered MacBridan.

"That's right," agreed Father Collin. "She's become very attached to it and finds it hard to believe that it could pose any kind of threat to her."

"It was the phrase 'giving her direction' that clicked for me, and thanks to that, we may have our answer," said MacBridan as he turned to the paintings. "If I were asked to describe these, I'd say that we have five poorly executed landscapes of the estate, all painted from the perspective from a room on the second floor of the house. But our painter could have cared less about what anyone thought of his abilities with a brush. In plain sight of everyone, he wrote down the location where he believed Balgair had hidden his stolen loot."

"Mac, please, I've stared at these pitiful things to the point where my eyes hurt," said Cori. "I don't see what you're getting at."

"Our artist was a sailor. For years he'd found his way across the sea by using coordinates, latitude, and longitude. Now take another look at these paintings, but this time, ignore the landscapes. What do you see?"

All three leaned forward, trying to discern what MacBridan had discovered. After a couple of minutes, Father Collin spotted it, and a smile began to take root on his face. "The witch board," he said.

"Exactly. It's not very prominent, and you only see a small portion of it, but it's in each and every painting. He wrote the location down by painting the coordinates, piece at a time, on the witch board, which is why it was imperative to know the order in which they'd been painted. Rather than some complex code, he used an illusionist's trick."

"An illusionist's trick?" asked Cori.

"Misdirection," answered Father Collin, "sleight of hand. Using something else to draw the focus away from what they're truly trying to achieve. In this case, he used landscapes to draw the focus away from the figures on the witch board."

"Precisely. Look closely. In the first picture, you only see a corner of the board, with the 5 being the only discernible number. He added in a couple of symbols, but they're meaningless. In the second painting, you can see that the witch board has changed location. Now it shows up in the lower left hand corner, but again, with only a small portion of it being visible. Here the numbers 7 and 4 being legible, and so on, and so on, from painting to painting," explained MacBridan.

"I'm embarrassed that something this simple went right by me," stated Father Novak. Cori got up to get a closer look at them.

"None of us spotted it," said MacBridan, "so don't feel too bad. He even painted the witch board in the shadows, using dark tones so as not to draw attention to it, but in each one, you can faintly see numbers or letters."

"This is embarrassing," said Cori. "It's been right in front of us the whole time."

MacBridan picked up a pad of paper and, starting with the first painting, began writing down the numbers and letters in the right order. When he was finished he had: 57° 42' 20.41" N, 5° 10' 21.88" W.

"And you don't think Kaseem has figured this out?" asked Father Novak.

"I'm pretty sure he hasn't," said MacBridan. "Kaseem's people kept trying to steal the painting itself. If they'd figured it out, all they'd need is a photo, and they'd have what we have."

"Now all we have to do is figure out who it is that's working against us from the inside," said Cori.

"Whoever it is correctly guessed that the key might be hidden somewhere in these paintings but couldn't unravel the riddle on their own. When they went shopping for help, I'm guessing that the lure of ancient artifacts pillaged by the Templars during the crusades drew Kaseem and his bunch out of the shadows. I'll wager they were given photos of the paintings but also failed to come up with an answer. When the family announced that they'd be leaving Virginia for a while and returning to Scotland, our inside person learned that there was another painting by the same ancestor. However, because Marston did such a good job at keeping the estate secure, Kaseem figured that snatching this piece in transit would be the easiest, giving them the opportunity to tear it apart for its secrets."

"Well done, James," said Father Collin, "well done."

Cori was already back at the table where Father Collin had spread out a large map of Scotland, as well as a detailed plot map of the estate. "Mac," said Cori, "let me see those coordinates."

It did not take her long to determine the location. "I was afraid of that," said Cori.

"What's the problem?" asked Father Novak.

"If we're right, our X marks the spot appears to be located at the chapel, or at least just off to the right of it," said MacBridan.

"Well, have fun," said Cori. "I got my fill of that place the first time, and after what happened to you last night, I'm in no hurry to go back there."

They were all quiet, taking in what they'd just learned. "What do you suggest we do?" asked Father Collin. "I can't see Lord MacKinnon digging up all of his ancestors to look for a treasure that for all practical purposes may not even exist."

"Unfortunately, Kaseem won't walk away from this," commented Father Novak. "No matter what's involved."

"Cori and I will be talking with Dolinski and updating him," said MacBridan. "But I think our next step is pretty clear. We have to return to the chapel and see what we can find."

Chapter 28

"Mr. MacBridan, please continue to hold. I'll let him know you're still waiting." The cold, distant demeanor of Ester King was one of the few consistencies in life that MacBridan found he could always depend on.

"I'm pretty certain she has a thing for me," MacBridan told Cori, "but to her credit, she tries really hard to keep her feelings hidden."

"Oh yes," replied Cori. "I mean, it's so obvious. Most people would have heard the tone of her voice as one being filled with disdain, potentially even bordering on contempt. And yet you're keen ear is able to pierce right through that false demeanor and penetrate her tightly veiled emotions."

"Most *ordinary* people would have heard it that way," MacBridan corrected her, "but my years of exhaustive investigative training and extensive personal experience with the fairer sex has enabled me to sense the passion that burns for me in her bosom."

Cori laughed at this, which surprised her. She suddenly realized how long it had been since she'd anything to laugh or even smile about. "Your self-confidence knows no bounds, and I want to point out that I phrased that as nicely as I could."

MacBridan gave an exaggerated sigh. "I'm continually surrounded by skeptics who do not appreciate my many talents."

"Not to change the subject, but let's see if we can focus that keen insight elsewhere for a few moments," said Cori. "Have you noticed a difference in how Faith has been acting today?"

"Now that you mention it, she hasn't been her normal, flirtatious self, although I really haven't given it any thought," answered MacBridan. "Why? Did she say something to you?"

"That's just it," said Cori. "Ever since we arrived, she's been open and friendly, especially with you. But today's been different. She's been very quiet, not talkative at all, even with her aunt."

"Cori, this entire household has been put through the mill. Whether they want to admit it or not, Wallace's death has shaken them to the core."

"I appreciate that, and that may be all it is, but this seems to run deeper with her. It's like she's closed herself off. At lunch, she barely said two words and stayed pretty quiet all the way over to the clinic while we were there and then on the way back."

MacBridan leaned back in his chair as he thought this over. They'd decided to call Dolinski from Lord MacKinnon's office. Cori was using the green leather chair while MacBridan had moved one of the beige overstuffed chairs by the fireplace and put it next to the desk. The crackling fire and wood smoke kept playing with his memory, making him think of camping with his dad. If Ester kept them on hold much longer, chances were he'd be asleep.

"Father Collin told me that he and Father Novak had a mild confrontation with Faith," related MacBridan.

"When was this?"

"Much earlier this morning. He said that when they were trying to convince Aunt Jean that she should get rid of the witch board that Faith sprang to her defense," explained MacBridan.

"Aunt Jean does seem to be pretty attached to that thing," said Cori.

"True. But Father Collin felt that it actually hit Faith harder than her aunt and that it took some doing to calm her down."

"Interesting, perhaps you're right," said Cori. "Maybe her closing herself off is just her way of coping with all that's been happening."

Although the drapes were open, the office remained heavily cloaked in shadows. Thick, dark clouds brooded across the sky, the wind rattling the windows. Fergus had let them know that a strong storm was heading their way.

"Try to look at things from Faith's point of view," said MacBridan. "She's been living in a pampered, protected environment here at the estate. Then out of the blue, things take a one-eighty, and the ugly, violent side of life erupts right in front of her, physically invading her home. All things considered, I expect most people would be acting a little differently."

"And that brings up something else that has me concerned," said Cori. "Most people would be affected by all this, but not you. We've experienced things that should never be seen outside of a nightmare, and yet it doesn't seem to bother you. You just keep on going. My foundation has been completely rocked by the things that have happened here. I'm more than exhausted, if that's even possible, and I'm not embarrassed to say that I'm scared to death. How? How do you do it?"

MacBridan looked at her for a moment and smiled gently at her. "Believe me, Cori, it may not show, but we're all feeling it, even me."

Before Cori could respond, Ester came back on the line. "I'll put you through now."

They could hear the phone start to ring on the distant end, and Dolinski immediately picked up. "Good morning," he said, "or I guess I should say good afternoon?"

"At this point, I'm not really sure," said MacBridan. "It's been too long since my head's hit the pillow."

"There'll be time for you to catch up on your beauty sleep later," said Dolinski. "How are things going?"

"It's been a full twenty-four hours," said MacBridan.

"We're pretty certain we now know what they're after," said Cori, "but unfortunately, things have taken a violent turn."

"Can't say I'm surprised to hear that," said Dolinski. "Things have been pretty intense since they tried to snatch that painting from you at the farm. So where do we stand?"

Together, they began to fill Dolinski in on all that had happened. With MacBridan doing most of the talking, he told him of their ruse to draw the bad guys out into the open, his confrontation with Talon, and the chase through the woods ending in Wallace's death in the churchyard.

"I've talked with Lord MacKinnon. He's on his way back from Rome now," said MacBridan.

"Any idea who it was that killed Wallace?" asked Dolinski.

MacBridan looked at Cori before he answered. It was one of those times when the truth would do anything but set you free. "No, but we're certain that they're tied into Kaseem."

"I'll try to reach Lord MacKinnon," said Dolinski. "Poor man. The death of a child, no matter how old, has to be devastating."

"While I was with Wallace at the chapel, they also took a run at Aunt Jean. We're still in the dark as to why, but if it hadn't been for Cori, the family would be planning a double funeral."

"Mac, no matter how good you may think you are at hiding it, I know that tone," said Dolinski. "Wallace has been a challenge for Lord MacKinnon ever since I've known him. On more than one occasion, the Hawthorne Group has had to step in to help clean up his messes. Remember, it was Wallace who put himself in harm's way, not you."

"You're beginning to sound like Father Collin."

"Then he's a wise man. Mac, I have no doubt that you did all that you could to help him."

"Did I? I keep replaying that scene in my mind over and over again. He wasn't far from me. I hesitated. In the end, I couldn't save him. It's not a performance one is proud of."

"This is a messy business, Mac, you know that. You and Cori have had your hands full from day one, and you've done a good job. Unfortunately, sometimes people get killed. But don't start trying to take on responsibility for someone else's stupid actions," growled Dolinski. "You said they also took a run at the aunt. Tell me about it."

Cori started to relate the events surrounding the attack but, like MacBridan, had trouble telling Dolinski all she'd experienced. There was simply no way she was going to tell him that the shadow people who haunt the estate had come after them. MacBridan watched her fumble for words. Her story became so disjointed that it was obvious she was holding something back. MacBridan intervened, finishing the narrative for her.

"After lunch, she was taken to a local clinic, and fortunately, everything checked out okay," said Cori.

"Are you all right?" asked Dolinski.

"Yes, it's just the lack of sleep catching up with me," said Cori. "I haven't been this tired in a while."

Dolinski didn't respond. MacBridan knew that he wasn't buying it, but fortunately for them, Dolinski put a great deal of trust in his people. He'd once told MacBridan that if a good operative held something back, it was usually for a good reason.

"So where does this leave us?" he asked.

"We do have some good news for a change," said MacBridan. "We finally know why they've been after that ridiculous painting. Believe it or not, it's been about buried treasure from the beginning."

"I'm listening," said Dolinski.

"The MacKinnon ancestor who did the paintings made his living as a sailor. His reputation was not the purest, and it's been suggested he engaged in piracy once or twice. Nevertheless, his travels took him to some pretty interesting places, and somehow he learned the location where Balgair MacKinnon buried a cache of gold along with some priceless religious artifacts."

"Who is Balgair?" asked Dolinski.

"He is the number one black sheep of the MacKinnon clan," explained MacBridan. Mac then told Dolinski what they'd learned about Balgair, his reputation and his potential tie in to the Templars. Cori took over from there, bringing Dolinski up to date on the ancestor who had done all the paintings. Once learning of where the treasure was buried, he went back to the estate, but soon became too ill to look for it. As his illness progressed, he became concerned that he might forget the location but didn't have anyone who he could trust. He'd been boasting to anyone who would listen that he knew where it was, about how rich he was going to be, so he couldn't simply write it down for fear of someone beating him to it."

"And so he found a way to hide it in the painting," said Dolinski.

"Precisely," confirmed MacBridan.

"But how did he do it? After they tried taking it in Virginia, our experts took that painting apart, even the frame. They couldn't find a thing," said Dolinski.

MacBridan finished the story, giving Dolinski the rather simple but clever method that had been employed to hide the treasure's coordinates in plain sight. "One of the MacKinnons, or possibly one of the estate staff, guessed that he'd hidden the location in the paintings but couldn't figure it out, so they went looking for help. Word of possibly being able to find the gold and the missing artifacts made it back to Kaseem's people. When they learned that another painting had surfaced in Virginia, they figured that due to the security measures Marston had implemented at the estate, it would be easiest to steal the painting in Virginia while in route back to Scotland."

"I trust you've already determined the location that the coordinates point to," said Dolinski.

"We have," answered MacBridan, "and that has further helped to give our theory credibility. The location is here at the estate, very close to the chapel."

"Has Father Collin weighed in on your theory?"

"He and Father Novak are in lockstep with us," said Cori.

"Sounds like you've nailed it, well done. Do you need more manpower?" asked Dolinski. "I can get Truecourt back up there in a heartbeat with some additional men if you need them."

"That would be helpful," said MacBridan. His answer surprised Cori. Mac rarely asked for help, even when she knew he needed it. "We're stretched pretty thin, and we have to beat Kaseem to the treasure. Once we've secured it, we'll be able to take the MacKinnon family out of the line of fire."

"Consider it done," snapped Dolinski. "Anything else?"

"No, we're good," said MacBridan. "I lost my phone last night, but Cori and I both brought backups."

"Plus I have a satellite phone in addition to my cell," said Cori.

"All right then," said Dolinski. "I don't need to tell the two of you to be careful, but know that I want you both back in one piece. Regarding Kaseem and Talon, you have a green light from me to use deadly force. Based on what little we've found on Kaseem, it looks like he's collected quite a body count over the years. I'll get a hold of Truecourt now." With that, Dolinski ended the call.

"So what's the plan?" asked Cori. At that very moment, a loud crack of thunder shook the house, causing both of them to jump. The rain followed on the heels of the thunder, violently lashing out against the house.

"Once the sun sets, it is back to the chapel. The treasure, which still sounds theatrical to say, is either there or nearby. Wherever it is, we have to find it before Kaseem does."

"That chapel is the last place I want to be in when it's dark," said Cori.

"It's the best chance to go unobserved."

"What do we do about Aunt Jean?" asked Cori. "We can't very well take her with us, and they may try to come after her for leverage."

"You'll stay here with her."

"You can't go to the chapel alone. It isn't safe."

"I'll talk to Father Collin and see what he wants to do. I'd like to have Ubel with me."

"Don't feel that you need to protect me," said Cori, her eyes flashing with anger. "I'm quite capable of taking care of myself."

"I have never thought otherwise," said MacBridan. "I need you here. Unless we're both wrong, and I don't think we are, they'll take another run at her. Cori, you are very good at what you do, and because of that, you need to be here, at the house, protecting her. Ubel is a killer, plain and simple. His talents, if you will, will be better served with me at the chapel. I'm positive Kaseem's watching the chapel, as well as the house."

"Very well," said Cori, standing up and looking at her watch. "It's nearly time for dinner. I'm going to clean up some, and then I'll meet you in the dining room."

"I'll see you there," said MacBridan as she left the office. The stress chemicals in their blood were probably near toxic limits. He saw what the stress was doing to Cori and realized how much he cared for her. There were forces at work here he didn't understand. For the first time in a long time, he began to have doubts that things would end well.

Although his chair silently urged him to stay, he managed to get up. The wind rattled the windows, small hail had begun to fall, and lightning lit up the sky almost like a strobe. MacBridan needed to find Father Collin. He hadn't gone two steps when his cell phone began to ring. Pulling it out of his pocket, he assumed either Cori or Truecourt was calling and didn't look to see who it was.

"This is Mac," he said.

"MacBridan?" It was a woman's voice.

"Yes?"

"I need your help." Her voice was strained, taunt with pain and fear. Although not yet hysterical, she was well on her way.

"Talon?" asked MacBridan.

"I have very little time," she said. "He's going to kill you, and if he catches me, I'm dead too." She talked in short, breathless bursts.

"Who's going to kill you? Where are you?"

"You know who I'm talking about," she said, nearly screaming into the phone. "This is not the time to act cute."

"Talon, come to the main house. We'll protect you."

"Sure, that's a laugh. And maybe you can have DS Wetmoore kindly lock me in a cell to protect me even more. I'm not an idiot."

"Why would Kaseem want you dead?" asked MacBridan. "You're working with him to get the painting, and if memory serves, he still hasn't got it."

"That's just it," said Talon. "It turns out that he doesn't need it anymore, so he doesn't need me. I watched them kill that poor man from the village. After two hours, he begged them to let him die. I won't let that happen to me. And that Goliath of an animal Mukhtar, what he did to those defenseless dogs, I'll never be able to get that image out of my mind."

"Talon, listen to me. Where are you?"

"Wait...wait, don't hang up." MacBridan listened intently. It sounded as if she was running, the phone brushing up against her. Finally she came back on.

"*Mon dieu*, I think they've found me," she said. Panic was taking over. "I'll call you back. Please I need your help to get out of here."

"Where are you?"

"Get out of that house, MacBridan. He plans to kill you, to sacrifice you, as well as Cori and those stupid priests. He's going to take revenge on anyone who's gotten in his way. There's no stopping him. He controls this thing. It's not human! I'll call you back." MacBridan heard a lot of noise in the background. He couldn't tell what was going on, but he thought he heard a man's voice, faintly. Suddenly, the call went dead.

Talon was gone.

Chapter 29

The storm continued its unrelenting assault on the estate. The wind and the rain struck with such intensity at times that MacBridan wondered if the windows would be able to hold against the beating they were taking. An hour before dinner, the estate lost all power. This kept Fergus and the staff busy lighting candles in all the rooms and along the hallways. The estate had its own backup generator, but for some reason, it had failed to come on, and Fergus could not get it started. Father Novak said the weather was obeying Kaseem's wishes because of the dogs. Despite everything, MacBridan had trouble believing that.

The warmth that radiated from the fireplace in his room felt wonderful, and despite the storm, MacBridan caught himself starting to doze off a couple of times. A light tapping at his door got him up and off the bed.

"Mind if I come in?" asked Cori.

"Please do," said MacBridan, letting her in and closing the door behind her. "Good thing you came by. Between the warmth of the fire and my amazingly comfortable bed, which I've rarely gotten to use, I might have missed dinner."

"Just got off the sat phone with Truecourt. The bad news is that this storm is blanketing most of the Highlands and won't be moving out any time soon. All flights into Glasgow over to Edinburgh and north of there have been canceled, and there's more than one road that's underwater."

"Which means we're on our own," mused MacBridan. "Have you tried reaching Wetmoore?"

"Not yet, but I will. Fergus told me that most of the village has also lost power. So depending on how well the cell towers are working, we may not be able to reach him."

"This also means that Lord MacKinnon won't be able to get back here," said MacBridan. "That, actually, may be a good thing."

"Why do you say that?" asked Cori.

"He wants Kaseem dead in the worst way. Given the opportunity, no matter how ill-advised, he might go and try something stupid and get himself hurt."

"That's all we need."

"I talked with Father Collin and Father Novak a little while ago, and I believe we're set for this evening's work," said MacBridan. "Father Novak is surprisingly bothered by this storm. Also, he plans to stay with you and Aunt Jean this evening."

"Why is he upset by the storm? Does he have some kind of phobia?" asked Cori.

"I couldn't get either one of them to elaborate, but he intimated that it's all a result of evil powers at work."

Cori shook her head. "Despite all the impossible things I've seen and experienced here, I have serious trouble buying into that."

MacBridan shrugged. "Same here. Nevertheless, you'll be having company. Maybe you can have Faith join you and get a game of bridge going."

"I do not know how to play bridge and have no desire to learn. At this pace, Aunt Jean's going to need a bigger room," said Cori. "Is Father Collin going with you?"

"Yes." MacBridan nodded. "He feels he needs to be there in case we do locate the artifacts."

"Doesn't trust you around all that gold?" teased Cori.

MacBridan smiled at her. "He didn't say it, but I think he's more worried about what we might find in the way of artifacts. My performance with the witch board didn't inspire his confidence in me. Whatever the reason, it'll be good having him there."

"Ubel?"

"He'll be going with us," said MacBridan. "Father Collin said he should be here soon."

"What a diverse little team we have," said Cori. "Ready to head down for dinner?"

"Not yet," said MacBridan. "There's one more thing we need to discuss. Just after you left the office, Talon called me."

"Kaseem wants to surrender?"

"Quite the contrary," answered MacBridan and told Cori all that she'd said. "She sounded scared and asked for help."

"There's a new tactic," said Cori. "You believe her?"

"I'm not taking anything at face value," said MacBridan. "It may indeed be some kind of trick, but for now, we'll just keep this in the back of our minds."

"Agreed," said Cori. "Come on, I'm starving. Let's go."

"Go on down," said MacBridan. "I'll meet you there."

Once Cori left, MacBridan ambled into the bathroom and stood there, staring at his reflection in the mirror. It wasn't pretty. He hadn't shaved in a couple of days, and there were dark circles under his red-rimmed eyes, which were as bloodshot as they could be. Leaning over the sink, he splashed cold water on his face. As tired as he was, he knew it was hardly the time to let his guard down.

Clipping the 9 mm automatic to his belt at the small of this back, he put on a lined jacket, turned, and started for his door. Thinking of what might be lying in wait for him, he stopped, went back to his suitcase, and put on an ankle holster, which held a .25 caliber Beretta. Now he was ready. Hopefully, Cori would be able to reach Wetmoore. He'd feel better having a couple of officers here with her.

As he stepped into the hall and closed his door, he caught sight of something moving out of the corner of his eye. Sitting in a chair next to the grandfather clock was Dillon. Dressed the same as always in what MacBridan believed to be his uniform, Dillon smiled and waved at him.

"You really startled me last night," said MacBridan as he walked toward the older man. "I nearly shot you. What were you doing out there at such an hour?"

"I told you, Mr. MacBridan. I've had trouble resting, so I went for a walk."

"Do you often stroll in the wee hours?"

"The burden of my worry hasn't let me rest," said Dillon.

"I'm glad you made it back here safely. I was just heading down for some dinner. Are you going to get something to eat?" asked MacBridan.

"No, not all that hungry," said Dillon. "I thought it would be best to keep an eye on Aunt Jean's room."

MacBridan moved closer to him and looked directly into Dillon's eyes. "You know about that thing I saw in the churchyard last night. You know what it is."

"That's why I warned you."

"What exactly is it?" asked MacBridan.

"It's the gatherer," said Dillon as a simple matter-of-fact.

"I don't know what that is. What is a gatherer?"

Dillon shrugged his shoulders and looked down at his shoes. "He's the gatherer," he repeated, his voice just above a whisper. "You need to be very careful of the gatherer, Mr. MacBridan. He's still out there."

MacBridan studied Dillon carefully. As always, Dillon maintained a quiet smile on his face. By his relaxed demeanor, you would have thought that they were discussing the different kinds of roses in the garden, not some nightmarish creature that kills."

"I promise, I'll be careful," said MacBridan. "I want you to be careful too. Will you be here tonight?"

"Oh yes, most certainly."

"My associate, Cori, will be spending some time with Aunt Jean this evening. Perhaps, you can join them."

"She's a very brave girl. She's also a very bonny lass. You're a lucky man to have her."

"Couldn't agree with you more. I'm very glad she's here with me."

"Well, you can count on my looking in on them."

"I appreciate that. When I come back up from dinner, I'll introduce you to Cori," MacBridan said.

"That would be lovely," said Dillon, his soft pleasant smile in place.

In contrast to the weather outside, the mood at dinner was far more lighthearted than it had been all day. Father Collin and Father Novak kept the conversation light and alive, and Aunt Jean appeared to have mostly recovered from the previous night's ordeal. Father Collin turned out to have a large selection of amusing anecdotes about priests, and Aunt Jean kept the family in stitches with stories about Virginia in the 1960s and 1970s.

After dinner, as MacBridan and Cori had found to be their custom, the family retired to the study for drinks. MacBridan joined them for perhaps the best single malt scotch he'd ever had before saying good night. He explained that although he didn't expect trouble, he was going to get some well-needed rest and would be relieving Cori later so that she too could get some sleep.

Faith, who had remained quiet through most of the evening, surprisingly raised her glass to MacBridan. "This has been a terribly trying time in my life," she said, looking at MacBridan and then at Cori, "but I want to thank both of you. You've helped me in ways you'll never understand."

"Here, here," said Barclay, raising his glass, and they all toasted them.

"Usually at this point, I'd get on my horse and ride off into the sunset," said MacBridan, "but if I tried that tonight, I'd probably drown the horse." At this, they all laughed. "Fortunately for me, I get to rest this evening. I'll see you in the morning."

MacBridan left the study and took his time going upstairs. He passed Fergus on the staircase and then saw Laria, the maid who had claimed she saw the spirit of Balgair when they'd first arrived. He passed her coming down the hallway by the door to his room. MacBridan made a point to speak to both of them. It was exactly what he needed. He now had two witnesses who would corroborate to everyone his going to his room to sleep. Before going in, he glanced down the hall. Dillon was gone.

Once inside, he continued to prepare for the evening in front of him. Digging into his suitcase, he took out a waterproof jacket that had a hood attached to it and a powerful G3 Nitrolon flashlight and slipped a finely sharpened six-inch pocketknife into his pants pocket. *If there be bear in these woods*, MacBridan thought to himself, *I'll be ready.*

MacBridan tried to take advantage of the little time he had, resting in one of the chairs by the fireplace. Just before 11:00 p.m., he got up and quietly left, passed the door to Aunt Jean's room, and went down the rear stairs, commonly used by the household staff. Once downstairs, he cautiously made his way to the back of the house, taking care not to be seen. As he approached the back door, Ubel stepped out of the shadows.

"Father Collin should be here in a few minutes," said Ubel, his Slavic accent more pronounced this evening. MacBridan guessed that maybe that was something that happened to Ubel when he felt stress. Good to know.

"How long have you been waiting?" asked MacBridan, spotting a small puddle of rainwater where Ubel had been standing.

"Not long. Earlier, I followed Fergus out to the backup generator when the power failed. After he left, I examined it. All the ignition wiring had been cut."

"So someone planned to leave us in the dark tonight, storm or no storm. And of course, we can't rule out that that someone could be Fergus. He may have cut the wires and went out to check on it purely for show."

"Possible," said Ubel. "I wasn't close enough to see what he was doing, but I did spot someone watching the house while I was out there."

"Where are they?" asked MacBridan.

"They were in the carriage house they use for their cars," answered Ubel, "but they aren't going to be a problem."

"Really?"

Ubel reached into his coat pocket and brought out a small but powerful walkie-talkie. "He had this on him. In the time I've had it, no one has tried to contact him. My guess is they also have someone watching the front of the house."

"What if he's to check in at certain times? If they don't hear from him, that could signal that something's up," said MacBridan.

Ubel merely shrugged. "In my experience, it is never wise to leave anyone who can come at you from behind."

Pointing at the walkie-talkie, MacBridan said, "Don't you think he's going to miss that when he comes to?"

Ubel offered the briefest trace of a smile, but his cold, reptilian eyes didn't give away any sign of any emotion. "He won't be coming to."

When the good guys are like this, the bad guys are unimaginable, MacBridan thought to himself.

Both men turned as they heard someone approaching. Quickly stepping back into the shadows, they waited to see who it was. The family rarely used this door, which was why very few candles had been lit, keeping most of the hallway in darkness. "What a miserable night. I think I have everything I need," said Father Collin, clutching a small black bag. "As bad as it's going to be, I suggest we use the path through the woods. Like you, Mac, I'm positive that Kaseem is having the house watched."

"As it turns out, Kaseem now has one less man on his payroll. Ubel has already taken care of the man watching the back of the house," said MacBridan.

"Did you recognize him?" asked Father Collin.

"He was one of the men backing up Karl at The Hanging Man pub. He pulled a gun, so I was forced to kill him, quietly of course."

Father Collin never broke eye contact with Ubel as he took this in. It was too dark for MacBridan to clearly see the expression on the priest's face. Father Collin bowed his head, crossed himself, and muttered a brief prayer.

"We need to move out," directed MacBridan.

"Did you tell Ubel of your call from Talon?"

Looking at Ubel, MacBridan said, "Before dinner this evening, Talon called me on my cell phone. She sounded desperate, scared, and told me that she was afraid for her life as Kaseem no longer needed her."

"Why has he given up on getting the painting?" asked Ubel.

"My guess is that he's ether determined the location of the treasure in some other way or he's decided to take a more direct approach," said MacBridan.

"Such as?" asked Ubel.

"One that I'm sure would appeal to you," said MacBridan. "Kick in the door, kill the first few things that move, and then torture the survivors until you get your answers."

"That approach is not without its merits," said Ubel.

MacBridan stared at Ubel for a moment before continuing, "Whatever the case, she told me that he plans to kill everyone who's opposed him. She asked for my help to escape but was cut off before she could tell me where she was."

"It could all be theater."

"My head says yes. My heart says no. That said, she talked about how they killed Karl and the misery that they put him through. She said she wouldn't allow that to happen to her. In Kaseem's eyes, she has failed him more than once. Staying on this line of reasoning, it's important to remember that he didn't hesitate to put the fake Truecourt facedown in the Glasgow bay for failing to take the painting off the ship."

"I'm not so certain that her call for help wasn't genuine," said Father Collin. "This is how Kaseem operates. He never leaves anyone behind who can identify him, and he has little to no regard for women."

"We really need to get a move on," said MacBridan.

Father Collin nodded. "Yes, let's go."

"We'll keep our flashlights off until we get into the trees," said MacBridan. Opening the door, he stepped out into the storm.

Chapter 30

After MacBridan left, Cori spent a good part of the evening in the study talking with Barclay, although it was rather a one-sided conversation. He did his best to draw her out, but her lack of sleep over the last twenty-four hours, combined with the nervous strain of all she'd been through, made it hard for her to focus, much less participate. In fact, she was so out of it that it wasn't until about thirty minutes into their conversation did she even realize Barclay was hitting on her, laying down the best lines of a Scottish player. She smiled widely as she reconciled this oversight with the fact that in addition to spending time with Barclay, she'd also been keeping an eye on Aunt Jean.

Father Novak joined Aunt Jean and Faith by the larger of the two fireplaces while Father Collin and Kerr manned the bar. Fergus discreetly moved through the room, making sure that everyone had what they needed. Father Novak kept the two women captivated, regaling them with his many stories. Pulling out the cross he wore around his neck, he held it so that both women could get a good look at it. Faith leaned forward and gently reached for it, holding it closer to the light, studying its intricate engravings. Only then could Cori see that it was a Celtic cross. Cori loved Celtic designs. She vowed to herself that once they'd cleared things up with the MacKinnon family, she was definitely going shopping.

One mild incident caught Cori's eye. After looking at her watch, Faith got up and hurriedly left the study, nearly running into Fergus at the door. Fergus, having successfully navigated around a collision with Faith, crossed the room and set a cup of steaming hot tea on the small table next to where Cori was sitting. Its bergamot aroma was heavenly. Earl Grey was her favorite!

"This is the stoutest black tea that we have," Fergus told her. "I hope you find it to your liking."

"Thank you, Fergus. I really appreciate you getting this for me," said Cori.

Fergus smiled gently and winked at her. "Please let me know if you'd like some more."

As Fergus departed, Father Collin joined Cori and Barclay, smiling and shaking his head. "We are like bees drawn to the most enchanting of flowers."

"How's that?" asked Cori.

"I just thought that I'd join the rest of the red-blooded males around here, Ms. Hopkins," said Father Collin in a teasing tone of voice. "You have obviously been casting a spell on all the men here."

Coir laughed and said, "Father, you are so good for my self-esteem."

Not appreciating the intrusions by Fergus and now Father Collin, Barclay asked, "Where's Kerr? By the way you two were going at it, I assumed you were at the very least solving world hunger."

"Nothing near so virtuous I'm afraid," said Father Collin. "Our debate solely focused on which tonic is best for the soul, a stout, Scottish single malt, or the velvety smooth flavor of fine Irish whiskey."

"Not to cast dispersions, Father," said Cori, "but I would have to guess that it was an unfair and unbalanced argument, with you having had so much more firsthand experience than Kerr on that particular subject."

"And proud of it, I am," said Father Collin, chuckling at this as he patted her arm. "Yes, the good Lord has been abundant in his blessings over the years, providing me with many a fine bottle of Ireland's heavenly nectars."

"So where is Kerr?" asked Barclay, pressing the original point of his question.

"I'm not sure. He got a call and scooted out of here," said Father Collin. "By the way it affected him, it seemed to be rather urgent."

About that time, Faith came back into the study and went over to Aunt Jean. "I think it's about time for us to head on up."

"We can't, at least not at the moment. Father Novak is right in the middle of an absolutely astounding story about the old Soviet Union," said Aunt Jean. "Did you know that he actually met Nikita Khrushchev?"

"It was a long time ago," said Father Novak, "in a very different world. In those days, I spent a great deal of time in Russia."

"I had no idea," said Faith.

"Why don't I walk up with you?" suggested Father Novak. "If you're not too tired, perhaps we can continue our conversation in your room."

"In Aunt Jean's room?" said Faith, her tone clearly voicing her disapproval.

"Oh for pity's sake, Faith. At my age, what could you possibly be worried about?" asked Aunt Jean. "And on top of it all, the poor man's a priest!"

"I'm not worried about that," said Faith, mildly embarrassed. "I just don't want you to overdo it."

"Please, child, don't be silly. I'm just fine."

"Then it's all settled," said Father Novak, getting up from his chair and offering Aunt Jean his arm. "May I escort you?"

"That would be lovely," said Aunt Jean, and they left the study, closely followed by Faith.

Father Collin, Cori, and Barclay had watched the entire exchange. Father Collin, sipping his Jamison, chuckled and said, "The man's a wonderful priest, just wonderful, but had his walk in life taken him down a different path, he would have made a remarkable ladies' man."

"You are terrible," scolded Cori. "I think Father Novak is very sweet and is simply being gallant."

"Is that how you saw it, Barclay?" laughed Father Collin, winking at the younger man.

"*Gallant*'s not the word that immediately came to mind," answered Barclay.

"You're both terrible," said Cori, getting up from her chair. "If you'll excuse me, I have some work to attend to. Once that's done, I hope I can stay awake long enough for Mac to relieve me."

"Would you like some company?" offered Barclay, recognizing that his last chance for the evening was slipping away. "I'd be more than happy to offer my assistance."

"Normally I'd take you up on an offer like that," said Cori, "but tonight, I'm afraid I wouldn't be very good company."

"I think I'm going to call it a night as well," said Father Collin. "I plan on doing a little reading and then turning in for an early night." Turning to Barclay, he said, "Especially in light of the storm, Father Novak and I truly appreciate you putting us up for the evening."

"My uncle wanted you to stay with us from day one," said Barclay. "You are more than welcome."

Cori said good night and started her rounds of the house. Forty minutes later, she'd confirmed that all of the doors and windows were securely bolted. She also made sure that the security system installed by Marston was on and functioning. Although the system ran on its own battery-backup power, she had no way of determining how much time the system would be able to continue to run if the power remained out. With her rounds completed, she felt reasonably secure from any intruders who might try to break into the house. She'd have felt even better if she knew who the traitor was on the inside.

Her mind raced along several paths as she headed back to her room, examining the odd bits of behavior she'd seen that evening. Who had called Kerr with something so urgent that he had to rush out in such a hurry? What had caused Faith to run off while the family was having drinks, nearly crashing into Fergus? And then there was Barclay. Up until tonight, she hadn't noticed any level of romantic interest coming from him at all. Had his feelings for her finally taken flight, or were his intentions to keep her distracted? And worst of all, why was she all of a sudden so cynical and so paranoid about the smallest of actions by the people around her? The reasonable side of her mind tried to point out that Kerr had probably just gotten a better offer from a young lady in the village. After too many cups of tea and sherry, Faith had probably just had an urgent need to use the restroom with Fergus inadvertently getting in the way. As to Barclay, she wondered why it had taken him so long. After all, she was a catch. The one thing she was certain of was being so tired her body ached.

Chapter 31

Despite the quality of his rain gear, the intense weather still found its freezing way through the smallest of openings. With no gloves, MacBridan feared his hands might be too numb to accurately use his gun. There were no lights anywhere to help guide them, and along with the heavy wind and rain, it was hard to find where the path through the woods started. They passed it by a couple of times before finally locating it, shouting to one another to be heard. Occasionally, small pellets of hail fell, pecking their cheeks like maddened birds.

MacBridan led the way into the woods followed by Father Collin, with Ubel bringing up the rear. It was hard to see even with their flashlights, the path extremely slick in places. They trudged on, step at a time, head to the wind. Halfway through, Father Collin tripped on a root, which sent him flying forward. He'd have fallen flat on his face had he not grabbed onto MacBridan, which nearly brought down both men. Although MacBridan broke his fall, Father Collin still landed firmly on his knees. Fortunately, other than being a muddy mess, he was uninjured.

Emerging from the trees, they crossed the lane and carefully made their way toward the chapel, keeping their flashlights off. The tall wall surrounding the churchyard acted as a windbreak, bringing them some welcome relief from the storm. However, when they got to the gate, they discovered that they were not alone. Shining like a beacon in the darkness, the chapel was lit up from the inside by the soft light of candles. The storm had moved the action back to an earlier era where the light of reason didn't keep the fear of dark at bay.

Huddling together, MacBridan had to yell to be heard, "Looks like there's a larger attendance for this evening's service than we expected."

"Perhaps Talon was telling you the truth after all," said Father Collin. "It looks like Kaseem has found the location to the treasure. If there's any good news in this, it further confirms what we concluded regarding the treasure's location."

"I could have gone all night without this kind of good news. At least we won't have to wonder where Kaseem is or what he's doing," said MacBridan.

"He won't be alone," said Ubel.

Looking at MacBridan, Father Collin asked, "What do you suggest we do?"

"We have to work under the assumption that they're expecting us. Thanks to the storm, we have zero chance of sneaking in on them, so we'll go in fast and hard. Anything that moves in an unfriendly way, shoot it."

Ubel nodded in agreement. "If we don't, they'll most certainly kill us."

"Don't misunderstand me," shouted MacBridan over the storm. "I do not want a mass execution. We will take prisoners, but they only get one chance to cooperate."

"There is one more critical element," interjected Father Collin. "We can't forget about the demon that killed Wallace. Stay close to me as we cross the churchyard. If either of you see the creature, get behind me, and I will try to protect us."

"You will try?" exclaimed MacBridan. "At this point, I'd really appreciate you saying something with a little more strength behind it, like, 'I'll take care of it.'"

"Faith, Mr. MacBridan, put your trust in faith."

MacBridan and Ubel leaned into the heavy iron gates. The one on the right slowly swung open. Its hinges made a terrible grinding noise, but no one in the chapel could have possibly heard it over the raging wind. Staying almost side-by-side, they worked their way around the headstones, constantly on the alert for the gatherer. Several times, the light from the chapel's windows, mixed with the leaves and debris being whirled around by the wind, caused them to stop, mistakenly thinking that the specter was almost upon them.

MacBridan breathed a silent prayer of thanks when they reached the chapel doors without incident. While Father Collin kept watch, MacBridan took off his rain jacket, and Ubel removed his overcoat, both men dropping them on the ground next to the door. MacBridan, gun in hand, looked at Ubel. Ubel nodded. He was ready.

Gripping the door handle firmly, MacBridan pushed down on the latch and threw his full weight into the door. It swung open, crashing into the wall. MacBridan rushed in, cutting to his right. Ubel followed, moving quickly toward the left hand side of the chapel.

The entire altar area blazed from the light of dozens of candles, with more candles burning in sconces along both sides of the chapel. Cold drafts of wind that rushed through the old structure gave added life to the candle flames, causing their light to dance across the walls. MacBridan spotted Talon slumped in one of the pews near the front, her head bent forward. She was alive! A dark-skinned man with a large handgun stood next to her. Her head snapped around, her face pale, highlighting the bruising and small cuts that blossomed high on her left cheek. The man guarding her raised his gun to fire, but a shot from Ubel caught him high in the chest, sending him flying over the pew and onto the floor.

Another man was kneeling in front of the altar, pounding on the stone floor with a large, heavy iron hammer. Dropping the hammer, he slowly stood up, gradually turning around. The slow pace of his movements conflicted with the violence taking place all around him. He seemed oblivious to the storm or his colleague's death. A mocking, arrogant smile of triumph streaked across his bearded face.

MacBridan took aim at him but didn't say anything. The man standing before him had to be one of the biggest men MacBridan had ever seen. Standing nearly seven feet tall, he easily weighed in at three hundred pounds, if not more, very little of which was fat. His large hands were clenched in fists the size of cantaloupes, his eyes ablaze with fanatical insanity.

"Where's David when you need him?" MacBridan said under his breath.

He and Ubel quickly moved to the front of the chapel, keeping their guns trained on the giant. MacBridan noticed that the door leading down to the crypt was partially open, slightly moving as drafts of air swirled around it. Father Collin, staying a few steps behind him, followed MacBridan down the right side, tightly gripping his small black bag. MacBridan glanced at Talon. She'd clearly been slapped around, her hands were cuffed, but he couldn't tell how badly she'd been hurt.

Father Collin stood next to MacBridan. "Where's Kaseem?" he asked.

The large man briefly glared at Father Collin before returning his gaze to MacBridan. He spat out some words in a language none of them could understand. It sounded like a prayer or mantra.

"He's not here," said Talon. Her voice sounded weak, strained. "He's at the manor house."

"Why?" asked MacBridan, never taking his eyes off the big man who stood about fifteen feet away from him.

Resting her head back the pew, she said, "He got a call from someone there. He knows you've located Balgair's treasure but not where."

"Then your call for help was all an act," said MacBridan.

"Does my face look like I was acting?" said Talon angrily, her eyes still closed. "He lied to me and then let me get away long enough to call you. He hoped it would flush you out."

"Not too original on his part, attempting the same plan I used on him."

"Perhaps, but for him, the plan has worked. He now knows that what he seeks is at the chapel," said Talon. "You are to show Mukhtar where it's hidden."

"So Goliath's name is Mukhtar. Judging from our earlier conversation, he and I might have trouble communicating," said MacBridan.

"That's why you are to show him, not tell him."

"That's not going to happen," said MacBridan.

Talon grimaced as she painfully straightened up. She carefully reached over to a small leather case next to her on the pew. Ubel redirected his aim at Talon. Reaching into the case, she slowly brought out a walkie-talkie similar to the one Ubel had taken off the man behind the house.

"He said that you might not want to cooperate. If that turned out to be the case, he told me to give you this."

Ubel took it from her, quickly examined it, and then walked over to MacBridan, keeping two pews between him and Mukhtar. But the giant's gaze never strayed from MacBridan. Once he'd given the walkie-talkie to MacBridan, Ubel crossed back to where he'd been, keeping Mukhtar in a cross fire.

Not wanting to be distracted, MacBridan handed it to Father Collin. "Father, would you be so kind as to turn this thing on?"

Father Collin took the walkie-talkie, worked with it for a couple of moments, and then handed it back to MacBridan.

"Ubel," said MacBridan, "be ready."

"Always," answered Ubel.

Pressing a red button on the side, MacBridan said, "Kaseem?"

It didn't take long for Kaseem to respond. "MacBridan, the gods have placed you at their altar at the right time. Their plans work so much better than yours or mine." Father Collin had turned the volume up so that he too could hear what Kaseem was saying. Mukhtar kept repeating his mantra. MacBridan figured that he was either high or in a trance.

"Show's over, Kaseem," said MacBridan. "We have your trained gorilla, and the treasure is now out of your reach." The windows of the chapel rattled as a strong gust of wind shot across the churchyard.

"It is time you learned more about me, MacBridan. I am not a patient man," said Kaseem. "The show, as you put it, is hardly over. We watched you and your confederates leave via the back of the house. I thank you for leaving it so completely unprotected."

A cold dread began to spread through MacBridan. "I assure you, it's anything but unprotected," said MacBridan.

"Of course not," laughed Kaseem. "You left things in the capable hands of an old priest and a mere woman. Like so many of your kind, you disappoint me. Give your weapons to Mukhtar, show him where the treasure is, or we will start killing the people here."

Kaseem's words were not lost on him, but MacBridan was determined not to let Kaseem get a rise out of him. "All I ever see you do is hide behind women," said MacBridan. "If they're not doing your dirty work for you, you're using them as a shield. You're nothing but a coward, Kaseem."

"Enough!" shouted Kaseem. "Tell Father Collin that I will personally slit the old priest's throat. The pitiful cross that he wore around his neck will hang from our god's altar as a trophy. Shall I read for him the inscription on the back of it?" Father Collin's face paled. Uttering a groan, Talon collapsed, falling across the pew. Ubel took it all in, his aim never wavering.

"Give your weapons to Mukhtar now," rasped Kaseem's voice over the walkie-talkie, "or I will put a bullet in Cori's head but will first let you listen to her beg for her life."

MacBridan gripped his gun so hard that his hand hurt. This couldn't be happening! He glanced at Father Collin. The priest looked sick. The next move was clearly left to MacBridan, and he had no idea what to do. How could he have been so stupid?

"You need to make sure you stay away from the poker tables, Kaseem. You really don't lie all that well. Even on the off chance you are at the house, what guarantee could I expect from a coward like you? How could I trust that you wouldn't go ahead and kill them anyway, no matter what we did?" asked MacBridan. Logic was what took men away from the Middle Ages; logic was the tool for now.

This time there was no response, just empty static.

MacBridan knew that he couldn't afford to let too much time pass. Just as he raised the walkie-talkie to his mouth, he heard a soft but distinct popping sound inside the chapel. Ubel grabbed his neck, spun around, and hit the floor.

At almost the same time, MacBridan felt a sharp sting, like that of a bee, hit him just under his jaw. Dropping the walkie-talkie, his hand flew to his neck. He could feel the small dart protruding from his skin. His vision immediately started to blur. Just before his knees buckled, he looked over at Talon. Sitting straight up in the pew, she held a dart gun firmly with both hands, aiming it directly at him. MacBridan didn't feel himself hit the floor as all went black.

Chapter 32

Looking at her watch, she estimated that MacBridan was probably well on his way to the chapel with Father Collin. The mere thought of that place sent chills through her. She stopped in her room long enough to check her satellite phone and then headed back out. Quietly she approached Aunt Jean's room and was surprised to hear the low murmur of voices coming from within. Lightly tapping on the door, she turned the knob and went in.

Aunt Jean, Faith, and Father Novak were all sitting near the fire. They smiled at her, and Faith said, "Come on in. Join the party."

Cori shut the door and walked over to them. "I wasn't sure anyone would still be up." Looking at Aunt Jean, she said, "When I heard voices in here, I thought I'd better take a peek. How are you feeling? You and I had a rather rough time of it last night."

"You and Faith must think I'm made of the most fragile material there is," scolded Aunt Jean but smiled at both of them. "I'm feeling surprisingly well, thank you. There are some spots here and there that are a little sore, but to be honest, as old as I am, I'd be more concerned if I wasn't sore in a couple of places."

"You sit right here," said Father Novak, bringing over another chair and putting it near the fireplace. "Robena just brought us a tray with the most wonderful tea. Shall I pour you some?"

"That sounds wonderful," said Cori as she settled into her chair.

The evening carried on. Cori sat back, admiring Father Novak as he skillfully held their attention telling one amazing story after the next. If he was tired in any way, he clearly wasn't showing it.

Finally, Aunt Jean surrendered to the late hour. "I hate bringing the evening to an end. I've had such a wonderful time, but I'm afraid I'm done in."

"Cori and I will step out into the hall while you get ready for bed," said Father Novak, "and then, we'll say good night. At that time, I'd like to pray with you if that's all right."

"That would be lovely, Father," said Aunt Jean.

Once in the hall, Cori said, "I have no intention of leaving her alone tonight. We can't risk it. She and I already talked about my staying with her earlier today, but that may have slipped her mind."

"It would be good if you can come up with an idea on how to get us both in there with her. Father Collin and I are certain that they'll come for her again."

"Let's hope not. I'm not sure my mind could handle a repeat performance of last night. If Mac and Father Collin are successful, then hopefully we won't have any uninvited guests."

About twenty minutes later, Faith opened the door, and they went back in. Aunt Jean was in bed, slightly propped up with pillows, the covers nearly to her chin. "Thank you for waiting," she said. "It's been such a lovely evening."

"It's not completely over," said Cori. "While we were waiting in the hall, Mac called and suggested that I stay with you. As he said earlier, we don't expect any problems tonight, but we also don't want to take any chances."

"Is that really necessary?" asked Faith. "All I'm saying is that you too have to be exhausted. I'd be happy to stay here with my aunt."

"I'll be fine," said Cori. "Plus, it's what we do. Also, Father Novak has offered to sit with me for a while and enjoy the fire."

"Should Cori start to nod off, I've been instructed to give her a good yet gentle nudge."

"I'm perfectly fine with you staying," said Aunt Jean. Looking at Faith, she said, "I'll actually rest better, knowing they're here with me tonight."

"Let us pray," said Father Novak, "and then we'll let you get to sleep." As he prayed, it was necessary for him to raise his voice in order to be clearly heard over the wind that raged against the windows. He had never seen a storm like this in all his travels. He knew the barriers that kept them separated from the shadow worlds, and this one was wearing thin. He prayed for strength and well-being, for protection of the house. He gave thanks for the many years of happiness the family had known here.

When the prayer finished, Faith kissed her aunt good night and walked to the door with Cori. "I'm probably just as scared as my aunt, but she hides it better," said Faith. "Although I doubt I'd be much help if something does happen, if you need me for anything, I'm just down the hall."

"We'll be okay," said Cori. "Other than the storm, we're really not expecting any problems tonight. My being here is just a precaution."

Faith smiled at her appreciatively and left. Cori bolted the door and then joined Father Novak back where they'd been sitting. The room was dark other than the light from the fire.

Cori leaned forward in her chair and whispered to Father Novak, "I wish I knew how things were going at the chapel."

"Not to worry. I have complete confidence in Father Collin as well as Mr. MacBridan. Hopefully, they'll be able to finally bring this nightmare to an end." With that, he settled back in his chair to begin their night vigil.

Cori barely felt the hand that took hold of her shoulder and began to gently shake her. Startled, she jumped and started to rise up out of her chair, reaching for her gun.

"It's okay," whispered Father Novak. "It's okay. You dozed off for a few moments."

"Sorry," muttered Cori as she stood up and stretched. "Thanks for waking me."

She'd apparently been out for some time as she noticed that the fire had died down to just a bed of glowing coals. Father Novak placed a small log on the fire and went to get another.

"Do you think we really need to build the fire up?" asked Cori.

Father Novak turned to her, and in the dim light coming from the fireplace, she could see the concern etched in his face. "You'd better have a look," he said.

He guided her to the window but was careful to stay to the side of it. "The storm has been doing a nice job of keeping me awake," he whispered. "But about twenty minutes ago, I began to feel very uneasy, so much so that I had to get up and move around." Pointing out the window, he said, "Wait for the lightning, and focus on the grounds below."

"What is it?" asked Cori.

"Just watch."

Anxiously, Cori stared out the window into the nearly pitch-black night. The wind had slowed down a little but still continued to pound against the window. Suddenly, a strong bolt of lightning flashed across the sky, clearly illuminating the ground below. Cori's eyes widened; a deep chill raced through her. Her first instinct was to run, to get away, but she held her ground.

"Oh my god," she breathed out. "Did you see them?"

"Watch," answered Father Novak. "Get one more look."

This time, the lightning held a little longer, confirming for Cori the horror her eyes had beheld. On the grounds below, the shadow people had returned, standing absolutely motionless in the storm. There was no way to count how many were there, but she guessed that there had to be well over a hundred of the grotesquely shaped creatures spread out all across the lawn looking up at them.

"What do we do?"

"I'm not sure," answered Father Novak. "I was standing at the window looking out, and the grounds were empty. Then with the next flash of lightning, they appeared."

"Why aren't they moving? Last night, they were trying to force their way in here."

"They almost seem to be waiting for something, like some kind of signal," answered Father Novak. "Come, we must make the most use of the time we have."

Cori glanced over at Aunt Jean. Blessedly, the old woman was sound asleep. Cori followed Father Novak back to the fire. The logs he'd placed on it had already caught and were putting out more light. He began to pull things out of his robe and place them on the table.

"Why don't you build up the fire a little more," he suggested. "Those vile creatures thrive in the darkness. I fear that we're going to need all the light we can get."

Cori quickly put more logs on the fire, then went over and checked the door. She then checked her gun, and even though it reassured her, she doubted that it would do her much good.

"You knew this would happen. I don't understand. Why have those things come back?"

Father Novak had returned to the window. Bowing his head, he prayed and then began to sprinkle holy water on the frame and the latch. Once finished with that, he looked at Cori and said, "I too am terribly disappointed that they've returned. The short answer is I don't know why, but we're certain that it's somehow important that they take Aunt Jean. Cori, it's up to you and me to protect this dear woman. I'm afraid that we are now the last line of defense."

"What are you saying?" asked Cori, trying to deny what she'd already guessed.

"It's clear that their presence here does not bode well for what may have happened to our friends at the chapel. Come. I need your help."

CHAPTER 33

As consciousness started to return to MacBridan, he could feel the hard, flat surface against his back. The pain in his head throbbed terribly, radiating from his temples and working its way around behind his eyes. Reaching up, he began to gently massage his forehead. Without warning, rough hands grabbed his shoulders and pulled him up into a sitting position. The sudden, jerking movement doubled the pain, sending waves of nausea washing over him. MacBridan tried to open his eyes, but even the faint light from the candles was too much. After a few moments, he tried again, this time squinting, and discovered that he was sitting on the front pew in the chapel.

As the pain began to subside, he tried to leaning forward to rest his head in his hands. But before he was able to accomplish this, someone threw cold water in his face. Surprisingly, this actually seemed to help a little. A deep voice, in a language he couldn't identify, muttered something.

"Yes, I see that," a man answered, fortunately in English, with a heavy Middle Eastern accent. "Welcome back, Mr. MacBridan. You recovered from our little sleep potion faster than most. I do apologize about the pain in your head, but you won't have to suffer it for very long."

MacBridan tried opening his eyes a little wider, and this time managed to keep them open. Mukhtar, who'd been hammering at the floor in the front of the chapel when they'd first come in, was now standing just to his right, keeping guard over him. Up close, he looked even bigger than when MacBridan first laid eyes on him. Father Collin was on the floor in front of the altar in a half-sitting, half-kneeling position, his head sagging into his chest. The man Ubel had shot had been drug off to the side. Ubel was lying on the floor next to MacBridan, still unconscious. Talon stood next to a tall, slender man with strange markings on his face, both of whom were leaning against the altar. In her hand, she still held the dart gun she'd used on MacBridan.

"While you were resting, I've been having a nice chat with Father Collin. Unlike this pitiful priest of Rome, you have actually been a modestly successful antagonist," said the man next to Talon. "Allow me to introduce myself. My name is Kaseem."

"I understand that this thing standing next to me is called Mukhtar," said MacBridan. "I'm not clear on Scottish law, but I do believe that there are restrictions regarding apes as pets."

"It is fortunate for you that his understanding of the English language is most limited. Yes, this is Mukhtar, a most devoted disciple. Like me, he has been anxious to meet you."

"Yes, your errand boy. Talon's told me some interesting stories about the two of you. I understand he's not the brightest bulb in the pack, but then, I'm not really being very fair am I? I mean, let's be honest, you haven't exactly done anything to knock my socks off." MacBridan was well aware that their situation was next to hopeless. As painful as it might become for him, trying to get under their captor's skin was the only tool he had available. When people became angry, they made mistakes.

Kaseem's face clouded over, and Mukhtar stepped in, preparing to backhand MacBridan across the face. "Mukhtar, no!" snapped Kaseem. "Not yet. Not until Mr. MacBridan and I have had a chance to catch up. He needs to fully understand what an utter failure he's been."

Mukhtar glared at MacBridan but didn't strike him, stepping back to where he'd been standing. MacBridan kept eye contact with Mukhtar the entire time, giving Mukhtar a triumphant, mocking smile. Then, to push things further, MacBridan winked at him. Rage filled the giant man, and what little hold Kaseem had over him was nearly lost.

"Mukhtar," Kaseem barked again, stepping up closer to the two men. "Do not be so easily manipulated by this infidel."

"You might try feeding him more," said MacBridan. "That almost always seems to calm animals down."

"Mr. MacBridan," breathed Kaseem, his voice low and threatening. "Tonight you will certainly—"

"You can call me Mac," interrupted MacBridan. "After all, you did say I could call you Kaseem. Unless, of course, your last name is Kaseem, then I'm being completely rude. Please tell me your name's not Kaseem Kaseem."

"You will most certainly die tonight. The only remaining question is how. Up to now, I have admired you as a surprisingly worthy opponent, which would compel me to offer you a merciful, respectful death. Keep pushing, and I'll turn the matter over to Mukhtar's discretion."

"He the one who slapped Talon around, or were you brave enough to handle that yourself?"

"I'm pleased to say that Talon and I have been able to resolve our minor differences. While I have little tolerance for failure, neither of us anticipated your involvement. You can be quite annoying, Mr. MacBridan."

"I get that a lot," said MacBridan, "especially from deranged deviants, or cowards, who like to pick on people weaker than themselves. I'm pretty sure you qualify in both categories."

Kaseem stared at MacBridan for a moment and then gave MacBridan a tight smile. But the smile ended at his lips; there was no humor in his eyes. Turning away, he walked back toward Talon, passing beside Father Collin. Without warning, he turned and viciously backhanded the priest firmly across the cheek bone. The force of the blow sent Father Collin sprawling to the floor landing hard on his side. As he tried to get up, Mukhtar grabbed him by the collar of his jacket and, with one hand, pulled the priest back up into a sitting position.

"Tonight will culminate a dream," said Kaseem, "a dream my order has pursued for centuries. Tonight, we will take possession of a talisman so precious, so powerful that it will sway the balance away from the god of Rome and to the one true god, our Lord Satan."

"Satan is not a god," spat out Father Collin, his voice tainted with pain. MacBridan had not been able to get a good look at Father Collin's face. Now he could clearly see him, and it was obvious that they'd been working on him for some time. "Read the Bible, Kaseem. James 2:19 tells us that even Satan knows that Jesus Christ is the one and only God, and he fears him."

"You are in no position to be giving sermons," hissed Kaseem.

"In the end, Satan, a fallen angel, will again be defeated," continued Father Collin. "He will have no power but will share the horrors of an eternal hell with all the damned."

Kaseem leaned down, his face inches from Father Collin's. "Tonight, Priest, you will meet the Lord Satan up close and personal. To satisfy the entity who guards the talisman, there must be two sacrifices, and you will be one of them. Tonight, two souls will be taken for our Lord Satan, one from a true blood relative of the entity and one to satisfy our lord's thirst for revenge."

At that point, Ubel began to wake up. Mukhtar walked over and easily lifted his limp form up off the floor as if he weighed nothing at all. Mukhtar took the semiconscious man and dropped him on the other front pew across the aisle from MacBridan. Mukhtar then reached into the black case Father Collin had carried with him, tore off the cap on one of the bottles of holy water, and squirted it in Ubel's face. Leaning back in the pew, Ubel tried to open his eyes, but like MacBridan, the dim light from the candles was too much for his eyes.

"Well, if there was any doubt before, its official now, you've absolutely lost it," said MacBridan, trying to take Kaseem's attention away from Father Collin. "You're nothing more than a whack job wrapped in fanaticism, using your perverted beliefs to justify your need to hurt people. And even then, you don't have the guts to do it yourself. You leave it to this off-the-leash moron."

The rage that lived just beneath the surface in Kaseem turned its focus on MacBridan. "Your death will be exceptionally unpleasant," whispered Kaseem. "Mukhtar will see to that."

Kaseem turned to Mukhtar and once again addressed him in the same language MacBridan had heard earlier. An ugly smile spread across Mukhtar's face as his eyes fixated on MacBridan.

"I have given you and the priest's servant to him. It has made him very happy," said Kaseem.

"Simple minds are so easily amused," said MacBridan. "As I now pose no threat to you, I do have a question I'd like answered. Let's put aside the raving nonsense about an ancient talisman. Like every other lowlife who's ever tried, you're after the gold, assuming that the part of the legend about the gold is even true. No, you're just a madman who is here out of greed and is hell-bent on killing two more people, Father Collin and a blood relative of the entity. And that's the part where you lost me. A blood relative of whom?"

Ignoring MacBridan's taunts, Kaseem managed to reign in his temper. "In light of the circumstances, that is a fair and remarkably astute question. I would be only too pleased to share with you all that we have learned. I'm referring to a blood relative of the entity who guards the talisman, of course."

"Of course," said MacBridan. "Tell me, what hallucinogenic drug does one use to find the family tree of an entity?"

"I'm guessing by the way that you say these things, that you believe this is what passes for wit," said Kaseem.

"You guys are a tough audience."

Kaseem studied MacBridan for a moment. "For centuries, my order has sought this particular talisman. Our own people lost it to the infidels when Jerusalem fell to the Christians during the first crusade. The Templars discovered it under the temple rock in Jerusalem and took it back to France. But they didn't understand what it was or the power it contained. Interestingly, it was the power of this talisman that over time led the Templars away from the Christian god and ultimately to their demise. Frankly, we believed that it was lost to us forever."

"He's referring to the severed head that the Templars are believed to have found," said Father Collin.

"Precisely," confirmed Kaseem. "When the story of Balgair was brought to our attention, it was as if a veil had been taken from our eyes. The trail of the talisman no longer ended in France but led to the Highlands of Scotland. Naturally, we jumped at the opportunity to finally retrieve that which had been lost. The only thing that stood between us and the successful completion of our quest was to take possession of one painting, one worthless, insignificant painting. With that in hand, we would have been able to piece together the clues left by the MacKinnon ancestor and quietly take back that which is ours. Then you entered the picture. MacBridan, you have more than earned the death you have coming to you."

"I'm flattered but still not real clear on who we're talking about. I'd ask you to walk me through that again, but I'm afraid you would. Who, in your mind, is the blood relative of this guardian entity?"

Kaseem appeared to be caught up in his own narrative. MacBridan wasn't sure he'd even heard him. "Balgair MacKinnon helped to betray the Templars. By giving Philip the testimony he wanted to hear, he played a role in the events that ended the

Templar order forever. In the midst of it all, he and his small band of followers made off with as much of the Templar's ill-gotten gains as they could carry. It is important to understand that years before this, Balgair had become a follower of the god Satan, which led him to his wife, a priestess in the cult of Lilith. When they arrived in Scotland, Balgair wisely hid everything, his beliefs, the talisman, and the treasure. Then, as soon as he could, he took steps to further secure the treasure, along with the artifacts, in a burial chamber specifically prepared for him. It is Balgair's spirit, willingly given over to Satan, that is the entity who haunts this land. The talisman that he brought with him anchored his soul to this place. Tonight, his minions, the damned souls of darkness that he has gathered over the years, will claim their final victim. With that death and the ritual killing of this priest, the spirit of Balgair will grow in power and be released. He will finally be able to freely roam the land, gathering more and more souls to our god's service."

The final pieces were now falling into place. A sense of dread and frustration spread through MacBridan as he realized the name of Kaseem's intended victim. By accident of birth, she had been a target all along. MacBridan now felt even more frustrated and defeated. Unless a miracle happened, the lunatic beliefs of Kaseem's cult would claim two more innocent lives, and there was nothing he could do about it.

MacBridan's eyes locked with Kaseem's. He could almost see the madness that ruled him. "You're after Aunt Jean." It was not a question but a confirmation.

"Tonight, she will join what has so quaintly become known as the shadow people," said Kaseem, "serving Balgair through eternity." Looking at Mukhtar, he said, "It is time. Let's get the good priest down into the crypt, and then they are yours." Kaseem, catching his own mistake, repeated himself, this time in Mukhtar's tongue.

"Who's been helping you, Kaseem? Who within the MacKinnon household brought you into this?" asked MacBridan. As much as he wanted to know, he was continuing to stall for time, trying to keep Kaseem talking. He still didn't have any kind of plan but knew that the longer he could put things off, the better chance they all had to escape.

"No more questions," said Kaseem. "Your time on this earth is over. Talon, keep your gun trained on them. If either tries to get up, shoot them with another dose of the sleeping potion. I'm sure Mukhtar will find an amusing way of waking them up."

Kaseem walked over to the door leading down into the crypt, closely followed by Mukhtar who half drug, half carried Father Collin down the stairs.

"How are you doing?" asked MacBridan, looking over at Ubel.

"Been better. My head is killing me. We have to help Father Collin," answered Ubel.

"I'm open. What do you have in mind?" MacBridan looked at Talon. She hadn't moved, staying close to the altar. As directed, she kept the long barrel of the dart gun leveled at them.

"Try anything, and I will use this," she said.

"Talon, you're not one of them. You're not a cold-blooded killer."

"They've made things pretty clear," said Talon. "Either I do as Kaseem says or he'll hand me over to that overgrown pig. I don't understand all that's going on here, but like I told you, I've seen some of the things they've done to people, and it terrifies me. I get the rest of my money tonight, and then I'm out of here."

"Talon, Kaseem is 101 percent loony tunes. Even assuming he finds what he's after, he's going to kill you, he has to."

"He no longer needs me to steal that stupid painting. If he was going to kill me, he would have done so by now. Sorry, MacBridan, but I'm not taking any chances."

"All you are to him right now is a useful tool. Once he has what he wants, you're dead. You're one of the few left who can identify him. He cannot afford to leave you behind. We'll protect you."

"Oh yes, I can see that," said Talon. "You can't even help yourself. I don't like the position I'm in, but right now, it's the only chance I've got."

A low, rumbling sound echoed up the stairs from the crypt and then stopped. Talon moved over to the crypt's door and opened it wider, listening. The sound started again, louder this time, the heavy grinding of stone against stone was unmistakable. It was the same sound MacBridan and Cori had heard during their first visit to the chapel when they'd been stuck on the crypt's staircase.

"What is that?" mumbled Ubel.

"I don't know," answered MacBridan.

"He's opening the door that leads to the hidden chamber, Balgair's tomb. Mukhtar discovered it yesterday. Apparently, Kaseem performed some kind of ritual, summoning that thing that he calls the entity. They were able to follow it back to the chapel and figured out where the door to the tomb was hidden."

"If Kaseem found the tomb yesterday, why didn't he just take what he's after and get out of here?" asked MacBridan.

"I asked the same question," answered Talon. "Apparently, it's not that easy. Whatever is down there, he and Mukhtar fear it. He told me that it is the tomb everyone has been searching for but that it is too dangerous to just go in and take what they want. He said there's a price in blood extracted from anyone who tries to enter that tomb."

"So what is he doing?" pressed MacBridan. "Is he going to force Father Collin to go in there and bring out the things he wants?"

Talon shook her head. "It's far more complex. Kaseem had originally planned to go to the manor, kidnap Father Collin, and bring him here. There's a ritual he needs to perform before anyone can enter the tomb, and the priest plays a key role. Kaseem had people watching the manor. When you left this evening, they let him know that you were heading toward the chapel. It couldn't have worked out better. As we were already here, you stumbled right into his hands."

"In one way, you were lucky," continued Talon. "Kaseem repeatedly let us know that we were to capture you alive. Had he not stressed that you would have died the minute you walked through the door. Kaseem gave me the dart gun and told me that I was to shoot you. He explained that it would not kill you, just put you out. Mukhtar was to be your distraction. Kaseem hid on the stairs to the crypt, with the door partially open. My signal to shoot you was when Kaseem shot that guy," she said, nodding at Ubel.

"What about Father Collin?" asked MacBridan.

"As I told you, Kaseem needs him as a sacrifice for the ritual he'll do after opening the tomb. You should have seen him describing it to me. He acted like a child who knows they're getting the toy of their dreams. He said that the sacrifice of a Catholic priest would satisfy the entity, the gatherer. Kaseem will then be able to enter the tomb without risk."

"You can't possibly be buying into all these," said MacBridan. "All he's doing is making you an accessory to murder. Surely you know how deranged he is."

Talon looked at MacBridan. He could see the fear she was feeling in her face. "I've seen that thing," she said, her voice nearly a whisper as if the creature could hear her. "It is real. Kaseem told me how it killed Lord MacKinnon's son in the churchyard." Her voice cracked. Up until now, MacBridan hadn't realized how close to the edge she was. "Kaseem said that it took his soul." Silent tears spilled down Talon's face.

"Talon, give me the gun. It's not too late. We can stop him and free everyone from this nightmare."

Talon looked down the stairs into the crypt and then at MacBridan. Despite the circumstances, she was as much of a prisoner as MacBridan and Ubel. Finally she turned and walked over to MacBridan, stopping about eight feet away from him.

"You can stop him?" she asked. "You can really protect me?"

"Together, we can," answered Ubel. He was now sitting up straight as the drug they'd been hit with continued to dissipate.

"I want to trust you," said Talon. "I'm just not sure. If you fail, he'll kill me."

MacBridan looked into her eyes. "Doesn't really matter. Whether Mukhtar returns and kills us or you help us and we fail in our attempt to stop them, you won't leave here alive. I'm all but certain that he's already promised you to Mukhtar. Your only hope is with us."

Before she could answer, Mukhtar reappeared in the doorway to the crypt. None of them had heard him coming, and Talon jumped, nearly dropping the gun. In a deep, guttural voice, he barked something at her.

Mukhtar quickly moved to her side, snatching the gun out of her hand. "Kaseem," he said and pointed at the stairs. "Kaseem, go."

Talon's face paled at the thought. "I'm not going down there. Kaseem said I could stay up here," she pleaded.

Mukhtar snarled at her as one of his massive hands shot out, grabbing her roughly around the back of her neck. Nearly dragging her to the door, he once again pointed down the stairs and shouted, "Go!"

Talon looked pleadingly back at MacBridan, but there was nothing that either he or Ubel could do. Talon hesitantly started down into the crypt. Mukhtar watched until she reached the bottom of the stairs and moved out of sight. He then turned his attention to MacBridan and Ubel.

Although MacBridan was feeling better, the pain in his head was still there, and he felt weak. Mukhtar walked over and stood before them. MacBridan estimated that he was around 6'10", if not taller, and had to weigh well over three hundred pounds. Sadly, most of it appeared to be muscle. His broad shoulders were well defined, the muscles hunching up around his neck like a bear. The dart gun looked like a child's toy in his massive hands.

Mukhtar held the gun up before them. Holding it in both hands, he smiled at them, his broken teeth a ruddy yellow. He said something and, then without any obvious effort, bent the long barrel of the gun, rendering it useless. He then turned and tossed the gun away behind him.

At that moment, Ubel chose to attack. Lunging out of the pew, he charged directly at Mukhtar, but the drug was still very much in his system, throwing his equilibrium off and causing him to nearly trip over his own feet. Mukhtar easily sidestepped Ubel, grabbed him by the shoulder and, using his own momentum, hurled Ubel toward the altar. Before Ubel hit the floor, MacBridan joined in the attack.

Taking his cue from Ubel's off-balanced performance, MacBridan went in low, aiming his right shoulder at Mukhtar's knees. Despite his lightheadedness, he connected right where he'd been aiming, but the drug had sapped his strength. Instead of bringing the big man down, the impact merely caused Mukhtar to stagger a few steps before regaining his balance. For MacBridan, it was much worse. He felt as if he'd tried to tackle a telephone pole. Pain lanced across his right shoulder and down his arm, but he was still able to wrap his arms around Mukhtar's waist.

Mukhtar growled at this annoyance. Swinging around, he tried to dislodge MacBridan, but MacBridan held tight. Ubel had landed hard but was already up on all fours, trying to regain his feet. Mukhtar spun around again but could not shake MacBridan off. Mukhtar wedged his arm underneath MacBridan's hands and jerked upward, easily breaking MacBridan's grip. This caused MacBridan to fall to his knees. Mukhtar quickly turned around, bunched the front of MacBridan's jacket in his left hand, and lifted him to his feet. He cocked his right arm back, balling his hand into a fist, and brought it around at MacBridan's face.

Using the crook of his arm, Ubel intercepted the blow just before it landed and, with his left, shot a vicious blow into the side of Mukhtar's neck. This sent the big man back a couple of steps, dragging MacBridan with him. Shoving MacBridan to the floor, Mukhtar turned his focus on Ubel. Ubel stayed in close, following up quickly with two more blows in quick succession, one to the bridge of Mukhtar's nose, then a hard uppercut to his chin. Both landed solidly, but Mukhtar stayed on his feet, absorbing the blows. With his left, Mukhtar backhanded Ubel, snapping his head around. Ubel's knees started to buckle, but before he could fall, Mukhtar hit him again, slapping him openhanded with this right. Ubel landed hard on his back, his head bouncing off the stone floor. The impact took the fight out of him, nearly leaving him unconscious.

Mukhtar sensed MacBridan moving in on him and whirled around. MacBridan did his best to stay out of Mukhtar's reach, but there was little room to maneuver, and his legs still were not fully cooperating. Seeing an opening, MacBridan launched two quick jabs into Mukhtar's face with his left and then connected with a hard right cross. Mukhtar staggered back as blood erupted from his smashed nose. Screaming in rage, Mukhtar charged MacBridan, wrapping both muscled arms around MacBridan's waist. Lifting MacBridan off the floor, he began to squeeze. To MacBridan, it felt like steel bands slowly crushing his ribs. Twice he slammed both fists into the sides of Mukhtar's head, but the blows didn't seem to have any visible effect. Mukhtar tightened his grip, steadily increasing the pressure on MacBridan's back.

MacBridan couldn't breathe. He glimpsed Ubel lying motionless on the floor. Black spots started to dance before his eyes. He heard a popping sound but didn't feel any pain. Although he was starting to lose consciousness, his mind latched on to the sound, trying to understand what had happened. If something in his back had broken, he should have felt a tremendous amount of pain. Instead, the pressure suddenly stopped; Mukhtar released him, and MacBridan slid to the floor, ending up in a semisitting position. Cool, sweet air rushed back into his lungs, and his eyes began to clear.

Mukhtar stood before him. The big man looked confused. Staggering back a step, his hand reached up behind his neck. He felt around for a moment then angrily pulled on something. Looking at his hand, he now seemed more confused than ever. MacBridan couldn't see what he was holding but could tell that Mukhtar was in trouble. Mukhtar slowly turned around and looked at the door to the crypt. It was then that he and MacBridan spotted Talon. She was holding another dart gun. Mukhtar took one awkward step toward her, stopped, and fell on his face.

Giving him wide berth, Talon moved around Mukhtar and went to help MacBridan. Together, he was able to get up off the floor and onto a pew. "Are you all right?"

"No, I'm not, but then, I also didn't expect to have a pulse at this point. Check on Ubel. I'm more concerned about him."

Talon quickly crossed over to Ubel and knelt at his side. His eyes were open, but he made no effort to get up. MacBridan managed to get up off the pew and slowly made his way toward them. He tried to determine if any of his ribs had been broken but couldn't find one spot on his body that didn't ache.

Looking down at him, MacBridan said, "Ubel, can you hear me?"

"Yes, I can see you too. That's not the problem. I'm just not sure if I can get up."

"Do you want us to try and help? We can let you rest on one of the pews," said MacBridan.

"No, let me stay here a little longer. I need to try and figure out what's working and what's not," answered Ubel.

"Talon, I have never been so happy to see anyone as I was to see you. What brought you back? Why didn't you stay with Kaseem?"

"I knew what you were saying was right," she said. Her voice was tired, and she'd nearly reached her limit. "When Mukhtar ordered me to go to Kaseem, it confirmed what I'd feared all along. I knew I had to get away but couldn't figure a way out. Kaseem had already opened up the back of the crypt, and I could see a tight passageway leading off into the darkness. I couldn't go in there. Then I saw it. Lying on the floor, just in front of the passageway, was Kaseem's dart gun. It was the only chance I had, and I took it."

"You saved our lives. Thank you," said MacBridan.

Looking up at him, she said, "You're welcome, but only on the condition that you now save mine. We need to get out of here as fast as we can."

"I can't leave Father Collin," said MacBridan. "I'm going to need you to—"

"This can't be happening," screamed Talon, pointing toward the crypt.

MacBridan snapped his head around. Despite getting hit with the dart, Mukhtar had amazingly made it to his feet. He clearly wasn't firing on all cylinders, but he was standing. Mukhtar turned, tried to focus on them, then staggered backward. The wall beside the door to the crypt saved him from falling, and he leaned against it. The whole time, he never took his eyes off them. Everything inside the chapel went still, waiting for what would happen next. The rage MacBridan had witnessed earlier once again filled Mukhtar's eyes as he began to move toward them.

Reaching down, MacBridan took the dart gun away from Talon. Dropping to one knee to steady himself, he fired at

Mukhtar. The dart caught him in the throat. Mukhtar clawed at the dart, his eyes bulging out as his air was almost immediately cut off. Once again, he staggered backward. Struggling against the effects of the dart, he backed through the doorway to the crypt and fell down the stairs.

All went silent. Taking the dart gun with him, MacBridan carefully followed Mukhtar down into the crypt. As with his first visit, the candles along both walls were lit. MacBridan stood over Mukhtar, looking down at him. The man's neck was clearly broken. "You get up after this, and I quit," muttered MacBridan.

Still hurting, MacBridan made his way back up the stairs as quickly as his ribs would let him. He was pleasantly surprised to find Ubel sitting up on the floor, supported by Talon.

"Is he dead?" asked Talon.

"I certainly hope so," said MacBridan. Looking at Ubel, he asked, "How are you doing?"

"I'm afraid I'm not going to be much help to you," he said. "Something's wrong with my head."

MacBridan helped Ubel to his feet. "You two need to get out of here. This is a long way from being over, and we need help. Talon, take Ubel and get as far from this chapel as you can. Try to get ahold of Wetmoore. Have him get his men out here as fast as possible."

"What are you going to do?" asked Talon.

"With the help of Kaseem's dart gun, I'm going after Father Collin."

"That's insane," said Talon. "Kaseem is raising that thing up, and I'm telling you, nothing can stop it. Besides, Father Collin's probably already dead. Loyalty's great, but going down there is suicide, plain and simple."

MacBridan did the best he could to smile. "Let's hope not. Now get going. If Wetmoore's too late to help me, he and his men will certainly be needed at the manor."

MacBridan helped them to the front door. The storm continued in its unrelenting pace, but Talon was only too happy to get out of the chapel. Leaning heavily on her, Ubel struggled to keep his balance. Shutting the door behind them, MacBridan turned and walked back down aisle. Lying on its side on the floor up by the altar, the bag that Father Collins had brought with him was spotted by MacBridan. Moving carefully, MacBridan knelt down, favoring his left side. As quickly as he could, MacBridan salvaged the few items that were there. He had no idea what was waiting for him down in the crypt, but on the off chance he'd find Father Collin alive, he thought it might be a good idea to bring the man some of his tools. Satisfied that he'd gotten what was left to be had, he headed to the door. For the last time, MacBridan started down the stairs into the crypt.

Chapter 34

"Well, the good news is they haven't moved any closer to the house," said Father Novak, looking out the window, continuing his watch over the lawn where the shadow people had gathered.

Cori paced in front of the fireplace, struggling to keep her nerves under control. The situation was beyond maddening. They'd not heard anything from MacBridan, and despite her satellite phone, she hadn't been able to reach Wetmoore. In her rational mind, she credited all of this to the outrageous storm. In her irrational heart, she blamed the devil. Every horror movie she had ever watched as a teen was reprocessed as documentary. Fortunately, if there actually was a fortunate side to this, the intermittent flashes of lightning enabled them to keep tract of the shadow people.

"If that's what you call good news, then we're in pretty bad shape," snapped Cori. Whimsy before death seemed in bad taste.

"The bad news is I believe they're growing in number."

"Does that mean anything, Father? Are twenty unkillable, unstoppable creatures worse than ten?" snapped Cori.

Father Novak actually bit his lip.

For at least the ninth time Cori went over to check on Aunt Jean. She envied the woman for simply being asleep. *Maybe I'll get lucky and faint*, Cori thought to herself.

A small clicking sound behind her grabbed her attention, and she looked around, trying to determine where it was coming from. It took only a moment to catch sight of the doorknob slowly turning. Someone was trying to get in.

Putting her hand on the handle of her gun, she quietly made her way to the door. "Psst," she said, trying to get Father Novak's attention. He looked over at her, and she mouthed the words, "We've got company."

Father Novak stayed where he was, his right hand instinctively reaching for the crucifix he wore around his neck. Cori stood still, waiting, listening. Once again, the doorknob started to turn. Lightly placing her hand on the doorknob, Cori gradually tightened her grip. Flipping back the dead bolt, Cori yanked the door open as hard as she could. Her tactic worked, completely catching their uninvited guest off balance, causing them to plunge head first onto floor just inside the bedroom. Quickly rolling over onto their back, they looked up to find Cori standing over them, her gun pointed at their head.

"Don't shoot! It's me," cried Faith, holding her hands up in front of her. "Please, help me."

"What were you doing out there?" demanded Cori. "Why didn't you just knock if you wanted to come in?"

Faith was crying. "I need your help. They're here!" she sobbed. "They're outside, and I didn't know what to do. I knew you were with Aunt Jean, so I got here as fast as I could."

Cori looked out into the hallway. As best as she could tell, Faith was alone. "So answer my question. Why didn't you just tap on the door? Why try to sneak in?"

"When I got to the door, I couldn't hear anything. I didn't want to wake anyone, especially Aunt Jean. She doesn't need this. Please, I don't want to be alone, not with them out there."

Leaning over, Cori helped her to her feet. Joined by Father Novak, they brought her over to one of the high back chairs by the fire. Cori then went back and secured the door, making sure that the dead bolt was firmly in place. Glancing at Aunt Jean,

Cori could see that she'd slept through their momentary burst of excitement. *That lady is one sound sleeper,* she thought.

"Ever since I was a little girl, Aunt Jean has told me stories about them, that they are real, but I never believed her," said Faith. Her breathing was still ragged, but she'd stopped crying.

"Who is real?" asked Cori.

"The shadow people," whispered Faith. "She told me that they're the souls of the damned, here to do the work of the gatherer. I always thought it was just another Scottish ghost story like Loch Ness or phantom pipers. Now I know different. Please, look out the window if you don't believe me, they're outside, all over the place!"

"Drink this," said Father Novak. "It will help."

Cori caught the distinct aromatic scent of what Father Novak handed her and asked, "Where did you get that?"

"Father Collin swears by Irish whiskey, but I never go anywhere without a little medicinal brandy." He showed Cori a small silver flask.

"Keep that handy," said Cori, "I'm not all that far from where she is."

Faith tentatively sipped the brandy, slowly leaning back in her chair. No sooner had she started to relax when she bolted up and looked around behind her at Aunt Jean's bed. "How's Aunt Jean? Has she seen them? Does she know they're out there?"

"Mercifully, she has so far slept through everything," said Father Novak.

"Father, what are those things?" asked Faith.

"They are creatures of darkness, and you're right to fear them," he answered. "But we've taken precautions that should make this room reasonably safe."

"Precautions?"

"I have washed the windows and doors with holy water, and I have asked the Lord to send angels for our defense."

Faith said, "I don't see any angels. I would feel better if I saw angels."

"How did you come to know that they were out there?" asked Cori.

"Because I saw them," answered Faith, puzzled by the question. "Is that what you're asking?"

"Why did you go and look out your window in the first place? What was it that made you think something was outside?"

Father Novak looked at Cori, surprised by her tone. Why was she questioning Faith in such a way? He didn't know what she was driving at but suddenly felt as if he'd missed something.

"Oh, I see. Had it not been for the storm, I probably wouldn't have. Typically, I sleep with my windows cracked to let in fresh air. With all the rain we've had, I've been keeping them shut. When I went to bed tonight, I couldn't sleep, and the lightning certainly wasn't helping any. I tossed and turned for some time, but it was no use. So I got up to pull the drapes, and just as I started to close them, there came another flash of lightning. That's when I saw them," said Faith, quickly looking toward her sleeping aunt and not Cori.

"What did you do?" pressed Cori.

"I'm not proud of this, but I screamed and fell to the floor," said Faith. She lowered her head for a moment and then looked up at both of them. "I've never known such fear. At first, I didn't know what to do. I just knew I had to get away. As quickly as I could, I crawled back to my bed, trying to think of where I could hide. But then, I remembered Aunt Jean's stories. If they were coming for me, there was no place I could hide where they wouldn't find me."

"Why would you think that they might be after you?" asked Father Novak.

"Because of the family curse," answered Faith. "It only affects MacKinnon women. Aunt Jean is terrified of them. She told me that over the past few days, she thinks she's seen them, once even inside the house."

Father Novak nodded his head and murmured, "Her fear is not without good reason."

Cori caught the movement out of the corner of her eye and looked at the window. Her mouth went dry, and she had trouble finding her voice. "Father Novak," she hissed. "They're here."

Father Novak spun around and faced the window. Faith sprang to her feet, stifling a scream as she ran to her aunt's bedside. The shadow people were outside the window, their grotesque forms fighting with each other, clamoring for a way into the room, but something as transparent as glass stopped them. Their shadow claws burned with a shadowy flame as they touched a spiritual barrier. Father Novak removed a large silver crucifix from one of his deep pockets. He immediately went to his knees and bowed his head in prayer, all the while holding the silver cross up before him and in the direction of the window.

Cori stood rooted to the floor. Although she didn't remember reaching for it, her gun was firmly in her hand. Her eyes kept darting from the window to Father Novak. She wanted to scream, to yell at the priest to do something, but realized he was doing all he could. The preparations the priest had attended to earlier seem to be working, at least for the moment.

Cori managed to pry her eyes away from the window long enough to glance over at Aunt Jean. The old woman still slept peacefully. In fact, as best as Cori could tell, she hadn't moved. Faith stood at her bedside, her left hand on her aunt's shoulder. Lightning filled the sky, and Cori gasped. The number of shadow people nearly filled the window, so many more than they'd seen the previous night, maybe a hundred; she could see them as much with her mind as her eyes. They hated her for being alive; their dull green eyes reflected each living thing in the room as though they were yellowish flames. She felt pity as well as fear.

Something kept nagging at the back of Cori's mind. Faith was too quick, too poised. Looking back at Aunt Jean, she turned in time to see Faith pull something out of her pocket and slide it under Aunt Jean's pillow. Faith then leaned over and gently kissed her Aunt's forehead. When she saw Faith's face, a terrible chill shot through Cori, causing her to shudder. To Cori's normal vision, Faith was acting the part of a concerned relative, but with the vision that saw the shadow people, Faith's eyes were hungrier, more savage than the demonic hoard outside. Faith smiled down at her Aunt, but it was a ghastly smile, her eyes filled with malice. She stepped quietly away from the bed and turned toward Cori. Their eyes locked.

"What have you done?" asked Cori.

Faith put her scared face back on, but she could see that Cori wasn't buying it. "Comforting my aunt."

Cori quickly moved toward the bed. Faith stepped in her way, trying to keep Cori away from her aunt, but Cori was in no mood to be messed with. Grabbing Faith's arm, she stepped in and pushed her backward, sending her to the floor. She then slid her hand under Aunt Jean's pillow, searching for whatever it was Faith had placed there. Her hand quickly found a cold oval-shaped object.

Pulling it out from under the pillow, Cori found that it was a medallion, surprisingly heavy for its size. A strange design had been deeply engraved on one side. Cori knew she'd seen it before but couldn't remember where. Faith was back on her feet, glaring at Cori.

"Put that back," she growled. "You'll ruin everything."

"Stay right where you are," said Cori. "I don't know what game you're playing, but I don't want you near her."

Slipping the medallion into her pocket, she reached down and touched Aunt Jean's face, then quickly moved her hand to the side of her neck. There was a pulse, but it was faint. Placing her hand on Aunt Jean's shoulder, she gently shook her, trying to wake her up. There was no way any healthy person could be sleeping now.

"Aunt Jean," she said in a loud voice. "Aunt Jean, I need for you to wake up." The old woman didn't move, didn't respond at all.

"She's been drugged," said Cori. "What did you give her?"

"I've given her a peaceful way out," said Faith.

Cori took a step toward her. "You're going to tell me what you gave her, and you're going to tell me now."

Faith's smile was reptilian in its coldness. "It doesn't matter. It'll soon be over, and you will have failed, all of you." Faith pointed at the window. "They've come for her, and they will have her. They cannot be stopped. They have come because you're helpless. Mr. MacBridan has also failed."

Cori took another step toward her. "If Mac is dead, I'm all in favor of you escorting him into the next world. Why was it so important that you put this medallion under her pillow?"

Either the wind or the shadow people, she didn't know which, suddenly slammed against the window. Father Novak stood up, still holding the cross before him. Cori could see that the shadow people were nearly frantic in their assault on the window. The glass was actually starting to bulge inward, and parts of the window frame were cracking.

"Cori, get rid of that thing," yelled Father Novak. "It's drawing them in!"

Before Cori could respond, pain exploded across the side of her head. The few seconds in which her focus had been drawn away and toward the window was all the time Faith had needed. Grabbing a flower vase from the small table beside the door, Faith swung it at Cori as hard as she could, shattering it against the side of her face. Cori fell to the floor, blood flowing from the cuts on her cheek and above her eye. The medallion shot out of her pocket and awkwardly wobbled across the floor toward Father Novak.

Faith held the jagged end of the vase in her hand. She stood over Cori, ready to strike her again, but she could see that Cori was out. She then looked up and found Father Novak standing by the window, looking at both of them. Coldly smiling at the priest, her eyes bore into to his. "Now it's your turn, Priest," and started for him.

Chapter 35

MacBridan moved as quickly and quietly as he could. The crypt was amazingly quiet as compared to the chapel, with most of the noise from the storm having been left behind. Candles burned in their sconces, giving him all the light he needed. Moving to the rear of the crypt, he saw how one side of the rear wall had swung inward, like a door, revealing another passageway. Although at first glance it looked like a cave, MacBridan could see marks where the stone had been chipped away. He guessed that this had been carved out of the bedrock centuries ago when the chapel had first been built, probably providing an escape route if need be. The chamber smelled of sandalwood and patchouli, the air thick with smoke and vibrated with an unseen energy.

The passageway was utterly dark. MacBridan pondered this for a moment as he had no idea where the flashlight he'd carried with him had ended up. Taking one of the candles down off the wall, he entered the tight opening, having to crouch down a little to keep from hitting his head. The passageway snaked its way through solid rock, becoming so narrow at some points that MacBridan had to wedge his large frame through in order to continue on. He protected the flame burning on the short wick of his candle as best he could from the water seeping through the rocks, as well as from the occasional gusts of wind that blew by. The wind was the biggest threat, for if he lost the light from the candle, he had no way of relighting it.

Between the lingering effects of the drug and the beating he'd taken from Mukhtar, MacBridan staggered and shook. The passageway continued on, taking him deeper into the earth. He soon lost track of time but doggedly continued on. Coming around a tight bend, the path surprisingly straightened out, angling sharply upward. At the far end, MacBridan could see a reddish light. He prayed that he'd caught up with them.

To make sure he wasn't seen, MacBridan blew out the candle and began to make his way toward the light. Stopping every so often, he listened but could hear nothing from the chamber above him. The incline made the going harder, and he tried to control his breathing as his ribs protested with every breath. His hope was that Kaseem was alone. He didn't know how many shots were left in the dart gun. If Kaseem did have help, things could get dicey. Physically, he was in no shape for a confrontation.

The path broadened a little as he approached the light, opening into a large chamber with torches mounted around the walls. Staying in the shadows, MacBridan's gaze was drawn to a coffin set upon a stone dais in the center of the room. An old kerosene lantern had been placed at the foot of the coffin. The coffin was closed, and in the dim light, he could make out angular markings all along the side of it. Edging forward a little more, he saw that there were five other coffins in the chamber, placed in equal distance from one another all surrounding the coffin in the center of the chamber. They too were closed. A second kerosene lantern burned dimly on the floor of the passageway next to where he stood.

Father Collin was sprawled on the floor, his back leaning up against the dais at the foot of the coffin. His chin rested on his chest, but from where MacBridan stood, he could not determine if he was breathing. Once again, MacBridan scanned the room, but there was no sign of Kaseem or anyone else. MacBridan checked the dart gun. Although he was not all that familiar with this kind of weapon, he was pretty sure that it was ready to fire. Stepping out of the passageway, he cautiously entered the chamber, carefully going down some irregular steps that had been carved out of the rock. He quickly crossed over to Father Collin.

Kneeling beside the priest, he glanced around, but fortunately, they were alone. MacBridan gently moved the priest's head up off his chest, feeling for a pulse in the man's neck. It was there, but it was weak. Reaching into his pocket, he pulled out one of the bottles of holy water that he had taken from the priest's bag. Opening it, he poured a small amount on his palm and gently wiped off Father Collin's face. The priest stirred, and his eyes fluttered open.

"That's better," said MacBridan. "I know this isn't what it was originally intended for, but I want you to drink this." He held the bottle of holy water up to Father Collin's lips to help him get it down. The priest choked a little at first but then sipped some more. "Any idea of where Kaseem went?"

"No, I'm sorry. I don't," rasped Father Collin. "Getting here was pretty tough on me. When we arrived, Kaseem recited something and then forced me onto the floor here. Something answered him. I remember him starting to light the torches. He said some mantra as he lighted each, then the room felt strange, and I passed out. We are not in normal time here. Like the mass in holy time, we are in the opposite."

"Drink a little more of this. Then, let's see if we can get you on your feet."

"Where is Ubel?" asked Father Collin. "How did you get here?"

"Ubel's fine, the rest I'll fill you in on later. For now, all you need to know is that gorilla, Mukhtar, is dead."

Father Collin regained some color. MacBridan had strong doubts about getting him back to the kirk. If it turned out that Father Collin couldn't walk on his own, MacBridan was pretty sure he wouldn't be able to carry him. He wanted to give the priest all the time he could to recover but knew they desperately needed to get out of there.

As he waited for Father Collin to recover enough to try and make a run for it, MacBridan looked more closely at the coffin and the markings on its side. Some of the markings belonged on the talisman he had seen before, an inverse pentagram, and there were words in some barbarous tongue. The texture of the coffin itself looked odd, and he reached out to touch it. Although greatly tarnished from years in a subterranean crypt, MacBridan discovered that it was made out of lead. It seemed too big to have been carried down here by normal means, but MacBridan knew that normal and this place didn't intersect.

A numbing cold suddenly burst into the chamber, carrying with it an odor that nearly made MacBridan choke. This was quickly followed by an intense pang of fear. The cold and the odor were exactly what he'd experienced in his room the night he'd had his nocturnal visitor. His eyes shot around in all directions, and at first, he didn't see anything. Then, coming from under the few steps he'd descended when he first entered the chamber, he saw a faint light from what appeared to be another passageway that up until now had been lost in the shadows.

"Time we got out of here," said MacBridan, putting both hands under the priest's arms, lifting the wounded man off the floor. MacBridan's ribs screamed in protest, and it was all he could do to keep from dropping him. Father Collin was now on his feet, but he was weak and had to lean against the coffin to keep from falling down.

"Are you able to walk?" asked MacBridan. "We've got to get—"

"Not leaving so soon are you?" asked Kaseem. He was standing behind them. Using both hands, he held a small ornate casket. Judging from the strain in his face, MacBridan guessed that it was pretty heavy. The light from the torches, as well as the two lanterns, dimly reflected off its golden sides and the small gemstones imbedded in its seams. "MacBridan, why is it that I'm not surprised to see you?"

"Mukhtar sends you his regards," answered MacBridan, raising the dart gun and pointing it at Kaseem. It was all he could do to hold it steady as the severe cold in the chamber penetrated every part of his body. "In fact, he told me he'd like you to join him."

Looking at the dart gun, Kaseem smiled and said, "I'm impressed. Either you bested Mukhtar in hand-to-hand combat, which I sincerely doubt, or Talon made a fatal decision regarding her loyalty. Before the night's end, I'll send something to take care of her."

"Nah, nothing like that at all. He just got tired of the wet, cold Scottish weather and left in a rather dramatic fashion for a far hotter climate," said MacBridan. "Now why don't you put that chest down and keep your hands where I can see them."

Kaseem's smile broadened a little. "Of course, I'll put it down. You wanted to see the treasure, the loot. This is what several lives have paid for, and I would have gladly paid ten times as much. It is what we have dreamt of."

Kaseem slowly lowered the casket to the floor and knelt beside it. His hand went to the latch, and as he started to open it, Father Collin held up his hand in protest and tried to say something but couldn't get the words out in time. Kaseem quickly reached into the casket. Grasping it by the hair, he slowly stood up, holding a woman's head before him. The putrid odor of decay thickened the air. A green mist encased the head and gradually started to spread over Kaseem's hand, slowly moving up his arm. MacBridan could only guess at how long the head had been in the casket and yet was amazed at how well preserved it appeared to be. The head was that of an old woman. Her gray matted hair hung down well below the jawine, mingling with tendons that dangled from its neck. The eyes were closed, but the lips and nose were remarkably in tack. At first glance, she almost appeared to be asleep.

"The legends were true! This is the head stolen by the Templars, the witch of Endor," said Kaseem triumphantly. "It is through this holy relic that we will be able to directly communicate with our Lord Satan. Behold the death of Rome!"

Both men stared at the head as the green mist started to radiate outward. Father Collin crossed himself but couldn't take his eyes away. Even MacBridan nearly found himself overwhelmed by its presence. Using all the strength he could muster, MacBridan steadied his aim and tried to pull the trigger. At that very moment, the head's eyes flew open. Though the sockets were empty, they burned with a deep, nauseating green light. An overpowering malevolence flowed from the eyes, piercing into their minds. This wasn't simple hatred. This was pure intelligence, a will that had survived for thousands of years.

Kaseem stepped forward, still holding the head and, with his other hand, slapped the gun from MacBridan's grip. The gun clattered across the stone floor, ending up against the far wall. Kaseem then backhanded MacBridan, the force of the blow sending him staggering backward. He tripped and fell onto the stone steps by the entrance, coming down hard on his side. The pain from his injured ribs wracked his body, breaking him out of the near trance he'd been in.

"MacBridan, don't pass out on me. I need for you to pay attention," said Kaseem, staring down at Father Collin. "You are about to witness a soul being sent to hell. You will witness the beginning of the end of Christ's rule."

Kaseem began to move the head closer to the helpless priest. MacBridan tried to get up, but his ribs wouldn't allow it. His eyes frantically searched the room, but there was nothing within his grasp that he could use as a weapon to defend Father Collin. He'd run out of ideas, and there was nothing he could do.

Chapter 36

Father Novak couldn't tell how badly Cori had been injured, but he was in no position to help her. The storm raged against the windows, and above it all, he could now hear the mournful, desperate wailing of the shadow people. The evil within the room called to the evil outside the room.

The medallion that had spilled out of Cori's pocket lay on the floor next to the leg of one of the wingback chairs. It was drawing the shadow people in, and Father Novak's mind raced as he tried to figure out how to get rid of it. But first, he had to deal with Faith.

"Faith, listen to me," said Father Novak. "I don't know what Kaseem has promised you, but you must understand. In his eyes, you are expendable."

"Promised me?" laughed Faith as she steadily advanced on the old priest. "Kaseem works for me. In exchange for some stupid religious trinket that he wants, I will gain tremendous wealth, at least that was the original plan. Thanks to you and MacBridan's bungling things, when my uncle passes, I may actually end up inheriting the entire estate."

"You sold your family for money," shouted Father Novak. "At least Kaseem believes what his family has known for thousands of years. You must understand. You are toying with evil incarnate. You had love in your life, a chance to better yourself, but you've done all this for what? For money? For land? My daughter, you are a worse evil than Kaseem. Turn back now before he sends you to the damnation you have earned."

Faith came around the chair, leaving her about six feet away from him. As best as he could tell, she had not yet spotted the medallion, which was nearly touching her foot.

"Don't talk to me like I'm an idiot, you miserable priest. I've studied these things, and I assure you that I am well protected. The medallion will direct them to my aunt. It is her death that will give Kaseem what he wants and fulfill our contract."

"Faith, please, you are on the road to damnation," pleaded Father Novak. "It is not too late! You can stop all these. Let me help you. You must understand. Your very soul is at risk! It is not the medallion which draws the shadows, but your evil!"

"Don't you dare try and preach to me, hypocrite," she screamed. "The Catholic Church has a long history of sin, and its priests, even now, are as sinful as Kaseem's people. Look to your own soul."

"Yes," said Father Novak, "I am a sinner. We are all sinners, but the difference is that we recognize our shortcomings and pray for his forgiveness. We serve the God of light, the God of salvation! Faith, all of us are sinners because we are human." Pointing out the window, he said, "Those things are not human. Those vile creatures are straight out of the pit. You have no idea what they are capable of."

"Well, why don't we let them in, and we'll see what they can do. My soul's secure for I am as honest in my desires as they are, but once they finish with my aunt, they will feast on you too." Her voice had changed into something that harmonized with the wail outside. With that, Faith moved to the window and reached for the latch.

Father Novak charged at the young woman and, despite his age, was surprisingly strong. His body slammed into hers, and his hands went around her throat as they both hit the wall between the window and the fireplace. Faith reached up, grabbed his wrists, and slowly began to break his grip. She could feel herself growing stronger. Part of her mind warned her, but her lust for the things of this world overwhelmed all reason.

Cori moaned and rolled onto her side. Although she was having trouble seeing out of her left eye, she was able to watch as Faith twisted around and punched Father Novak hard in the stomach. The old priest released his hold on her as he doubled over. Her hands went to his neck, and she began to strangle him. Father Novak tried to fight back, but he was simply no match for her. Dropping to one knee, his face turned bright red. Cori tried getting up to help him, but the pain in her head wouldn't let her.

With a loud, cracking boom, the bedroom's heavy oak door exploded open, swinging all the way around and slamming into the wall, one hinge completely breaking away from the frame. Completely shaken by this, Faith let go of Father Novak, who dropped to his hands and knees gasping for breath.

In the doorway stood a man in a servant's livery. Cori tried to focus on him but was still having trouble seeing clearly. From what she could see, he appeared to be in his late fifties with gray hair but could not remember having seen him before. Wrath and anger blazed across his face, and strangely, there seemed to be a faint glow of soft blue light all around him. Pointing his finger accusingly at Faith, he shouted, "Enough! Be gone from here!"

Faith recoiled from him as if she'd been struck, and for the first time that night, she felt true fear. Panicked, she turned around, rushed to the window, and began to fumble with the latch, trying to get it open. Father Novak saw what she was doing, but his damaged throat wouldn't let him call out to her. Reaching out with his left hand, he picked up the medallion and then struggled to get back up to his feet.

Cori had managed to pull herself up to a sitting position but could go no further. She was fighting the pain, the vertigo, and the nausea that came with her head injury. She too watched Faith at the window but could do nothing to stop her.

Finally, Faith released the latch and stepped back. The windows instantly burst open. The wind and rain preceded the wailing shadow people who began to rush into the room.

Father Novak gave a gurgling scream of desperation and, once again, lunged at Faith. Cori watched in horror as the priest struck Faith in the lower back wrapping his arms around her waist. Faith had not seen him coming, and his momentum hurled them both through the open window.

The shadow people turned and followed Faith and Father Novak to the ground below. Over the howling of the wind, Cori heard a gut-wrenching, high-pierced scream. Cori crawled to the window, pulled herself up to the windowsill, and looked down. At first, she couldn't see anything, but a flash of lightning lit up the grounds below. There, in a tangle of arms and legs, lay Faith and Father Novak. Neither one of them moved. The shadow people were gone.

Cori carefully let go of the windowsill and eased herself back down onto the floor. She sat there with her back against the wall, just below the window. The rain spilling in washed over her and, along with the cold wind, helped to clear her head. She cried as she hadn't cried since her mother's death.

She carefully leaned her head back, letting it rest against the wall for support. Sitting there, her eyes came to focus on Aunt Jean's bed. Next to the bed stood the servant who had saved them, the blue light a little more pronounced. Cori saw that he was looking at her. The fierceness he'd displayed at the door was gone and had been replaced by a gentleness she found amazing. He smiled at her, somehow conveying to her that he too was watching over Aunt Jean. Cori closed her eyes, surprised at the comfort she took from his smile.

Chapter 37

The green mist surrounding the head that Kaseem held up before them continued to work its way up his arm, almost reaching his shoulder. Kaseem began to chant what sounded like the same phrase over and over again, his voice steadily building in volume. His eyes rolled back in his head. Not believing what he was seeing, MacBridan watched as a macabre smile formed on the old woman's face. Then, abruptly, the chanting stopped.

The mist now encased Kaseem's arm and moved on up his neck, stopping as it covered his mouth. "So this is the way of the world now. Satan's minions think I will work for them, I who defied heaven. And you priest of the self-sacrificing God, you think he will save you? Mankind is mine, not God's, not Satan's. Blessed are you to see the age of my rule!"

Although it was Kaseem who spoke, the voice belonged to someone else. It was the weathered voice of an old woman, a voice filled with ageless hatred.

"Fall to your knees and worship the goddess that sets men free from the tyrant above and the coward below." She wasn't speaking English, but everyone understood her words.

Surprisingly, Father Collin obeyed, going down on both knees, bowing at the waist.

"Father! No!" managed MacBridan.

Keeping his left arm as close to his side as he could, Father Collin carefully brought his hand up to his face. Although it was out of Kaseem's line of sight, MacBridan could see that Father Collin still held the bottle of holy water that he'd given to him to drink a few minutes ago. He watched as the priest raised the bottle to his lips.

A slender tentacle of the green mist peeled itself away from the head and extended out, slowly arching toward Father Collin. "Raise your head and look at me, Priest. I will consecrate you as my priest. I will give you the voice I promised my weak-willed husband."

Father Collin's head jerked up and, with all his remaining strength, spat the holy water at the abomination held only inches in front of him. His aim was perfect, catching it squarely in the center, just above the nose. The result was swift and terrible. The face immediately shriveled up, drawing in on itself as if it had been hit by acid. A horrible scream of agony exploded in the chamber as the head burst into blue flames. The flames rapidly shot up Kaseem's arm. He tried to throw the head away but couldn't let go of it.

Reaching behind him, MacBridan grabbed the kerosene lantern sitting on the step and threw it at Kaseem. The old glass shattered against Kaseem's chest, spilling kerosene down the front of him. This too ignited, completely engulfing Kaseem, turning him into a living ball of flame.

MacBridan pushed himself up off the steps and rushed to Father Collin's side. They watched as Kaseem twisted and fell into the passageway he'd emerged from earlier. Screams of utter torment filled the chamber as the floor shook and small pieces of the ceiling started to fall. Helping Father Collin to his feet, MacBridan put one arm around the priest's waist and, with the other, grabbed the remaining kerosene lantern at the foot of the coffin.

"No idea what you just did," said MacBridan, "but this place is coming apart. Come on, Father, time we got out of here."

They made it to the steps but had to slow down, taking them one at a time. MacBridan was doing all he could to help Father Collin as larger pieces of stone began to break away from the ceiling, crashing to the floor. A large rock broke away from the wall on the far side of the chamber, its sharp edge piercing into one of the coffins. The force of the blow broke the coffin's seal, and MacBridan saw flames spurt out of the ancient grave.

Father Collin tripped on the last step and would have gone down had it not been for MacBridan holding him up. It was tight, but they entered the passageway together and started down its steep decline.

The sound of all that was happening behind them was terrible. The coffins were being destroyed by the collapsing chamber. With the breaking of each coffin's seal, a new voice was added to the wail of pain and torment. MacBridan and Father Collin continued to work their way down the passageway, putting as much distance between them and the chamber as they could. Just as they reached the part of the passageway that angled to the left, the entire chamber collapsed, the roar of falling rock overpowering everything else. The ground where they stood shuddered, but fortunately, the passageway held firm.

MacBridan stopped and gently leaned Father Collin against the wall. He then set the lantern down on the stone floor. Every part of his body ached, some parts more than others. Leaning against the cold rock wall for support, he shut his eyes. It was over. Somehow, they had survived.

Opening his eyes, he looked at Father Collin. The priest had been watching him and gave a grateful smile. The lantern at their feet burned steadily, filling the passageway with soft, reassuring light.

"That is one mean spitball you've got there, Father," said MacBridan. "You put some nice trajectory on it."

"Remnants of an ill-spent youth," answered Father Collin. He then lowered his head and began to pray. MacBridan watched him for a few moments and then, although very much out of practice, closed his eyes and joined him.

Chapter 38

The sun burned through the early morning mist, entering its third consecutive day of clear skies over the estate. Since they'd arrived, the sun had been a rare commodity. MacBridan felt certain that for Abbotsbury, this had to be some kind of record.

The past few days at the estate had been a mixture of mourning for those who had passed and a time for healing for those who had survived the terrible ordeal. The weather relented enough the day after the final assault to allow Lord MacKinnon to return to the estate arriving just before noon. Despite the tragedies that greeted him, he quickly stepped in, attending to all the challenges facing his family and his home. MacBridan, who already had a great deal of admiration for Lord MacKinnon, watched the man display an inner strength that few would have been capable of during a period of such personal loss. Gazing out the window, MacBridan seemed to reaffirm, by the warmth from the sunlight through the glass, that the evil they'd faced was truly gone.

"I'm very pleased with how well you're doing," said Dr. Gordon to Cori. "At this point, I don't believe you have anything to worry about. As to your cheek, I expect that most of the bruising and puffiness will go away over the next few days. I doubt the stitches will leave much in the way of a scar, but that said, I'm sure that the doctors back in the States will be able to put it right."

MacBridan turned and watched Dr. Gordon finish his examination of Cori. Their first concern had been that she'd suffered a concussion. Fortunately, all the tests the doctor ran on her came back negative. Despite the good news, she continued to suffer severe headaches, which had only started to lighten up yesterday. This morning, she began to feel human again.

"My being worried about a small mark on my face seems so petty in light of all that has happened," said Cori. "And thank you for the pain pills you gave me. I wouldn't have made it without them."

"You really need to talk to her about sharing those," said MacBridan. "She hoards them like there's no tomorrow."

"Speaking of which," said Dr. Gordon, "how are you feeling?"

"Better," answered MacBridan. "I still feel like a truck hit me but didn't break the skin, but most of my aches and pains are starting to go away. If I have anything to complain about, I'd say the ribs on my right side are the most tender."

"I can give you something for the pain if you'd like," offered Dr. Gordon.

"That's not necessary," said MacBridan. "Push comes to shove, I'll steal some from her."

"In your weakened condition?" laughed Cori. "I'd like to see you try."

"Excuse me," said Fergus as he entered the room. "They're getting ready to move Aunt Jean back to her room, and Nurse Macaulay asked that I let you know."

"Thank you, Fergus. I believe we're finished here," said Dr. Gordon, closing up his medical bag. Looking at Cori, he said, "I'll look in on you tomorrow."

Fergus stepped aside as Dr. Gordon left the room. Nodding to MacBridan, he walked over to Cori who was seated by the fireplace. "Is there anything I can get for you? Some hot tea perhaps?"

Cori smiled at Fergus. "When you get the chance, some tea would be very nice, but please do not make a special trip."

"Not at all, madam, it is my pleasure. Also, Aunt Jean asked that I convey her greetings to you. She wanted me to let you know that if you're feeling up to it, she'd like for you to join her in her room later this afternoon."

"Oh, Fergus, that is so good to hear," said Cori. "She must be doing so much better today."

"She is much improved," confirmed Fergus. "The crisis has passed."

"Please let her know that I'll be down to see her in about an hour or so. There are a couple of things that Mac and I need to go over."

"Very good, madam. May I say how pleased I am at your recovery."

"Thank you, Fergus. You've been most kind," said Cori.

MacBridan watched Fergus leave. "Keep that up, and you're going to need someone to start tasting your tea for you before you drink it."

"What are you talking about?"

"Don't give me that innocent act. You've been blatantly throwing yourself at Fergus since we arrived. Be careful, or Robena may put something special in your tea, not to mention your food."

"You have a sick, pathetic, and immature mind," said Cori. Leaning back in her chair, she closed her eyes. "Have you seen Father Collin?"

"I spoke to him day before yesterday," answered MacBridan. "I'm not sure where he is. Apparently, the church called in a private physician for them out of London. Ubel suffered a pretty bad concussion but is expected to fully recover. As to Father Collin, he got banged up a little worse than I did. Fortunately, none of his injuries were serious. He did say that he'd be out to see us before we leave. He also asked that I tell you that you are in his prayers."

Cori's eyes filled with tears, and she looked away. "Priest or not, I doubt he'll ever forgive me."

"Forgive you? For what?" asked MacBridan.

"You know what I'm talking about," said Cori. "He and Father Novak tried to tell me about the dangers we were facing, and I mocked them. Even now I have trouble believing everything that happened. I should have listened to them, but no, I couldn't. Why couldn't I have at least tried to keep an open mind? If it weren't for me, Father Novak would be alive today."

MacBridan went over and sat down in the chair across her and took her hand. "Cori, first off, Father Novak died fighting the enemy he had always fought, and he died in grace. Secondly, you reacted much the same as I did when I first met Father Collin a couple of years ago. I didn't believe what he tried to tell me either. For that matter, I didn't even trust him. Like you, I had to pass through my own trial to understand what he was telling me and to see what a tremendous ally he really is.

"When you consider all that we've been through," continued MacBridan, "all that we were up against, it is amazing that any of us survived. And through it all, you held your ground. You did a remarkable job. None of us even suspected Faith. You did all that you could against an impossible situation, all that anyone could have done. It is because of your actions that Aunt Jean is alive and well."

"I didn't save her," said Cori. "One of the servants did, and my mind is so addled that I can't even tell you which one it was."

"Yes, well, we'll come back to the part about the servant," said MacBridan, "but you're leaving some pretty important details out of the story. It was you who became suspicious of Faith when she returned to Aunt Jean's room that night. It was you who kept a close eye on her and caught her planting that medallion under Aunt Jean's pillow. Father Collin told me flat out that if you hadn't removed that from under her pillow, the shadow people would have taken Aunt Jean."

"I couldn't help him, Mac," cried Cori. "I sat there on the floor and watched that brave old man sacrifice his life, and there was nothing I could do." Silent tears streamed down her face. MacBridan knelt on one knee, took her in his arms, and held her as she cried.

A voice behind them said, "If this is any example of your bedside manner, then it's a good thing you didn't go into medicine." They both looked up to see Father Collin standing in the doorway, the Irish lilt in his voice as strong as ever. "The idea is to cheer the patient up, not cause them to completely breakdown."

Cori straightened up in her chair, grabbed a tissue, and tried to wipe away the tears. Father Collin walked over and stood in front of them, his back to the fire.

"I didn't know you were coming by today," said MacBridan.

Father Collin smiled, standing between them and the fireplace. "The fire feels good. We have a great deal to talk about, and I've been so anxious to see both of you. Forgive me for eavesdropping, but Cori, you have nothing to be ashamed of. You and Father Novak did everything you could to protect an elderly, defenseless woman against tremendous odds, and you succeeded."

"We are both so sorry about Father Novak," said MacBridan. "He was a very brave yet a very gentle man."

"I thank you for that," said Father Collin. "He was an amazing individual and a good friend. I've never met a man more dedicated to Christ's teachings or caring for his flock. Over the years, he accomplished so much in the fight against the dark side. It is interesting to note that it also took him quite awhile to fully come to grips with all that we are truly up against."

"Really?" asked Cori.

"Father Novak was not always a part of the order I belong to. In his younger years, he spent most of his time in the Soviet Union, bringing the word of God to the people there, quite often putting himself at great risk. It wasn't until he became involved in an incident in Poland that he was approached by my cardinal to join us. He was more skeptical about the demonic side of things than my friend here," he said, pointing at MacBridan.

The logs in the fireplace crackled and popped. Father Collin took a small log out of the bin and placed it on the fire. Turning around, he held his hands out toward the flames, his fingers spread to absorb the warmth. "I've been chilled ever since we came out of that miserable crypt. I was so cold for so long that night, body and soul."

"What happened in Poland?" asked MacBridan. MacBridan wasn't sure where this was going, but he knew that Father Collin rarely engaged in idle chatter. All this was leading to a point, and MacBridan was certain that the priest was waiting for one of them to ask the obvious. Obligingly, he did his part.

"Father Novak possessed a brilliant mind. Like so many people trained in science and logic, he did not accept the concept of supernatural entities. It's funny when you think about it. We love and follow a supernatural God, the Bible tells us of several supernatural events, and yet you'd be surprised at how many priests struggle with that very concept. It has nothing to do with their faith, which is as strong as can be. It's just that this kind of thing, even for them, is so far outside the realm of possibility. Nevertheless, it is difficult for most of us to accept that there are entities beyond the human realm. That there are, what we shall say, creatures that certainly do cause things to go bump in the night."

"In Poland, he came face-to-face with a severe case of demonic possession. My order was brought in to help. Before the ordeal was finished, one of the priests Father Novak had been working with was killed during the exorcism. All that he witnessed affected him significantly. He returned to Rome and spent the next nine months recovering, coming to understand the many faces of evil that walk this earth."

"Cori, it was because of this phase of his life that he was so drawn to you. He recognized and understood the dilemma you were struggling with. Your world was turning upside down, and there was no escape from what you were witnessing. Father Novak knew from firsthand experience how mentally devastating that could be. He couldn't get over your courage. For you to be willing to go back to Aunt Jean's room the very next day and potentially face the shadow people again, absolutely awed him."

"But, Father," said Cori, "why is there a supernatural side? Why does Satan play major games over individual souls?"

Father Collin said, "We don't know. Some of my order believe that evil is like a substance that enters the world much like pollution from a smokestack. The demonic effulgence is in the air so that when a Hitler or a Pol Pot tries his evil plan, he is filled with charisma, which is what Lilith called the voice when she offered it to me. I don't know. I just know that we must fight in the manner we are called and that you have fought well."

Cori sat quietly, staring into the fire. "Thank you, Father," said Cori. "I needed to hear this. I'm just going to have to think this through and find a way to come to terms with it."

Father Collin smiled at her. "I understand. I truly do. Just promise me that you won't try doing this by yourself. Let us help. Sadly, we have a great deal of experience in this area."

"I may take you up on that," said Cori, doing her best to smile.

"Remember," said Father Collin, "God never gives us more than we can handle."

"I understand Ubel is feeling better," said MacBridan. "Without his help, I never would have made it to you. How's he doing?"

"Fortunately, his head is nearly as hard as yours," answered Father Collin. "He's doing much better. Talon was able to get Ubel back to his car that night and drove him to the village clinic. Once she got him inside, she left him there and took off with his car. As far as I know, neither she nor the car has turned up."

"Tell him that he shouldn't feel too bad about letting Talon slip through his fingers or losing the car. In fairness, she is a thief," said MacBridan, smiling ear to ear.

"I'll be sure to pass on your kind words."

MacBridan smiled at the thought of that. "I'm sure it will make his day."

Father Collin chuckled as MacBridan pulled over a third chair for him. "Before coming upstairs, I spent some time with Lord MacKinnon. Despite everything, he's actually doing pretty well. Kerr and Barclay are staying close to him, which frankly is what he needs right now. I think the thing that puzzles him the most is Faith."

"Greed's a powerful force," said MacBridan. "Whatever relationship she may have had with Lord MacKinnon, I'm sure she had well-founded doubts as to what would have happened to her if and when the title went to Wallace."

"I do imagine that that had to have played a part in the equation," agreed Father Collin. "Still, I believe Lord MacKinnon is far more disappointed in her betrayal than in Wallace's poor judgment. Her greed made her a lightning rod for the forces at play. That is why we didn't notice her."

"What I need is for someone to give me clarification on what was real around here and what wasn't," said Cori. "The spooky stuff started the minute we walked in the front door. How much of that was Faith trying to scare us and how much of it was Kaseem?"

"In point of fact, things actually started up before you arrived. When you and Mac kept them from stealing the painting in Virginia and then stopped them again on the docks in Glasgow, Kaseem realized that this was not going to be as easy as he first thought."

"Mac told me what Kaseem said to him at the chapel," said Cori. "That's something else I have to reconcile. If we hadn't stopped them, they would have found what they were looking for and quietly slipped away. It seems that our intervention led to several deaths."

"Well, you can eliminate that thought from your mind right this minute," said Father Collin. "Kaseem was sent by Sathanas, grand master of the Cult of the Shadow, to retrieve the head that they believed Balgair stole. Believe me when I tell you that for Kaseem, it was truly a do-or-die mission. The followers of his cult never do anything quietly and always leave a trail of death behind them."

"I remember your telling us of your run-ins with this cult before," said MacBridan.

"Over the years, we've faced them many times. Each time, we have learned the hard way that they have little to no respect for human life. Had you two not appeared on the scene, at a minimum, Faith and Talon would have been killed. Even if Kaseem had succeeded in stealing the painting but then failed in his effort to decipher the code, he would have proceeded just as he did, and Aunt Jean would have died also. Actually, it's hard to say what the final body count would have been, but I assure you, there would have been far more innocent victims than bad guys."

"But what was real and what was contrived?" pressed Cori. "Did Kaseem control the creature Mac saw in his room, or was that somehow put on to scare us away? What was it that we experienced in the crypt? Was that a trick? Was it the creature, the shadow people?"

"All good questions," said Father Collin, "which is why I wanted us to talk."

"As to the creature, controlled is far too generous of a word. Kaseem merely set things in motion. Once that was done, he could sometimes tap into the evil that was already here, directing it just as he tried to do with the medallion. Remember, this cult dates back far before the time of Christ with Satan as their god. For centuries, they've practiced dark rituals, performed human sacrifice, and have knowledge of ancient grimoires that, to a point, enabled them to manipulate demonic forces. The forces of the shadow respect power and intelligence. They are not loyal. When a stronger sorcerer shows up, they switch sides. So they are always in danger from the very forces they unleash."

"So they use us as bargaining chips, tokens of their power," said MacBridan. "The more death they cause, the tougher they look to their demonic overlords."

"Precisely, but we're getting ahead of ourselves. Again, the failed thefts let Kaseem know that he might have to find the artifact another way. So as is their practice, he decided to try locating the grave through the evil that has plagued these grounds for centuries. To do this, he had Mukhtar steal several dogs in the area, including Lord MacKinnon's, and then, one at a time, sacrificed them in a beckoning ritual."

"What is that?" asked Cori.

"It is a blood sacrifice. You've read the *Odyssey*? Discarnate spirits thirst for the blood that once bound them to life. Spill some blood, they show up for a drink. They were as glad to work for Kaseem now as they had been for Balgair centuries ago. It is the very same evil that, centuries ago, helped to destroy the Templars and has cursed the MacKinnon clan for generations. If successful, the evil would reveal itself to Kaseem." Father Collin reached into his jacket and handed MacBridan a small leather-bound book tied with a dark blue ribbon. "You'll want go through this."

"What is it?" asked MacBridan.

"Fortunately for us, Faith kept a diary and was rather diligent in her updates," answered Father Collin. "She recorded everything, from her first meeting with Kaseem up to her final entry when she was preparing to leave her room and put the medallion under her aunt's pillow."

"How nice," answered MacBridan. "Has Lord MacKinnon seen this?"

"No, and I don't think we'll show it to him. She was a very disturbed young lady. It would only serve to hurt him. Fergus found it, brought it to me, and asked what he should do with it. I told him that I'd give it to Wetmoore, which I will do when we're finished with it."

"But you haven't given it to Wetmoore. So by saying that you're going to do something, but then not really doing it until you're good and ready, that's more than just bending the truth." said MacBridan. "I've always been under the impression that you guys aren't supposed to do that kind of thing."

"I am not bending the truth," corrected Father Collin. "Think of it as more like telling him the truth in advance. Ultimately, Wetmoore will get the diary."

"Does Faith mention Marston in there?" asked Cori.

"She most certainly does. It was she who poisoned him and was quite proud of her accomplishment. She goes on for nearly a page and a half regarding the poison she formulated and how pleased she was with herself when it went undetected."

"So the garden of illegal pleasures that Cori and I found was hers."

"Yes, it not only ties in to her pharmaceutical studies, but she was fascinated at her ability to concoct what she referred to as her little potions. She wrote about a couple of the staff here at the estate that she experimented on, putting her concoctions in their food or their drink. She would carefully take note of their reactions, ranging from a mild rash to cramps, each time learning and further refining her potions. Her primary goal was that the victim never caught on, never figured out that they had been poisoned or that she'd been the one who'd given it to them. At first, she was very scientific and practical, but as she began to channel the demonic forces, she took glee in causing others pain. She didn't even seem to notice when she knew things about herbs that she had never studied. This is part of the witching way. As you do evil, knowledge and power seep into your soul like water into a sponge.

"With Talon's failure to get the painting, Faith decided on her own that Marston had to go. She thought that that would make things easier for them. She had no idea that Lord MacKinnon would ask the two of you to stay on. When that happened, from her perspective, she'd lost the devil she knew only to be replaced by the devil she didn't," said Father Collin. "When you read through, there you'll find that she was mixing up something special just for you Mac."

"How nice," said MacBridan. "It's actually kind of funny. Not ten minutes ago, Cori and I were talking about how one of us might need a food taster."

"So who did the maid see the night Marston died?" asked Cori. "Was it Faith in costume or the dark lord like everyone believed?"

"We'll never really know," said Father Collin. "There's no mention of it in the diary, so it's hard to speculate. However, by the time that evening rolled around, Kaseem had already completed the beckoning ritual, so the evil that lurked here was on the prowl."

Looking at MacBridan, Father Collin said, "Kaseem told me that he started targeting you almost immediately. When Faith let him know that you were in Balgair's old room, he had her place a small medallion there. Whether or not that caused the apparition to appear in your room that night is open for debate, but all things considered, you were lucky events played out the way they did."

"Then it really was a ghost that Mac saw in his room," said Cori.

"No, much worse, it was a demon of sorts. Balgair gave himself over to the dark side long before coming to Scotland, damning his soul for all eternity. We know now that the night the villagers attacked, he and his most loyal acolytes escaped to the chapel, going down into the crypt and ending up at the secret burial chamber they had prepared. My guess is that they all committed suicide. However they died, Balgair's spirit was transformed, taking on demonic form, remaining here to watch over the very artifact he'd stolen from the Templars."

"So with Kaseem having done his stuff, the dark lord truly was walking the grounds," said MacBridan.

"It's a good example of the danger that so few people understand and why Father Novak and I were so concerned when we saw the witch board. That particular board has evil embedded in it. We know that, but even the spin-off that was made from them is dangerous. How many years have Ouija boards been sold as a game, most being used by young people intent on scaring themselves?" Father Collin shook his head. "Believe me when I say it's anything but a game."

"All things considered, and I'm not arguing, I had one as a kid," said Cori. "True, my grandmother hated it, but my parents didn't seem to care. For us, it was a game. We never had a problem with it."

"And fortunately that is true for most, but there have been those few who were not so fortunate. Accidents happen all the time," said Father Collin. "So here's the problem. When people sit down to play with an Ouija board, be they adults or young people, they focus their minds on it, doing whatever comes to mind to call upon the board to answer their silly questions. They certainly do not intend to call forth a demon. It is a rare human that can be a great sinner, just as it is a rare human that can be a saint. When that one in a thousand humans asks a question angels and fallen angels will answer it. Once contact is made, the human lives in a dangerous world. They may put their silly board game away, but hovering near them, just over their left shoulder is a demon. When I think back on the exorcisms that I've participated in, many of the families we were working with had an Ouija board somewhere in the house and had been using it before the trouble started. The sorcerers of old were safer. They acknowledged the demon and didn't entertain it unawares."

"What will become of the witch board now?" asked Cori. "It's been with the family for a long time, and we all know how attached Aunt Jean is to it."

"Lord MacKinnon and I discussed that," answered Father Collin. "It's agreed that I'll take it back to Rome for more study. If we determine that it no longer poses a threat, we'll return it to the family."

"I sense more telling the truth in advance," said MacBridan.

"Perhaps," said Father Collin with a small smile. "The good news for the MacKinnon family is that now there shouldn't be any other recurrences of either the dark lord or the shadow people. The head that Kaseem located in burial chamber was the focal point of the evil, and it has been destroyed, burnt, and buried under tons of rock."

"Wetmoore told me that they aren't even going to try to recover Kaseem's body," said MacBridan. "Not only would it cost a small fortune, but Lord MacKinnon wants things left as they are."

"Lord MacKinnon understands that it was Kaseem who got Wallace killed," explained Father Collin. "Over the last few days, we've been able to determine that the passageway leading to the burial chamber extends well beyond the wall surrounding the churchyard, so the chamber is not on holy ground. Lord MacKinnon feels that it is just that Kaseem spend eternity with the remains of the evil he tried to resurrect."

"I'm sorry. I'm still not clear. What was that down in the crypt with us the day Mac and I went to examine the chapel?" asked Cori.

"Here's a long answer to a short question," said Father Collin. "In her diary, Faith wrote about Kaseem's daily attempts to locate the burial chamber. Each day, he would attempt to call forth the demon, hoping to see from where it emerged."

"Which would in turn lead him to the burial chamber," ventured MacBridan.

"To a point, yes, at least he'd be close," said Father Collin. "He performed the ritual a few times near the manor, accurately guessing that the burial chamber was hidden somewhere on the grounds surrounding the house. When that failed, he moved to the chapel area and, as we know, was eventually successful. It's interesting to note that he located it about the same time that we did."

"Using distinctly different methods," said MacBridan.

"Indeed," agreed Father Collin. "So, Cori, in answer to your question, it is my opinion that the two of you may have almost fallen victim to an unfortunate coincidence."

"Coincidence?" said Cori.

"You both told me that you heard stone grating against stone," said Father Collin. "My guess is that you were hearing the stone at the back of the crypt that concealed the passageway opening up. In short, I believe you were in the wrong place at the wrong time coinciding with Kaseem performing a beckoning ritual. Once again, thanks to MacBridan's hardhead, you were able to escape in time. By getting back into the chapel, you were in a consecrated sanctuary and safe from any demonic presence."

"Not to nitpick, but that would be thanks to my hard shoulder," corrected MacBridan. "I did not hit my head against the door."

"Oh, I do apologize, did I say head?" asked Father Collin, feigning innocence. "I must have been thinking of your hardheadedness, your tenacity in tight situations."

"Father, you don't really believe it was a coincidence, do you?" asked Cori.

"No, I don't. I think divine grace was extended to you and Mac. Kaseem thought it was MacBridan's karma. In his heart, Mac knew two things. It is important to help and important to know when to ask for help. This makes him a warrior of the light."

"Not that it matters now, but I wonder how the MacKinnon ancestor who did the paintings found out about the location of the burial chamber," said MacBridan. "My guess is that one of Balgair's cronies escaped, and our guy, centuries later, stumbled across the information."

"When the black sheep ancestor began to engage in piracy, he opened himself to evil. He went from a thief to a rather notorious torturer. He felt Lilith's call and gained some special abilities including second sight. But it burned through his body. He painted the pictures so that he would remember his visions. Had the same thing happened to a McKinnon woman, she would have been one of the greatest witches we have known in modern times."

"So women are tougher than men?" asked Cori.

"Do you think Mac or I could survive childbirth?" asked Father Collin. "When women do good, they usually do greater good than men. When they do evil, hell itself is often impressed."

"How did the holy water kill her?" asked MacBridan.

"The holy water didn't kill her. The grace of the Lord killed her. At the time she was beheaded, John the Baptist had not introduced the sacrament of baptism. Holy water restores matter, for an instance, to its prefallen state. Her head briefly belonged to God, so there was nothing for her spirit to hold on to. Her spirit was drawn to the place of evil. It was as natural a fall at that moment as Newton's apple."

"Mac," said Cori, "do you have any idea what we're going to tell to Dolinski? He's going to expect a report from us."

"He and I have already been through most of it, so he's pretty much up to speed," said MacBridan.

"You're kidding. He believed all this?"

"As to the supernatural events, I just told him that there were some things we simply couldn't explain," said MacBridan. "Between Faith's background in pharmaceuticals and Kaseem's shady cult association, he has settled on drug-induced delusions. He seems content with that, so I really didn't see a reason to argue."

All three settled into their chairs and gazed into the fireplace. A large bed of coals had built up, and the warmth they radiated acted almost like a blanket of comfort. It was the quiet after the storm, and for the first time in days, they could actually let down and relax.

"Cori, I have a gift for you," said Father Collin. Reaching into one of his pockets, he brought out a small box and handed it to her.

"What is this for?" asked Cori.

"Over time, your memories of this will blend into a combination of the power and goodness of the light and the abominations the dark side is capable of. I want you to keep this with you to remind you that in the end, the light of goodness will always win out."

Cori opened the box and looked inside. Turning it over, she poured into her hand a chain of smoky white beads with a gold cross at the end. "Thank you, Father. I'm afraid I'm not Catholic, but of the rosaries that I've seen, it's very beautiful."

"It's also very old," said Father Collin. "It was Father Novak's and had once belonged to his mother. I think that he would be pleased to know that you have it."

Once again, tears welled up in Cori's eyes. Reaching for a tissue, she said, "Thank you. This means a great deal to me." She wiped her eyes then balled the tissue up in her hand. "I don't know what's wrong with me. I haven't cried in years, and now I can't stop."

"Perhaps it's been too long," suggested Father Collin. "Let God come into your life, and you will never be alone. You will have no need to ever fear the darkness again."

"It has been too long," agreed Cori. "I'll be taking you up on your offer to help. Thank you." Gently holding the rosary in her hand, Cori once again leaned back in her chair, deep in her own thoughts.

"Not to take advantage of your emotional state," said MacBridan, "but can I have one of your pain pills?"

"Not a chance," said Cori, not taking her eyes away from the rosary.

Chapter 39

The door to Aunt Jean's room was open, but they lightly tapped on the door anyway before going in. MacBridan and Cori found her sitting in one of the tall wingback chairs by the fireplace, a quilt draped across her legs. Her face was pale, and there was a certain fragileness about her, but the sparkle in her eyes was as strong as ever. On the end table next to her where three oversized, thick books that looked like scrapbooks.

"You up for some company?" asked MacBridan.

"Heavens yes! It is so good to see both of you," said Aunt Jean, her smile lighting up her entire face. "Ronald has already shared with me in great detail all that happened. And yesterday, I had a wonderful visit with Father Collin, which helped a great deal. It seems quite an understatement, but I owe you my life and more."

She held out her arms, and Cori went to her, and they hugged each other. "You too, Mr. MacBridan," said Aunt Jean. "You're not too big to be hugged." MacBridan leaned down and was surprised at the strength in the old woman's arms.

"How are you doing?" asked Cori, sitting down in the chair next to her. MacBridan stood next to the fireplace, leaning against the mantel.

"Physically, I'm doing just fine. Of course, with Dr. Gordon hovering over me like a mother hen, getting well is the only way to be rid of him. As to the rest, that will take in some time."

"We're sorry about Faith," offered MacBridan. "I wish things could have turned out differently."

"Yes, I'm having such a hard time with that on so many levels," said Aunt Jean. "I don't have any doubts about how she felt about me, as to whether or not she loved me. That's not it. It's just so sad that something as ignorant as greed could have completely taken her over the way it did. She and Wallace, both so young to be lost in such a senseless way. Ronald's doing his level best not to show it, but I know how badly he's hurting. Why is it that a Scotsman believes that he can't let down in front of others, just show his emotions? It certainly wouldn't make him any less of a man."

"Don't ask him," said Cori, looking at MacBridan. "The last time I saw Mac even come close to something resembling emotion was because some sports team lost a silly game."

"It was *not* a silly game," said MacBridan. "It was the Super Bowl."

"Men can be maddeningly annoying," said Aunt Jean, patting Cori's arm, "but then, what would we do without them?"

Changing the subject, MacBridan said, "No pun intended, but it looks like you're getting ready to do some heavy reading."

"These are some old photo albums of the family," said Aunt Jean. "Barclay checked in on me yesterday evening, and somehow, we got to talking about my childhood and what it was like in those days to grow up here. People don't realize how important pictures become over time. It's actually pretty interesting to see how little the manor house has changed. I asked Fergus to get them out for me so that I could show him."

"I'd like to see them myself," said Cori.

"How about you, Mr. MacBridan?" asked Aunt Jean. "Any interest in seeing a collection of old pictures?"

"Absolutely, I'd love to look at them. I'm a huge history buff and couldn't agree with you more, pictures are invaluable. Besides, Cori and I really haven't had the chance to walk around and see all that's here. The pictures will let us know what to look for."

Cori scooted her chair closer to Aunt Jean's. MacBridan brought over a chair and placed it just behind the small end table between the two women where the photos albums were stacked. All black and whites, the first album was full of pictures of the MacKinnon family participating in events in Abottsbury, festivals the village celebrated. Aunt Jean's father was prominent in most of the pictures. The second album focused more on the estate, the chapel, and pictures of the family at play. They weren't too far into the second album when Aunt Jean had to take a break.

"I need for you to excuse me for a moment," said Aunt Jean. "Cori, would you please walk with me? I'm afraid that I'm still a little unsteady."

Cori helped her out of her chair and held her arm as they walked to the bathroom. While Cori waited outside the door, MacBridan sat back down and thumbed a few pages ahead. He was starting to turn the page when a picture of a man with a little girl caught his eye. Leaning over, he studied it closely.

"Well, I'll be," said MacBridan. "The more I see, the less I understand."

"What is it?"

"Here comes Aunt Jean. There's a picture here I want to ask her about. It'll be interesting to see what she says, but whatever you do, don't overreact." MacBridan turned the pages back to where they had left off.

"I'm getting stronger," said Aunt Jean as Cori helped her walk across the room and settle back into her chair, "but I still don't completely trust myself to do much walking without help. All I need right now is to fall again."

They picked up where they'd left off and, in a few minutes, made it to the page holding the picture MacBridan had singled out.

"Aunt Jean," said MacBridan, "is that you?"

Looking at it, Aunt Jean smiled. "Yes, that's me. I think I was eight when that was taken. Behind us is the new carriage we'd just had delivered."

"Who is that standing next to you?" asked Cori, her voice nearly a whisper. Her eyes had grown wide with disbelief when she focused in on the photo, but to her credit she was able to keep all that she was feeling bottled up inside.

The man in the picture looked to be in his fifties, was smiling broadly, and had his hand resting gently on her shoulder. He was impeccably groomed in a servant's livery.

"What a dear, sweet man he was," answered Aunt Jean. "At that time, he was the head butler and always drove the carriage whenever the family went anywhere. He wasn't supposed to, but sometimes, he let me sit up front with him and drive the carriage. We were very close."

"What was his name?" asked MacBridan.

"I always called him Mr. Byrne, but his full name was Dillon Byrne," answered Aunt Jean. Cori's face paled as she and MacBridan looked at each other, confirming what MacBridan had already guessed. "He was an Irish gentleman and was with our family for years. My father told me that the name *Dillon*, in Ireland, means *faithful*. He died tragically, at the chapel, just before we left for America. It was a terrible day."

Cori swallowed hard and struggled a little to keep her voice steady. "That's very sad," said Cori. "What happened?"

Aunt Jean proceeded to tell them what happened to her that day in the churchyard, everything that she experienced, and how she watched Mr. Byrne die right in front of her. "Do you know that until today, I've never shared the details of what really took place with anyone else, of all that I saw," said Aunt Jean. "In America, I had come to disbelieve it myself. Considering what we've all just been through, I feel safe that you won't think it was just the wild imaginings of a young girl."

"What a terrible thing for a child to have to experienced," said MacBridan. "No, Aunt Jean, we don't doubt a word of what you are telling us. As to Dillon, I'd say that the meaning of his name is very much on the mark."

"That's very nice of you, Mr. MacBridan. What makes you say that?"

"I've come to depend heavily on first impressions, how a person looks, how they act. Based on what you've told us and his expression, posture, and his attitude toward you in this picture, I'd say he loved you greatly. I'll bet he was the kind of man who would have done anything to protect you," said MacBridan.

Aunt Jean studied him closely, trying to determine if there was more to his opinion than mere speculation. Deciding not to press him, she smiled and leaned back in her chair. "Thank you. That makes me feel good. I've always believed the same."

They stayed with her a while longer, looking at the albums, then left to meet with Lord MacKinnon downstairs in the library. As they walked along the hall, passing their rooms, Cori remained absolutely silent, refusing to make eye contact with MacBridan. He waited patiently, knowing that she was still trying to work out what they'd just discovered. Finally she asked, "How did you know?"

"That it was Dillon who burst into Aunt Jean's room that night? I didn't. I was guessing. It's just that each time I talked with him, there was something odd about it all, something not right, but I couldn't pin it down. The night I chased Wallace into the churchyard and ran into Dillon by the lane, I began to wonder whose side he was actually on. Trust me, the thought that he might not be among the living never entered my mind. Until I saw that picture, I had zero thoughts along that line."

"Where's Father Collin when we need him?" asked Cori. "So Dillon is a ghost?"

"Perhaps, but I don't think so. No, my guess is that he was a good spirit, a force for good, terribly devoted to Aunt Jean. My mom always told me that we all have guardian angels. Maybe that's the answer."

They continued down the main hallway, finally coming to the staircase. Cori stopped just before they started down. "Mac, I know that Scotland is beautiful, and I don't want to hurt anyone's feelings, but as soon as we can, I'm ready to get out of here."

MacBridan smiled and put his arm around her shoulders. "I understand. Believe me, I understand. You should come up to my lodge in Kentucky for a rest. I need to fish and stare at clouds."

"I could stand to stare at a few clouds," said Cori.